Rebecca Winters lives in Salt Lake City, Utah, USA. With canyons and high alpine meadows full of wildflowers, she never runs out of places to explore. They, plus her favourite vacation spots in Europe, often end up as backgrounds for her romance novels—because writing is her passion, along with her family and church. Rebecca loves to hear from readers. If you wish to email her, please visit her website at cleanromances.com

An ex au—pair, bookseller, marketing manager and seafront trader, **Jessica Gilmore** now works for an environmental charity in York. Married with one daughter, one fluffy dog and two dog—loathing cats, she spends her time avoiding housework and can usually be found with her nose in a book. Jessica writes emotional romance with a hint of humour, a splash of sunshine and a great deal of delicious food—and equally delicious heroes.

Kandy Shepherd swapped a career as a magazine editor for a life writing romance. She lives on a small farm in the Blue Mountains near Sydney, Australia, with her husband, daughter, and lots of pets. She believes in love at first sight and real-life romance—they worked for her! Kandy loves to hear from her readers. Visit her at www.kandyshepherd.com

Brides of Summer

REBECCA WINTERS
JESSICA GILMORE
KANDY SHEPHERD

MILLS & BOON

First Published in Great Britain 2019
by Mills & Boon, an imprint of HarperCollins*Publishers*
1 London Bridge Street, London, SE1 9GF

BRIDES OF SUMMER © 2019 Harlequin Books S. A.

The Billionaire Who Saw Her Beauty © 2016 Rebecca Winters
Expecting The Earl's Baby © 2015 Jessica Gilmore
Conveniently Wed To The Greek © 2017 Kandy Shepherd

ISBN: 978-0-263-27657-2

0619

MIX
Paper from
responsible sources
FSC™ C007454

FSC
www.fsc.org

This book is produced from independently certified FSC™
paper to ensure responsible forest management.

For more information visit: www.harpercollins.co.uk/green

Printed and bound in Spain
by CPI, Barcelona

THE BILLIONAIRE WHO SAW HER BEAUTY

REBECCA WINTERS

This is for my super-marvellous father,
Dr John Z. Brown, Jr, who was adored by
his many thousands of patients during his long career.
I've praised him before in other books
because he was the best!

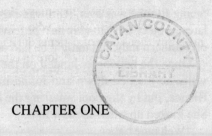

CHAPTER ONE

"Signor Montanari?"

Rini was just getting in the limo. He looked around in the direction of one of the reporters who'd followed him outside the doors of the fourteenth-century Palazzo Colonna in Rome. Dozens of them had assembled to cover the European Congress of Businessmen.

"A moment of your time, *per favore*—one piece of news I can use for my lead story in *La Repubblica*?"

Why not?

"Since Italy imports almost all of its hydrocarbon demand, a doubling of domestic production would help the country reduce its energy bill. I'm planning to find them in Italy."

"Where?"

"That's my secret for now."

The reporter beamed for having been given a partial scoop. "*Mille grazie, signor.*"

He nodded and closed the door before his driver took him to the heliport for the flight to his mountaintop villa in Positano, on the Amalfi Coast. Now that the two-day September conference covering the economic problems facing Europe was over, Rini was eager to explore his latest project. On Monday he'd be leaving for the coast of Southern Italy, but tonight he had other plans.

Once the helicopter landed on the pad behind his villa, he jumped down and found his housekeeper, Bianca, out by the pool watering the tubs of flowers. She looked up when she saw him.

"Welcome back."

"It's good to be home."

"How's your father?"

"Well as can be expected." Rini had flown to Naples after yesterday's session and spent the night with his *papà*, who seemed to be handling the loss of Rini's mother a little better these days. She'd been the heart of their home and Rini would always miss her happy, optimistic spirit.

"Was the conference beneficial?"

"I'm not sure *beneficial* is the right word. *Chilling* would be more accurate. Europe is in trouble economically, but I'd rather not think about that tonight."

"Do you want dinner?"

"I'd love one of your meals, but I'm meeting Guido tonight. It's his birthday." His best friend from childhood, the son of Leonides Rossano, who owned Rossano shipping lines, had texted him earlier in the day:

The parents are throwing a party for me on the yacht. Please say you can make it. I know you're at a conference, but I need your advice about something serious. By the time you arrive it will be breaking up so we can talk in private.

The message sounded serious, even for Guido, who clearly wasn't in a celebratory mood. He obviously had no plans for the weekend with a woman. His friend was as bad as Rini, who had no plans in that department, either. The two of them made quite a pair, but for entirely different reasons.

Guido was still looking for the right woman who hadn't come along yet. Rini didn't have the same problem. The right woman wasn't out there for him because she wouldn't want him when he had to tell her he was infertile. An old soccer injury he'd suffered in his youth had made it impossible for him to give any woman a child.

The pain of that realization had grown worse with every passing year, increasing his dissatisfaction with his own personal life. Whenever he did meet a woman he cared about, he held back, not allowing the relationship to develop into something deeper. It always came down to his fear she would reject him if she knew the truth.

He'd been denying his deep-seated needs for such a long time, he'd forgotten what real fulfillment was like. Since his sister Valentina—the mother of two children and now ecstatically married—had recently moved out of his villa, his unhappiness had deepened.

She'd lived with him through her whole pregnancy. He'd helped her with the baby when she'd first come home from the hospital. He'd loved every minute of it, but he'd carried a secret pain in his heart because he knew *he'd* never be able to be a birth father. When she'd married Giovanni and moved out, Rini felt the emptiness of the villa. It echoed the emptiness in his soul for what could never be.

Valentina's happiness, not to mention that of his younger brother, Carlo, who enjoyed a wonderful marriage and had a little girl, heightened his awareness that the key element in his life was missing. He envied his brother for being able to give his wife a child. Rini's doctor had told him he was a fool to let that prevent him from falling in love. "The right woman will be able to handle it," he'd reminded him.

Rini didn't believe it as he walked through the villa to his suite and stripped for a shower to get ready. After slipping into his black tuxedo, he reached for the wrapped gift he'd bought for the occasion. Once he'd said goodbye to Bianca, he left for the helicopter. The new hand-tied fishing fly he'd purchased for Guido was reputed to bring results. They often fished the mountain streams for trout. He thought his friend would be pleased.

Twenty minutes later he landed on board the Rossano luxury superyacht moored in the Bay of Naples, reminding him that not everyone was feeling the economic crunch. The yacht boasted seventeen staterooms and all the amenities of a five-star hotel, including a swimming pool and dance floor.

Twilight had descended, lending magic to the spectacular surroundings of one of the most beautiful and photographed bays in the world, with Mount Vesuvius in the background. He told his pilot to come back later and jumped down as Guido strode over to him.

"I've been waiting for you. Saw you on the evening

news. Impressive stuff. I was afraid you wouldn't be able to make it. Thanks for coming."

"As if I'd miss your birthday." He pulled the small package out of his jacket and handed it to him. *"Buon compleanno."*

They gave each other a hug, then walked into the salon-cum-bar for a drink. He opened his present and held up the lure. "Just what I need."

"Good. Let's go fishing next weekend. I'll clear my schedule for next Saturday." Rini had been working himself into the ground and needed a break.

"Perfect." With a smile of satisfaction he put the present in his pocket. With dark blond hair, good-looking Guido could have his pick of any woman. The money behind his family name made him sought after and somewhat cynical, as he feared no woman saw him for himself. Guido was the best friend Rini could ever have had. He hoped the only son of Leonides Rossano would end up one day with a woman worthy enough to win his heart.

Rini's name and wealth made him a target, too. Women came on to him, causing him to question if any of them loved him for himself. Coupled with his problem of infertility, Rini imagined it was possible he'd end up a bachelor for good.

"Was it a nice party?"

"Different. One of the big fashion houses asked Father for permission to film a show on the yacht. You missed the whole thing."

"Sorry about that. The meeting in Rome went longer than anticipated."

Rini followed him down the steps to the deck, where he greeted his friend's parents and family, who made up some of Naples's most elite socialites and were beautifully dressed. Rini was well acquainted with many of them. An orchestra played music and the drinks were flowing.

They moved over to the area where a smorgasbord had been set up. By now he was hungry. After filling his plate, he joined his friend at one of the tables away from the others, where they could eat and talk alone.

"Your text said you wanted advice. What's going on with you?"

Guido started to say something when his father broke in on them. Two attractive women with long hair he hadn't seen before were with him. Rini exchanged a glance with his friend, who looked annoyed at the interruption. They both got to their feet.

"Dea Loti and Daphne Butelli, may I present my son Guido and his best friend, Rinieri Montanari."

"How do you do," Rini said, eyeing both of them.

"You missed their show, Rini," the older man interjected.

"As I indicated earlier, I was unavoidably detained on business."

"Well, you're here now. They have to leave on the tender in a few minutes. Maybe you could give them a dance before they go?"

Guido's father never stopped hoping his son would meet the woman he couldn't live without. Rini knew his friend was upset at being railroaded, but agreed to the request. "It would be our pleasure."

He gravitated toward the woman closest to him, who was dressed in purple. After walking her over to the dance floor, he drew her in his arms. "I've never been to a fashion show before. I'm sorry I missed it."

"I doubt it's the kind of thing the CEO of Montanari's generally does on the weekend." By now Guido was dancing with the other model.

"I understand it's hard work. Did you have a chance to eat yet? We don't have to dance if you're hungry."

"Thank you, but no. I don't want anything. I have to watch my figure."

"Well, your discipline definitely shows."

She flashed him a beguiling smile. "Do you live in Naples?"

"No, but I work here."

It surprised him when her hands slid up his chest and around his neck. "Daphne and I are going to be in Naples one more night because of an afternoon show at the Grand Hotel Parker's, then we have another show in Rome. Perhaps we could get together tomorrow evening for dinner after the show?"

Her eyes stared up at him in unmistakable invitation.

"I'm afraid my plans are indefinite at the moment, but I've certainly enjoyed this dance with you."

She held her smile. "Well, if you straighten them out, call me around seven at the Grand Hotel Vesuvio, where I'm staying, and ask for Signorina Loti." In the next breath she planted a hungry kiss on his lips he hadn't been prepared for. Then she darted away.

Rini went back to the table to wait for Guido. In a few minutes his friend joined him. "Sorry my father did that to us." One eyebrow lifted. "After the kiss she gave you just now, are you going to see her again?"

"No." Her pushy style had put him off. "What about you?"

"Not interested. You know damn well Papà told her you're the most eligible bachelor in Italy, next to me, of course." He said it without mirth.

Rini shook his head.

Guido studied him. "Maybe she decided to try the direct approach to get beneath your armor."

"I'm afraid it didn't work."

An exasperated sigh escaped. "Papà doesn't know when to give up. In fact it's because of him I need to talk to you. I've made a decision to take a year off from the family business to invest in something I really want to do. He won't like it, but I want your opinion. Come on. Let's get a drink in the bar."

Rini followed him, wondering what was on his friend's mind.

After a dive with colleagues that produced no new finds, twenty-eight-year-old Alessandra Caracciolo returned home late Monday afternoon. Bruno Tozzi had left his scuba gear in the cruiser with hers and would come by for it in a day or two. Instinct told her he'd done it on purpose so he'd have an excuse to see her again.

Since their last dive, when Bruno had buddied her, he'd made it no secret that he wanted to be with her all the time, but she didn't have romantic feelings for him. Though she dove with him and their friends for their work, that had to be the extent of their relationship. The next time they were together, she would make it clear she wasn't interested and never could be.

She tied the boat to the dock of her family's private pier. Garbed in flip-flops and a man's long-sleeved shirt that she'd thrown over her blue-and-white polka-dotted bikini, she headed for the Land Rover with her duffel bag.

Once in the car, she drove on sand past the helipad and around to the front of the castle. When she reached it, she would take a shower and wash her hair. Alessandra wore it neck-length because she spent so much time in the water. It dried fast and the natural curl made it easy to take care of.

As she pulled up near the main entrance, she saw a limo parked in the courtyard, making her curious. All vehicles came across the causeway from the mainland at Metaponto, a port town of Basilicata, Italy. But after five o'clock, any visitors were escorted out by staff.

Their family's castle on the tiny island of Posso off the Ionian coast dated back to Queen Joanna of Naples, who ruled in 1343. Besides tourists from Bari and Taranto, who were allowed visits to the castle four hours a day on Tuesdays and Wednesdays with a guide, dignitaries from the world over called on her father, Count Onorato Caracciolo, asking favors because of his influence in the region.

Alessandra got out of the car and hurried inside past the tapestry of the queen hanging on the wall in the huge front foyer. She headed for the grand staircase, eager to make herself scarce until she'd cleaned up.

The moment she reached the first step, a deep male voice called to her. *"Signorina?"*

She whirled around to see a tall, incredibly gorgeous dark-haired man in a charcoal-colored business suit walking toward her, his dark brows furrowed. Still holding the duffel bag in one hand, Alessandra clutched the railing with the other.

He stared at her so strangely. "I thought I was hallucinating, but it *is* you. Since Saturday night you've cut your hair. I don't understand. How did you know I was coming here today? On the yacht you told me you had another show to do in Rome," he murmured.

The way his piercing black-brown eyes played over her face and figure, she knew he had a history with her identical twin, Dea. He was the most striking male Alessandra had ever seen in her life. She found herself envying her beautiful sister for having met him first and couldn't fault her taste. Men had never been able to resist her.

Alessandra cleared her throat. "I'm sorry, *signor*, but I'm not Dea."

Embarrassed to be caught looking so messy and disheveled after her diving trip, she ran up the steps without looking back. Her sister would never allow herself to be seen like this. All the way to the next floor she felt the man's penetrating eyes on her retreating back and bare legs, causing her to tremble.

Had her sister finally met the one she'd been looking for? Dea had always kept their family identity private. Because she was a model, she called herself Dea Loti so no one would know she was the daughter of Count

Caracciolo. For her to divulge her secret to this man
meant their relationship must have turned serious, otherwise he wouldn't have known where she lived.

No doubt she'd invited him to come. Did she want
the family to meet him? But his scrutiny of Alessandra
led her to believe he hadn't looked pleased to see her
here. Maybe Dea hadn't told him she had a twin. Alessandra didn't know what to think.

If only she hadn't arrived back from her dive trip
until tomorrow, this wouldn't have happened and she
wouldn't be haunted by that man's image engraved on
her mind. It shocked her to realize that at long last there
might be an important man in her sister's life. Alessandra knew her sister's quest had been to find the perfect
man while she made the most of her modeling career.
Their parents would be overjoyed.

Six years ago she and Dea had gone through a terrible experience involving a man, one Alessandra had
hoped to marry. But when he met Dea, he fell for her
and followed her to Rome. Their relationship didn't last,
but the pain of betrayal had cut Alessandra like a knife
and it had taken a long time to recover. Since the falling out with her sister, no man of importance had come
into either of their lives.

In the last two years she'd tried to put the past behind her and get back the friendship they'd once shared.
Dea came and went from home according to her hec-
tic schedule and their family had enjoyed some good
times. Evidently this past summer Dea had found romance after she'd gone back to Rome. Love on a yacht,

no less… If that gorgeous man owned it, then he could keep her in the lifestyle she desired.

But for some reason Alessandra had been oddly upset by the encounter in the foyer, unable to understand why. *Except that she really could…* These days her own love life was nonexistent.

Once inside the bedroom, Alessandra plopped the duffel bag on the floor and got out of her clothes. Her mind was still on Dea, whom she hadn't seen for six weeks. Her sister had developed an interest in fashion and modeling at an early age and that hadn't changed.

Alessandra led a different life altogether. She couldn't remember when she didn't have an interest in the archaeology of this region of Italy. The island castle itself was built on an ancient archaeological site. Since college she'd been involved in several multidisciplinary studies in the field of archaeology within a Mediterranean perspective, with particular emphasis on Southern Italy.

Without being able to scuba dive, she could never have achieved her dream to do the necessary underwater work with friends she'd made among the archaeological staff at the University of Catania. Scuba diving wasn't for everyone. Dea couldn't understand her passion for it, but it didn't matter because their parents approved and supported both her and Dea in their individual endeavors.

After a shower and shampoo, she blow-dried her hair, then dressed in pleated tan pants and an ivory-colored linen blouse. With an application of coral frost lipstick, she left the room on khaki wedges and went in search of her parents. They'd married for love and were very close. Unlike many couples, they did everything together whether it was for business or pleasure. Though Alessandra had never discussed it with Dea, their parents' happy marriage had been the ultimate role model for both sisters.

On the way to their apartment she saw Liona, the wiry housekeeper who'd come to work for them at eighteen and had been with them ever since. She was like another member of the family and ran the large staff with precision.

"If you're looking for your *mamma,* she left for Taranto two days ago to help your aunt, who fell and broke her hip."

"Oh, no! Poor Fulvia."

"She'll be all right, but your mother will probably be gone for a few more days."

"I need to call them."

They started down the staircase together. "I'm glad you're back. You know how your father worries."

Liona was the one who worried about Alessandra. She thought scuba diving was dangerous. Alessandra gave her a hug. "It's good to see you. How's Alfredo?" Liona's cat had been sick.

"The vet says he's getting old and shouldn't go up and down stairs."

"I'll help carry him for you."

"Bless you. Did you have any luck on this last diving trip?"

"I wish."

"Oh, well. Another time. Are you hungry? I'll tell the cook."

"Please don't bother her. I'll find something to eat later. Thanks, Liona."

She hurried toward her father's office, wondering if the male visitor was still with him, then scoffed with impatience because the man was on her mind at all.

"Ciao, Papà."

"Alessandra!" Her grayish blond father stood up from his desk and hugged her. "You were gone too long this time."

"It was only a week."

"We always miss you. Did you have a good time?"

"Yes, even if we didn't find anything of significance." She walked around to sit in one of the leather chairs facing his desk. "I'd much rather know about you and mom. Liona told me Zia Fulvia broke her hip and Mom went to Taranto to help her."

He nodded. "Your aunt will make a full recovery. Your mother could be back tomorrow."

"Oh, good. So tell me what else has been happening while I've been away."

His brows lifted. "Something unexpected. I'm glad you're back so we can talk. More than anyone else I want your input because you have a fine mind."

"I got it from you and Mamma." Her comment produced a chuckle. So maybe her assumption had been right. "It wouldn't have anything to do with the man I saw in the foyer earlier this evening, would it?"

He cocked his head. "Actually it would. When did you see him?"

"I'd just come in the castle when he spoke to me."

"Did he introduce himself to you?"

"No. It wasn't like that. On my way up the staircase he mistook me for Dea before he headed for your office, that's all."

Her father nodded. "I guess I shouldn't be surprised. Her face is everywhere."

"Papà—" She smiled at him. "Are you pretending with me?"

"About what?"

"Was he here because of her?"

The count blinked. "Not that I know of."

"Oh." She needed to keep her thoughts to herself. "Who is he?"

He smiled. "If you didn't live in your world of books and ancient underwater artifacts, you would have recognized him as the CEO of Italy's most powerful engineering dynasty, Rinieri Montanari."

She stirred in the chair. "Of course I recognize the Montanari name. Who wouldn't?" It explained the man's aura of authority.

Her father sat back and touched the tips of his fingers together. "His family has accumulated great wealth. He's the brilliant one driving the company to new heights. A week ago he made an appointment to come and see me about a business proposition."

"That sounds interesting."

"I'll give you a little background. Night before last he was on the news following the European Congress of Businessmen held in Rome. I saw the gleam in his eyes. He said he had secret plans to grow the economy.

Today we talked and arranged for him to come back tomorrow to get into the details."

He'd aroused her curiosity. "What is he after?"

"He'd like to drill for oil on our property."

Alessandra shifted in the chair. "He and dozens of others who've wanted the same thing for the last half century," she muttered. "Since he knows it's not for sale, why is he coming back?"

"This man is different from all the others. He wants to lease the land."

Lease? "Are you considering letting him?"

"I'm thinking about it."

"Wow."

Her father eyed her curiously. "Why do you say that?"

"I thought our property was inviolate."

"Leasing isn't the same thing as selling."

"You're right."

"Alessandra, something's on your mind. Why did you ask if he was here because of Dea? Has your sister confided in you about him?"

"No, Papà. In fact I haven't spoken to her for almost two months."

"Hmm. If he'd met her before, he didn't mention anything about meeting her to me."

"Why would he if he didn't know anything about our family?"

"But what if he does know? It makes me wonder what came first, the chicken or the egg?"

"What do you mean?"

"He might have met Dea before he ever called me."

Alessandra was trying to understand what her father was getting at. "Why is this troubling you so much?"

"I'm your loving *papà*. My daughters were born princesses of the Houses of Taranto and Caracciolo. Because of our family history, you know I've always wanted to protect you from unscrupulous men."

His explanation surprised her. "That sounds like medieval thinking. Papà, you don't honestly think the CEO of Montanari Engineering fits in that category?" *That gorgeous man? The one she'd envied Dea for meeting first?* Alessandra didn't want to believe it. Something about him had impressed her deeply.

"Though we don't use the titles anymore, there are some men who try to calculate the monetary worth of our family. There's nothing they would like more than to acquire your bank accounts and assets more than your love."

Alessandra frowned. "The man comes from his own family dynasty and doesn't need more."

"One would assume as much, but for some men one dynasty isn't enough." His gaze swerved to hers. "I don't want to think it. But if he has targeted Dea to marry her and eventually gain possession of our property, I don't like the thought of it."

She didn't like it, either. Not at all. "Personally I don't believe it." Alessandra didn't want to believe it. Not about that man. Whatever history her sister and Signor Montanari might have together, she didn't want to think about it. To be with a man like him…

Alessandra got to her feet. "Don't let it bother you, Papà. Have you had dinner yet?"

"No."

"I'll bring you something."

"*Grazie*, but I'm not hungry."

"I'm afraid I am. I haven't eaten since I got back. Excuse me while I grab a sandwich. If you want me, I'll be in the library."

Alessandra left the office and headed for the kitchen to find something to eat. Afterward she walked to the castle library on the main floor, the repository of their family history where she could be alone. Years earlier she'd turned one corner of it into her own office, complete with file cabinets and a state-of-the-art computer and printer, plus a large-screen television for viewing the many videos she'd compiled. This had been her inner sanctum for years.

She sat down at the desk and got back to work on the book she was writing about Queen Joanna. Just as she'd settled down to get busy, the phone rang. It was her father.

"Papà?"

"I just wanted to let you know I've got business in Metaponto. The pilot is flying me in a few minutes."

"Do you want company? I'll go with you."

"Not tonight, *piccola*." Her father's endearment for her. When Alessandra was born, she was the younger twin by three minutes and the name *little one* stuck. "I'm sure you're tired after your scuba-diving trip, so you get some sleep and we'll talk in the morning. I could be gone a couple of hours and will probably get back late tonight."

"All right."

While she got back to work she heard her father's helicopter fly away. She kept busy for another hour, then went upstairs to get ready for bed. But when she slid under the covers, she didn't fall asleep right away. Memories of the past with her sister filtered through her mind.

Though their personalities were entirely different, she and Dea had been as close as any two sisters until college, when Francesco had come into Alessandra's life. She'd fallen in love and they talked about getting married. But before they got engaged he met Dea, who was more confident than Alessandra and had already started her modeling career.

Her sister had a beauty and lovability that had drawn guys to her from her teens. By contrast, Alessandra felt rather dull and unexciting. Certainly she wasn't as attractive. But she'd always accepted those truths and never let them affect their friendship. Not until Francesco had laid eyes on Dea. From that moment everything changed. Alessandra felt herself lose him and there wasn't anything she could do about it.

He followed her sister to Rome and she never saw him again. Francesco sent Alessandra a letter explaining he couldn't help falling in love with Dea and hoped she wouldn't hate him too badly. As for Dea, Alessandra didn't see her for two months. When her sister came home, she told Alessandra she was sorry for what had happened. She explained that Francesco had done all the running, and she'd soon found out he was a loser. Alessandra was lucky to be out of the relationship.

The trauma of being betrayed by Francesco and her

sister had completely floored her. It had taken a long time to work past the pain. Though they'd shared sisterly love in the past, from that time on they'd had a troubled relationship and two truths emerged. Alessandra didn't know if she could trust a man again and Dea would always be the beautiful one who usually got the best of Alessandra. People seemed to love her the most.

Alessandra had to live with the knowledge that she was known as the clever one, a scholar with a sense of adventure. She'd thought that by the age of twenty-eight she would have finally gotten past her jealousy of Dea's ability to attract men. But it wasn't true. Otherwise meeting Signor Montanari, who'd met Dea first, wouldn't have disturbed Alessandra so much.

If her father was right, what a sad irony that this man might be using Dea to get what he really wanted, making both sisters appear as poor judges of character. First the chef Alessandra had fallen for who couldn't remain faithful once he'd laid eyes on Dea. Now Signor Montanari, who looked like the embodiment of a woman's dreams. But what if her father learned this man had a secret agenda? The troubling thought kept her tossing and turning all night.

CHAPTER TWO

ON TUESDAY MORNING Alessandra awakened and headed to the bathroom for a quick shower. She dressed in jeans and a blouse. After brushing her hair and applying lipstick, she walked down the hall past the stairs to her parents' apartment wearing her sandals.

She knocked on the door with no result, so she opened it and called out, "Papà?" He was probably in the sitting room drinking coffee while he read his newspapers, but the room was empty. Frowning, she retraced her steps to the staircase and hurried downstairs to the small dining room where the family ate breakfast. Maybe she'd find her father there.

The second she opened the doors, she received a shock. Her sister stood at the antique huntboard pouring herself a cup of coffee.

"Dea! What a surprise! It's good to see you!" She looked beautiful as usual in a stunning blue dress and high heels. Alessandra rushed over to hug her. "Where's Papà?"

"In the office."

"I didn't know you were coming home." She reached for a glass of juice and a roll.

"Neither did I until I got a phone call from him last night."

"You did?" That was news to Alessandra. He must have called her on his way to Metaponto.

Dea's eyes darted to her without warmth. "He told me Rinieri Montanari had come to the castle to do business with him and wanted to know if I had been dating him. He seemed concerned enough that I decided to make a quick trip home to talk to him about it."

"He's always trying to protect us, you know that."

They both sat down at the banquet-size table. "What I'm curious about is how *you* know Rinieri Montanari." The tone of her sister's point-blank question had an edge. There had to be another reason her sister had made a sudden flight home. Alessandra didn't begin to understand what was going on.

"I don't! Didn't Papà tell you? Signor Montanari was in the foyer when I came in from my scuba-diving trip yesterday. As I started up the staircase he called out to me. I had no idea who he was. He thought I was you."

"Did he say anything else?"

"Only that he acted surprised you were here at the castle and commented that you'd cut your hair since he'd been with you on the yacht. He said you'd told him you had another show to do in Rome. I took it that's why he seemed shocked to find you here. I told him I wasn't you, then I went up the staircase. That's it."

Dea sipped her coffee slowly. "So he mentioned the yacht."

"Yes."

She could hear her sister's mind working. "Is that *all* he told you?"

Dea sounded so worried, Alessandra was perplexed. "I swear it."

Her sister's mouth tightened.

"Have you worked this out with Papà?"

She put down her empty cup. "Not yet, but I will when we fly back to Metaponto in a few minutes."

"But you just got here last night!"

"I have to return to Rome for another show. As soon as Papà finishes up business with Signor Montanari, he's flying me to the airport." She checked her watch. "They've been together for the last half hour."

With nothing more forthcoming, Alessandra knew she'd been dismissed and rose to her feet, feeling chilled. "Then I'll say goodbye to you now." She leaned over to kiss her cheek.

Until Alessandra could talk to her father alone, she would have to wait to know what had gone on. Dea was going back to Rome without clarifying anything about her relationship with Rinieri Montanari. In fact she hadn't been this cold to Alessandra in a long time.

She left the dining room without saying anything and rushed down the hallway to the library, where she could get to work.

When her phone rang two hours later, she saw that it was her father and clicked on. "Papà? Where are you?"

"At the airport in Metaponto, waiting for your mother. She's flying in from Taranto."

Thank goodness. Alessandra needed to talk to her. "Has Dea gone back to Rome?"

"After our talk this morning I put her on the plane."

"You sound more calmed down. Is everything okay?"

"There was a misunderstanding that was all my fault, but I've spoken with Signor Montanari and it's been cleared up."

Except that Alessandra still knew next to nothing. She gripped her phone tighter. "I'm relieved for that. How did Dea seem? She was chilly with me."

"That's because I upset her. After I apologized for minding her business, I explained it was my way of being protective to prevent her from being hurt in case Signor Montanari wasn't being sincere. You did absolutely nothing wrong, so don't worry about it. Now the main reason for my call. Do you have plans for the rest of the day?"

"I'm working on my book."

"Would you have time to do me a favor?"

"Of course."

"Signor Montanari is going to be our guest for the next few days."

What? Alessandra almost fell out of her chair. The change in his attitude toward the other man was astounding.

"He needs someone knowledgeable to show him around today. Since I don't know how long I'm going to be gone, you're the only one I trust to drive him and answer his questions. Your work with the institute has given you vital insight into the importance of any changes or disturbances to the environment here in the south. Will you do it?"

His compliment warmed her heart, but it was already getting a workout because it meant she would be spending time with a man whose name was renowned throughout Italy. Her father had yet to explain what he'd found out about Dea's relationship with Signor Montanari.

"Yes." But Alessandra was so attracted to him, she would have to be careful it didn't show. No way would she give her sister a reason to suspect her of coming on to him when she'd met him first.

"Get him back in time, *piccola*. I've asked him to join us for dinner. Liona has put him in the guest apartment on the third floor. He's probably eating lunch right now. Your mother's plane is arriving so I have to get off the phone. *A piu tarde, figlia mia.*"

Rini had just finished a second cup of coffee when the beautiful woman he'd seen yesterday on the stairs walked in the dining room. He should have realized right away that she wasn't quite as slender as Dea, but he preferred her curves. "Signor Montanari? I'm sorry if I've kept you waiting. I'm Alessandra." She sounded slightly out of breath and looked flushed.

Earlier in the morning, after the count had asked him about his relationship with Dea, he'd left the castle for the airport. Rini thought it odd to be questioned about her, but he let it go.

At that point the count said that while he was gone, his daughter Alessandra would give him a tour of the property. According to him, she understood the impact of drilling on the environment better than anyone else and he would be in the best of hands. If she was an engineer, Rini had yet to find out.

He got up from the table. "We meet again. I've never met identical twins before."

"Dea's the older sister by three minutes."

"Which accounts for the difference," he teased. "I can see that." He smiled and walked toward her. "Call me Rini."

After a slight hesitation she shook the hand he extended. "*Benvenuto a Posso*, Rini. Papà told me you'd be our guest for a few days and asked me to show you around today."

"That's very kind of you, but I don't want to inconvenience you." He couldn't read her thoughts.

"It's all right. Papà said this was important."

She'd dressed in a simple short-sleeved peach top and jeans. Her tanned olive skin indicated she spent a lot of time in the sun. His gaze traveled from her cognac-brown eyes to her neck-length slightly tousled brown hair rippled through with golden highlights.

As she pulled her hand away, he noticed she didn't wear nail polish. The reason she looked so natural was her lack of makeup. Except that she did wear lipstick, a coral color that blended with the golden tone of her skin and drew his attention to her voluptuous mouth.

He remembered Dea's mouth being sculpted the same way before she'd kissed him. How remarkable that identical twins could look so much alike, yet on closer inspection were so different.

"Your father said you're the one who knows everything."

"Oh, dear. I hope he really didn't say it like that."

Rini got the idea he'd embarrassed her. "He meant it as a compliment."

"I'm his daughter so he has to say it," she commented in a self-deprecating manner. "If you're ready, we can go now."

"Please lead the way."

He followed her ultrafeminine figure out of the castle to a Land Rover parked near the main doors. Rini had done his homework. Her island home was renowned as an Italian treasure. What a coincidence the castle was home to both women!

Before Rini could credit it, she climbed in the driver's seat. "You'll need to move the seat back all the way to accommodate your legs," she said after he opened the passenger door.

One corner of his mouth lifted as he did her bidding and climbed in. They attached their seat belts and she took off across the causeway to the mainland. She drove with expertise, as if she could do it blindfolded. After leaving the small town of Metaponto, they headed for verdant hills that were covered in ancient olive groves.

"My father explained why you're here. Now that we're on Caracciolo property, tell me why the CEO of Montanari Engineering wants to lease this particular piece of property in order to drill. A lease means taking on a lot of controls." She didn't mince words and was all business.

"Your land may not be for sale, but a lease means compromise that benefits both parties and could be lucrative." Rini looked out over the mountainous, sparsely populated province of Basilicata. "Hidden in the arch of Italy's agricultural boot is the home to Europe's biggest on-shore oil field."

"That's what I've heard."

"Italy produces one hundred and twelve thousand barrels a day, one tenth the North Sea's level. My goal is to double Italian oil production within the next five years. If not on your land, then I'll find others because as you know, the south is underdeveloped."

"Your goals are very ambitious."

"Agreed, but the potential of this particular untapped oil field is huge. We're hoping to drill for the billion-plus barrels of crude oil that lie beneath it. Your father and I are hammering out ideas to preserve the existing environment while drilling for oil to boost the suffering Italian economy."

"You sound like a politician."

"Everyone should be concerned over our country's unemployment problems. I'm particularly anxious for us to bring down the country's twelve-percent jobless rate through new employment. The goal will be to obtain oil, yet maintain sustainable development of agriculture that will offer real career paths for the future."

"I have to admit you make a good case." She kept driving to the top of a ridge that overlooked the huge valley. Onorato Caracciolo was a clever man to send Rini out with his daughter first. Rini had a hunch it would be a smart idea to win her over to his idea since her father appeared to place great trust in her knowledge and intelligence. But after the misunderstanding involving his other daughter, he needed to walk carefully.

"If you wouldn't mind stopping, I'd like to get out and look around."

She pulled off the road and turned off the engine. While he walked a ways, she climbed down and rested one curving hip against the front fender to wait for him. When he returned she said, "I know you see oil beneath the property. But what I see is a fertile field that has been here for centuries. Your plan would create giant, unsightly scabs."

His eyes narrowed on the features of her beautiful oval bone structure. "If you're imagining dozens of derricks, you'd be wrong. My gut instinct is to build several right here in the shadow of the mountain out of sight. The existing road to the south travels straight to the sea, where the oil would be transported to tankers. One would barely be aware of the activity."

"And if you find it, does that mean more derricks?"

"We'll make that decision later."

Her softly rounded chin lifted. "What if you don't discover any?"

"Preliminary reports from this part of Italy indicate vast reserves. We'll find it, but we'll proceed slowly with your father having the final say in how long we are allowed to drill. Let me ask you a question."

"Go ahead."

"If I were to appeal to Queen Joanna herself and explain the benefits, what do you propose she would say? Forget how long ago she ruled. Your father tells me you're a historian writing a biography on her. Your research means you know her better than any other living person today. Was she a risk taker?"

He could hear her mind working.

"She backed Antipope Clement VII against the unpopular Urban VI. For that she was given this papally owned land eventually bequeathed to our family. So yes, I'd say she was a risk taker."

Rini's lips twitched—he was fascinated by the knowledge inside her brain. "You think she would have granted me an audience?"

She stared at him. "I have no idea."

"Humor me and put yourself in Joanna's place."

A smile broke the corners of her mouth he found more and more enticing. "It was a man's world. I wouldn't have trusted any of them. You, particularly, wouldn't have been given a second audience."

"Why single me out?"

"Because you're handsome as the devil, increasing the odds of Joanna being tricked. Give me a little more time to think about your ideas that have persuaded my father to give you a hearing."

"You mean you're not tossing me out on my ear just yet?"

She opened the driver's door. "Of course not. That's for Papà to do." On that note she climbed in and started the engine.

He went around to the other side, glad to hear she wasn't shutting him down yet. "In that case, let's take the road that leads to the sea. En route you can tell me more about the subject of your future best seller."

"I'd rather you gave me more reasons why you think this project of yours outweighs the many negatives. My father will want a report to run by my mother and her sister, Fulvia. The property comes through my father's line, but he always leans heavily on the opinions of his wife and sister-in-law."

"Who makes the ultimate decisions?"

"When it comes to business, the three of them go back and forth until there's a consensus."

"He's a man surrounded by women."

She smiled. "As my Aunt Fulvia says, behind every successful man *is* a more successful woman."

Food for thought. "Do your parents love each other?"

"Very much."

"That's nice. Before my mother died, my parents had the same kind of relationship."

"I'm sorry for your loss. It sounds like you've been lucky to have great parents too," she murmured on a sincere note as they started down into the valley. "What does *your* father think of this latest idea of yours?"

"Though he and I are always in consultation over business, this is one time when he doesn't know where I am, or why." He angled his head toward her lovely profile. "I've taken this time to do reconnaissance work on my own. I told no one where I was going, not even my best friend. That's why I was so surprised when I thought you were Dea. I couldn't figure out how you could have known my destination."

She darted him a questioning glance. "So it really was pure coincidence that you had business with our father?"

"I was introduced to her as Dea Loti. But the mis-understanding has been cleared up. The simple fact is, I thought you were she. But I shouldn't have called out to you before I'd met with your father for an explanation, then none of this would have happened. To be honest, I wasn't ready for you to disappear on me the way you did."

Her pulse sped up. *Did he just say what she thought he said?*

"I was a mess and hoped no one would see me sneak in the castle."

"Not from where I was standing."

She swallowed hard and appeared to grip the wheel tighter. "When Dea and I were younger, we got taken for each other a lot. Not so much now that she's become a top fashion model. She's the true beauty. I've always believed I looked different even though we're identical. But I'm aware other people can't always tell the difference. Under the circumstances I understand why my shorter hair gave you a shock."

Not just her hair. As he was coming to learn, many things about her were different from her sister and other women. She was so genuine and charming, it knocked him sideways. "Your hair is attractive and suits you."

"Thank you."

"I can see why your father wants to protect you." Rini decided not to argue the point further when her physical beauty was self-evident. But Alessandra Caracciolo had been born a twin and he'd heard it could be a blessing and a curse, so he left it alone.

They'd reached a crossroads that would take them back to Metaponto and the causeway, but Rini wasn't ready to go home yet. To his surprise he found he wanted to get to know her better. *Much better.* Besides her intelligence, she spoke her mind and was like a breath of fresh air. "Do you have time to drive us along the coast? I want to inspect the shipping access."

"We could do that, but if you want to get a real feel, you should view everything by boat."

That idea sounded much better. "When we reach Metaponto, let's find a marina where I can charter one for tomorrow."

"You don't need to do that. I'm sure my father will want to take you out on our cruiser so you can talk business."

"Then let me buy you dinner in town in order to repay you for driving me around today."

"Thank you, but that's not necessary. My parents are expecting you to eat with them and I have plans after we get back."

He had no right to be disappointed that she'd just turned him down. She was probably involved in a relationship right now. Why not? She was a stunning woman. He imagined that men flocked to her.

After having shown him around the property for her father, she'd done her duty and had other things to do. Though it was none of his business, for some odd reason the possibility of her being interested in another man didn't sit well with him.

Wednesday morning Alessandra was just getting out of the shower when her phone rang. She reached for her cell and checked the caller ID. "Mamma?"

"*Buongiorno*, darling."

"I'm so glad you're back home. How's Zia Fulvia?"

"I thought she was better. That's why I came home yesterday. But after your father and I finished having dinner with Signor Montanari last evening, we got a call from her. She's having a bad reaction to her new pain medication and it has frightened her. I told her we'd fly to see her this morning. Your father and I are on our way to the airport and will stay with her for another night to watch over her."

"I can't believe you've already gone," Alessandra said in surprise. "I haven't even seen you yet." She needed to talk to her.

"I know. Where did you disappear to last evening? I expected you to join us for dinner."

"I'm behind on my book. After I brought Signor Montanari back to the castle, I went straight to the library to work."

Before Signor Montanari's explanation about Dea, Alessandra had tried hard to hide her attraction to him. But once she knew he and her sister were not involved and never had been, the news had thrilled her so much, she might have given herself away if she'd gone to dinner with him.

"I'm sorry we missed you, darling. I want to hear all about your scuba-diving trip, but it will have to wait another day." Alessandra had already forgotten about that. "Your aunt is really distressed."

"The poor thing. Give her my love and tell her I'll visit her soon."

"She'll love that. By the way, your father wants to know if you would be willing to show Signor Montanari around again? Today he wants to explore the coast by boat. Would you take him out on the cruiser?"

She sucked in her breath. "First let me ask you a question, Mom. What do you think about his idea to lease the property for drilling?"

"To be honest, I don't like the idea at all."

"I didn't think so."

"It seems a travesty to change anything about the land or what lies beneath it. Your father knows how I feel. Though your father believes Signor Montanari's ideas have merit, I'm not persuaded. There's a great deal to discuss before anything is decided."

"It sounds like Papà doesn't feel as strongly as you."

"Let's put it this way. He likes Signor Montanari's vision and is willing to hear more. What's your opinion?"

"He talked a lot about bolstering the economy by providing more jobs. My suspicion is that he's hoping to run for a high-level government position and this could be the feather in his cap."

"He's a brilliant man. That's what brilliant men do." *But not with Caracciolo land.* That's what her mother was really saying. The time Alessandra had spent with him yesterday had persuaded her he was worth listening to, but these were early days. "Alessandra? What's wrong? You don't sound yourself."

"I just wish I hadn't brought Dea into the conversation when I was talking with Papà. He ended up phoning her."

"Your father told me what happened. But when he learned that Signor Montanari had been a guest of Leonides Rossano on his yacht the other night and happened to get introduced to Dea, your father realized he'd made something out of nothing and overreacted. It certainly didn't have anything to do with you."

"But I didn't know the truth until Signor Montanari told me as much while I was driving him around."

"I'm sorry. It's understandable you thought he and your sister were involved."

"I didn't know. When I saw Dea at breakfast yesterday, she didn't explain anything."

"Well he made it clear to your father that meeting Dea was like ships passing in the night."

"But maybe Dea had hopes it could be more." Already Alessandra knew a man like Rinieri Montanari only came along once in a lifetime. She and Dea weren't twins for nothing.

"Why do you say that?"

"If their chance meeting had been so insignificant, how come she flew home last night?"

"Because your father was worried."

"He was," she conceded. "But she didn't even come in my room to talk to me."

"Alessandra—during dinner I got the impression that the CEO of Montanari Engineering is a force to contend with. If he'd been interested in your sister, he would have made future plans to let her know how he felt."

"You're right, but what if she finds out I'm showing him around?"

"What if she does?" After a silence, she asked, "You're attracted to him, aren't you? Otherwise you wouldn't think twice about this. There's nothing wrong with that! I'll admit my heart skipped several beats when I met him at dinner last night."

Her mother's instincts were never wrong.

"He said he truly enjoyed being shown around by you. I could tell he meant it. Don't blow up a simple misunderstanding your father has apologized for into something major."

"You're right. I'm being foolish."

"You are. Go ahead and show Signor Montanari around until we get back from Taranto. I'll call you tonight."

"Okay. Love you. Give Zia Fulvia a hug from me."

Alessandra hung up, realizing she was transparent to her mother, who understood the situation completely. She felt better after their talk. The longing to be with Signor Montanari again was all she could think about.

She pulled on a pair of pleated khaki pants and a blouse with a small tan-on-white geometric print. Once dressed, she went downstairs to the kitchen for coffee and a roll. The cook made her some eggs. While she ate, Liona poked her head in the door. "Alessandra? Did you see Alfredo when you came down the stairs?"

"No."

"He ate his food, but now I can't find him. He usually stays on the main floor while I'm working around. Maybe he's gone off sick somewhere."

"I'll look for him." She ate a last bite, thanked the cook, then began a search, wondering if Signor Montanari was around. "Alfredo—" She called his name several times. When she reached the front foyer, she worried that he'd slipped past some visitor at the entrance.

She opened the door and almost ran into the gorgeous man who'd haunted her dreams. He was just coming in. The sight of him made her heart leap. He held the big marmalade cat in his arms.

"*Buongiorno*, Alessandra," he said with a white smile. "I've been waiting for a limo and found him lying outside the door wanting to get back in."

"Liona will be so relieved. Here. I'll carry him to the kitchen."

"I'll be happy to do it."

"I don't mind."

She could tell he didn't want to give up the cat, who seemed perfectly happy to be held by him. It surprised her because Alfredo didn't like many people. "Then follow me." She opened the door and showed him the way.

Liona was thrilled to see them walk in the kitchen. The housekeeper reached for her cat.

"He found Alfredo outside the castle," Alessandra explained.

"The poor thing is getting confused. I'll take him back to my apartment. *Grazie, signor.*"

"*Prego, signora.*"

Alessandra trailed him out of the kitchen. "That was very nice of you. Her cat is getting old." She followed him to the entrance, but there was no sign of a limo yet, only three tour buses bringing tourists to tour the part of the castle open to the public. "I hope the driver didn't already come and leave."

"I'll call to find out." He reached in his jeans pocket.

Her eyes traveled over his rock-hard body. His blue
crewneck shirt had the kind of short sleeves that only
looked good on a man with a well-defined physique. In
a minute he clicked off. "It'll be a while due to an accident near the causeway."

"What were your plans?"

His veiled gaze slid to hers. "To charter a boat."

"There's no need to do that," she said on impulse.
"Since my father isn't here to take you, he suggested I
drive you where you want to go in our cruiser."

"But that means interrupting your work."

"It's all right. As Papà reminded me, you're a busy
man. Since you're here, you need to make the most of
the time. I'll do my own work later." The talk with Alessandra's mother had taken away the guilt she'd been har-
boring over Dea. There was nothing she wanted more
than to spend more time with him.

"Then I'll call off the limo."

"While you do that, I have to run in and get a few
things. I'll meet you at the Land Rover in five minutes."

Alessandra hurried inside and up the staircase to her
room. Her heart raced abnormally hard to think they
were going out on the boat together. She filled her duffel bag with some necessary items, then rushed back
down to the kitchen and stashed water and snacks in
the top of it. She never knew how long she'd be gone,
so she never left without being prepared.

When she walked out to the car beneath a semi-
cloudy sky, she found him waiting for her with his own
backpack. It had been years since she'd felt this alive
around a man. This time when she unlocked the door

with the remote, he opened her door and relieved her of her duffel bag so she could get in. He walked on around and put their things in the back before climbing inside.

"Our cruiser is docked on the other side of the island." She started the engine and drove them the short distance.

"It's right in your backyard!"

She smiled. "I know. Can you believe how convenient?"

Once she'd pulled up to the pier, they both got out. He obviously knew his way around a boat. After depositing their bags, he undid the ropes while she got on board and found them both life preservers. She put hers on first.

"Who's the scuba enthusiast?"

"You're looking at her."

His piercing dark brown eyes scrutinized her. "How long have you been a diver?"

"Since I was nineteen. Have you ever done it?"

"I learned at fourteen. It's probably my favorite activity."

His admission excited her no end. To scuba dive with him would be like a dream come true. "Mine, too," she admitted. "Excuse me for a minute."

She disappeared below and pulled out a special oceanography chart of the area for him to look at. When she came up on deck she discovered he'd climbed on board and had put on his preserver. "Here." She put the rolled-up chart on the banquette next to him. "You can look at this as we proceed." Alessandra started the engine at a wakeless speed and drove them toward open water.

"This cruiser is state of the art."

She nodded. "A huge change from our old boat I took everywhere until my father bought this for me so I could go on longer trips."

"For pleasure?"

"It's always a pleasure, but I'm part of a team working for the Institute of Archaeological and Monumental Heritage."

Her response seemed to surprise him. "Where did you go to college?"

"I received my master's degree from the University of Catania. Our job is to identify and retrieve buried structures of archaeological interest."

"Living on an archaeological wonder, you come by your interest naturally."

She nodded. "My area of academics is to study the advanced techniques for nondestructive testing and remote sensing. Hopefully our work will expand our knowledge and help restore the historical buildings above and below the water in this area of Italy."

He sat on the banquette across from her with his hands clasped between his knees. She felt his eyes probing her with new interest. "It's no wonder your father told me I would be in good hands with you. You're an archaeologist. I thought maybe you were an engineer.

"Your father knew that you're exactly the person I need to consult while I'm here. Like you, I'm anxious to identify where the drilling will cause the least amount of destruction to the environment, both on land and water."

"Tell you what. After I give you a tour of the coastline, we'll go to my office at the castle. Since you're an engineer, you can watch a series of videos we've produced that will open your eyes to the many roadblocks you'll have to consider in order to drill and transport oil."

"I'm indebted to you, Alessandra."

"You have no idea what kinds of snags you're up against, so don't get too excited, *signore*."

"Call me Rini," he urged for a second time in his deep male voice that affected her insides. "I like snags. They make life exciting."

Though she agreed with him, she needed to be careful not to let this man get under her skin. Alessandra had a hunch he wasn't just talking about the search for oil. He had a way of infiltrating her defenses no matter where she turned. She had a feeling that if she got involved with him, he had the power to hurt her in ways that she would never get over.

"Why don't you consult the map I brought up? It will explain a lot as we go."

As they cruised along the coast, she glimpsed a half smile that broke the corner of his compelling mouth before he did her bidding and unraveled it for his perusal. He was such a breathtaking man, she could hardly concentrate.

It was hard to believe he wanted to be with her and not Dea. For some reason Rini Montanari hadn't been interested in her sister. She couldn't comprehend it.

Probably Dea hadn't been able to comprehend it, either. But Alessandra didn't know what went on in her sister's mind and would be a fool to make any more assumptions about anything.

Just be excited that he wants to be with you, Alessandra.

CHAPTER THREE

By five in the afternoon Rini had seen as much as he needed for a preliminary assessment. Alessandra had been a fountain of knowledge. Depending on Onorato's willingness to continue their talks, he wanted to bring out a team from the Naples office to begin an in-depth exploration.

But at this point business wasn't on his mind. During their outing he'd grown hungry. She'd brought along water and snacks, but he wanted a big dinner and intended to surprise her by taking her out for a meal. He'd seen a helipad at the side of the castle and went below deck to call for a helicopter.

With her expertise she guided the boat to the pier and shut off the engine. He discarded the life preserver and jumped to the dock to tie the ropes. In a moment the rotors of the helicopter sounded overhead.

Alessandra looked up. "I guess my parents are back. That's a surprise. Mother told me they could be gone for several days." She removed her preserver.

"I think that's *my* helicopter."

She blinked. "You sent for yours?" Did he see disappointment in her eyes?

"I chartered one to take us to dinner. Last night you turned me down. Tonight I decided not to take any chances on another rejection."

Her eyes slid away from his. "Where are we going?"

Good. She'd decided not to fight him. "That's my surprise. Bring what you need and leave the rest in the boat. We'll retrieve everything later."

"You don't want to change clothes?"

"There's no need."

She nodded. "I'll only be a moment." Before long she came back up on deck having applied a fresh coat of lipstick.

Avoiding his help, she climbed out of the boat and they made their way to the helicopter in the distance. But she couldn't refuse him when he opened the door to assist her into the back. Their arms brushed and he inhaled her light, flowery fragrance, which made him more aware of her.

Within seconds they lifted off and the pilot flew them due east. For the next little while her gaze fastened on the landscape below. When they started their descent to the city of a hundred thousand, she darted Rini an excited glance. "I love Lecce! It's a masterpiece of baroque architecture."

"I haven't been here in several years, but I remember a restaurant near the cathedral and hope it's still as good."

He'd arranged for a limo to drive them into the city nicknamed the Florence of the South. They got out and started walking along the narrow, shop-lined streets to the square for their dinner.

Lots of tourists, plus music from the many eating

places, put him in a holiday spirit, something he hadn't felt in years. Alessandra stopped in front of every shop and boutique, all of which were made from the soft local limestone. The facades were a mass of cherubs. She delighted in their faces as well as the displays. He hadn't felt this carefree in years.

"Oh, Rini. Look at that precious cat! It reminds me of Alfredo." They'd stopped in front of a souvenir shop selling the famous *Cartapesta* items of saints and animals made out of papier-mâché and painted.

"I think you're right. Let's buy it for your housekeeper." Without waiting for a response, he lifted the three-inch orange crouching cat from the shelf and walked inside to pay for it. The clerk put it in a sack. When he exited the shop, Alessandra stared up at him.

"She'll be thrilled."

He handed her the gift. "Will you keep it until we get back to the castle?"

"That was very kind of you," she said in a quiet voice. After sliding it in her purse, they walked out to the square.

"If my memory serves me correctly, our restaurant is on the right, halfway down the colonnade. We'll eat what they bring us. There's no menu." After the call to arrange for the helicopter, he made a reservation at the famous restaurant. When they reached it, the maître d' showed them inside to a table that looked out on the square.

Mugs of *caffè in ghiaccio con latte di mandorla* arrived. She smiled between sips. "I'm already addicted to that wonderful almond flavor."

"Agreed. How about the antipasto?"

She experimented. "These are fabulous. I could make a whole meal on the salmon-and-oyster bruschetta alone."

"I like the little tortillas with olives."

"There's nothing not to like, Rini." Soon they were served angel-hair pasta with sardines. If that wasn't enough, they were brought mouthwatering apple crostinos for dessert.

"I'm so full, I don't think I can move. Thank you for bringing us here. I haven't had a meal like this in years."

He loved it that she enjoyed her food. "It's the least I can do after everything you've done for me. I'm in awe of your knowledge. Not only that, you're a master sea woman." He put some bills on the table, then got up and escorted her out of the restaurant. Night had fallen, adding to the beauty of the square.

"A *sea woman*? Sounds like a new species." Her soft laughter charmed him.

"Until your father gets back, I'm hoping to spend a few more days on the water with you. It's true I'm here on business, but I've decided to take a few days to mix pleasure with it."

He led them through a street to find a taxi so they could head back to the helipad at the airport. Once on board they took off, then he turned to her. "Your scuba equipment has been calling to me. How about we pick up some gear for me tomorrow and you take us where you go diving. I'll charter us a boat."

"That would be ridiculous when we can use my boat."

"I wouldn't want you to think I'm taking advantage of you."

"Can we just not worry about that?"

"That's fine with me. What I'd like to do is camp out. I'll be your buddy. Could I tear you away from your work that long, or would it be asking too much?"

After they reached the island and got in the car, she eyed him speculatively. "After the exquisite meal, it pains me to have to turn you down. I'm afraid I'm behind on my project, but you're welcome to take the cruiser and go exploring on your own."

He didn't believe her excuse. She could be warm and engaging, but if he got too close, she'd retreat. After finally meeting a woman who thrilled him in so many ways, he couldn't take the disappointment that she put other plans first. It was driving him crazy.

"If you don't go with me, I won't have a buddy. You're so smart and know so much, a trip without you wouldn't be fun. What if we go out early after your work is over for the day? Say two o'clock?"

"I'm not sure I can be finished by then." She got out of the car and started walking to the entrance in an attempt to elude him.

He caught up to her. "Then we'll play it by ear."

"You never give up, do you?" But she said it with a smile. "All right."

Those two little words gave him hope, but the minute they went inside the castle, Liona and her cat were there to greet them. "You have a visitor, Alessandra. He insisted on waiting for you. I've put him in the small salon."

Him? Maybe Rini had been right and she was seeing someone.

"Thank you, Liona." She pulled the sack out of her
purse. "This is for you. Signor Montanari bought it for
you."

The older woman smiled. *"Veramente?"* She opened
the sack and pulled out the cat. "This looks like *you*,
Alfredo. You must have bought this in Lecce!"

Rini nodded. "It caught our eye."

"Mille grazie, signor. Come on, Alfredo. Let's look
at this treasure together." She put the cat in her arms.
"Buona notte," she called over her shoulder.

Alessandra's eyes darted to him. "You've made her
night."

He cocked his head. "But it appears yours isn't over
yet, so I'll leave you to your guest and see you tomorrow. *Dormi bene.*"

After wishing her good-night he headed for the stairs,
which he took two at a time to his room on the third
floor. Full of adrenaline because she'd finally agreed to
be with him tomorrow, he pulled out his phone and returned Guido's call. Though it was late, his friend would
probably still be awake. On the third ring he answered.

"Rini? I'd given up and was headed for bed."

"Sorry. I just got back to my room."

"Where are you?"

"In a castle on the island of Posso."

Guido chuckled. "Sure you are. So what's happening? Are we still on for Saturday?"

"I'm not sure."

"Don't tell me it's work again."

"Not this time."

"That sounds serious."

"I am. Have you got a minute?"

"Since when do you have to ask me a question like that? Go ahead. I'm all ears."

For the next little while he unloaded on his friend, leaving nothing out. When he'd finished, Guido whistled in response.

"In my gut I know Alessandra likes me, but she's keeping me at a distance. I asked her to go scuba diving tomorrow and she finally gave in, but she's not easy to understand. She doesn't wear a ring, but tonight a man was waiting for her when we got back from dinner."

"Then the first thing you need to find out is if she's committed."

Rini's brows furrowed. "I don't think she is. The housekeeper referred to the man as a visitor."

"All's fair then. Are you thinking she's being hesitant because you met her sister first? You know, that kind of unwritten law thing."

"Maybe."

"The only way to find out is go after her and learn the truth for yourself."

"I'll do it. Thanks for the advice."

After a long silence, his friend said, "I've been wondering when this day would come."

Guido wasn't the only one...

"I'll call you later in the week to make final plans for Saturday. Ciao."

He rang off, but he was feeling restless and decided to go for a walk before trying to get some sleep.

* * *

Alessandra waited outside the castle entrance while Bruno drove to the dock to get his scuba gear. When he came back, she approached the driver's side of his van. "Did you find everything?"

He nodded. "I'm sorry to have bothered you so late. I have to leave on the diving trip for the institute in the morning. I wish you'd join us. We'll be out there for another three days at least."

"What spot this time?"

"The same one. We haven't begun to explore that area thoroughly."

"I agree."

"Will you come? I know you're busy on your book, but we need your expertise." His gray eyes urged her to say yes. "I'd rather buddy with you than anyone else."

I know. But she didn't feel the same. "Bruno? Please don't take this wrong, but I want to keep our friendship on a professional basis and won't be buddying with you again."

He looked surprised. "Does this mean there's someone else?"

Exasperated, she said, "It means I'd prefer to keep my work separate from my personal life. I hope you understand."

Tight-lipped, he accelerated faster than necessary and took off.

"Someone didn't seem very happy," a deep male voice said behind her.

She whirled around in shock. "Rini, I—I thought you'd gone to bed."

"It's a beautiful night. I was afraid I wouldn't be able to sleep, so I decided to go for a walk around the castle. Did the fact that my kidnapping you to Lecce upset certain plans you had with your visitor?"

"If I'd had plans, I wouldn't have gone with you. That man was Dr. Tozzi from the archaeological institute. He came to get his scuba gear out of the cruiser. Tomorrow he's going on another exploratory dive with the others for a few days."

"You two dive together a lot?"

"There's a whole group of us. Last week we went out on our boats from Metaponto. He happened to be my buddy that trip, so that's why his scuba gear ended up in the cruiser. Tonight I told him he'd have to find another buddy because I would like our relationship to stay completely professional. "

"He doesn't have his own boat?"

"Yes, but he forgot to transfer his equipment after we'd finished. The institute has a state-of-the-art oceanography boat, but he won't bring it out until we've made a positive find."

"I see. Are you supposed to go out with them again?"

"Yes, but I have to divide up my time."

His dark brows lifted. "You're a very important person, besieged on every side, so I have an idea for tomorrow. While you work on your book for part of the day, I'll run in to Metaponto to get me some gear. Then we'll join your group. En route you and I can talk over your father's business. That way you can please everyone, including me. What do you say?"

She let out a sigh. Already he was reducing her to

mush. "I'll get up early and work until lunch, then we'll leave for Metaponto. The dive shop will have the gear you need. From there we can head for the dive site and meet up with the others."

"I'd like to stay out overnight and camp."

"I would, too. It's one of my favorite things to do."

"Good." His eyes blazed. "I shall look forward to it. I'll see you at lunch."

He took off for another run around the tiny island without giving her a chance to say anything else. Alessandra hurried inside the castle, secretly excited to go diving with him. Thoughts of buddying with him left her breathless. The idea that they would protect each other was so appealing she couldn't wait.

At six the next morning she showered and dressed quickly before heading to the library to work on her book. While she was knee-deep in research, Liona entered the library.

"Alessandra? Signor Montanari is eating his lunch in the dining room."

Her head lifted. "It's that time already?"

"*Si.* One o'clock."

"I can't believe I lost track of time. Tell him I'll be right there."

She raced out of the room and up the stairs to freshen up, then hurried back down with her packed duffel bag. When she entered the dining room he stood up to greet her. The man looked amazing in white cargo pants and a dark brown crewneck shirt.

"Sorry I'm late."

His dark eyes traveled up her jean-clad legs to her

white pullover, then found her gaze. "We're in no hurry. Sit down and eat lunch."

"I'd rather not take the time now. While you rent scuba gear, I'll grab us some food and drinks at the nearby deli to hold us over until tomorrow."

"With the announcement of an overnight on the water, you've made my day, *signorina.*"

Everything he said and did made her pulse race. Her feelings for him were spilling all over the place. She didn't know how to stop them. *She didn't want to stop them.*

He followed her out of the room with his backpack and they left for Metaponto in the cruiser. At the dive shop they loaded up with extra tanks. Once they'd bought drinks and groceries, they gassed up the cruiser and headed west. She handed him the special ocean chart he'd looked at before.

"We'll be diving at the midway point between Metaponto and Crotone. Some of the finds date back to the Magna Graecia. We're looking for some columns from the sixth century before Christ reputed to be there.

"If we're really lucky, we'll see the remnants of a temple dedicated to the goddess Hera. This area of the Ionian is a treasure trove, but as you realize, all the artifacts are buried, making them almost impossible to discover."

Rini looked up from the chart to flash her an intriguing smile. "It's the *almost* impossible that fires your blood, *non è vero*?"

She nodded. But artifacts weren't the only thing that fired her blood. The flesh-and-blood male who was a living Adonis had made her come alive without even trying. She'd taken one look at him that first evening in the castle foyer and had fallen so hard, she feared she would never recover.

It was too late to wish he'd gone back to Naples. Already she hated the idea that he would have to leave at all. Her thoughts were crazy. This was the renowned Rinieri Montanari she was talking about, not just any man.

Alessandra imagined that every woman who met him couldn't get enough. Even her mother had been bowled over by him. But the fact that he was still a bachelor meant there was a big reason he didn't have a wife.

Maybe he'd lost a great love and could never bring himself to marry. Or he enjoyed women, but couldn't commit to one for fear of feeling trapped. So no matter how attentive he was being right now, Alessandra would be a fool to think *she* would be the one woman in Italy who could do what no other female had done and win his love.

She glanced at him. "How long has it been since you went diving?"

Rini folded up the chart. "A year, but don't worry. You can count on me." Deep down she knew she could trust him. He engendered a confidence she'd never felt around other men. It didn't bother her that he'd just said he wasn't concerned about the time that had passed since his last dive.

"How have you stayed away from it so long?"

"Too much work."

"But there are lots of marvelous diving sites in the

Naples area. Surely you could have taken some time off."

"True, but even though the office is there, I don't live in Naples and am always anxious to fly home at the end of the day."

That was a surprise. "Where is home?"

"Positano."

"Oh—such a glorious spot with fabulous diving opportunities."

"My friends and siblings did it with me for several years, but for most of the last year my sister Valentina lived with me while she was expecting her baby. That meant no diving for her. As I told you earlier, we'd just lost our mother in a car accident. I divided my time between visiting my father at our family home in Naples and staying around the villa for my sister in order to keep her company."

Alessandra hadn't realized he'd carried such a load. She was touched by the way he cared for his family. "Did she have her baby?"

"*Si.* My nephew, Vito, is thriving. The man Valentina married has adopted him. They live in Ravello with his son, Ric. Both babies were born the same day at the same hospital."

"You're kidding—"

"What's really amazing was that the babies got switched. Valentina brought the wrong baby home while the man she married took home Valentina's son."

"What?" She almost lost control of the wheel. "How awful! Where was the mother?"

"They were divorced. At birth she gave up her mother's rights to Giovanni. It was a nightmare after the babies were returned to their birth parents. By then Valentina and Giovanni had bonded with the children. At that point they began to see each other so they could be with both babies and they fell in love."

A smile lit up her face. "That's the greatest love story I ever heard. How hard to love the wrong baby, but how sweet they were able to make everything work out. The person I feel sorry for is the mother who gave her child away. I can't comprehend it. I love my mother so much, I don't want to think what it would have been like if she hadn't been there for me. In fact I can't wait until the day comes when I can have my own baby."

He seemed caught up in his own thoughts before he said, "Fortunately she came to her senses and has now worked out visitation so she can help raise her son."

"That's the way it should be!" But Alessandra couldn't help but wonder about the father of his sister's baby. Still, she didn't want to pry.

"I can read your mind, Alessandra. Vito's father was one of Valentina's engineering professors at the University in Naples, but he didn't want marriage or children. My sister suffered terribly, but today she's so happy, you would never know she'd been through so much trauma."

Alessandra could relate to the trauma. Her hands tightened on the controls. She was living proof you could get through a broken heart and survive the emotional pain, but not everyone could end up as happy as his sister.

"So she's an engineer, too."

"Yes. A brilliant one."

"What does her husband do for a living?"

"He's the CEO of the Laurito Corporation."

Alessandra smiled at him. "That's an amazing combination. Your sister was blessed to have a brother like you to watch over her." She was coming to find out Rini was an extraordinary man. He'd even bought that little gift for Liona.

"Our family is close."

Alessandra could say the same where her parents were concerned. Before long she could pick out the red-and-white scuba flags from two boats ahead. "There they are!" The group had already started diving in an area near the coast. "If anything of significance is found, Dr. Tozzi will bring out the institute's boat. Today we're still exploring."

Alessandra brought her boat to a stop and lowered the anchor. After she raised her flag, she looked back at Rini. He'd already slipped on his wet suit. By the gleam in his eyes she could tell he'd been anticipating this dive.

"I'll be right back." She took her wet suit below to change. Talk about excited. She could hardly keep her fingers from trembling before going back up on deck.

In a moment they'd put on their weight belts and buoyancy-control devices. He reminded her of the film phenomenon James Bond. She finished dressing and put her goggles in place. "We'll be going down eighty feet. Ready?"

"Si, bellissima."

He shouldn't have said that to her. The deep tone of his compliment curled to her insides, disturbing her concentration. She ended up jumping in the water after he did, almost forgetting to keep her goggles and regulator in place.

The air temperature registered eighty degrees, but the water was cooler. Once below the surface she pressed the button to let out some air. The weights carried her down, down. Rini stayed right with her, watching her as their ears adjusted to the pressure. She could tell by the way he moved that he was a pro. It made her feel perfectly safe.

Eight minutes later they reached the sea floor with its clumps of vegetation and only a smattering of tiny fish. He stayed with her as she moved toward the area where she could see the group working. They all waved to her. She motioned for Rini to swim with her beyond the circle and examine a nearby area. The ridge in the distance looked promising, but as she brushed some of the debris away, it turned out to be more debris instead of a column lying on its side.

Rini found some interesting spots and waved her over to him, but every investigation came up short. She got the feeling they were searching in the wrong area. After a half hour he tapped his watch. She'd been about to do the same thing because it was time to go up and it would take a while.

They started the ascent, listening to the rhythm of their breathing through their regulators. She felt like they were the only people alive and loved this dive that had been magical for her. The sheer pleasure of enjoying this experience with him, of depending on him, could never be equaled.

Once they broke the surface, he helped her onto the

transom before levering himself on board. Before she could sit down on a banquette, another boat approached them.

"Alessandra—"

"Ciao, Bruno." She waved to him and the three others from the institute who rode with him.

"I was hoping you'd make it. Who's your friend?"

"Bruno Tozzi, meet Signor Montanari." The two men nodded. She refused to tell him anything about Rini. "It's too bad we haven't turned up anything interesting yet."

"We'll have to keep searching tomorrow."

Another of the divers said, "Why don't you join us in Crotone for dinner?"

"Thank you, but I'm afraid we have other plans. We'll do another dive with you in the morning."

"Bene."

In a minute their boat drove off. Alessandra was glad he'd gone and hurried below deck to get out of her wet suit. When she came up on deck a few minutes, she found Rini already changed into his clothes. He'd organized their gear near the back of the boat and had taken down the flag.

His eyes played over her. "It's growing dark. Do you have a place in mind where we can camp?"

"Yes. A small, secluded cove five minutes from here. I'll raise the anchor." She turned on the boat lights and they headed for the coast. Her heart fluttered in her chest when she thought of spending the night out here with him. Because she knew this area so well, they arrived quickly. She cut the engine and the momentum swept them onto the sandy portion of the isolated beach.

Alessandra turned to him. "Do you want to eat on deck, or in the galley?"

"Since the food is already up here, let's stay put, shall we? I'll do the honors and serve you for a change."

"Well, thank you."

In a minute he had everything laid out on the opposite banquette and they could pick what they wanted—fruit, meat pastries, cheese rolls, drinks, chocolate and almonds.

He sat back in the chair opposite her and feasted. "After that dive, this is heaven," he admitted with satisfaction.

"I can tell you're a seasoned diver, Rini. It was a privilege to be with you today."

"Now you know how I feel to have joined you. I'm excited about tomorrow's dive. Maybe we'll find something, but even if we don't, it doesn't take away from the thrill of being with an expert like you."

His compliments sounded so sincere, she was in danger of believing them. "I loved it."

After a brief silence, he said, "Dr. Tozzi was upset to see you out here with me, so don't deny it."

"I wasn't going to." She reached for some more grapes. "I'm glad you were with me. I've told him I'm not interested in him. Now he's seen it for himself."

Rini's dark brows furrowed. "Is that the reason I was invited along?"

He couldn't really think that, could he? It would mean he felt vulnerable. She couldn't imagine him having a vulnerable bone in his body. She leaned forward. "Of course not!"

He bit into another plum. "Is there an important man in your life?"

Yes. I'm looking at him. "Not in years."

"Why not?"

"I could ask you the same thing," she blurted without thinking. "Why does Rinieri Montanari sail alone?"

"I asked you first," he returned. "A beautiful, fascinating woman like you has to have a history."

Alessandra wasn't used to hearing those adjectives attributed to herself. If he only knew it, she was totally enamored with him. "You don't really want to know."

"I wouldn't have asked otherwise." At this point he'd put the leftover food back in the sacks she would take down to the galley later.

"I fell in love with Francesco at twenty-two. He was a chef from Catania when I was in my last year of undergraduate school. He swore undying love for me and said he'd found his soul mate. I believed him. We talked about getting married.

"One weekend Dea came to visit. I was excited for her to meet him. She stayed in my apartment with me and the three of us spent time together. After she left for Rome, where she was pursuing a modeling career, everything seemed to change. He suddenly told me he had to go on vacation and would call me as soon as he got back. During those two weeks he didn't phone me once.

"I thought I'd lose my mind until I heard from him. I imagined every reason under the sun for his absence except the one he gave me. He didn't have the decency to tell me in person. Instead, he sent me a letter telling me he'd fallen in love with Dea and knew I couldn't forgive him."

Lines darkened Rini's features in the semidarkness.

"At the time it was terrible. Dea didn't come home for two months. When she did, she told me he'd followed her to Rome, but it was over between the two of them almost before it had begun. She thought he was a loser and told me I was better off without him.

"Though inwardly I agreed, my pain had reached its zenith because Dea always had this power to get the boys interested in her. But when it came to Francesco, who I thought was committed to me, something broke inside me. I suffered for a long time. But it happened over six years ago and is buried in the past." She took a drink of water. "Now it's your turn to tell me the secrets of your heart, dark or otherwise."

CHAPTER FOUR

RINI FELT LIKE he'd been stabbed in the chest. Too many emotions rocked him at once. There was someone he needed to talk to before he bared his soul to Alessandra.

"I'm afraid my story would take all night. Let's reserve it for tomorrow evening after another dive. If you don't mind, I'd like to sleep up here tonight."

"Then you'll need the quilt and pillow on the bed in the other cabin in order to be comfortable."

"I'll get them."

"You sound tired after that dive, Rini. I am too, so I'll say good night."

"Buona notte."

He waited an hour before going below to bring up the bedding. Once he'd made himself comfortable on the banquette at the rear of the cruiser, he pulled out his phone and called his sister. Rini knew it was too late to be phoning, but he had to talk to her.

After four rings he heard her voice. "Rini? What's wrong? Has something happened to Father?"

"No, no."

After a short silence she asked, "Are you ill?" He

could hear Giovanni's concerned voice in the back-ground.

"Not physically. But I'm wrestling with a problem that needs your slant. Do you mind?"

"What a question! After all you've done for me, I'd give anything to help you if I can. Tell me what's going on."

He raised up on one elbow. "Let me give you a little background." Without wasting words, he explained his dilemma from beginning to end.

"Ooh" was all she said when he'd finished.

"Forgive me if this touches too close to home, but you're the one person in the world who would under-stand her pain after Francesco went after her sister."

"Rini? I got over Matteo's womanizing and it sounds like she has gotten over her pain, too, so forget her past. You only have one problem. Let this woman know how you feel about her and prove to her that your love for her is everlasting. If Mamma were still alive, she would tell you to follow your heart and not let anything get in the way."

He could hear his mother saying those very words. "Alessandra was really hurt."

"So was I. It passes when the right man comes along. Trust me."

He breathed deeply. "You make it sound so simple."

"Nothing worthwhile is simple, Rini. But look what happened when I followed my heart instead of letting go of Ric, the baby I thought was mine…"

"You mean instead of listening to me tell you not to

get involved with Giovanni," he groaned. "I was a fool to interfere."

"Of course you weren't! I know you were only trying to protect me. But it all worked out and I'm now an ecstatic wife and the mother of two angelic boys."

His eyes closed tightly. "But from the start Giovanni wanted you enough to defy convention, too. That's why it worked."

"Rini, tonight you're alone with her on her family's cruiser. Do you seriously think that would have happened if she weren't absolutely crazy about you?"

"Her father asked her to show me around."

"But to dive? Camp out over night? Have faith, dear brother. A little patience wouldn't hurt until she realizes she can trust you with her life."

A lump had lodged in his throat. "*Ti amo*, Valentina."

"*Ti amo. Buona notte.*"

Rini lay back down, thinking about what she'd said. Even if a miracle happened and her attraction grew into love, she didn't know about his infertility, an insurmountable hurdle in his mind.

The next thing he knew, the sound of gulls brought him fully awake. Clouds blotted out the sun. He sat up to check his watch. Seven thirty. Was Alessandra still asleep? He gathered the bedding and took it below to the other cabin. Her door was still closed.

One thing he could do was fix them his favorite prosciutto ham and eggs to go with their breakfast. As he was putting their plates and mugs on the table, she appeared in the doorway wearing jeans and a T-shirt that molded to her beautiful body.

"You've got color in your cheeks."

"I went for a walk."

He'd had no idea. What a wonderful bodyguard he'd made! "If you'd wakened me, I would have gone with you. Sit down and I'll serve you."

"Umm. Everything smells good."

He poured them coffee and sat opposite her.

She took a sip. "How did you sleep?"

Rini stared at her through shuttered eyes. "There's nothing better than spending the night under the stars. What about you?"

"It's fabulous out here, but I confess diving makes me tired. I fell asleep once my head touched the pillow."

"That's good. How soon do we need to join the others?"

"They'll be out there by nine o'clock."

He swallowed the last of his eggs. "Just for the fun of it, what would you think if we enlarged the search area by traveling a quarter of a mile farther east from them to dive at the same distance from the coast?" He wasn't ready to share her with the others yet. "I consulted the chart. The depth of the sea floor isn't quite as great there. Maybe seventy feet. Who knows? We might make a discovery."

Her lips turned up at the corners. "Your mother must have gone crazy to have a son who went around with such an excited gleam for adventure in his eyes."

Rini liked the idea that she'd noticed. "Is that what I have?"

"Oh, yes. It probably got you into a ton of trouble."

He chuckled. "So what do you say?"

"I like your idea. Later on this afternoon we can join the others for another dive."

"Sounds like a plan." Pleased she was willing to go along with him so they could be alone a little longer, he got to his feet to clean up the kitchen. She cleared the dishes and they made quick work of it. He'd never experienced this kind of togetherness with a woman before. Rini couldn't imagine letting her go.

"Thanks for fixing the delicious breakfast. I'll change into my wet suit and meet you on deck."

He bounded up the stairs to put on his own gear. To spend a whole day with her doing something they both loved couldn't have excited him more.

In fifteen minutes they'd arrived at the spot he'd suggested for a dive. They had the whole sea to themselves for the moment. She lowered the anchor and erected the flag. Together they put on all their equipment. "Ready?" he called to her.

Her brandy eyes clung to his, pulling at his heart strings. "Let's go!"

They jumped in the water. He experienced delight as they sank lower past more tiny fish. Once they reached the bottom, they explored around all the vegetation that grew taller and was more plentiful than at the other spot. He saw traces of some deep-sea-fishing tackle caught by the undergrowth. It was like playing hide-and-seek as they swam here and there like little children let out to play.

His eyes followed her as they moved through a new chute. He was so mesmerized by the fun he was having, he almost ran into her because she'd suddenly stopped.

When he looked beyond her, he saw a large round-ish shape like a big boulder covered in debris ahead of them.

The hairs lifted on the back of his neck and knew she was feeling the same electricity. Something was here that didn't belong. He swam to one side of it and waited for her to approach the other side. She was the expert.

Her hands began to brush away the layers of silt. He helped her. After five minutes of hard work, they uncovered part of what looked like a sculpted mouth. Alessandra's eyes stared at him with a glow through her goggles. This was a fantastic find and they both knew it.

While he marveled, she tapped her watch. He'd been too engrossed and forgot the time. They needed to go up to the surface now! It was hard to leave after what they'd just discovered, but they would be back later.

Rini knew the rules by heart. Keep his breathing steady as they rose, but it was hard when his adrenaline was gushing. He could only imagine Alessandra's joy. This was her life!

They broke the top of the water and swam toward the boat. Like déjà vu he helped her on board the cruiser, then climbed in himself.

"Oh, Rini," she cried, having removed the belt and breathing apparatus. "We found something that could have belonged to the Temple of Hera. We've got to find Dr. Tozzi and bring the others here!"

Without conscious thought he grasped her upper arms, bringing her close to his body. "Congratulations!"

Her eyes, the color of dark vintage brandy, searched his. "It was your inspiration that brought us here."

For a moment he was caught up in the wonder of her beauty that went soul deep. "I'll never forget the experience of winding through that undersea garden with you."

"Neither will I," she whispered.

He pulled her closer and closed his mouth close over hers. The unexpectedness of it must have caught her off guard because she began kissing him back with a fervency he could only have dreamed about.

Hungry for her, Rini drove their kiss deeper, marveling over her response to him. Sensation after sensation of desire caused him to kiss her senseless. Only the wake from a passing boat that bounced the cruiser reminded him how far gone he was.

Alessandra seemed to feel it, too. She tore her lips from his and moved out of his arms. "If—if you'll mark this spot on the chart, I'll drive," she stuttered.

He didn't like it that she'd headed for the controls, leaving him bereft. So much for him practicing the patience Valentina had talked about. Rini hadn't been able to keep himself from crushing her in his arms. He'd wanted that divine fusion to go on and on.

While Alessandra raised the anchor and started the engine, he reached in his backpack for a pen. He found the rolled-up chart on the banquette and sat down to fill in the information, but it was difficult. To his surprise the wind had kicked up. He looked overhead and noticed that more clouds had been amassing. Three hours ago it had only been overcast and there hadn't been this breeze.

She drove as fast as the elements would allow. Finally

in the distance he saw the flags of the three boats. They drew closer and waved to several groups of divers in two of the boats. Soon Alessandra drew alongside one of them. "How long has Dr. Tozzi been down?"

"He and Gino should be coming up any minute."

"Did you find anything?"

They shook their heads.

"Well, all is not lost. We have some amazing news." She cut the engine and lowered the anchor while they waited in the rocking crafts for the head of the institute to appear. Rini shared a private glance with her. He could feel her eagerness to impart their finding.

Rini watched until he saw two heads pop out of the water. The divers reached their boat and climbed in. The second the good doctor removed his headgear, his gaze shot to Alessandra.

"You missed this morning's dive."

"We did our own dive farther east and raced here to tell you what we found." In the next breath she told everyone about the head.

"You uncovered a mouth?" The doctor sounded incredulous.

"I wish we could show it to you now, but the weather is acting up. Maybe by early evening we can do another dive. In the meantime, why don't you follow us to the cove where we spent the night on the beach? The site is right off the coast from there and a little east where we can eat before you leave for the port."

Everyone agreed it was a good idea. Alessandra raised the anchor and started the engine. Once again they took off for the cove. While he stayed on the cruiser, Alessandra climbed out to chat with the others. They decided the storm wouldn't hit until evening, but it would be better not to go out diving again today.

"Are you staying here again tonight?"

"I'm not sure what our plans are, Gino, but we'll definitely be here tomorrow at nine to show you the dive site, unless the weather is worse."

Rini had checked ahead. There'd be a storm later. On impulse he picked up the chart and got out of the boat to show it to them. "In case we don't get together, I've marked the coordinates on here if you want to write them down."

Dr. Tozzi glanced at it and made notes on the pad in his pocket before handing it back to Rini. "Thanks."

"You're welcome."

The group prepared to leave. Nothing could have made Rini happier. So happy, in fact, that he handed Alessandra the chart, then helped push the other boats back in the water and waved everyone off.

Alessandra had to suppress a smile. Rini couldn't have been more helpful. How could any man measure up to the famous CEO who could scuba dive and read ocean charts with the best of them?

In a few more days, when he'd finished up business with her father, he'd fly off to Naples and his busy life that sent him all over the country. She had to remember he was only here in the south of Italy for a few more days. To think of him leaving was killing her.

If it turned out her parents agreed to let his company do some drilling, Rini would send out their experts.

From time to time she'd see him coming and going from the castle. But for today and tomorrow, they would be together and it thrilled her heart.

She turned to him. "How would you like to do something fun?"

He cocked his dark head. "What kind of a ridiculous question is that to ask a man alone with a beautiful woman?"

"Just checking," she teased and got back in the boat with her heart thudding in her chest. "If you're game for a bumpy ride, I know a place where the food is divine. By boat it will take us about an hour and a half. When we get there we'll enjoy an early dinner and stay overnight."

"That good, hmm?"

"Yes."

"Only if you'll let me drive us. So far *you've* done all the work."

"I don't mind, but if that's what you want."

"It'll relieve my guilt."

"Over what?"

"I like to feel useful."

"You were amazingly useful when you pushed all the boats off the sand. You reminded me of Hercules."

His deep laughter resounded in the air.

"I'm not kidding. They would have had a terrible time in this wind without your help."

"If I impressed you, then it was worth the pain."

Her eyes scrutinized him from head to toe. "You did it so effortlessly, I doubt there's a sore muscle in your body."

He returned her gaze, sending the color flooding into her cheeks. "I guess it comes from both of us living in and out of the water."

She looked down. "Would you believe I still need to get out of my wet suit?"

"Do you need help?"

She felt the blush break out on her face. "I think I can handle it."

"While you do that I'll push us off and we'll get going."

Her chest fluttered as she hurried below deck to change and freshen up. After ascertaining that her parents had left her aunt's and had gone back to the castle, she joined Rini. He'd changed clothes and was seated in the captain's chair wearing his life preserver. "Tell me where to go."

Alessandra reached in the cubbyhole for her regular map and opened it, but the wind made it difficult to keep steady. "We're here. Keep following the coast past Metaponto, then we'll cut a diagonal and head straight for Taranto."

"That's where your aunt lives?"

"Yes. Our mother's titled family descends from the Duca di Taranto, although the title is now defunct, like my father's."

"Ah. It's all making sense." He put the map back and handed her a life preserver. "Sit across from me so we can talk."

She grinned. "Aye, aye, sir, but I don't think we'll be able to hear each other."

"As long as we're together, I don't care."

The man could read her mind. She sat on the banquette and stared out at a sea full of white caps. The moderate swells slowed them down, but she was having the time of her life. Since he hadn't vacationed in a year, Alessandra suspected he was happy, too, especially after he was the one to have picked the area where they'd made an underwater find. Every time he looked at her, his dark eyes burned with charged energy, melting her to the spot.

Outside Metaponto he stopped long enough to switch gas tanks. "I remember seeing Taranto's naval base and shipyards from the air."

"Then you know it's a big commercial city and port. Our Taranto relatives live in one of the eighteenth-century palazzi in the old town center. I've let my aunt know we're coming to see her. She broke her hip and has a nurse around the clock, but she loves visitors. Be warned she'll insist we eat dinner with her before we leave."

"I don't want to impose."

"She'll love it, Rini. Since you're a seafood lover, get ready to enjoy the most luscious roasted oysters you've ever eaten in your life. The cook prepares them in a special sauce followed by sea-bream-and-mussel soup. It's out of this world. Mother would steal her if she could."

He eyed her speculatively. "What's the other reason you're taking me there?"

You could never fool a man like Rini.

"She's mother's brilliant older sister by nine years and was married to a general who died two years ago. When Mamma was thirty, she almost died giving birth to me and Dea. Fulvia couldn't have children and was there to do everything. She won my father's devotion. As I told you earlier, her opinion goes a long way with both of them. I'd like you to tell her your business ideas for developing the property."

His features sobered. "Are you saying your mother doesn't approve?"

"I'm afraid not. Both of them were raised to be purists and believe that the former papal legacy should remain untouched."

"What about *your* opinion, Alessandra?"

She took a deep breath. "I've listened to my father and think your idea is an important one. If a lot of oil is found, it *will* help the economy. But what's important is what Zia Fulvia has to say."

Those dark eyes searched hers. "Why are you trying to help me?"

A good question. "I believe in you *and* an even playing field."

"I'm humbled by your faith in me." He rubbed his jaw where the shadow of his beard was showing. She thought him irresistible. "Will I find her difficult?"

"Yes."

She loved the bark of laughter that came out of him.

"But you told me you like snags because they make life more exciting."

When he smiled, she felt herself falling toward him. "I did say that, didn't I? Let's go and get this over with. It couldn't be worse than a visit to the dentist."

Alessandra kept chuckling as the cruiser pounded the white water on its way to Taranto. She'd never met anyone with a sense of humor like his. He was getting to her with every minute they spent together.

Due to the wind they made slow progress. It was after five when they passed through the outer and inner sea to pull into the private dock reserved for her aunt's family. Alessandra called for the limo that drove them to the Taranto palazzo in the old town.

"Tarantos have lived here for over four hundred years," she explained as they turned into the court-yard with its fountain supported by Taras, the son of Poseidon from Greek mythology. "You'll think you've entered a fabulous museum. Fulvia and Mamma were raised princesses and Fulvia still lives like one."

"She won't shudder at the sight of us fresh off the boat?"

At seventy-seven Fulvia was still all woman and would probably faint when she saw the gorgeous male Alessandra had brought with her. "No. She's used to my showing up a mess after a day at sea."

Rini helped her out of the limo. "Lippo," she called to the older man who opened the ornate front door at the same time. *"Come stai?"*

"Bene, grazie, Alessandra."

"Please meet Signor Montanari."

"Piacere di conoscerla."

She looked at Rini. "Lippo and Liona are cousins. Our families couldn't live without them."

"Your families are close-knit in many ways," Rini murmured. "Does he have a cat, too?"

Alessandra chuckled. "He would, but my aunt has allergies."

"Signora Fulvia is in the drawing room, but she's tired since your parents left and is still off her food."

"We won't stay long."

"After you've spoken with her, dinner will be served in the small dining room."

"*Grazie*, Lippo."

Alessandra led Rini through hallways of marble floors and walls lined with gilt-framed portraits to her aunt's favorite room. Still a beauty, she sat in a wheel chair surrounded by the mementos of her deceased husband, who'd enjoyed a distinguished military career.

"*Buonasera*, Zia. I've missed you." She hugged her aunt. "I'm so sorry about your hip."

"A hazard of old age. Don't let it happen to you, *cara*." Her brown eyes flicked to Rini, assessing him with uncommon interest. No woman could help it. "Your fame as an engineer precedes you, Signor Montanari. Alessandra, why don't you see if your dinner is ready while I have a chat with him? Then I'll ask the nurse to take me to my room."

Her aunt had to be more miserable than she looked in order to get down to business this fast. "You poor thing. Please don't overdo it. I'll be right back." She shared a private glance with Rini before leaving the room. Though she felt the slightest bit apprehensive, he seemed perfectly at ease.

She didn't think anything could throw him. If he couldn't achieve his goal with her father, Alessandra knew he'd look elsewhere for oil because he was a man on a mission.

* * *

By nine thirty the bad weather had turned ugly. Rini
felt the rain as he helped Alessandra into the limo and
gave the driver instructions to return them to the private
dock. Though she'd told him they could stay the night
at the palazzo, the illuminating conversation with her
aunt had turned him inside out and he'd wanted to leave.

Her aunt had told him something that had nothing
to do with his business meetings with the count. She'd
brought up an alarming personal issue that had a direct bearing on Alessandra and her sister. He needed to
think long and hard about it for the good of the Caracciolo family before he shared it with Alessandra, *if he
ever did*. The only solution was to kill his feelings for
her. In order to do that, he needed to leave the castello
and search for hydrocarbons elsewhere in the south.

"I'd rather get back to the cruiser. It will do fine
while we wait out the storm." He imagined it would
last all night.

"Well?" she asked with a smile after they'd gone
below deck to the small room she used as an office. The
rain pounded down outside. He stretched out in one of
the chairs and extended his legs, crossing them at the
ankles. Across from him sat the woman he considered
the greatest beauty of the Taranto family bar none.

The humidity had curled the tips of her delightful
hair. With her pink cheeks, she reminded him of one
of the adorable cherub faces from Lecce. Her physical
looks were a given. But what he found truly exquisite
was her spirit—she had decided to give him a fighting

chance to carry through with an idea, although it would never see the light of day now.

"I loved the tour of the palazzo and the meal was superb."

"It always is, but I'm talking about your chat with my aunt. How did it go? She was too tired to talk to me before she went to bed."

None of it was meant for Alessandra's ears. "I thought I was talking to a strong minded woman."

Laughter bubbled out of her. "She's tough all right."

Choosing his words carefully he said, "We talked pro and con. Her knowledge and directness impressed me before she asked to be excused to go to bed."

She eyed him curiously. "That's all you can tell me?"

Tight bands constricted his chest. "There isn't anything else."

"Oh, dear. It doesn't sound like it went well."

"I have no idea. But be assured I enjoyed meeting her and I'm indebted for your help. Since it's getting late, why don't you go on to bed? I've got business calls to make. Sleep well."

After they'd left her aunt's palazzo the night before, Alessandra couldn't believe the change in Rini. He seemed to have turned into a different man, and was aloof, preoccupied. What on earth had they talked about that made him so unapproachable?

She went down to her cabin and cried herself to sleep over the way he'd just shut her out. She'd been waiting for him to kiss her again, but it never happened. What he and her aunt had talked about had changed him in some way.

When Alessandra woke up the next morning, Rini was already at the wheel. The weather had to be better, otherwise the cruiser wouldn't be skimming across the water with such speed.

Why hadn't he knocked on her door to waken her? Anything to let her know he was aware of her.

She couldn't understand it and got out of bed to dress. After making coffee in the galley, she went up on deck with her duffel bag in the hope he would be in a better frame of mind to talk to her.

But the second she saw the set jaw of that handsome face, she knew instinctively that now wasn't the right time. He was in no mood to confide in her. She walked over him. "I thought you might like this."

He eyed her briefly before taking the cup. "Thank you. You're an angel. As you can see, the storm has passed over. We'll have you home soon."

Home?

Her fear that something terrible was wrong had come to fruition. She frowned. "I thought we were going to dive. It's a great morning for it."

"I'd like to, but I'm afraid something came up while I made some business calls last night. I need to discuss them with your father. Please don't let that stop you from joining your group once you drop me off."

Diving was the last thing on her mind. She moved around and straightened the scuba equipment. They were almost to the island. Soon he eased the cruiser to the dock. When it was safe, she jumped out with her duffel bag and tied the ropes, leaving him to shut down the engine.

He joined her at the Land Rover. Their silent drive to the castle only took a minute, proof he was surprised she hadn't stayed in the boat before taking off again. Alessandra had the impression he couldn't wait to get away from her.

Sure enough, as soon as she'd parked the car, he reached for his backpack and got out. Alessandra followed him inside the foyer of the castle. He looked back at her. "I phoned your father earlier. He's waiting for me. Thank you for showing me your world. I loved every second of it."

So did I. Why are you acting like it's over? Rini— what's going on?

But he kept her in the dark. Without lingering, he walked toward her father's office.

With a heart that had fallen to the floor, she went up the staircase to shower and change into clean clothes. Her mother was probably in the day room so she hurried downstairs to talk to her. She would know what was going on with her father and Rini. This was a nightmare.

When she wasn't there, Alessandra went to the dining room and found it empty. "Hey, Alfredo. Are you looking for Liona?" She picked up the cat. On her way to the kitchen she heard the rotors of the helicopter. Someone must be arriving from the mainland. She kept on walking to the kitchen. No one was in there.

She lowered the cat to his food and water dishes, then she took off for her father's office. Maybe her mother was in there and she would find the three of them deep in conversation. After hesitating, she knocked on the door, unwilling to stay away any longer. "*Scusi*, Papà."

"Come in, *piccola*."

She found her father alone. "Where is everyone?"

"Your mother drove Liona to Metaponto for her dentist appointment." That explained why Alfredo looked lost.

"I—I thought Rini Montanari was still with you," she stammered.

He sat back in his leather chair. "He was here earlier to tell me that after thinking everything over, he decided that erecting oil derricks on our property would be a scab on the legacy Queen Joanna left to the family."

Those were the very words Alessandra had used. To hear her father say them brought inexpressible pain.

"He says he's off to search for another area to drill. After thanking both you and me profusely for our time and hospitality, he called for a helicopter and left."

Her legs started to buckle. She grabbed the first chair before she fell. "That's it? No other explanation?"

Her father smiled warmly. "Only to say that you discovered a large head while you were diving yesterday and he presumes it'll make you famous."

Except that Rini was the one with the inspiration to know where to dive.

"Oh—one more thing. He told me you're the most charming, lovely, intelligent woman he ever met and he understood why I wanted you to show him around. I could have told him that about you, but it's nice he discovered it for himself. As for the oil-drilling proposal,

I have to admit I'm glad he withdrew it. Neither your mother or Fulvia were in favor of it."

"I know." A boulder had lodged in her throat.

"Fulvia phoned your mother early this morning. We were surprised to learn you'd taken him to see her. It made her very happy to see you while she's recovering."

But the visit had turned out to be devastating for Alessandra. Once again her world had been destroyed. This time she knew she'd never be able to put it back together.

Alessandra took a quick breath. "Since the weather kept us from making another dive, I decided to pay her a visit. She was tired, but seems to be getting along fine."

"She was very impressed with Rinieri's honesty."

Honesty? What on earth did that mean?

Feeling ill, she got up from the chair. "I've been away from my work too long, so I'd better get busy or my editor will lose his patience. I'll be in the library if you need me." She hurried over to give him a kiss on the cheek before leaving the office.

When she reached her desk, she buried her face in her hands and sobbed. Several messages came in on her phone, all from Gino wanting to know if she would be joining them for the afternoon dive. None were from Rini.

Alessandra texted him that she couldn't make it, then left the castle in the Land Rover and drove to the mainland. After grabbing some food, she drove to the ridge where she'd taken Rini on that first day. The recent downpour had greened up the fields. She walked around, playing back their conversation in her head.

Alessandra was convinced that the excuse he'd given her father not to drill wasn't the real reason he'd backed off.

Deeply troubled, she returned to the castle and got busy on the historical biography she was writing on Queen Joanna. But by Saturday morning she couldn't stand it any longer. Rini had been cruel not to have contacted her, if only to say goodbye. After what they'd shared scuba diving, she wasn't about to let him walk away until he'd listened to a few things she had to say.

If this was how he ended every relationship with a woman, no wonder he was still a bachelor. He'd been clever to abort their growing attraction before it burned out of control. Rini had been every bit as hungry for her as she'd been for him when they'd kissed. So why had he done this?

He'd been the one to pursue her, to want to scuba dive with her. There'd been no stopping him getting his way because she'd wanted to be with him so badly, too, and still did. So what had changed everything? Alessandra needed answers and she wasn't going to let him get away with it.

After telling her parents she'd be home late, she drove the Land Rover to Metaponto and took a commercial flight to Positano. Without her father's knowledge she'd looked up Rini's home address on his computer.

She could have gone to the Montanari office in Naples, but figured he'd be home on the weekend. If she walked in on him entertaining another woman, that was too bad. She needed answers.

Three hours later the limo she'd hired wound around

the lush vegetation of his property. It stopped in front of a magnificent two-storied, ochre-colored villa, probably built at the turn of the century. Good heavens, the hilltop town above the Amalfi Coast was gorgeous beyond belief!

Alessandra marveled to know that Rini lived in this flower-filled paradise. The exterior was drenched in purple and red bougainvillea, robbing her of breath. So did the view of the sea from such a dizzying height.

A warm midafternoon sun shone down on her as she got out of the back. "Stay here, please," she said to the driver. She walked past several cars in the courtyard on her way to the front entrance. Alessandra hoped that meant Rini was home.

After using the bell pull, she waited for someone to answer and heard female voices inside. One said, "I'll get it, Bianca."

The moment the door opened, Alessandra knew she was looking at Rini's sister, who was a real blond beauty. Even though their coloring was different, the extraordinary family resemblance brought Rini to mind with a pang.

"*Buon pomeriggio, signorina.* Can I help you?" She'd answered the door in a bathing suit covered by a short lacy wrap.

Her heart was pounding too hard. "I hope so. I'm here to see Rini."

She studied Alessandra for a moment. "Aren't you the famous Diorucci model?"

CHAPTER FIVE

THIS WAS DÉJÀ VU all over again.

"That's my sister, Dea. I'm Alessandra Caracciolo."

"Well, you're both absolutely stunning."

"Thank you."

"I'm afraid my brother isn't here. I'm Valentina Laurito. Was he expecting you?"

"No." She swallowed hard. "I wanted to surprise him."

A mischievous smile broke the corners of his sister's mouth. "So did I. Bianca informed me he went fishing this morning and hasn't come back yet, but she's expecting him soon so I stayed."

Fishing…

While she took in the disappointing news, an older woman appeared in the foyer carrying a darling blond baby boy, the image of his mother. She made the introductions. "Have you come far?"

"I flew in from Metaponto."

"That's quite a ways. Won't you come in and wait with me while I give my son a bottle? We're out by the swimming pool. Vito loves his Zio Rini and keeps waiting for him to walk out."

Alessandra knew the feeling well. "If you don't mind, I'd love to."

"Tell your driver to come back for you later."

She did the other woman's bidding, then walked through Rini's elegant villa. The patio furniture included tables, chairs and a large swing. Alessandra saw plastic toys in the water. Valentina took the baby from the housekeeper and settled him in his baby swing with a cover to shield his eyes.

"We have extra bathing suits if you'd like to change and take a dip."

"Thank you, but no."

"You might like it after your flight."

"It didn't take that long. Besides I get in plenty of swimming." Valentina was so easy to talk to, Alessandra needed to be careful what she said to her. Rini was a private person who wouldn't appreciate her getting too familiar with his family. Especially not after he'd left the castle permanently.

She found a lounge chair close to the swing to watch the darling baby. In a minute she heard rotors overhead and her pulse leaped. What would Rini think when he found her out here with his family? Maybe she shouldn't have come, but it was too late now because moments later her gaze darted to the tall, dark figure striding toward them from the other end of the pool wearing jeans and a T-shirt.

"There's your *zio*!" Valentina cried.

"Vito—" Rini called to him. The baby turned his head toward his uncle and lifted his arms.

That's when Rini saw her and his eyes narrowed. "Alessandra," he murmured.

Without missing a beat he came close and picked up the baby in his arms, kissing him. "What a surprise. Two visitors in one afternoon."

"Alessandra has flown here from Metaponto, but I can't persuade her to take a swim."

"That's because she scuba dives for the archaeological institute from Catania and probably enjoys a break from swimming."

Valentina's head swung toward her. "Rini's a master diver, too!"

"I know. Your brother was instrumental in helping me make a find the other day. I'm indebted to him."

"Rini," his sister virtually blurted with excitement. "You didn't tell me about that." Her eyes took in the two of them.

With enviable calm he explained, "While I was looking for new oil fields, I tagged along with Alessandra. She lives on an archaeological treasure."

"Zio Salvatore called me when he couldn't find you at the office. You know how upset he gets."

He played with Vito, avoiding Alessandra's eyes. "I'm back from Calabria now and got in touch with him."

"That's a relief. So how was fishing?"

"Good. Guido caught two trout with the lure I gave him. We ate them for lunch."

"Lucky you. I'm glad you came home when you did. Vito and I waited as long as we could, and now we've got to get back to Ravello. Giovanni will be wondering where we are." She turned to Alessandra. "It was so nice to meet you."

"You, too. Your little boy is wonderful."

"Thank you. I think so, too. I have another son, Ric, but he's with his birth mother today." She took the baby from her brother's arms and disappeared into the villa.

Alessandra was left alone with Rini. Her pulse raced at the way his eyes ignited as he studied her for a moment without saying anything. She was glad she'd worn her white dress with the blue-and-green print, a favorite of hers. For once she'd knocked herself out trying to look beautiful for him. She'd even worn some eye makeup and had spent time on her hair.

"I think you know why I'm here," she said, answering the question he hadn't asked. "You didn't say goodbye." Her accusation hung in the air.

His hands went to his hips in a male gesture. "If you'll excuse me for a minute, I'll be right back."

"Promise?" she responded. He'd arrived dressed in outdoor gear with a navy crewneck shirt. With that hint of a dark beard on his jaw, she was almost overcome by his male virility. Alessandra had missed him so terribly, it hurt to look at him.

A nerve throbbed at the corner of his compelling mouth. "I swear it."

He left the patio on a run. She found a chair under the umbrella table and took in the sight of his own private Garden of Eden. So many species of flowers and trees astounded her, as everything looked perfect. All her life she'd lived in a castle surrounded by sand and water.

Alessandra loved the isolation, but being here in Rini's home made her appreciate what she'd been missing.

The fragrance from the roses intoxicated her. She got up and walked around to smell the various varieties. Soon she heard footsteps behind her. When she turned, she discovered that the woman Valentina had introduced her to had come out on the terrace. She pushed a cart of food and drinks to the table. "Rinieri will be right out, *signorina*."

"*Grazie*, Bianca."

From the corner of her eye she saw a baby sandal left on one of the chairs. She started to retrieve it when Rini came out on the patio dressed in tan trousers and a silky black sport shirt. Freshly shaved, he looked and smelled fabulous.

Alessandra held up the sandal. "Your sister left this in her wake. I'm afraid her fast exit was my fault."

"You're wrong." He took the little sandal and put it on the table. "She couldn't wait to join her husband. They're crazy about each other." Rini held out a chair for her. "Sit down and we'll eat. One trout apiece wasn't enough for the appetite I've developed."

"I'm hungry, too. They only served snacks on the plane."

In a minute they filled up on shrimp salad with penne, dried tomatoes and slices of grilled eggplant that melted in her mouth. Rolls and lemonade with mint leaves made their meal a feast, but clearly Rini was a fish man.

Filled to the brim, she sat back in the chair. "I'm waiting for an explanation."

He wiped the corner of his mouth with a napkin before his gaze fell on her. "All along there's been something I should have told you about myself, but I never seemed to find the right time."

"What? That you lead a secret life? That you have a wife hidden somewhere?"

"Nothing like that. After the visit to your aunt's, I decided that I'd wasted enough of your family's time and thought it best to leave so you could get on with your dive."

She shook her head. "You're a man who was raised with good manners, so your excuse doesn't wash. Something happened during your private talk with my aunt that put you off your desire to drill on my family's property. I deserve to know the truth. It's only fair after providing you the opportunity to talk to her."

His eyes glittered. "You're treading on dangerous ground to ask for the truth."

Her hands gripped the sides of her chair. "Now I know I'm right. As you can see, I'm a grown woman and can take whatever you have to tell me."

Lines darkened his striking face. "I'm not so sure."

"Are you afraid I'm too fragile if you tell me a secret about yourself I don't want to hear?"

He eyed her somberly. "I have no desire to bring hurt to you."

Bring? Such a cryptic comment brought a pain to her stomach. "What do you mean? In what way?"

"You need to leave it alone, Alessandra."

Anger sparked her emotions. "I don't accept that."

"I'm afraid you're going to have to." He sounded so remote, her insides froze.

"In other words you really meant it to be goodbye the other day."

Rini leaned forward. "I'd hoped I'd made that clear when I left the island the other morning without letting you know my intentions."

The forbidding CEO of Montanari's had spoken. *Don't you dare break down in front of him.*

She struggled for breath. "Don't worry. You've made me see the light. You and Francesco aren't that different after all. After he disappeared from my life, he sent his goodbye in a letter rather than face me. You flew off and left it to my father to do the honors. What is it about some attractive men? They seem to possess every quality except the one most vital."

A white ring appeared around his lips. She was pleased to see he wasn't completely impervious to her judgment of him. "Don't worry. Keep all your secrets! I'm leaving." She started to get up.

"No, Alessandra—you want the truth of everything, so I'll tell you. I never planned to, but since you've come all this way, I can't handle seeing you in this kind of pain. No one deserves an explanation more than you do."

"Go on."

"Where your aunt is concerned, we only talked business for a moment. The main thrust dealt with you."

"Me?"

Rini nodded slowly. "She loves you."

"I love her, too, but what does that have to do with anything?"

"She wanted clarification and asked to know what happened when I met Dea."

The moment he'd spoken, she stirred in the chair and averted her eyes. "I—I can't believe she brought up something that was none of her business." Her voice faltered. "Mother must have said something." After a long pause she said, "How uncomfortable that had to be for you."

"Not uncomfortable. I found it refreshing. You're a lot like her, you know. If I didn't know better, I'd think she was your mother."

Alessandra's head lifted. She blinked. "You're kidding—"

"Not at all. You and your aunt have a sense of fair play I admire very much. It's clear you both want the best for everyone. I told her nothing happened. Guido's father asked us to dance with the models he'd introduced us to. I had one dance with Dea, then she left. That was it. After my explanation, your aunt wanted to know my intentions toward you."

Alessandra shot out of the chair. "She had no right! I don't see how she could have asked you that when we hardly know each other!"

He stared up at her. "That's not true, Alessandra. Your aunt told me you've never taken a man to meet her before and what we had was something special. Naturally she's aware you've been showing me around for your father."

"So?"

"She realizes we would have learned a great deal about each other already."

"Well yes, but—"

"Her concern for both you and Dea is commendable," he interrupted. "So I had to be brutally honest and tell her that I didn't feel a connection to her. Since you and I met under the most innocent and extraordinary circumstances, she demanded to know if I felt a connection to you."

Alessandra paled.

"Don't you want to know what I said?"

"It's none of my business," she whispered.

"That's not an answer and you know it."

She turned away.

"I told her that my attraction to you was immediate and has been growing out of control." Her groan resounded in the air. "You feel it, too. I know you do. Out of loyalty to both her nieces, your aunt vetted me to make sure I wasn't using *you* to gain access to the legacy."

"That's absurd. I would never have thought that about you."

"But it's a mercenary world. She knew how hurt you were years ago and wanted to protect you."

"So you withdrew the proposal to prove to my family you had no ulterior motive? That's why you walked away from me?" Her voice rang out.

Instead of answering her, he reached for her and drew her over to the swing, pulling her down on his lap. "Look at me, Alessandra."

She shook her head. "I'm afraid to."

"Because you know I want to kiss you. The other morning while we were on the sea floor uncovering the mouth on that head, I was reminded of you. When I kissed you on the boat, I was half out of my mind with desire. My motives *are* ulterior, but intensely personal."

"No, Rini. We mustn't. Not out here where Bianca can see us."

"*I* must, *bellissima*."

He curved his hand against the side of her face and turned it toward him. Obeying blind need, he covered her trembling mouth with his own. She tried to elude him, but he drove his kisses deeper and deeper until her little cry allowed him the access he craved. Maybe he was dreaming because she slowly began returning his kisses with a heart-stopping hunger that caused him to forget everything except the heavenly woman in his arms.

His hands roved over her back and shoulders while they gave and took pleasure from each other's mouths. He felt her fingers slide up his neck into his hair. Every touch fed the fire enveloping him.

"Alessandra," he moaned. "I can't get enough of you. Do you have any idea how much I want you?"

"I want you, too," she confessed, covering his face with kisses.

"During the dive I was dying to grasp your hips and pull you into a secret cave where we could make love for months on end."

"Our wet suits would have presented a problem."

"But not now." He eased her down on the swing, where he had the freedom to look at her to his heart's content while he kissed the living daylights out of her.

Rini had never known this kind of all-consuming

desire before. The way she responded to him let him know something earthshaking had happened to her, too. She'd already had one love affair in her life, but it had been a long time ago. He was thankful it hadn't worked out because he was convinced she'd been reserved for him.

But what if she couldn't handle what he needed to tell her? He kissed her nose and eyelids. Before things went any further, she deserved to know the whole truth about him. Though terrified of her reaction, he couldn't stop now.

"You're the most divine creature this man has ever met. Since your aunt wanted to know my intentions toward you, it's only fair I tell you something about me first."

"You don't have to do this, Rini. You don't owe me anything. Please. I never dreamed my aunt would get personal with you like that."

"I'm glad she did. It woke me up to something I've been unwilling to face for years."

Her anxious eyes searched his. "What do you mean?"

"I've remained a bachelor for a reason."

"If you're allergic to marriage, you're not the only man. Until my father met Mother, he decided he'd always be single."

"That hasn't been my problem. In truth I've never gotten to the point in my adult life when I needed to state my intentions. But with you, it has become necessary."

She lifted a hand to caress his jaw. "Why?"

He kissed her succulent lips. "You're not just any

female I happen to have met. I'm not talking about the fact that you were born titled from both sides of your illustrious families. This is something that affects you as a woman. Don't you know you're head and shoulders above any woman I've ever known? Your pure honesty demands the same from me."

"Papà said my aunt was impressed with *your* honesty." She shivered. "What honesty is that? If your intention is to frighten me, you're doing a good job."

"*Frighten* might not be the best word." He sat up and got off the swing. "What I tell you will change the way you view me, but this has to come from me. I'll understand if you say it's been nice knowing you before you go your own way."

"For heaven sakes just tell me!"

Rini had angered her. This was going wrong. "From the time I could remember, I played soccer. By seventeen I was playing on a winning team with my friend Guido. On the day of the championship game, I got injured. At the hospital tests were done and I was told I was infertile. Over the years I've undergone tests, but the diagnosis is always the same…"

Her haunted eyes had fastened on him. She didn't move or cry out, but he saw pain break out on her face.

"Like anyone, I grew up thinking that one day I'd get married and have children. It was something I took for granted. Even after my first diagnosis, I didn't really believe it. I thought that surely in time the problem would go away and I'd be normal like everyone else. But every year I was tested, I was told that nothing had changed."

"I'm so sorry," she whispered, sounding agonized.

"So am I, Alessandra, because the diagnosis has impacted my life."

"So *that's* why you left me without saying goodbye? You thought I wouldn't be able to handle it?"

His lips thinned.

"Of course a woman wants babies with the man she marries. But there are other ways to have children."

"It's not the same. The other day when I was telling you about Valentina, you said you couldn't wait until you could have your own baby. It's a natural urge to want to procreate."

"Yes, but—"

"But nothing. I can't give any woman a baby, so I've been living my life with the reputation of being a dedicated bachelor. No one but my doctor, and now *you*, know I'm infertile."

"It happens to people, Rini. How tragic that you've let it rob you of the joy of life! It kills me that your fear has prevented you from settling down with a woman because you can't give her what you think she wants.

"I know you'd make a marvelous father, Rini. That's why there's adoption. Thousands of couples do it. For you to have lived your life since seventeen with such a dark cloud hanging over your head doesn't bear thinking about."

"You're very sweet, Alessandra, but you're not in my shoes." Her incredible reaction was all he could have hoped for and let him know her support would never be in question. His doctor had told him the right woman would be able to handle it.

But there was still something else to keep them apart.

All of it stemmed from his conversation with her aunt and her implied warning. Even now he held back, thinking it was better that she believe his infertility presented the biggest problem for them.

Alessandra stared at him. "What you're saying is that you're going to let this stand in the way of our having a relationship. If you really mean that, then you need counseling before you deny yourself the greatest joy in life."

"Therapy won't help me," he responded bleakly. He rubbed the back of his neck. "Combined with the conversation I had with your aunt, a relationship with you won't work."

"We're back to my aunt again?"

"She told me some things in confidence I can't share. Don't be upset with her. It's because she loves you."

"Rini—" she cried out, aghast. But she'd felt him withdraw emotionally from her. It had been a huge mistake to fly here after all.

Alessandra pulled out her cell and called for the limo to return to his house. Once off the phone she got up and walked over to the table to drink the rest of her lemonade. "Please tell the cook the food was delicious. Now if you'll excuse me, I'm going outside to wait for my ride."

Rini moved faster than she did and caught up to her outside the front door of the villa. "Alessandra—"

"It's all right, Rini. Though your explanation wasn't the one I expected, I got my answer, so thank you. Please forgive me for barging in here uninvited. I give you my promise it will never happen again."

When the limo turned into the courtyard, she rushed

to get in the backseat on her own. Rini was right there, but she refused to give him the satisfaction of meeting his eyes and closed the door herself. As the limo drove off, Rini's heart plummeted to his feet.

"Where do you wish to go, *signorina*?"

"The airport, *per favore*."

Alessandra didn't look back as they turned away. *No more looking back.*

Just now she'd wanted to comfort him over his infertility, but she sensed he wouldn't have been willing to listen to her. For him to have revealed his agony to her had been huge for him. Now that he'd told her the truth, he'd backed away, certain that she—like any other woman—wouldn't see him as a complete man.

Was that image of being incomplete the reason for his meteoric rise in the business world? Had he worked day and night to compensate for what he saw as an inadequacy? She'd detected the love in his voice when he'd talked about his sister and her babies. Pain pierced her heart to realize that every time Rini eyed his nephew, he was reminded that he could never give a woman a child from his own body.

She'd seen the way he'd kissed and loved Valentina's baby. The man had been there for her throughout her pregnancy. Yet all that time, he'd been gutted by the knowledge that he'd never be able to look forward to having a baby from his own body. Her heart ached for him.

As for his conversation with her aunt, that was something else again. If he'd been sworn to secrecy, then she wouldn't be getting an explanation out of him. Alessandra could go to her aunt and demand to know the truth, but it wasn't her right.

On the flight back to Metaponto, she stared out the window of the plane. Rini Montanari had been an earth-shaking interlude. But interlude was all he'd prepared for their association to be and became the operative word in her romance-less life.

Sunday evening the helicopter dipped lower over Ravello. Rini was late for his brother Carlo's birthday party, which Valentina and Giovanni were hosting.

For the last three weeks Rini had traveled to four areas of Calabria in Southern Italy, exploring the possibility of developing more oil sites. But he'd been in agony since Alessandra had left his villa and couldn't concentrate.

Nothing he'd visited turned out to be as promising as the land owned by the Caracciolo family. But he'd written that off. Unfortunately, blotting Alessandra from his heart was another matter entirely. With love in her eyes, she'd reacted to the news that he was infertile as if it was of no consequence to her. She'd assured him it didn't matter. The way she'd kissed him, as if he was her whole life, he'd believed her.

But her aunt's fear that a relationship with Alessandra might cause a permanent rift between the twins had prompted him to back away. Fulvia had told him how close the girls had been growing up, how much fun they'd had as children. But everything changed when Alessandra fell in love and then was betrayed by her sister and the man she'd thought she would marry.

The girls had finally gotten past it, but now they'd reached another impasse because Dea had met Rini first. Apparently she'd been devastated when he didn't want to date her. Hearing that Alessandra had been showing him around the property had upset her.

Though the situation was totally unfair, Fulvia had looked him in the eye and asked him if he wanted to be responsible for bringing on more pain between the two of them that might last. It was his decision to make.

In the end, Rini couldn't do it, so he'd had to let Alessandra go. All he could do was watch news clips on television about the discovery of the Temple of Hera beneath the waters off Basilicata in the Ionian.

Dr. Bruno Tozzi and his team had been given credit for the find and Alessandra's name had been mentioned. Every few days more information was being fed to the media about more discoveries of a courtyard and temple walls.

Rini was proud of Alessandra and the amazing work she was doing. Thanks to the coverage, he was able to keep track of her without having to make contact with her father. But having said goodbye to her had thrown him into a black void.

Once Rini arrived at the Laurito villa, he was besieged by family. He played with Carlo's daughter, then took turns enjoying the two baby boys. Giovanni chatted with him for a while, but it was Valentina who sequestered him in the sunroom just off the terrace. He couldn't get out of it.

"I thought you'd be bringing Alessandra with you. She's fabulous!"

"That's over."

"Why? I know you're in love with her."

His eyes closed tightly. "It can't work."

"Rini—are you saying she doesn't love you?"

He inhaled sharply. "She's never said the words."

"Have you?"

"It doesn't matter."

"Yes it *does*! Alessandra came to your house unannounced. I saw the look in her eyes when you walked out on the patio. If ever a woman had it bad…"

"There are things you don't know and I can't tell you. Don't make this any harder on me."

"Okay." She patted his arm. "I'll leave it alone. Keep your secrets and come on back out. Papà wants to talk to you and find out what new areas you've found for drilling."

"I wish I had better results to report."

Together they joined the others. Near midnight he flew back to his villa and did some laps in the swimming pool before going to bed. To his chagrin, sleep wouldn't come. He spent most of the night outside on a lounger.

Three weeks… If he didn't see Alessandra again soon, he'd go mad. But he had certain knowledge that bound him to stay away from her. Early Monday morning he put his emotional needs in the deep freeze and left for his office, prepared to announce some new sites for drilling that would please the board. He worked steadily until Thursday, when his secretary put through a call from his sister.

"Valentina?"

"Have you heard the news?" She sounded frantic.

His gut clenched. "What is it?"

"The seismic research facility in Malta registered a six-point-nine quake in the Ionian. The impact was felt all along the coast. It affected the diving site where Alessandra has been working with the institute."

Earthquake? He broke out in a cold sweat. *If anything happened to her, his life wouldn't be worth living.* To hell with what her aunt had told him. He needed to go to her and wouldn't let anything stop him.

"According to the news, apparently two or three divers were injured and transported to chambers at various hospitals on the coast. I found out the institute's oceanography boat docks at Crotone, so I'm sure some of the victims were taken there."

"I'm on my way. Bless you, Valentina."

He alerted his pilot and flew to the Naples airport, where he took the company jet to Crotone. En route he phoned to make certain a rental car was waiting. Following that he made calls to the three hospitals in the town, but no one would give him information about the injured because he wasn't a relative. Other injuries over the southern area had been reported and hospitals all along the coast were filling.

Emergency vehicles and fire trucks filled the parking area of the first hospital. He made it to the ER and learned that one diver had been brought there. No one would give him information, but one of the ambulance crew helped him out by telling him they'd transported a male diver here.

Thanking him, Rini drove to the next hospital. Again it was the wrong one. He made the rounds until he reached the last hospital. When he spotted Bruno Tozzi in the waiting room, he knew Alessandra had to be here. Avoiding conversation with him, Rini walked through the hospital to the director's office. He'd do whatever it took to be granted permission to see her.

"I'm fine," Alessandra assured her parents after she'd spent six hours in the chamber.

"Are you in pain?"

"No, not at all. The doctor told me I have a light case of the bends."

"Dr. Tozzi wants to see you."

"He worries about all the team, but I'm not up for visitors. Tell him I promise to call him tomorrow when I'm feeling better."

"All right. We'll find him out in the reception area and be back in two hours. The doctor said you'll be here overnight. We'll stay with you and drive you home in the morning. Try to rest in the meantime. Love you." They kissed her before slipping from the room.

No sooner had they gone than the door opened again. It was probably the nurse coming in to check her vital signs. When she saw who entered the room, her heart fluttered dangerously fast.

"*Rini*—what are you doing here?" After three weeks of not seeing him, the sight of his tall, well-honed body wearing a navy blue business suit was too much to handle in her weakened state.

"When I heard what happened, I couldn't stay away."

She turned on her side, trying to hide from him. "Did you talk to my parents?"

"They don't know I'm here."

Her breath caught. "You shouldn't have come. We've said all there is to say."

"I had to be sure you were going to recover," he said, his voice throbbing.

Tears stung her eyes, but she refused to let him see them. "I don't see how you found out where I was."

"A simple deduction after Valentina phoned me with the news about the epicenter of the quake."

She sighed. "How did you get past the desk? No one is allowed in here."

"I have my ways. Alessandra, you could have died out there. The doctor said you lost consciousness. It could have been fatal. Do you have any idea what I've been going through thinking I might have lost you?"

"Maybe now you know how I felt when you let me leave Positano and I knew it was over with you." A bitter little cry escaped her lips. "My parents will be taking me home in the morning. The only reason I can imagine you're being here is because of your guilt.

"What a surprise I'm going to survive! Surely it's a relief to you. That way you don't have to tell me what you've been holding back. It would only add to your guilt."

"Alessandra—" His mournful voice reached that vulnerable place inside her before he'd come around the side of the bed. She felt him cup her face with his hand. "*Grazie a dio* you're alive and safe."

She kept her eyes tightly closed. "I admit I'm happy about it, too."

His fingers toyed with her hair, sending fingers of delight through her exhausted body. "I once came down with a case of decompression sickness and know how it feels."

"One of the hazards when you're having fun."

"You don't need to pretend with me. I know you've had a fright and need sleep. Do you mind if I stay here with you for a little while?" He leaned down and kissed her lips. It felt like the touch of fire.

"The doctor won't like it, but that's up to you."

Peering at him through slits, she watched him draw a chair to the side of the bed next to her. He looked like a man with the weight of the world on his powerful shoulders. She needed him to go away and never come back, but she couldn't find the words.

In a minute a nurse came in to bring another bag for her IV. She checked Alessandra's vitals and left without saying a word to him. The man could get away with murder. "What did you do to get permission?"

"I told the administrator that Montanari Engineering would make a generous donation to the hospital if they'd let me in to see you."

There was no one like him, her heart cried out. "Rini Montanari. That was a naughty thing to do."

"It worked. That's all that mattered to me. To find you alive means everything. These last three weeks without you have been a hell I never want to live through again," he admitted, his voice breaking.

His pain was tangible. "Now you'll have to make

good on your offer and work all hours of the day and night to recoup the loss."

"It'll be worth it since the hospital helped save your life. You're the most precious thing in my world. I love you, *bellissima*," he said in the huskiest voice she'd ever heard. "Now go to sleep and don't worry about anything."

When Alessandra woke up in the middle of the night, she decided she'd been dreaming that Rini had come to visit her. Had he really said he loved her? There was no sign of him. The night nurse came in and helped her to the restroom, then walked her back to bed.

CHAPTER SIX

THE NEXT MORNING Alessandra awakened to find her parents in the room. They'd brought her a fresh change of jeans and a soft top, which she slipped into. At 11:00 a.m. the doctor discharged her with the proviso that she rest, stay hydrated and do no diving for at least fourteen days.

It felt good to be wheeled outside to her parents' limo. They made her comfortable before driving her back to the castle. Yet not at any time had they or the medical staff mentioned that Rini Montanari had been a visitor.

She'd really experienced a whopper of a dream to imagine he'd left his office to fly to Crotone in order to find out if she was all right. Alessandra was terrified it would take years, maybe a lifetime, to get over him. But what if she couldn't? The ache in her heart had grown acute.

Instead of going upstairs, she told her mom she wanted to stay in the day room and curled up on the couch under a quilt to watch television. Supplied with water and nuts, she didn't lack for the creature comforts. Alfredo wandered in and jumped up on her lap. He supplied the love she craved.

"Alessandra?" She lifted her head to her mother. "Are you up for company?"

"If it's anyone from the diving group, could you tell them I need a few days?"

"It's Rinieri Montanari."

She reeled in place.

"He said he visited you at the hospital, but the nurse put something in your IV and you fell asleep. He's anxious to know how you are."

Rini *had* been there!

She hadn't dreamed it after all and couldn't believe it. Thrilled, yet tortured by what her mother had told her, she couldn't concentrate on anything else. "I—I look terrible."

"That would be impossible," her mother assured her, "but if you want me to send him away, I will."

"No—but don't tell him to come in yet. Could you hand me my purse? It's over on the credenza."

Her mother did her bidding. Alessandra's hand trembled as she brushed through her hair and applied a coat of lipstick.

"Ready?"

Alessandra nodded. While she waited, she checked her phone to find a dozen texts from friends, one of them from Bruno, who wanted to know how soon she'd be back. Fulvia had sent her love and condolences. She wanted a good talk with her when she was feeling better.

Alessandra's editor was thankful she was all right

and told her not to feel pressured about delivering the book. He hadn't given her a deadline. But there was no message from Dea, the one person Alessandra wanted to talk to. The pit grew in her stomach as she realized her own sister hadn't tried to contact her. Why?

"You don't look like you've been sick," said the deep, familiar male voice she was dying to hear.

She looked up at the sinfully gorgeous man. "You're right. I'm a fraud."

Rini walked over to her. He'd dressed in jeans and a pullover sweater in slate blue. Combined with the soap he used in the shower to assail her, his presence had put her senses on overload. He reached down to scratch behind the cat's ears. "You have the right instincts, Alfredo. I'd trade places with you if I could."

In the next instant he leaned down and pressed a warm kiss to her mouth. "Welcome back to the land of the living. Your doctor told me you lost consciousness down there."

"Only for a moment. My buddy Gino knew exactly what to do. It all happened so fast."

"We can be thankful the divers with the institute are experts." He stood there looking down at her with an intense expression.

She squirmed. "Rini?" Her voice shook. "Why are you here?"

"Though I had my reasons, I treated you badly when I left here the first time without saying goodbye. My behavior was worse when you flew to Positano to see me and I wouldn't explain myself. I thought I was doing the right thing both times, but your accident has changed the way I feel about everything.

"I love you and I've never said that to another woman in my life. Almost losing you has made me realize I could no longer let my reason stand in the way of being with you, so I'm back to find out if you'd be willing to start over again with me."

While she sat there in shock, Liona wheeled in a tea cart laden with a meal for them. "If Alfredo is bothering you, I'll take him out."

"Oh, no. I love him right here. Thanks, Liona."

After she left, Rini got up and served both of them a plate of food and her favorite iced tea. His gaze found hers. While they ate he said, "Life has given both of us a second chance. What I'd like to do is invite you to my villa for a week where we can spend real time together."

Alessandra couldn't believe what she was hearing. She said the first thing that came into her head. "Can you take a vacation?"

"Of course. I want to get to know you without work or interruptions getting in the way. The nice thing about being CEO is that I can arrange it when I want. The doctor told me you shouldn't dive for at least two more weeks. You've shown me your world. Now it's time I showed you mine."

She smiled. "Like fishing?"

"Only if you'd want to."

"Rini, I adore the outdoors. Hiking, camping, all of it."

"The mountains are beautiful this time of year.

Could you talk to your editor and ask for an extension to turn in your book?"

"He already told me to take all the time I need."

If only Rini knew she loved him so much she felt like she could move mountains for him, but she was afraid. "When the week is over, *then* what? Will you consider you've done everything possible to obtain my forgiveness?

"Will we say goodbye like sensible people who've enjoyed their interlude together but knew it had to come to an end? You'll go your way because you can't offer me any more than what you've already done? I'll go mine?"

His jaw hardened. "Why don't we stop worrying about the future and just take things one day at a time? I need help because I've never done anything like this before."

She took a deep breath, surprised to hear the vulnerability in his voice. "Like what?"

"Invite a woman I care about to stay at my house."

"I've never done anything like it, either." Talk about needing help…

"The doctor told me you need rest and that you shouldn't fly until tomorrow. So if I leave you now, will you think about my invitation? I'll call you in the morning. If you decide you want to come, I'll arrange to pick you up in the limo and we'll fly in the company jet to Positano." He stood up.

"Where will you be in the meantime?"

"At the airport in Metaponto. I'm working in my office on the jet and will stay in the bedroom overnight.

I'll give you until ten a.m. to get in touch with me. If I don't hear from you by then, I'll be flying back to Naples."

She knew he meant it. This was it.

"If you'll give me your phone, I'll program my number for you."

Alessandra handed it to him. "Rini, whatever my answer is, I promise to call you."

Lines marred his arresting features. "I can't ask for more than that." He put the phone on the table. "You need rest now. Take care of yourself, *adorata.*"

The second he disappeared from the day room she wanted to call him back and tell him she'd go with him right now. But she needed to keep her wits about her. The decision to spend a week with him would change her life forever.

She kissed the cat's head. "Who am I kidding, Alfredo? My life changed beyond recognition the day he approached me in the foyer."

He said they'd take things a day at a time. She had no choice but to do what he wanted because at this point she knew she couldn't live without him. If it was only for a week, so be it. The man was so complicated it was driving her crazy. Somewhere in the mix, Rini's inability to give a woman a child had stunted his vision of life. She wanted to help him explore the world of adoption so he'd realize he could know total fulfillment.

With her heart ready to burst from the joy his invitation had brought her, she lay down and didn't awaken until hours later, when she heard her parents' muffled voices talking about her sleeping her life away.

Alessandra sat up, disturbing Alfredo, who jumped to the floor. "What time is it?"

"Time for you to be in bed. Let's get you upstairs."

Later when her mother tucked her in bed she told her about Rini's invitation. "I want to accept it, but I'm afraid."

"Don't let what Francesco did keep you from reaching out for your own happiness."

If her mother only knew this had nothing to do with Francesco. But at least she had her parents' blessing.

Liona brought her breakfast at eight, after which Alessandra pressed the button programmed to phone Rini.

"Am I going to hear what I want to hear?" he answered in that deep voice. She thought she heard a trace of nervousness and loved him for it.

"Maybe, unless you've had a change of heart during the night."

"Alessandra—don't keep me in suspense."

Her mouth had gone dry. "I want to come, but I need time to pack."

"How much?"

She chuckled. "Do we have to leave by ten?"

"I don't care when we leave today as long as you're with me."

"Then can we say noon?"

"I'll be at the castle at twelve and we'll eat on the plane during the flight."

"It sounds wonderful. Ciao, Rini."

After ringing off, she hurried around her room to get ready for her trip. She needed to pack everything under the sun. Normally she traveled light, but not this time. Besides sportswear for their outdoor activities, her plan was to bring a few new bikinis and evening dresses that would knock his socks off.

She turned on her radio to some light rock music. The cat wandered in her room and probably thought she was out of her mind as she danced around filling her two suitcases.

"Alfredo? You should see his gorgeous villa."

"Whose villa would that be?" asked a familiar female voice.

Alessandra spun around. "Dea!" After being caught off guard, she hurried over to her sister and hugged her. "I didn't know you were coming." With Rini coming for her, she couldn't believe the bad timing.

"Evidently not. Papà told me about your accident so I came home to see how you are. I thought you'd still be in bed recovering. I never expected to find you flying around your room having a conversation with the cat. What's all the packing for?"

"I—I'm going on a trip," she said, her voice faltering.

"I gathered as much." Dea's eyes looked at the bags on the bed. "I do believe you've emptied your drawers and closets. Are you finally giving Bruno Tozzi a chance? He's been after you for over a year."

"Not Bruno. I've never been interested in him that way. Actually I'm going to be a guest at Rini Montanari's villa." She'd had no choice but to tell her sister the truth.

At the mention of his name, any goodwill Alessandra had hoped could be resurrected between her and Dea on this visit had vanished. Her sister paled. Rini really had hurt her by not asking her out again. "Are you talking about the one in Naples or Positano?"

Of course her sister would know all about Rini. She'd danced with him on his friend's yacht. "I assume Positano."

"Is this because you showed him around the property for Papà?"

"Dea? Please sit down so we can talk." Alessandra closed the lids on her bags. "He'd been scuba diving with me. It's a sport we have in common. When he heard about the earthquake, he flew down. Yesterday he came by the castle to invite me to stay with him for a week."

"You mean he hasn't been here all month?"

"No. He's been gone for weeks on business. I was surprised to see him again." So surprised she'd thought she'd been dreaming when he came to her hospital room.

Dea's eyes followed her around while she packed her cosmetics. "I was shocked to learn he had business with Papà in the first place."

"Let's agree it was a shock all the way around." Alessandra was so uncomfortable she could hardly bear it.

Her sister studied her for a minute. "Be honest with me. Are you going with him because of what happened with Francesco?"

"No, Dea—not at all! How can you even think that?" Alessandra cried. "Whatever happened is long since buried in the past." She sank down on the end of the bed. "What do you want me to say?"

"Have you fallen for him?"

"I care for him very much."

"As much as you did Francesco?"

"You can't compare relationships. Francesco was my first boyfriend. I was young. As you reminded me, he ended up being a loser."

"Don't you know why I told you that?"

Alessandra frowned. "What do you mean?"

"He wasn't interested in me. Within a day of his arriving in Rome, he was chatting up another model."

"Oh, Dea—I didn't know that."

"I thought Mother would have said something. I'm telling you this to warn you about Rinieri Montanari."

Alessandra didn't want to hear it.

"On the yacht, his best friend's father, Leonides Rossano, confided in me that Rinieri was Italy's most eligible bachelor—as if my best friend, Daphne, and I didn't already know it. I read between the lines and deduced he'd been a player for years. Alessandra—he might end up breaking your heart after he gets what he wants from Papà."

"You're wrong about that, Dea. He doesn't want anything from him," she replied, defending Rini. "He withdrew his proposal weeks ago and has been looking elsewhere for oil in the southern part of Italy."

"I didn't know that. Sorry." Dea stood up, but Alessandra could tell the revelation had shaken her. "How soon is he coming for you?"

"At noon."

She looked at her watch. "It's almost that time now. I don't want to be around when he arrives, so I'll join the parents while you get the rest of your packing done. I'm glad you're recovered. Even gladder that I wasn't the one under the water when the quake struck."

A rush of warmth propelled Alessandra toward her sister. She put her arms around her again. "Thank you for coming. You don't know how much it means to me."

Dea hugged her back. "You've always been the brave one." She kissed her cheek before disappearing from the bedroom. Alfredo followed her out the door.

The brave one?

An hour later those words were still chasing around in Alessandra's psyche as Rini helped her out of the limo to board the Montanari jet.

Once they'd attained cruising speed, his steward served them an incredible lunch of lobster pasta with *sfogliatelle* for dessert. The shell shaped pastry had a divine ricotta filling with cinnamon. The wonderful flavor was beyond description.

They sat in the club area by the windows. His dark eyes never left hers. "I'm glad to see a smile. When I picked you up, you seemed preoccupied. For a moment I was afraid you still didn't feel well enough to come. We could have left tomorrow."

"I'm fine, Rini, but I have to admit I'm still a little tired."

"After what you experienced, that's understandable. When we get to the villa, you can rest all you want."

She looked out the window, wishing she felt the same excitement he'd engendered in her when she'd told him she would accept his invitation. But Dea's unannounced arrival had taken her by surprise. Though touched that she'd come to see her after her scuba-diving accident, her sister's questions about Rini had put a damper on this trip.

He was doing everything in his power to make her comfortable and had no idea Dea had been at the castle when he'd picked her up. She didn't want him to know, let alone tell him what her sister had said. Dea hadn't been unkind. Alessandra had been grateful for that, but she couldn't help feeling that her sister was suffering in some way.

Alessandra remembered how she'd felt when she'd first talked to Rini in the castle foyer. The immediate, overpowering attraction she'd felt for him had to be swallowed in the knowledge that he'd already been with Dea. She'd wondered then if she'd ever be able to get over him.

Yet today, her sister had to handle the news that Rini wanted to be with Alessandra enough to invite her to his home. If Dea had felt the same overwhelming attraction to him that night on the yacht, then who knew how long it would take her to get over Rini, especially if he ended up being in Alessandra's future. The thought haunted her.

"I think you really are tired." Rini got out of his seat and adjusted hers so she could lie back. "Our flight won't last long, then we'll put you to bed in the guest bedroom until you're feeling your old self."

"Thank you." But she no longer knew who her old self was. Life had taken on new meaning since she'd met him.

* * *

Something was wrong beyond Alessandra's fatigue. Rini had sensed it the moment she'd met him outside the castle doors with her suitcases. He'd expected to be invited in to speak to her parents, but she'd whisked them away as if she was in a great hurry. Rini hadn't questioned her about it. In time he'd get answers. They had a whole week. Today was only the beginning.

Once the jet touched down, the helicopter flew them to the villa. He carried her luggage while she made her way along the path that led to the back patio. She looked over her shoulder at him. "You truly do live in a garden. At home I smell the sea air. Here, I'm assailed by the most heavenly scents."

"After living in Naples with the occasional scent of sulfur from Vesuvius in the air, I chose this flower-filled mountaintop on purpose. Follow me through the house. Your room faces on the pool. You can walk out the French doors at any time and take a swim. Come on. Let's get you in bed."

He saw her eyes widen in appreciation when they entered the bedroom off the hallway. "It's a lovely room. Those blue hydrangeas on the coffee table take my breath."

"I'm glad you like them. Go ahead and freshen up. I'll be back in a minute." He put her cases down and left to get her a bottle of water from the kitchen. Rini had given Bianca the next three days off so he could be alone with Alessandra and wait on her himself.

When he returned, he found her sitting on the side of the bed still dressed in white culottes with a sharp front crease. She'd layered them with a multicolored blue silk top and looked so sensational, he couldn't take his eyes off her.

"I thought I'd find you under the covers. This is for you." He put the water on the bedside table before opening the shutters to let in the early evening light from the pool area.

She smiled up at him, but it lacked the joie de vivre he'd seen while they'd been out diving. "I'll sleep tonight. Now that I'm in your world again—but only because you invited me this time—I want to talk to you. Please sit down."

He sat in one of the upholstered chairs by the coffee table.

"Where's Bianca?"

"On a short holiday."

"So it's just you and me?" He heard a slight tremor in her voice.

He frowned. "Are you worried about being here alone with me?"

"Of course not." She got up from the bed and walked over to smell the flowers. "Can we have a frank talk? You said you wanted to start over again. I want that, too, but I need to understand you better."

Rini sat forward with his hands clasped between his legs. "Would I have brought you here if I didn't want the same thing? We've got all the time in the world. Go ahead. Ask me anything."

She darted him a curious glance. "You say that, but I wonder if you really mean it."

"Where's this doubt coming from?"

"I don't know exactly. Tell me about what happened when you first met Dea. Being twins, she and I have shared a unique past. Sometimes it has been eerie."

"In what way?"

"It's hard to explain, but there are times when even though we're two people, we think as one."

Rini got to his feet. "I've heard that happens to twins. But what does that have to do with me?"

"I'm not sure and am only feeling my way," she cried softly before turning away from him.

He put his hands on her shoulders and pulled her against him. "You sound frightened," he whispered into her fragrant hair.

"I am."

"Of what? Of me? Tell me." He shook her gently.

"I've been going over the conversation that my aunt had with you about me and Dea. You told her that you felt no connection with Dea, but it was different with me." Alessandra turned around in his arms. "But it doesn't provide all the answers."

"What more do you want?"

Her eyes searched his. "Will you bear with me a little longer and tell me your feelings when you realized I wasn't Dea?"

His hands slid to her face. "After I left your father's office and went back to my hotel in Metaponto that first night, I couldn't get you off my mind. Make no mistake. It was *you* I was thinking about. From a distance you had Dea's superficial features, the same features that had drawn me on the yacht. But the second you said you weren't Dea, I realized my mistake.

"You looked so adorable standing there in your shorter hair and man's shirt that didn't cover up your bikini. Tanned, no makeup, bare-legged, full of energy, duffel bag in hand. I thought, I've got to get to know this exciting woman! I told your aunt I felt a connection so powerful with you, I couldn't wait to get back to the castle the next morning to see you again."

He felt Alessandra's anxiety before she eased out of his arms. "Thank you for being so honest with me." She was shivering.

"Now that I have, do you want to tell me what's going on in your mind?"

"After I entered the castle, I heard a voice call out *signorina*. You'll think I'm out of my mind, but when I saw you walk toward me, it was like seeing the prince who'd haunted my dreams come to life before my very eyes. I felt your imprint on me before you said a word.

"But the second you started talking, I realized you thought I was Dea and my dream was crushed to grist. She'd had a history with you. She'd been there first. I'd never experienced such envy in my life. I've heard of love at first sight, but I never imagined it would happen to me. My pain that she'd met you first was too excruciating to bear."

Her eyes glistened with unshed tears. "Until I learned the truth of your relationship with Dea during our drive, I'd been forced to keep my feelings bottled up and pretend nothing was wrong in front of my father."

Her words shook Rini. *"Adorata."* He reached for her, but she took another step back. "I haven't finished. There's something else you need to hear."

Rini couldn't take much more and attempted to get his emotions under control. "What is it?"

"When Dea and I were little girls, we had many of the same likes and dislikes that in some cases baffled everyone. One of the things we had in common was to talk about the princes we would marry one day. We played our own form of house with a miniature castle and all the characters Papà had made for us.

"Our mother and aunt gave us beautiful clothes to dress our dolls. Dea always had the most glamorous and stupendous outfits because they knew how much she loved fashion. I was given a fabulous boat that would sail me and my prince around the castle and the world."

The lump was growing in Rini's throat.

"We played for hours about living in the castle all our lives and being happy forever with our princely husbands and children. In our case it wasn't pure fiction considering the lives of our titled parents and heritage."

"Alessandra—"

"Let me finish," she interrupted. "You were there when she first laid eyes on you. You saw what I can't see. Rini, I'm convinced that when Dea met you on the yacht, she had the same experience I did. She saw you sitting there and knew you were the prince of her dreams. It was one of those times we were both the same person. By the expression on your face, I can tell I'm right."

He closed his eyes tightly for a minute. *Incredibile!* This talk with Alessandra answered the questions that had lingered in his mind about Dea. In view of what he'd just learned, the way she'd linked her arms behind his head and the ardent kiss she'd given him when they'd stopped dancing as if she'd been claiming him for her own made a strange kind of sense. Her actions had borne out Alessandra's theory.

Guido had acted nonchalant about it, but Rini had seen the glint of envy in his friend's eyes. That was the only time he'd ever known him to show a side of emotion that surprised him. But Rini couldn't be that cruel to Dea or Alessandra by telling her what Dea had done that night to show her attraction to him. It had to be a secret he would take to the grave.

His head reared. "What you're saying is, Dea is now the one devastated."

"Maybe."

"Then we're back to where we were before. If your guilt is going to keep you from enjoying this vacation with me, then I'll fly you back home in the morning."

"No, Rini—that isn't what I want. I just needed to have this conversation with you."

"But it doesn't solve anything, does it?"

"I guess I want you to tell me what we should do."

"If you mean that, then I suggest we table our concerns and enjoy our vacation. We'll just have to hope that time and work will help Dea get over whatever disappointment she's feeling." But that wasn't going to be easy since he still hadn't forgotten the conversation with her aunt. He'd been burdened by it. "As for you and me, I'd hoped to take us on an overnight hike tomorrow."

"You know I'd love that."

"Then we'll pick you up a lightweight backpack and

sleeping bag in the morning." She nodded with a smile. "How are you feeling now?"

"Much better. I'm getting hungry and know you are. Why don't we go out to dinner someplace in Positano."

"I've been anxious to show it to you. If you're ready, we can go now."

CHAPTER SEVEN

As RINI HELPED Alessandra into the black BMW parked in front, he squeezed her waist and kissed the side of her neck. When he reached for her hand and held on, her heart pounded with anticipation of the night to come. He started the car and they wound through the lush greenery toward the town center. She could see the twinkle of lights from the fabulous villas half hidden behind cypress trees and palms.

The interior of the car smelled of the soap he used in the shower. She was so in love with him it was impossible to hide it from him. If she didn't put Dea out of her mind, she could ruin this incredible time for them.

"Whoa. We're right on the edge of the cliff."

Rini flashed her a smile and parked the car along the side of the narrow road. "We've arrived at my favorite place. You'll love the view from here." She could hear soft rock music as he helped her out. They walked up the rock steps lined with flowers growing out of the vegetation to the little restaurant perched high up. The view from the terrace, where a band was playing, opened to the sea below between two mountain sides.

She gasped and clung to him. "That's a steep drop."

"Kind of like dropping eighty feet with you in our own private world." Trust him to remind her. "Come on, *bellissima*."

He put his arm around her shoulders and guided her to an empty, candlelit table. The romantic ambience made her feel feverish. Rini seated her and asked for wine from the waiter who recognized him. "Will you trust me to order for you?"

"If you'll trust my cooking when we eat along the trail tomorrow evening."

"I can hardly wait." After the waiter walked away, Rini reached for her hand and pulled her onto the small dance floor, where another couple was dancing.

"There's no room for anyone else."

"That's the whole idea," he whispered before biting her earlobe gently. They danced in place, sending her body temperature skyrocketing. "If you knew the dreams I've had about holding you like this. Tonight there's no wet suit to separate us."

She chuckled. "I noticed."

"I never want to be separated from you," he admitted in a husky voice and crushed her to him. Alessandra closed her eyes and rocked in place with him. Never sounded like forever. Was it really possible? But that question led to the troubling question about Dea still hanging over her head, shooting more pain to her heart. So it was better not to think, just relish this night under the stars with Rini.

"I could stay this way indefinitely," she murmured, "but I can see our food has arrived. Let's get you fed."

"How lucky am I to be with a woman who understands me." He walked her back to their table and they plunged into an exquisite meal of octopus on creamed potatoes and prawns, followed by vegetables and *carpaccio* of swordfish with a dessert of *salame de chocolat*.

"If we keep eating like this, I'll have to buy me a larger wet suit," she quipped.

His dark eyes glinted with amusement. "We'll hike it off tomorrow. For now you need to get home to bed. It's been a long day for you."

"I have to admit bed will feel good tonight."

"I knew it." He paid the bill and ushered her out of the restaurant. "Careful as we go down the stairs. Hold on to me."

She didn't need his urging as she clung to him. He walked her to the car, keeping her hugged against his side. Before he opened the door, he lowered his head to kiss her. She'd been dying for it. The passion he aroused in her was so powerful, she almost fainted. Someone in a car driving by let out a wolf whistle, causing her to blush in embarrassment. Rini only chuckled and opened the door so she could hide inside.

"Sorry about that," he murmured as they drove back to his villa.

"No, you're not."

"Would you believe me if I told you I couldn't help myself?"

Yes, if his desire for her was half as great as hers for him. She rested her head against the back of the seat. "This has been a wonderful night. I rarely drink wine and am afraid I drank too much."

His hand reached out to give her thigh a squeeze, sending rivulets of desire through her body. "One glass?"

"Already you're a corrupting influence on me."

Male laughter rang inside the confines of the car. "Didn't you know you've become my addiction? You'd better lock your door tonight."

She rolled her head in his direction. "I trust you, Rini."

"Maybe you shouldn't."

"If I didn't, I wouldn't be going camping with you. Where are you going to take me?"

"Along the footpath of the gods."

"Did you just make that up?"

"No. It's the name of a trail formed by man years ago along the Amalfi Coast. In my opinion it's one of the most striking panoramas of this world. You'll know what I mean when we get going. We'll follow it part of the way through gorges and precipices, then veer inland into the mountains."

"You've given me goose bumps."

"When you uncovered the mouth on that head, it raised the hairs on the back of my neck."

She eyed him with longing. "I can't believe how you just happened to know where to dive."

"Pure selfishness. I wanted you to myself." He pulled into the courtyard and escorted her inside the villa to her bedroom. Putting his hands on her shoulders he said, "Tonight was the perfect way to start our vacation. I'll see you in the morning and we'll get going whenever you're ready. Sleep well."

He gave her a brief kiss before exiting the room. It was a good thing. If he'd lingered, she wouldn't have let him leave.

Before she went to bed, she hung up a few things in the closet, then checked her phone. Her mother had texted her to find out how she was feeling since her hospital stay. There was no mention of Dea, who was probably still there. Alessandra texted her back, telling her she felt fine and that they were going hiking tomorrow. She sent her love to her parents. But when she climbed under the covers, her heart ached for Dea, whom she knew was in deep pain.

The ringing of the house phone at the side of the bed awakened Alessandra the next morning. She checked her watch. Seven thirty a.m. He was a morning man who loved fish. Little by little she was learning those precious things about him. With a smile she reached for the phone. "*Buongiorno*, Rini."

"Hot coffee is waiting for you in the kitchen when you're ready, but there's no hurry."

The excitement in his voice was contagious. She swung her legs over the side of the bed. "If I told you I couldn't make it until noon, you know you'd have a heart attack."

"Please don't tell me that."

"You'll have to be patient with me," she teased. "Ciao."

She hung up the receiver and raced around the room getting ready, once she'd taken a shower. After diving into her suitcases, she pulled on jeans, a T-shirt and hiking boots. She packed a cloth bag she'd brought in her suitcase. Quickly she filled it with extra clothes, socks, a hoodie, a flashlight, matches, cosmetics and a brush—all the little things needed for their hike. She'd attach it to the backpack they were going to buy her.

When she hurried through his elegant home to the kitchen, she discovered she'd only taken eight minutes to get ready. Not bad considering the gorgeous male drinking coffee had assumed she would keep him waiting for hours.

The look of surprise on his handsome face was so comical, she thought he would drop his mug. Alessandra grinned. "Got ya."

His eyes blazed with intensity. In the next breath he wrapped her in his arms and whirled her around. "I figured five more minutes and I was charging in to get you."

"Now I wish I'd waited."

A bark of laughter escaped his throat before he kissed her fiercely. He didn't let her go until she struggled for breath. "I've made breakfast. Go ahead and eat while I take your bag out to the car with the food I've packed."

"You made food for our hike? I could have helped."

"Bianca always has my favorite meat and cheese pies on hand. We'll pack some to take with us."

"I'm salivating already."

She reached for a ham roll and grapes. After swallowing coffee, she hurried out to the car. Rini locked up the house and they left for the town to pick her up a backpacking frame. He knew exactly what he wanted for her and soon they were on their way to the outskirts of Positano, where he parked the car in an area reserved for hikers.

Rini was a master at assembling all the gear, which included a tent, fishing gear plus all the other things they'd brought. "How does that feel?" he asked after helping her adjust the straps. "Is it lopsided?"

"It's perfect and the day is absolutely glorious."

Through her sunglasses she stared at the striking male specimen standing before her wearing his own pack. He carried the bulk of their equipment as if it was nothing and smiled back at her through his sunglasses. "Get ready to be astounded by the sights."

"After you, Captain."

They were off. She followed him along a well-worn path for about a mile. Before she knew it they'd come to a section with a thousand-foot dropoff and no railing. "Rini," she squealed in awe.

"We're at the top of the cliff. You'll notice that people live up here and use this path coming and going."

"It's a miracle. Unbelievable." They continued walking and ran into farms and terraces that grew fruits and vegetables.

"Some people come here for a hike and decide to live here in one of the little houses on these mountains."

"I can see why. It's so peaceful up here, unconnected to anything else."

"You should be here during a storm. The clouds drift in from the sea and literally collide with the cliffs."

"The view from this spot is breathtaking. That water is so blue, I have to take a picture." She pulled the phone out of her pocket and insisted he get in it. They took turns so he could capture her, then they trudged on.

Alessandra really did feel she was walking on the footpath of the gods. One of them was right in front of her. He took such wonderful care of her every step of the way, she felt cherished.

They stopped at noon to eat lunch under a tree, then made a turn into the interior. Rini was an encyclopedia on the flora and fauna, let alone the history of the region governed by Byzantine rule from the third century when Amalfi was a trading post.

He took her past gorges and caves until they came to a mountain stream. "How are you at fly fishing?"

"I've only trolled for fish in the sea. You'll have to teach me."

"You're going to love it. Let's have a snack, then I'll set up our fishing poles and I'll show you how to cast."

It felt good to sit down and relax for a little while. He told her to look in his tackle box and see what kind of fly she'd like to use.

"Do they all work here?"

"Most of them. Look for a gray spider fly."

Alessandra rummaged around until she found one of that color. "This?" She held it up.

"That's it. I'll attach it and we'll walk down to the edge of the water to catch our dinner."

She watched him put her fly on the line before he chose a spot. "Show me how to cast."

He demonstrated five or six times so she could get the hang of it. "Okay. I think I'm ready to try." But it wasn't as easy as he made a look. She hit too low, too high and was too jerky. On her last cast she put the fly rod too far back and her line was snagged by a shrub. "Oh, no!"

Rini didn't laugh outright, but she knew he had to be chuckling as she scrambled up the side of the ravine to retrieve the fly. She made several attempts to no avail. "Help! I can't get it out!" He joined her and carefully extricated it from the prickly bush. "You're so good at this I bet you've never done that."

"You have no idea the mistakes I've made," he confessed after pressing a hungry kiss to her mouth. "Come on. Let's try it again."

"I'm embarrassed and want to watch you fish for a while."

He reached for his pole and aimed for a spot near a rock where the water pooled in the stream. On his third attempt to catch something at the same place, she saw a little fish grab his fly and he reeled it in.

"That was poetry in motion, Rini. I'll never be able to do that."

"Keep at it and you'll become an expert like you are at everything else." He got out his fish knife and removed the hook before throwing the fish back in the stream.

"Why did you do that?"

His eyes lit on her. "It was too small. Maybe he has a big brother or sister swimming around. Now it's your turn to try again."

She reached for her pole. "I'll aim for the same place you did." This time she threw it so hard, her pole landed in the water. *"Diavolo!"* she cried and jumped into the fast moving stream to catch it. But her boot tripped on a rock and she felt flat on her face. Her pole was carried farther downstream and got stuck around a bunch of rocks.

Like lightning Rini was there to help her up. By now they were knee-deep in the water. She lifted her head, not knowing whether to laugh or cry. His body was shaking with laughter, but being polite, he held it back. She loved him so much, she couldn't stay angry and started to laugh.

"Apologies for the slip."

His smile enveloped her. "Which one?"

"Both!" She broke free of his arms and made her way carefully downstream to recover her pole. "Ooh—a big trout just swam past me. I wish I could have grabbed it!"

Rini's deep male laughter poured out of him in waves. He moved toward her.

"No, no. I can make it back to shore myself. You're probably thinking, is this the scuba diver?" To her horror, the moment she said the words she slipped on a moss-covered rock and fell on her face, making another big splash.

When she stood up sputtering, there was Rini taking a picture of her. "That's not fair." Alessandra made a face. "This is ridiculous." She raised her rod and stomped out of the water, flinging herself down on a grassy spot. "Don't you dare laugh again."

Rini raised his hands. "I wouldn't dream of it. I was hoping we could hike farther to a small lake, but under the circumstances we'll camp here. I'll set up the tent so you can change out of your wet clothes."

"I'm all right. Let's keep going. Maybe I'll have better luck at the lake. I'll just troll for a fish by walking through the water and trailing my line."

One dark brow lifted above eyes that were dancing in amusement. "You're sure?"

"Let's go." She put on her backpack, deciding to carry her pole as is.

Rini started out first. All along the way she heard him chuckling, but he never turned around. A half hour later they dropped into a dark green gorge. With night falling fast, she was reminded of a primeval forest. The water from the stream emptied into a silvery narrow lake maybe a soccer field long. "It's shaped like a fat eel!"

"Spoken like a scuba diver. My father always thought it looked like a cigar."

"What about your brother?"

"A long blimp."

She laughed. "And you?"

"The Veil Nebula."

Alessandra blinked. "You love astronomy?" He nodded. "Did you ever consider becoming an astronomer?"

"No. The universe is too far away. With engineering I can get my hands on something once I design it."

"You like the tactile."

He nodded. "We'll set up camp here."

"I love this spot."

"Tomorrow we'll explore the other end of the lake. The water trickles down to become a waterfall and cascades to the sea."

"I wish we didn't have to wait."

His gaze trapped hers. "You know the old saying. All good things come to those who wait."

"But I don't want to. Aren't I awful?"

"Later tonight I'll tell you what I think."

His words filled with promise almost caused her legs to buckle. In seconds he'd found them a grassy area and pulled out the blue-and-white two-man tent. She helped him erect it. They worked along in harmony. Finally she was able to go inside and change into warm gray sweats and tennis shoes. All her clothes needed to be dried outside, including her boots.

While he built a small campfire, she laid their sleeping bags side by side. The whole time Alessandra worked, she feared he could hear her heart thudding through the walls of the tent. Tonight they'd be sleeping together. This was the kind of heaven she never imagined could happen to her.

The light from the flames flickered, revealing his tantalizing male features. He'd thrown on a tan crewneck sweater over his jeans. His beautiful olive skin and dark coloring had been bequeathed by his Neapolitan ancestry. She could feast her eyes on him all night.

He watched her approach. "Come and sit down. I've made coffee to go with our pies."

"You're wonderful." She kissed his jaw before making a place next to him. "I'm sorry I couldn't contribute anything for our dinner. I'll do better another time."

"I'm counting on it," he murmured.

Her pulse raced as she sipped her coffee from the plastic mug. "Did your mother camp with you when you came out here?"

"Many times. Valentina, too. It's dark in this part of the mountains. She would bring her hand telescope and pass it around. I remember the hours she taught us about the constellations. Then she and Papà would slip into their tent and leave the three of us to enjoy the wonders of the universe. When I grew old enough, I understood they sneaked away to enjoy the wonder of each other."

"Oh, I know all about that." Alessandra chuckled. "Our family went on expeditions to Sicily. One time at the Valley of the Temples, we'd set up our camp. I thought we'd explore that first night while there was still light. But our parents told us to run along and enjoy ourselves.

"My sister and I eyed each other. We could always amuse each other. But it was another one of those times when we were both thinking exactly the same thing. You could say that night contributed to our enlightenment. I never looked at my parents the same way again."

Rini ate another pie. "I can relate." He let the fire burn down.

She sat cross-legged in front of it. "You've never told me where you went to school."

"University of Naples, then MIT in Cambridge, Massachusetts."

"You didn't meet a special woman during those years?"

He swallowed the rest of his coffee. "Yes, but I had a goal to finish my education and didn't let anything get in the way."

"Still, you know what I mean."

"She didn't matter enough to distract me from my agenda since I knew I couldn't give her a baby."

"I'm glad it didn't work out. Otherwise I wouldn't be with you now."

Rini stirred and got to his feet. "I want to continue this conversation, but would rather do it in the tent. Give me a minute to put out the fire." While he went over to the stream half a dozen times for water to douse the flames, Alessandra put the food away, then found her flashlight and took a trip behind a fat bush.

She kept the light on for Rini. Once she'd removed her tennis shoes, she entered the tent and lay down inside one of bags. Before long he joined her having exchanged his sweater and jeans for a dark blue sweatshirt and pants. His dashing smile took her breath. "I'm having the most fun I've ever had in my life."

"So am I."

He zipped up the tent flaps and opened the little screened window for air. Then he stretched out on top of his sleeping bag and turned toward her. "Do you mind if we keep the light on for a little while? I want to look at you while we talk."

She rolled on her side to face him. "I love looking at you, but you already know that."

"Alessandra?" He reached for her hand and kissed the palm. "Though I want to make love to you and never stop, I can't wait any longer to tell you what's on my mind first."

"What is it?"

"I'm helplessly in love with you, *adorata*, and want to marry you."

A cry escaped her throat. "Rini—"

"That couldn't be news to you." He sat up to face her. "I fell in love with you that first day. You weren't the only one who had a surreal experience."

Joy permeated her body. "I hoped you felt that way, but I hardly dared to dream I would ever hear those words."

"I've been afraid to say them because of the burden it puts on you."

She raised up on one elbow. "What burden? If you're talking about the fact that you can't give me babies, we've already had this conversation. It doesn't matter."

He shook his head. "Of course it does. But putting the reality of adoption aside, I'm talking about something else that I should have discussed with you weeks ago."

Weeks?

With that word Alessandra got a sinking feeling in the pit of her stomach and sat up. "This has to do with my aunt, doesn't it?"

Lines marred his features, letting her know she was right, and her frustration grew. "Instead of going diving that morning, you drove us back to the castle because you said you had business with Papà."

"I did," he muttered.

"That's interesting. When I came down to the office later to find you, he told me you'd gone. I heard the helicopter. According to him you were no longer interested in drilling for oil on our property. As a footnote he said you thanked both of us profusely for our time."

Her voice quivered, but she couldn't stop it. "I thought I was in the middle of a nightmare."

Rini was quiet so long, she couldn't stand it. "What went on with my aunt behind closed doors that caused you to leave without even having the decency to say goodbye to me in person? If what happened was so terrible, why didn't you tell me immediately?"

"I held back because I didn't want to betray a confidence that could bring pain."

"You've said that before. To whom?" she demanded.

He stared her down. "Everyone involved."

"I don't understand." Her tears had started. He brushed them away with his thumbs.

"My feelings for you ran so deep, I was afraid to spend another moment with you. The only thing to do was get away and never see you again."

She shuddered. "Don't you know how cruel that was to me? I'd fallen hopelessly in love with you and you knew it."

"Listen to me." He grasped both her hands. "I slipped away because I thought it was the best thing to do considering that I never intended to see you again."

Alessandra couldn't take much more. "Then why did you come back?"

"You know the answer to that. When I heard about the earthquake and knew your diving team had been affected, I came close to having a coronary. Nothing could have kept me away, not even my reason for leaving you the way I did in the first place."

"The accident didn't turn out to be that serious."

"It could have been deadly," he argued. "Don't you

know *you* were the most important person in my life? To think of losing you was so terrifying, I flew out of my office and left for Crotone. I had to search for you at two other hospitals before I found you. The moment I saw you again and your doctor told me you would recover, I realized I couldn't walk away from you a second time."

"Even if what you're about to tell me will hurt everyone?" Her question rang inside the tent.

"Yes. I have to risk it because I've just asked you to be my wife. But I was premature and don't want your answer until you've heard the whole truth from me."

A groan came out of her. "How long are you going to make me wait? Please just tell me what it is and let it be the end of all the secrets."

The sick look on her face devastated Rini, but she needed to hear everything. He drank part of his bottle of water first, then screwed the top back on. "Did you know that Dea flew to Taranto to see your aunt the morning after being on the yacht?"

A delicate frown marred her features. "That's news to me. I thought she told you she had some fashion shows that kept her in Naples."

Rini nodded. "That's what she told me. Does your sister have a special bond with your aunt?"

"Yes. Many times over the years she's gone to stay with her. My aunt took care of her after she was born so Mamma could have a break from two children at once. I usually spent time with our mother. I adore my aunt, but I'm pretty sure Dea developed a deep attachment to Zia Fulvia that has lasted. Our aunt is very glamorous and exciting. Naturally it meant the world to her since she couldn't have children.

"I've always appreciated that Dea and I were raised to be individuals. Neither Mamma or Fulvia played up our twin status. We were never dressed alike or put in the same classes at school. They wanted us to be able to express ourselves in our own way and have our own friends. Dea gravitated to Fulvia."

"Yet interestingly enough, in some ways you're more like your aunt than she is."

"You told me that before." She took a ragged breath. "You still haven't told me why Dea went to see her."

After listening to the explanation of Alessandra's background, Rini was beginning to understand a great deal. "Your sister wanted to talk to her about me."

A haunted look crept into her lovely face. "I'm surprised my aunt would reveal something that private to you."

"So was I, until she explained herself. I'm convinced that what she told me was motivated out of pure love for both you and Dea."

Alessandra lowered her head. "What did she do? Ask you to stop seeing me?"

"No. That's exactly what she didn't do. For the first few minutes she told me a story about a wonderful, brilliant girl who fell in love with a chef from Catania named Francesco and got her heart broken. Fulvia feared this girl would never get over it and never be able to forgive her sister, whom she'd always felt was more beautiful and loveable than herself. To Fulvia's great surprise and joy, this girl *did* get over her heartache. She seized life to the fullest without blaming her sister for anything."

"What?" Alessandra's head flew back in shock.

"That's right," Rini murmured. "Then she told me a story about another exciting, bright girl who fell for an engineer named Rinieri Montanari. He represented her prince incarnate, but she discovered he didn't feel the same way about her and she wanted to die."

Alessandra's chin trembled. "Oh, Rini…"

"Oh, Rini is right. Your aunt asked me to think carefully before I took another step. She feared Dea might not be as strong and courageous in battling her heartache as was the scholarly twin she'd always envied."

"Dea envied me?"

The shock on her face was priceless and told him this was a woman without guile. "She left me with a question and a warning before she went up to bed. Her exact words were, 'Is the recent love you feel for Alessandra greater than the lifetime love between twin sisters? Whatever you decide, you'll have to live with the consequences forever.'"

Rini didn't know how she'd respond after telling her the truth, but he hadn't expected her to turn away from him and sob into her pillow. *"Cara—"* He lay down next to her with his arm around her shoulders. She convulsed so much, all he could do was hold her and kiss her cheeks and hair until the tears eventually subsided. "Talk to me, *bellissima.*"

After a long time she turned over, her face blotchy from crying. "The warning she gave you felt like someone just walked over my grave."

"Why do you say that?"

"Because when I found out you'd met Dea first, I determined to put you out of my mind. Nothing was worth coming between my twin and me since we'll be sisters forever. I was taken by surprise when Papà asked me to drive you around the property. Much as I wanted to be with you, I knew it would be taking a great risk. Fulvia's words have just confirmed my worst fears."

Gutted by her response, Rini shut off the flashlight and lay down on his back. "I'm sure your aunt didn't want me to reveal our conversation to you, but my world changed after your accident and I had to tell you."

"I'm thankful you did. I know she spoke to you out of love for Dea and me." He heard Alessandra's heavy sigh. "It took a lot of courage on your part to tell me and I admire you for keeping quiet about it for as long as you have in order to protect Dea."

"What worries me now is where you want to go from here."

"I don't know, Rini. In the morning I'll have an answer. Thank you for the greatest day I've ever known. *Buonanotte*."

He heard the rustle of her sleeping bag. She'd turned away from him physically and emotionally. Unable to lie this close to her without reaching for her, he stood up and went outside to walk around. A three-quarter moon lit up the night sky. He didn't need a flashlight or a fire to see the forested landscape. The lake shone a mystic silver.

She's not going to marry you, Montanari. I can feel it in my bones.

Rini felt like he was burning up with fever. The cool night air brought some relief. He eventually planted himself beneath the trunk of a pine tree close to the tent so he could keep an eye on her. Several times he nodded off, but was wide awake at six craving coffee.

After making it, he heated it on the ultralight stove. Once he'd downed a cup, he walked over to the stream. Though he cast his line half a dozen times, nothing was biting yet. Maybe it was an omen to prepare him for what was to come.

He could have kept the secret he'd shared with her aunt, but wouldn't have been able to live with it long. Alessandra's tearful breakdown proved to him he'd done the right thing telling her. But it was possible he'd written the death sentence on a future life together with her.

Near eight o'clock she stepped outside the tent with a false smile, dressed in another pair of jeans and a white pullover. One by one she produced their sleeping bags, all rolled up and snug in their cases. He didn't have to hear a word from her to know their vacation had come to an end.

Her eyes darted to his. "*Buongiorno*, Rini. I detected coffee. It smells so much better out in the forest, don't you think?"

Without saying anything he poured her a cup and handed it to her.

"*Grazie.*" She eyed his pole. "I heard your line snaking in the air. Evidently you didn't have any luck fishing this morning or you'd be cooking our breakfast."

Rini had all the chitchat he could take. "Why don't you just tell me what I already know," he groaned.

This morning she was dry-eyed. "Papà once said that Zia Fulvia was the wisest woman he'd ever known. After what we talked about last night, I'm convinced of it. I'm honored by your marriage proposal, Rini. No thrill will ever equal it. But even if I'll love you to my dying breath, I don't want to see you again. I'm ready to hike back to the car whenever you say."

CHAPTER EIGHT

A WEEK AFTER returning to the castle, Alessandra realized she couldn't go on in this state of limbo. Even if she could dive again, she didn't want to. The thought of working on her book was out of the question. She unpacked all the gorgeous clothes she hadn't worn and put them away. Rini was on her mind night and day.

Though her parents didn't question her when she returned home having cut her vacation short, she knew they wanted to. But her father didn't probe and she was thankful for that. Her aunt came to stay for a few days to enjoy a change of scene. Soon she'd be able to get around without the wheelchair.

Fulvia was as warm and loving as always, giving nothing away about her private conversation with Rini. They did some puzzles as a family and Alessandra learned that Dea was back in Rome after another sensational show in Florence attended by some VIPs in the television industry.

But talking about Dea had been like pressing on a thorn until she was bleeding all over the place. The day after her aunt flew back to Taranto, Alessandra told her parents she was taking the Land Rover to visit friends in Metaponto and wouldn't be back until evening.

She gave Alfredo a kiss on the head before leaving the castle. "I don't like lying, but this is one time no one can know where I'm really going."

Once she reached the airport, she boarded a flight for Rome. The plane landed at noon. After hailing a taxi, she asked the driver to take her to the elegant apartment complex in the heart of the city where Dea had been living for the last year. The five-hundred-year-old street where it was located was a warren of fabulous shops near the Pantheon and the Piazza Navona.

When Alessandra approached the desk manager, he called her Signorina Loti. "You've mistaken me for her. Would you please ring her room? I'm her twin sister and have flown a long way to see her."

The middle-aged man did a double take. "*Scusi, signorina.* It's astonishing how much you two look alike. Except for the hair... I suppose in this case it will be all right to let you in."

"Thank you, *signor.* You're very kind."

Dea had a fabulous apartment on the third floor. Fulvia had come to Rome to help her furnish it in a lavish style. After she'd been let in and freshened up, she went out again and left a note for the manager to give Dea when she came in from work.

Four hours later she returned to the apartment building having eaten and done a little book shopping while she thought about what she was going to say to her sister.

"*Signorina?* Your sister came in ten minutes ago."

"Grazie."

Her heart pounding with anxiety, Alessandra took the lift and knocked on her apartment door. Dea opened it looking gorgeous in harem pants and a filmy short-sleeved top of aqua. "This is a surprise."

"For me, too."

"Come in."

They hugged before she walked into the living room. She put down her sacks and turned to her sister. "Forgive me for not letting you know I was coming. I didn't decide until this morning."

"No problem. I thought you were still on vacation in Positano."

She shook her head. "I returned early."

Dea eyed her critically. "What happened to change things?"

"That's what I want to talk to you about. Do you have time, or do you have other plans?"

"Not tonight. If you want juice or fruit, it's in the fridge."

"Thanks, but I've already eaten.

Her sister sank down on the sofa. "Go ahead. What's on your mind that has brought you all the way here?"

"The last time we saw each other, you asked me if I was seeing Rini because of what happened with Francesco."

"And you told me no. Why are we talking about this?"

She sucked in her breath. "Because I'm tired of ignoring the elephant in the room and I have a feeling you're sick of it, too."

Dea averted her eyes. It told Alessandra her sister knew exactly what she was driving at.

Tears sprang into Alessandra's eyes. "I'm going to tell you something I've never admitted to you before. From the time we were little, I looked up to you as my big sister."

"Three minutes hardly qualifies me for that title."

"It did for me because you came out first and no one let me forget it. You were beautiful and made friends easily. Everything you did was elegant and perfect. As I grew older, I felt more gawky and insecure around you. By our teens guys flocked around you. I'm ashamed to admit I was so jealous of you."

She had to be getting through to her sister because Dea lifted her head and stared at her in disbelief. "You... were jealous of me?"

"Oh, yes. When Francesco followed you to Rome, I didn't want to believe it, but deep down I wasn't surprised. I'd seen the way he'd looked at you. He never looked at me like that."

"I'm sorry, Alessandra," she cried.

"No, no. Don't be. You didn't do anything to attract him. You don't have to. It always happens because you're you. For a long time after that I lived in denial about it. Finally I realized I needed to grow up and face the fact that I could never be like you. It meant I had to work on myself."

"But you're perfect just the way you are!"

It was Alessandra's turn to stare at her sister in wonder.

"It's true. All my life I've been the one jealous of

you. You're beautiful without even trying and you're smart. You write books and do all these amazing things with the underwater archaeological society. I've envied your love of adventure and hated it that I have so many stupid fears."

Alessandra shook her head. "I had no idea."

"We're a mess," Dea muttered. "Since it's truth time, want to tell me why you're not still with Rinieri? He's the most gorgeous hunk of manliness I ever saw."

"I agree," she said quietly. "But I wish I hadn't met him."

"That's the biggest whopper of a lie you've ever told."

"Dea—"

"It's true. You're mad about him. So what are you doing here with me?"

"Y-you know why," she stuttered.

"Because I had a giant-sized crush on him first? That's true, but he wasn't enamored of me no matter how hard I tried to entice him. It killed me that he didn't want to see me again. I even told Zia Fulvia."

Alessandra swallowed hard to hear the admission she already knew about.

"She laughed and said, 'Dea Caracciolo—do you want to conquer every man you meet? What would you do with all of them? It's not natural!'"

Alessandra's laughter joined Dea's.

"She gave me a simple piece of advice that made sense. 'When the true prince of your dreams comes along, it'll work. Until then, dry your tears and do your thing you do better than anyone other woman in the country.'"

"Fulvia's wonderful."

"She is. So are you, and Rini Montanari is absolutely smitten with you. Otherwise he wouldn't have invited you to his villa for a whole week. The famous bachelor has fallen to his knees. If you don't snap him up, then you're a fool."

"You mean it?"

"Oh, come here." Dea reached out and hugged her hard. "I have something else to tell you that should make you happy."

"What?"

"I made a play for him. He didn't bite."

"What kind?"

"On the yacht, I kissed *him* good-night right on the mouth."

"Good grief!"

"Don't worry. He didn't kiss me back and turned me down when I asked him to go out to dinner with me the next night. Only an honorable man would do that. You're a very lucky woman and I'll welcome him into our family with open arms."

"I love you, Dea, and want only the best for you."

"I know that, and I love you, too."

"Let's never let anything come between us again."

"Never."

"We're sisters forever."

Forever.

"Now let's go on a shopping spree and find you an outfit that will deliver the coup de grâce the moment Rini sees you. Why not show up at his office and dazzle everyone in sight?"

"I only want to dazzle *him*."

"Then let's do it!"

The Montanari office complex dominated a portion of a city block in the downtown business center of Naples. At four in the afternoon, Alessandra was met by whistles and stares as she stepped out of the limo in her Jimmy Choo heels. She was wearing the designer dress Dea had picked out for her. It cost a fortune but she didn't care because she felt transformed in it.

The solid off-white pullover dress with long sleeves had a row of trendy buttons up the side from the tulip-styled hem to the neck. Around her shoulders she wore a flowing ivory-and-tan print scarf that matched the tan-and-ivory lace of her shoes.

Her hair glinted with streaks of gold among the brunette. She wore new lipstick in a deep pink with a soft blush on her high cheek-bones and a touch of eye shadow Dea said brought out her eyes. She'd never been so decked out. Her sister said she'd never looked more beautiful. Alessandra felt like she was moving in a fantastic dream.

His office building was like a small city, forcing her to pass through security before she could approach the bank of elevators. Her pride in his accomplishments made her throat swell with emotion as she rode one of them to the thirty-sixth floor, where his headquarters was located. She approached the secretary in the main reception area.

"I'm here to see Signor Montanari."

The attractive, thirtyish-looking woman looked up, then blinked. "You're Dea!"

Alessandra smiled, not minding it at all. "No, but you're close. I'm her sister."

"Do you model, too?"

"No. I scuba dive."

"Oh." Her blue eyes rounded. "Which Montanari did you wish to see?"

"Rinieri."

"I'm sorry, but the CEO is in a board meeting and can't be disturbed. If you'd like, I'll make an appointment for you."

At least he was here and not out of town. "Thank you, but no. I'll wait until he comes out."

"It might be several hours."

"I don't mind." *I'd wait forever for him.*

She sat down on one of the love seats with her ivory clutch bag in hand. Twenty minutes later she saw an attractive, dark-haired man who bore a superficial resemblance to Rini walk into the reception area and hand something to the secretary. His brother? A cousin?

The secretary must have said something to him because he turned in Alessandra's direction. Their eyes met before he walked over to her. "I understand you're here to see Rinieri?"

"Yes, but he didn't know I was coming. I wanted to surprise him."

The flattering male admiration in his eyes made her efforts to look beautiful worth it. "He's going to be surprised all right. I'm going back in to the meeting. I'll let him know someone is out here waiting for him, but I won't give you away."

Her heart fluttered in her chest. *"Grazie."*

"Prego."

Twelve men sat at the oblong conference table. Rini's Zio Salvatore scowled at him from a few seats down on the right. "I think we're moving too fast. Look what's happened in Greece!"

"If we don't strike now, someone else will." Rini was tired of the deadlock. Tonight he'd reached the end of his rope. He was ready to take off for places unknown to forget his pain. Guido had tried to talk to him, but Rini was in such a dark place, he wasn't fit company for anyone. Something had to change or his life wasn't worth living.

"My son's right," Rini's father said. "With this uncertain economy, we have to take advantage of these opportunities while we can."

While everyone offered an opinion, Carlo came back in the room. His brother's brows lifted, a signal that he wanted to talk to him about something. It would have to wait until they'd resolved the issue before the board.

"Let's take a vote," his cousin Piero said.

"We're not ready yet!" This from Rini's great uncle Niccolo.

The arguing went on another fifteen minutes. Rini received a text on his phone. Just so you know, Octavia said you have one more appointment before you leave tonight. The person is waiting in reception.

Since when? Rini didn't have the time or inclination

to do any more business once he left this room, but he nodded in acknowledgement to Carlo, who sat at the other end of the table. When five more minutes hadn't yielded a consensus, Rini brought the meeting to a close.

"It's late. We'll reconvene on Monday and take a vote then." Salvatore couldn't have been more pleased that no action had been taken yet. He came from the old school, unable to abide the kind of progress Rini felt the company should be making.

After slipping out a side door into his private office, Rini rang Octavia. "Send in the person who's been waiting. Since they're infringing on my weekend, tell them I can only give them one minute. My helicopter is waiting."

"Yes, sir."

While he leaned over his desk long enough to sign a pile of letters ready to be mailed, he heard a knock on the door.

"Come in."

"Signor Montanari? Please forgive me for barging in without an appointment, but this is a matter of life and death."

He knew that voice and spun around, convinced he was dreaming.

"Cat got your tongue?"

The vision before him left him breathless. He *had* to be dreaming!

"The last time we were together, you asked me an important question. I couldn't give you an answer then, but I'm prepared to give you one now. But maybe too much time has passed and you'd like to unask it."

He could hardly breathe. "Remind me of the question."

"You asked me to be your wife." The tremor in her voice made its way to his heart.

"I remember. But you had an irreconcilable conflict that prevented you from answering."

Her eyes filled with tears. "Since then I've *un*-conflicted it."

His breath caught in his lungs. "How was that possible?"

"Two days ago I flew to Rome and had the conversation with Dea we've needed to have since she visited me in Catania. It was the heart-to-heart kind that immersed two sisters in tears. It was a time of love and forgiveness for all past hurts and misunderstandings. In the end she told me something I needed desperately to hear. So do you.

"She said, 'I wanted Rini Montanari to want me, so I made a play for him and kissed him good-night right on the mouth. He didn't bite.'"

Rini's head reared. "She admitted that to you?"

"Oh, yes. There's more. She said she invited you to dinner but you turned her down flat."

He shook his head. "I don't believe what I'm hearing."

"I do. That's because you're an honorable man, my darling. Not only for turning her down because you didn't have those kinds of feelings for her, but for keeping that secret to yourself in order not to hurt her or me. She thinks I'm the luckiest woman alive. I am! She said to tell you that she welcomes you to the Caracciolo family with open arms. That's a good thing because I plan to be your wife. I can't live without you!"

She ran into his arms, almost knocking him over while she covered his face and mouth with kisses. "*Ti amo*, Rini. *Ti amo*."

"Hey, bro?"

Rini's eyes swerved to the door. Carlo had just walked in on them, but he came to an abrupt standstill and a huge smile broke out on his face. "Well, look what my *fratello* snagged on his last fishing trip! I wouldn't have missed this for the world. Looks like Guido's the only living bachelor left in Naples. I'll make sure you're not disturbed."

He closed the door. By now Rini had sat down in his chair with Alessandra in his lap. They kissed long and hard until he started to believe this was really happening. She looked and smelled divine.

"How soon can we get married, *bellissima*?"

"Whenever you want. I think the chapel in the castle would be the perfect place. Dea and I had a chapel in our play castle. We always planned elaborate weddings with our dolls. We even had a doll priest. Did you know Queen Joanna married one of her husbands there?"

Rini hugged her hard. "I can't think of a place more fitting for you."

"And you, because you're my prince. We'll invite all our friends and family. We have room for everyone. The cook will plan a wedding feast with all the fish you can eat." He started chuckling. "Dea will help me find the perfect wedding dress and Fulvia will help Mamma do everything else. We'll ask your sister to bring her babies and we'll dress them up like little princes. Alfredo will walk around excited because there's going to be food. And Papà will play the host with a twinkle in his eye."

By now his chuckling had turned to deep laughter. "There's one thing *I* want to do. Plan the honeymoon," he whispered against the side of her neck.

"I was hoping you'd say that. Can we leave now and go somewhere private where I can kiss you as long and wickedly as I want?"

"What a ridiculous question to ask the man who's headlong in love with the most gorgeous woman alive."

"I hope you'll always feel that way."

It took them a while to stop kissing long enough to make it to the roof. Rini told his pilot to fly them to Positano. "We're getting married, Lucca."

He grinned. "Tonight?"

"Don't I wish. It'll be soon."

With a background of Vesuvius, the helicopter rose into the evening sky. Rini was so full of emotion, he couldn't talk. While they were in the air, he pulled a ring out of his breast pocket. He'd bought it a month ago and had been carrying it around, keeping it close to him like a talisman.

"Give me your left hand, *adorata*."

Her whole countenance beamed as she did his bidding. He slid the ring on her finger. "It's fabulous, Rini!" She held it up close to inspect it. "The diamond and setting—this is like the one on Queen Joanna's hand in the foyer of the castle!"

"The foyer was the place I fell in love with you. She's

the reason you and I met. In a way I owe her my life. I'm glad you noticed."

Her beautiful eyes rounded. "You silly man. How could I not notice? Just wait till you see the ring I have planned for you."

Joy was a new emotion for him. So new, he clung to her hand, unable to find words.

CHAPTER NINE

ALESSANDRA STOOD OUTSIDE the closed chapel doors with her father, where they could hear the organ playing. After waiting a month for her wedding day, she was so anxious to be Rini's wife, she'd started to feel feverish in anticipation.

"Papà? Why are we waiting?" Everyone was inside including her husband-to-be, whom she knew was equally impatient to be married at this point.

Her distinguished-looking father, outfitted in wedding finery and a blue sash befitting the Count of Caracciolo, turned to her with a gleam in his eyes. "Your aunt has worked her magic."

"What do you mean?"

"As you are a princess of the Houses of Taranto and Caraciolla, the Archbishop of Taranto is going to preside. We're giving him time to enter the nave through the side entrance."

A quiet gasp escaped her. "Rini's not going to believe it."

"He's going to have to get used to a lot of surprises being married to my darling *piccola.*"

She smiled at him. "You're loving this, aren't you?"

He leaned over and kissed her forehead. "Almost as much as you. After all the weddings performed in your playhouse castle, you're going to be the star in your very own. You look like an angel in all that white fluff and lace."

"Dea found it for me."

"Of course. That explains the long train."

"It's spectacular."

"So are you. I see your mother gave you her tiara to wear."

"Something old and borrowed. Papà? Do you like Rini? I mean really like him?"

"I think he's an exceptional man who has met his match in you."

While they stood there, Dea came around the corner toward them. She looked a vision in pale lavender carrying two bouquets. She handed the one made of white roses to Alessandra. "I outdid myself when I picked out this wedding dress for you."

"I love it. I love you."

"Do you know where you're going on your honeymoon yet?"

"Rini's lips are sealed."

"Lucky you." Dea kissed her. "It's time."

The doors suddenly opened and Dea took her place behind Alessandra and her father. Together they entered the ornate chapel with its stained glass windows, where a lot of history had been made. Every single person she loved was assembled. The archbishop added a solemnity to the occasion in his ceremonial robes. But she only had eyes for the tall, dark-haired man turned out in dove-gray wedding clothes standing near the altar.

The dazzling white of his dress shirt set off his olive skin coloring to perfection. He was her prince in every sense of the word. She prayed her heart wouldn't give out before she reached his side. His dark eyes seemed to leap to hers as she reached his side. While the archbishop addressed the congregation, Rini didn't remove his gaze from her.

"Surely heaven is shining down on these two people this day while they are joined together in the most holy ordinance of the church," the archbishop began.

Rini's hand held hers. He rubbed his thumb over her palm and wrist. She was trying to concentrate on the sacredness of the occasion, but his touch sent fire through her entire body. By the time they came to exchanging vows, he'd reduced her to a weakened state. Thank heaven the words were finally pronounced.

"I now pronounce you, Rinieri di Brazzano Montanari, and you, Alessandra Taranto Caracciolo, man and wife in front of God and this congregation. What God has joined together, let no man put asunder."

Her clear conscience over Dea had freed her from bondage. They both kissed with restrained passion, forcing themselves to hold back. But she was bursting inside with love for him. When she turned to face her family, her joy was so great she could hardly contain it.

"It won't be long now," Rini whispered in an aside. He squeezed her hand as he led them down the aisle and out the doors to the great dining hall that had once seen the courtiers of kings and queens. He reached around her waist and pressed her against his hip while they greeted their parents and guests. She saw her father hand something to Rini before they took their places at the head table.

Guido and his parents sat together before he took over the emcee job. "One good thing about this marriage. Alessandra has taken him off the market. Now *I'm* the most famous bachelor of Naples." He ended with a wonderful trail of anecdotes about Rini that had people bursting with laughter.

Dea took her turn. "Alessandra and I were joined at the hip in the womb. It feels strange to be on my own at last, but I couldn't be happier for her." She shared more nuggets of personal moments with Alessandra to delight their audience. Alessandra turned beet-red.

One by one, the members of both families paid tribute. Valentina brought tears to everyone's eyes in her tribute to Rini, who'd been so wonderful to her after their mother had died. Carlo reminisced over his own touching memories of Rini when their mother was alive.

There were more speeches, but she could tell Rini was restless. In a move that appeared to surprise him, she rose to her feet with some difficulty considering the length of her train. "Rini and I want to thank everyone for making our wedding day unforgettable. Zia Fulvia? What would we do without you? In fact, what would we do without our marvelous staff, my darling Liona and her cat Alfredo and the families we cherish."

Rini got to his feet. "I couldn't have said it better, but I hope you'll understand that we need to leave."

"Sure you do," Guido quipped loud enough for everyone to hear. Dea laughed at his remark. Alessandra hid her head against Rini's shoulder as they left the hall on a run. He led her through the hallway to the foyer. They raced out the doors to the Land Rover. He stuffed her inside and ran around to drive them to the helipad.

Their pilot was all smiles as he helped her on board. Once they were strapped in, they took off with Rini seated in the copilot's seat. "*Complimenti*, Signora Montanari."

"*Grazie*, Lucca. My husband won't tell me where we're going."

"We'll be there soon, *bellissima*."

"It was a beautiful wedding, don't you think?"

"Yes, but I thought it would never be over."

"Mamma said the wedding is for the bride. She was right."

The pilot flew east to the Adriatic, then dropped to a luxury yacht making its way through the water. Her eyes darted to Rini's in question.

"Guido's parents insisted on providing their yacht for our honeymoon. We can stop anywhere we want and scuba dive in Croatian waters. There are caves you'll love to explore."

"It sounds wonderful, but as you once told me, I don't care where we go as long as we're together."

Lucca set them down on the yacht's helipad with remarkable expertise. Rini jumped out and reached for her, carrying her across the deck to a stairway with the master bedroom on the next level down. She could see everything had been prepared for them ahead of time.

Flowers overflowed the living area of the suite, creating a heavenly perfume.

"At last." The way he was looking at her caused her limbs to quiver. He wrapped his arms around her and undid the buttons of her wedding dress, while he gave her a husband's kiss that never ended.

Somehow they gravitated to the bedroom, leaving a trail of wedding clothes and a tiara. The covers had been turned down. He followed her on to the mattress, burying his face in her throat. "Alessandra, I can't believe you're my wife. I've been lonely for you for years."

"You don't know the half of it. I love you so terribly. Make love to me, darling, and never ever stop," she murmured feverishly until they were devouring each other and conversation ceased.

For the rest of the night they communicated with their bodies, trying to show each other how they felt in ways that words couldn't. Rini took her to another world, where she felt transformed. When morning came she couldn't bear for the night to be over. Even though he'd finally fallen asleep, she started kissing him again to wake him up. His eyes opened.

"You've married a wanton. Forgive me."

In a surprise move he rolled her over so he was looking down at her. "I wouldn't have you any other way. You're perfect." Another long, deep kiss ensued.

"But was it…good for you?"

He moaned. "What a question to ask me? Can't you tell what you've done? I'll never want to go to work again."

"I don't know if I'll be able to let you go."

"Then our problem is solved. *Buongiorno, moglie mia.* Welcome to my world."

She pressed another avid kiss to his compelling mouth. "We're not dreaming this, are we? This is real. You really are my husband."

"You'd better believe it, but in case you're in any doubt, let me prove it."

To her joy he proved it over and over. Except for taking the time to eat, she drowned in her husband's love. They didn't surface for three days.

At the end of that time they planned to go up on deck. But before they left their room, Alessandra rushed around in her robe to pick up their wedding attire still all over the room. It would be too embarrassing for any of the ship's staff to see the hurry they'd been in after arriving in the helicopter after the ceremony.

"Darling? I found this in the pocket of your suit." He'd just come out of the bathroom with a towel hitched around his hips. She handed him an envelope.

"Your father slipped this to me at the castle."

"I wondered what it was."

Rini opened it and pulled out a letter.

"What does it say?

"'Alessandra's mother and I wanted to give you a wedding present, but it's for selfish reasons on our part. If you want to drill on our land, you have our permission. That way we know we'll see you part of the time when you have to be at the castle to supervise everything.'"

He looked shocked. Alessandra slid her arms up his chest and around his neck. "Now you know how much they love and trust you."

"I never expected this."

"That's one of the reasons why they did it. But my guess is, Fulvia helped Mother see that your vision can help our country."

"Is that what you think, too? Your opinion is the one that matters to me."

"You know I do. Otherwise I would never have taken you to see my aunt."

"We can thank providence you did. She proved to be the catalyst that helped you and your sister put away your demons."

She nodded. "One problem solved and one to go."

He kissed her with almost primitive desire. "We don't have another one."

"You're almost thirty-three and not getting any younger. Neither am I. If we're going to adopt children, we need to do something about it soon. These things can take time."

His brow dipped. "Are you desperate for a child already? Or tired of me already?"

"Rini... I'm not going to dignify either of those questions with a response. I'm simply looking ahead to our future. When I saw you playing with Ric and Vito a couple of days ago, I could picture you playing with our own children.

"I'm not saying we're ready now. Maybe the day will come when you'll want to consult one of the attorneys who work for you and we'll make an application to begin the process. But if it upsets you, I promise I'll never bring it up again."

He let out a ragged sigh and crushed her in his arms.

"I'm sorry I got so defensive. It's different when you know you can't have your own baby. I don't know if I could be a good father."

"No one knows if they're going to be able to handle it. I bet if you ask Carlo, he'll tell you he was nervous before their daughter was born."

"But he knew it was his."

"But he didn't see the baby until she was born. If we adopt, we won't see the baby until it's born. What difference will it make?"

He smiled. "You're right. It won't."

"Come on. Let's go on deck and soak up a little sun."

"I have a better idea. How would you like to fly to Montenegro for dinner? We've been away from the ship for three days. Wear that gorgeous outfit you showed up in at my office."

"You liked that one? I'll start getting ready right now."

"I like you in anything when you have to wear clothes, but if I had my way…"

"That works for me where you're concerned too." She giggled and ran into the bathroom, but he caught up to her before she could lock the door.

EPILOGUE

Eight months later

RINI WAS AT the drilling site when his cell rang. Hopefully it was Alessandra telling him she was back at the castle after her visit to her editor in Rome. Her book on Queen Joanna would be coming out shortly and the publisher wanted to set up some book signings.

But when he checked the caller ID, he saw that it was Maso Vanni, the attorney who'd helped him and Alessandra make application for adoption. The unmarried mother from Naples who'd been the right match for them was expecting her baby in a month. Rini hoped everything was all right. The last thing he wanted was to give his wife bad news.

He clicked on. "Maso? What's going on?"

"Lauretta Conti is in labor."

"What?"

"The doctor is trying to slow things down, but my advice is for you and your wife to get to the hospital as soon as you can."

"We'll be there!" He rang off and phoned Alessan-

dra, but her voice mail was on. He left her the message
that he was on his way to the hospital in Naples because Lauretta Conti might be having her baby in the
next little while.

After leaving instructions with the crew, he drove
to Metaponto for his helicopter flight to the hospital in
Naples. There was no time to shower or change out of
his khaki work clothes. En route he tried several times
to reach Alessandra. "Please answer as soon as you
can, *cara.*"

Once at the hospital he was shown to Lauretta's private room. The doctor said they couldn't stop the baby
from coming. "My patient needs a Caesarean. You're
about to become a father."

Rini had never felt so helpless in his life.

"The nurse will show you where to scrub."

The situation was surreal as he washed and put on
a gown. He was given a mask and gloves. Before long
he returned to the room and stood by the head of the
bed. He and Alessandra had met with Lauretta several
times in preparation for the baby's arrival. Where was
his wife?

Suddenly things began to happen. The anesthesiolo-
gist administered a spinal and a team came in while the
doctor performed surgery. Everyone seemed so calm.
When he heard a gurgling sound, a thrill shot through
him. A second later the newborn cry of the baby filled
the room.

The pediatrician took over and Rini was told to follow him to the room next door. "I understand you're
going to be the father of this baby."

"Yes." But fear held him in its grip.

"Where's your wife?"

"She's on her way." She would be when she got the message.

"He's strong for a preemie. Six pounds, twenty-one inches long. Seems to be breathing on his own. As soon as we clean him up, you can hold him."

The baby had a dusting of dark hair. Rini watched in fascination as the doctor checked him out. One of the nurses came in and put the baby in a little shirt and diaper, then wrapped him in a receiving blanket.

"Sit down, *signore*, so you can hold your son."

Nothing had seemed real until she placed the baby in Rini's arms and he was able to look at him. The sight of the beautiful boy caused his heart to melt. He didn't make a peep. Rini couldn't tell the color of his eyes yet. His little mouth made an *O*.

"You've got a cute *bambino* there," the nurse said. "Don't be afraid of him. He won't break. I'll get a bottle ready for him."

Taking her advice, he put the baby on his shoulder and patted his back. The warmth of his tiny body was a revelation. Emotion swamped him as he realized this baby would look to him forever as his father. Rini removed the mask and kissed his little head, wanting to be all things to him. A longing to protect him and give him everything possible filled his soul.

"Here you go." The nurse handed him the bottle. "He'll be hungry soon. Tease his mouth with the nipple and he'll start to suck."

He followed her advice. Like magic the baby responded and started to drink with gusto. "Hey, you like this, don't you? I like food, too. I'm a big eater. Always have been."

"Like father, like son." His wife's voice.

He turned his head. "Alessandra… How long have you been standing there?"

"Long enough to watch you bond with him. I knew it would happen."

Tears filled his eyes. "It did. I was terrified when I got here, but when the nurse put him in my arms…"

She smiled down at both of them. "Fatherhood took over."

"You need to hold him."

"I will in a minute. It's enough to watch the two of you. What did the pediatrician say?"

"He seems fine and his lungs are functioning even though he came early."

"We're so blessed." Her eyes glistened with moisture. "Can you believe we're parents now? I'm a new mom and didn't even have to go through labor."

"You're the most gorgeous mother in the world."

"And you're already a natural father. I can tell he's so happy to be there with you. He has almost finished his bottle."

She put her arms around his shoulders and stared down at the baby with her cheek against Rini's. "We're going to learn how to do this minute by minute. I love you for being willing to adopt. I know it wasn't an easy decision to make."

Rini was close to being overcome by his deepest feelings. "I never dreamed I would see this day."

"I know. It's a surprise since you're a true man of vision."

He cleared his throat. "I don't think you have any idea how much I love you for marrying me when you knew I couldn't give you a baby."

"But you *have* given me one, darling. He's in your arms and you're both in mine. What more could a woman ask for in this life?"

* * * * *

EXPECTING THE EARL'S BABY

JESSICA GILMORE

For Carla
A book about sisters, for my sister
Love Jessica x

PROLOGUE

'OH, NO!'

Daisy Huntingdon-Cross skidded to a halt on the icy surface and regarded her car with dismay.

No, dismay was for a dropped coffee or spilling red wine on a white T-shirt. Her chest began to thump as panic escalated. *This*, Daisy thought as she stared at the wall of snow surrounding her suddenly flimsy-seeming tyres, *this* was a catastrophe.

The snow, which had fallen all afternoon and evening, might have made a picturesque background for the wedding photos she had spent the past twelve hours taking, but it had begun to drift—and right now it was packed in tightly around her tyres. Her lovely, bright, quirky little city car, perfect for zooming around London in, was, she was rapidly realising, horribly vulnerable in heavy snow and icy conditions.

Daisy carefully shifted her heavy bag to her other shoulder and looked around. It was the only car in the car park.

In fact, she was the only person in the car park. No, scratch that, she was possibly the only person in the whole castle. A shiver ran down her spine, not entirely as a result of the increasing cold and the snow seeping through her very inadequate brogues. Hawksley Castle was a wonderfully romantic venue in daylight and when it was lit up at night. But when you were standing underneath the parapets, the great tower a craggy, shadowy silhouette looming above you and the only light a tepid glow from the lamp at the edge of the car park it wasn't so much romantic, more the setting for every horror film she had ever seen.

'Just don't go running into the woods.' She cast a nervous glance over her shoulder. The whole situation was bad enough without introducing the supernatural into it.

Besides it was Valentine's Day. Surely the only ghosts abroad today had to be those of lovers past?

Daisy shivered again as her feet made the painful transition from wet and cold to freezing. She stamped them with as much vigour as she could muster as she thought furiously.

Why had she stayed behind to photograph the departing guests, all happily packed into mini-buses at the castle gates and whisked off to the local village where hot toddies and roaring fires awaited them? She could have left three hours ago, after the first dance and long before the snow had changed from soft flakes to a whirling mass of icy white.

But, no, she always had to take it that step further, offer that bit more than her competitors—including the blog, complete with several photographs, that she'd promised would be ready to view by midnight.

Midnight wasn't that far away…

'Okay.' Her voice sounded very small in the empty darkness but talking aloud gave her a sense of normality. 'One, I can go into the village. It's only a couple of miles.' Surely the walking would warm up her feet? 'Two, I can try and scoop the worst of the snow off…' She cast a doubtful glance at the rest of the car park. The ever heavier snowfall had obliterated her footprints; it was like standing on a thick, very cold white carpet. An ankle-deep carpet. 'Three...' She was out of options. Walk or scoop, that was it.

'Three—I get you some snow chains.'

Daisy didn't quite manage to stifle a small screech as deep masculine tones broke in on her soliloquy. She turned, almost losing her footing in her haste, and skidded straight into a fleece-clad chest.

It was firm, warm, broad. Not a ghost. Probably not a werewolf. Or a vampire. Supernatural creatures didn't wear fleece as far as she knew.

'Where did you come from? You frightened the life out of me.' Daisy stepped back, scowling at her would-be rescuer. At least she hoped he was a rescuer.

'I was just locking up. I thought all the wedding guests were long gone.' His gaze swept over her. 'You're hardly dressed for this weather.'

'I was dressed for a wedding.' She tugged the hem of her silk dress down. 'I'm not a guest though, I'm the photographer.'

'Right.' His mouth quirked into a half smile. The gesture changed his rather severe face into something much warmer. Something much more attractive. He was tall—taller than Daisy who, at nearly six feet, was used to topping most men of her acquaintance—with scruffy dark hair falling over his face.

'Photographer or guest you probably don't want to be hanging around here all night so I'll get some chains and we'll try and get this tin can of yours on the road. You really should put on some winter tyres.'

'It's not a tin can and there's very little call for winter tyres in London.'

'You're not in London,' he pointed out silkily.

Daisy bit her lip. He had a point and she wasn't really in any position to argue. 'Thank you.'

'No worries, wouldn't want you to freeze to death on

the premises. Think of the paperwork. Talking of which, you're shivering. Come inside and warm up. I can lend you some socks and a coat. You can't drive home like that.'

Daisy opened her mouth to refuse and then closed it again. He didn't seem like an axe murderer and she was getting more and more chilled by the second. If it was a choice between freezing to death and taking her chances inside she was definitely veering towards the latter. Besides... 'What time is it?'

'About eleven, why?'

She'd never get home in time to post the blog. 'I don't suppose...' She tried her most winning smile, her cheeks aching with the cold. 'I don't suppose I can borrow your Wi-Fi first? There's something I really need to do.'

'At this time of night?'

'It's part of my job. It won't take long.' Daisy gazed up at him hoping her eyes portrayed beseeching and hopeful with a hint of professionalism, not freezing cold and pathetic. Their eyes snagged and the breath hitched in her throat.

'I suppose you can use it while you warm up.' The smile was still playing around his mouth and Daisy's blood began to heat at the expression in his eyes. If he turned it up a little more she wouldn't need a jumper and socks, her own internal system would have defrosted her quite nicely.

He held out a hand. 'Seb, I look after this place.'

Daisy took the outstretched hand, her heart skipping a beat as their fingers touched. 'I'm Daisy. Nice to meet you, Seb.'

He didn't answer, reaching out and taking her bag, shouldering it with ease as he turned and began to tread gracefully through the ever thickening snow.

'"Mark my footsteps, my good page,"' Daisy sang under

her breath as she took advantage of the pressed-down snow and hopped from one imprint to the other. Tall, dark, handsome and coming to her rescue on Valentine's Day? It was almost too good to be true.

CHAPTER ONE

Six weeks later...

DÉJÀ-VU RIPPLED DOWN Daisy's spine as she rounded the path. It was all so familiar and yet so different.

The last time she had been at Hawksley the castle and grounds had been covered in snow, a fantasy winter wonderland straight out of a historical film. Today the courtyard lawn was the pale green of spring, crocuses and primroses peeking out at the unseasonably warm sun. The old Norman keep rose majestically on her left, the thick grey stone buttresses looking much as they must have looked nearly one thousand years ago, a stark contrast to ye olde charm of the three-storey Tudor home attached to it at right angles.

And straight ahead of her the Georgian house.

Daisy swallowed, every instinct screaming at her to turn and run. She could wait a few weeks, try again then. Maybe try a letter instead. After all, it was still such early days...

But no. She straightened her shoulders. That was the coward's way out and she had been raised better than that. Confront your problems head-on, that was what her father always told her.

Besides, she really needed to talk to somebody. She

didn't want to face her family, not yet, and none of her friends would understand. He was the only person who this affected in the same way.

Or not. But she had to take the risk.

Decision made, smile plastered on and she was ready to go. If she could just find him that was…

The castle had a very closed-off air. The small ticket office was shut, a sign proclaiming that the grounds and keep wouldn't be open until Whitsun. Daisy swivelled trying to find signs of life.

Nobody.

There was a small grey door set at the end of the Georgian wing, which she recognised from her earlier visit. It was as good a place to start as any.

Daisy walked over, taking her time and breathing in the fresh spring air, the warm sun on her back giving her courage as she pushed at the door.

'Great.' It was firmly locked and there was no bell, 'You'd think they didn't want visitors,' she muttered. Well, want them or not she was here. Daisy knocked as hard as she could, her knuckles smarting at the impact, then stood back and waited, anticipation twisting her stomach.

The door swung open. Slowly. Daisy inhaled and held her breath. Would he remember her?

Would he believe her?

A figure appeared at the door. She exhaled, torn between disappointment and a secret shameful relief. Unless Seb had aged twenty-five years, lost six inches and changed gender this wasn't him.

Daisy pushed her trilby hat further back and gave the stern-looking woman guarding the door marked 'private' an appealing smile. 'Excuse me, can you tell me where I can find Seb?'

Her appeal was met with crossed arms and a gorgonish expression. 'Seb?' There was an incredulous tone to her voice.

The message was loud and clear; smiling wasn't going to cut it. On the other hand she hadn't been instantly turned to stone so it wasn't a total loss.

'Yes.' Daisy bit her lip in a sudden panic. She had got his name right, hadn't she? So much of that night was a blur…

'The handyman,' she added helpfully. *That* she remembered.

'We have an estate maintenance crew.' The gorgon sniffed. Actually *sniffed*. 'But none of them are named Seb. Maybe you have the wrong place?' She looked Daisy up and down in a manner that confirmed that, in her eyes, Daisy most definitely did have the wrong place.

Maybe it was the lipstick? Real Real Red wasn't a shade everyone liked. It was so very red after all but it usually made Daisy feel ready for anything. Even today.

It was like being back at school under her headmistress's disappointed eye. Daisy resisted the urge to tug her tailored shorts down to regulation knee length and to button up the vintage waistcoat she had thrown on over her white T-shirt.

She took a step back and straightened her shoulders, ready for war. She had replayed this morning over and over in her mind. At no point had she anticipated not actually seeing Seb. Or finding out he didn't exist.

What if he was a ghost after all?

Surely not. Daisy wasn't entirely certain what ectoplasm actually was but she was pretty sure it was cold and sticky. Ghosts weren't made of warm, solid muscle.

No, no dwelling on the muscles. Or the warmth. She pushed the thought out of her mind as firmly as she could and adopted her best, haughty public schoolgirl voice. 'This is Hawksley Castle, isn't it?'

Of course it was. Nowhere else had the utterly unique

blend of Norman keep, Tudor mansion and Georgian country home that ensured Hawksley remained top of the country's best-loved stately homes list—according to *Debutante* magazine anyway.

But Daisy wasn't interested in the historical significance of the perfectly preserved buildings. She simply wanted to gain access to the final third of the castle, the Georgian wing marked 'private'.

'Yes, this is Hawksley Castle and we are not open until Whitsun. So, I suggest, miss, that you return and purchase a ticket then.'

'Look.' Daisy was done with playing nice. 'I'm not here to sightsee. I was here six weeks ago for the Porter-Halstead wedding and got snowed in. Seb helped me and I need to see him. To say thank you,' she finished a little lamely but there was no way she was telling this woman her real motivation for visiting. She'd be turned to stone for sure.

The gorgon raised an eyebrow. 'Six weeks later?'

'I'm not here for a lesson in manners.' Daisy regretted the snap the second it left her mouth. 'I've been…busy. But better late than never. I thought he was the handyman. He certainly—' seemed good with his hands flashed through her mind and she coloured '—seemed to know his way around.' Oh, yes, that he did.

Nope. No better.

'But he definitely works here. He has an office. Tall, dark hair?' Melting dark green eyes, cheekbones she could have cut herself on and a firm mouth. A mouth he really knew how to use.

Daisy pulled her mind firmly back to the here and now. 'He had a shovel and snow chains, that's why I thought he was the handyman but maybe he's the estate manager?'

Unless he had been a wedding guest putting on a very good act? Had she made a terrible mistake? No, he hadn't been dressed like a wedding guest, had known his way around the confusing maze behind the baize door in the Georgian wing.

She was going to have to get tough. 'Listen,' she began then stopped as something wet and cold snuffled its way into her hand. Looking down, she saw a pair of mournful brown eyes gazing up at her. 'Monty!'

Proof! Proof that she wasn't going crazy and proof that Seb was here.

Crouching down to scratch behind the springer spaniel's floppy brown ears, Daisy broke into a croon. 'How are you, handsome boy? It's lovely to see you again. Now if you could just persuade this lady here that I need to see your master that will be brilliant.' She couldn't help throwing a triumphant glance over at her adversary.

'Monty! Here, boy! Monty! Here I say.' Peremptory tones rang across the courtyard and Daisy's heart began to speed up, blood rushing around her body in a giddying carousel. Slowly she got back up, leaving one hand on the spaniel's head, more for strength and warmth, and half turned, a smile on her face.

'Hi, Seb.'

It had been a long morning. It wasn't that Seb wasn't grateful for his expensive education, his academic credentials and his various doctorates but there were times when he wondered just what use being able to recite Latin verse and debate the use of cavalry at Thermopylae was.

Business studies, basic accountancy, and how to repair, heat and conserve an ancient money pit without whoring her out like a restoration actress would have been far more useful.

He needed a business plan. Dipping into what was left of the estate's capital would only get him so far. Somehow the castle needed to pay for itself—and soon.

And now his dog was being disobedient, making eyes at a blonde woman improbably dressed in shorts and a trilby hat teamed with a garish waistcoat. Shorts. In *March*. On the other hand... Seb's eyes raked the slender, long legs appreciably; his dog had good taste.

'Monty! I said here. I am so sorry...' His voice trailed off as the woman straightened and turned. Seb felt his breath whoosh out as he clocked the long blonde hair, blue eyes, tilted nose and a mouth that had haunted him for the last six weeks. 'Daisy?'

'Hello, Seb. You never call, you don't write.' An undercurrent of laughter lilted through her voice and he had to firm his mouth to stop a responsive smile creeping out. What on earth had brought the wedding photographer back to his door? For a few days afterwards he had wondered if she might get in touch. And what he would say if she did.

For six weeks afterwards he had considered getting in touch himself.

'Neither did you.'

'No.' Her eyelashes fluttered down and she looked oddly vulnerable despite the ridiculous hat tilted at a rakish angle and the bright lipstick. 'Seb, could we talk?'

She sounded serious and Seb tensed, his hands curling into apprehensive fists. 'Of course, come on in.' He gestured for her to precede him through the door. 'Thanks, Mrs Suffolk, I'll take it from here.' He smiled at his most faithful volunteer and she moved aside with a sniff of clear disapproval.

'I don't think she likes me,' Daisy whispered.

'She doesn't like anyone. Anyone under thirty and female anyway.' He thought about the statement. 'Actually anyone under thirty *or* any female.'

Seb led the way through the narrow hallway, Monty at his heels. The courtyard entrance led directly into what had once been the servants' quarters, a warren of windy passageways, small rooms and back staircases designed to ensure the maids and footmen of long ago could go about their duties without intruding on the notice of the family they served.

Now it held the offices and workrooms necessary for running the vast estate. The few staff that lived in had cottages outside the castle walls and Seb slept alone in a castle that had once housed dozens.

It would make sense to convert a floor of unused bedrooms and offer overnight hospitality to those who booked the Tudor Hall for weddings rather than chucking them out into the nearby hotels and guest houses. But it wasn't just the expense that put him off. It was one thing having tourists wandering around the majestic keep, one thing to rent out the spectacular if dusty, chilly and impractical hall. The Georgian wing was his home. Huge, ancient, filled with antiques, ghosts and dusty corners. *Home.*

And walking beside him was the last person to have stayed there with him.

'Welcome back.' Seb noted how, despite her general air of insouciance, she was twisting her hands together nervously. 'Nice hat.'

'Thanks.' She lifted one hand and touched it self-consciously. 'Every outfit needs a hat.'

'I don't recall you wearing one last time.'

'I was dressed for work then.'

The words hung heavily in the air and Seb was instantly transported back. Back to the slide of a zip, the way her silky dress had slithered to the ground in one perfect movement.

Definitely no hat on that occasion, just glittering pins in her hair. It was a shame. He would have quite liked to have seen her wearing it when she had lain on his sofa, golden in the candlelight, eyes flushed from the champagne. Champagne and excitement. The hat and nothing else.

He inhaled, long and deep, trying to ignore the thrumming of his heart, the visceral desire the memory evoked.

Seb stopped and reconsidered his steps. The old estate office was an incongruous mix of antique desk, sofa and rug mixed with metal filing cabinets and shelves full of things no one wanted to throw away but didn't know what else to do with.

Now, with Daisy's reappearance, it was a room with ghosts of its own. Six-week-old ghosts with silken skin, low moans and soft, urgent cries. Taking her back there would be a mistake.

Instead he opened the discreet doors that led into the front of the house. 'Let's go to the library.' It wasn't cowardice that had made him reconsider. It was common sense. His mouth quirked at the corner. 'As you can probably tell, the house hasn't received the memo for the warmest spring in ten years and it takes several months for the chill to dissipate. The library is the warmest room in the whole place—probably because it's completely non-modernised. The velvet drapes may be dusty and dark but they keep the cold out.'

Daisy adjusted her hat again, her hands still nervous. 'Fine.'

He pushed the heavy wooden door open, standing aside to let her go in first. 'So, this is quite a surprise.'

She flushed, the colour high on her cheekbones. 'A nice one, I hope.' But she didn't meet his eye. He stilled, watching her. Something was going on, something way beyond a desire for his company.

Daisy walked into the oak-panelled room and stood, looking curiously about her. Seb leant against the door for a moment, seeing the room through her eyes; did she find it shabby? Intimidating? It was an odd mixture of both. The overflowing floor-to-ceiling bookshelves covered two of the walls; the dark oak panelling was hung with gloomy family portraits and hunting scenes. Even the fireplace was large enough to roast at least half an ox, the imposing grate flanked by a massive marble lintel. All that the library needed was an irascible old man to occupy one of the wing-back chairs and Little Lord Fauntleroy to come tripping in.

She wandered over to one of the shelves and pulled out a book, dust flying into the air. 'Good to see the owner's a keen reader.'

'Most of the English books have been read. That's the Latin section.'

She tilted her chin. 'Latin or not, they still need dusting.'

'I'll get the footmen right on it. Sit down.' He gestured to a chair. 'Would you like a drink?'

'Will a footman bring it?'

'No.' He allowed himself a smile. 'There's a kettle in that corner. It's a long way from here to the kitchen.'

'Practical. Tea, please. Do you have Earl Grey?'

'Lemon or milk?'

Seating herself gingerly in one of the velvet chairs, the dusty book still in her hand, she raised an elegantly arched eyebrow. 'Lemon? How civilised. Could I just have hot water and lemon, please?'

'Of course.'

It only took a minute to make the drinks but the time out was needed. It was unsettling, having her here in his private space, the light floral scent of her, the long legs, the red, red lipstick drawing attention to her wide, full mouth. The problem with burying yourself with work twenty-four-seven, Seb reflected as he sliced the lemon, was that it left you ill prepared for any human interaction. Especially the feminine kind.

Which was rather the point.

'A proper cup and saucer. You have been well brought

up.' She held up the delicately patterned porcelain as he handed it to her and examined it. 'Wedgwood?'

'Probably.'

Seb seated himself opposite, as if about to interview her, and sat back, doing his best to look as if he were at his ease, as if her unexpected reappearance hadn't totally thrown him. 'How's peddling ridiculous dreams and over-blown fantasies going?'

Daisy took a sip of her drink, wincing at the heat. 'Business is good, thanks. Busy.'

'I'm not surprised.' He eyed her critically. 'Engagement shoots, fifteen-hour days, blogs. When you work out your hourly rate you're probably barely making minimum wage.' Not that he was one to talk.

'It's expected.' Her tone was defensive. 'Anyone can get a mate to point a camera nowadays. Wedding photographers need to provide more, to look into the soul of the couple. To make sure there isn't one second of their special day left undocumented.'

Seb shook his head. 'Weddings! What happened to simple and heartfelt? Not that I'm complaining. We are already booked up for the next two years. It's crazy. So much money on just one day.'

'But it's the happiest day of their lives.'

'I sincerely hope not. It's just the first day, not the marriage,' he corrected her. 'Romantic fantasies like that are the biggest disservice to marriage. People pour all their energy and money into just one day—they should be thinking about their lives together. Planning that.'

'You make it sound so businesslike.'

'It *is* businesslike,' he corrected her. 'Marriage is like anything else. It's only successful if the participants share goals. Know exactly what they are signing up for. Mark my words, a couple who go into marriage with a small ceremony and a robust life plan will last a lot longer than fools who get into debt with one over-the-top day.'

'No, you're wrong.' Daisy leant forward, her eyes lit up. 'Two people finding each other, plighting their troth in front of all their friends and family, what could be more romantic than that?' Her voice trailed off, the blue eyes wistful.

Seb tried not to let his mouth quirk into a smile but the temptation was too much. 'Did you just say plight your troth? Is that what you write in your blogs?'

'My couples say my blogs are one of the most romantic parts of their special day.' Her colour was high. 'That's why I do the engagement shoots, to get to know each couple individually, know what makes them tick. And no.' She glared at him. 'Even with the extras I still make well over the minimum wage and no one ever complains. In fact, one couple have just asked me to come back to document their pregnancy and take the first photographs of their baby.'

'Of course they did.' He couldn't keep the sarcasm out of his voice. 'The only thing guaranteed to waste more money than a wedding is a baby.'

Her already creamy skin paled, her lips nearly blue. 'Then you probably don't want to hear that you're going to be a father. I'm pregnant, Seb. That's what I came here to say.'

As soon as she blurted the words out she regretted it. It wasn't how she'd planned to tell him; her carefully prepared lead up to the announcement abandoned in the heat of the moment. At least she had shaken him out of the cool complacency; Seb had shot upright, the green eyes hard, his mouth set firm.

'Are you sure?'

Oh, yes. She was sure. Two tests a day for the past week sure. 'I have a test in my bag, I can take it here and now if you like.' It wasn't the kind of thing she'd usually offer to an almost stranger but the whole situation was embarrassing enough, another step into mortification alley wouldn't hurt.

'No, that won't be necessary.' He ran a hand through his hair. 'But we used… I mean, we were careful.'

It was almost funny—almost—that she and this man opposite could have spent a night being as intimate as two people could be. Had explored and tasted and touched. Had teased and caressed and been utterly uninhibited. And yet they didn't know each other at all. He couldn't even use the word 'condom' in front of her.

'We did.' Daisy summoned up all her poise and looked at him as coolly and directly as she could manage, trying to breathe her panicked pulse into submission, to still the telltale tremor in her hands. 'At least, we did the first and second time. I'm not sure we were thinking clearly after that.'

Not that they had been thinking clearly at all. Obviously. It was easy to blame the snowfall, the intimacy of being alone in the fairy-tale landscape, the champagne. That he had come to her rescue. But it still didn't add up. It had been the most incredible, the most intense and the most out-of-character night of Daisy's life.

A muscle was beating along the stubbled jawline; his eyes were still hard, unreadable. 'How do you know it's mine?'

She had been prepared for this question, it was totally reasonable for him to ask and yet a sharp stab of disappointment hit her. 'It has to be yours.' She lifted her chin and eyed him defiantly. 'There is no one else, there hasn't been, not for a long time. I usually only do long-term relationships and I split up from my last boyfriend nine months ago.' She needed to make him understand. 'That night, it wasn't usual. It wasn't how I normally behave.'

'Right.'

'You can check, have a test. Only not until after it's born. It's safer that way.'

His eyes locked onto hers. 'You're keeping it, then?'

Another reasonable question and yet one she hadn't even thought to ask herself. 'Yes. Look, Seb, you don't have to decide anything right now. I'm not here for answers or with demands. I just thought you should know but...'

'Hold on.' He stood up with a lithe grace, hand held out to cut her off. 'I need to think. Don't go anywhere, can you promise me that? I won't be long, I just, I just need some air. Come on, Monty.'

'Wait!' It was too late, he had whirled out of the door, the spaniel close to his heels. Daisy had half got up but sank back down into the deep-backed chair as the heavy oak door closed with a thud.

'That went better than I expected,' she murmured. She was still here and, okay, he hadn't fallen to his knees and pledged to love the baby for ever but neither had she been turned out barefoot onto his doorstep.

And wasn't his reaction more natural? Questioning disbelief? Maybe that should have been hers as well. Daisy slid her hand over her midriff, marvelling at the flat tautness, no visible clue that anything had changed. And yet she hadn't been shocked or upset or considered for even a nanosecond that she wouldn't have the baby.

Its conception might be an accident in most people's eyes but not in Daisy's. It was something else entirely. It was a miracle.

One hour later, more hot lemon and three pages of a beautiful old hardback edition of *Pride and Prejudice* read over and over again, Daisy admitted defeat. Wait, he had said. How long did he mean? She hadn't promised him anyway; he had disappeared before she could form the words.

But she couldn't leave without making sure he had a way of getting in touch. She hadn't thought last time, hadn't slipped her card into his hand or pocket with a smile and invitation. Had part of her hoped he would track her down anyway? Perform a modern-day quest in pursuit of her love. The hopeless romantic in her had. The hopeless romantic never learned.

But this wasn't about challenges. It was more important than that. Rummaging in her bag, Daisy pulled out one of her business cards. Stylish, swirling script and a daisy motif proclaimed 'Daisy Photos. Weddings, portraits and lifestyle.' Her number, website and Twitter handle listed clearly below. She paused for a second and then laid the card on the tea tray with a hand that only trembled a little. It was up to him now.

She closed her eyes for a moment, allowing her shoulders to sag under the weight of her disappointment. She had been prepared for anger, denial. Naively, she had hoped he might be a little excited. She hadn't expected him to just *leave*.

Her car was where she'd left it, parked at a slant just outside the imposing gates. If she had swallowed her pride and accepted the Range Rover her father had offered her then she wouldn't have been snowed in all those weeks ago.

Daisy shook her head trying to dislodge unwanted tears prickling the backs of her eyes. It had all seemed so perfect, like a scene from one of her favourite romantic comedies. When it was clear that she was stuck, Seb had ransacked the leftovers from the wedding buffet, bringing her a picnic of canapés and champagne. And she had curled up on the shabby sofa in his office as they talked and drank, and somehow she had found herself confiding in him, trusting him. Kissing him.

She raised her hands to her lips, remembering how soft his kiss had been. At first anyway…

Right. Standing here reliving kisses wasn't going to

change anything. Daisy unlocked her car, and took one last long look at the old castle keep, the grim battlements softened by the amber spring sun.

'Daisy!'

She paused for a moment and inhaled long and deep before swivelling round, trying to look as unconcerned as possible, and leaning back against her car.

Her heart began to thump. Loudly.

He wasn't her type at all. Her type was clean-shaven, their eyes didn't hold a sardonic gleam under quizzical eyebrows and look as if they were either laughing at you or criticising you. Her usual type didn't wear their dark hair an inch too long and completely unstyled and walk around in old mud-splattered jeans, although she had to admit they were worn in all the right places.

And Daisy Huntingdon-Cross had never as much as had a coffee with a man in a logoed fleece. The black garment might bear the Hawksley Castle crest but it was still a fleece.

So why had her pulse sped up, heat pooling in the pit of her stomach? Daisy allowed the car to take more of her weight, grateful for its support.

'Come back inside, we haven't finished talking yet.' It wasn't a request.

The heat melted away, replaced by a growing indignation. Daisy straightened up, folding her arms. 'We haven't *started* talking. I gave you an hour.'

'I know.' She had been hoping for penitent but he was totally matter-of-fact. 'I think better outside.'

'And?' Daisy wanted to grab the word back the second she uttered it. It sounded as if she had been on tenterhooks waiting for him to proclaim her fate. The kernel of truth in that thought made her squirm.

He ran a hand through his hair. The gesture was unexpectedly boyish and uncertain. 'This would be easier if we just went back inside.'

She raised her eyebrows. 'You think better outside.'

He smiled at that, his whole expression lightening. It changed him completely, the eyes softer, the slightly harsh expression warmer.

'Yes. But do you?'

'Me?'

'I have a proposition for you and you need to be thinking clearly. Are you?'

No. No, she wasn't. Daisy wasn't sure she'd had a clear thought since she had accepted that first glass of champagne, had hotly defended her livelihood as her rescuer had quizzed and teased her and had found herself laughing, absurdly delighted as the stern expression had melted into something altogether different.

But she wasn't going to admit that. Not to him, barely to herself.

'Completely clearly.'

He looked sceptical but nodded. 'Then, Daisy, I think you should marry me.'

CHAPTER TWO

SEB DIDN'T EXACTLY expect Daisy to throw herself at his feet in gratitude, not really. And it would have made him uncomfortable if she had. But he was expecting that she would be touched by his proposal. Grateful even.

The incredulous laugh that bubbled out of that rather enchanting mouth was, therefore, a bit of a shock. Almost a blow—not to his heart, obviously, but, he realised with a painful jolt of self-awareness, to his ego. 'Are we in a regency novel? Seb, you haven't besmirched my honour. There's no need to do the honourable thing.'

The emphasis on the last phrase was scathing. And misplaced. There was every need. 'So why did you come here? I thought you wanted my help. Or are you after money? Is that it?'

Maybe the whole situation was some kind of clever entrapment. His hands curled into fists and he inhaled, long and deep, trying not to let the burgeoning anger show on his face.

'Of course not.' Her indignation was convincing and the tightness in his chest eased a little. 'I thought you should know first, that was all. I didn't come here for money or marriage or anything.'

'I see, you're planning to do this alone. And you want me to what? Pop over on a Sunday and take the baby to the park? Sleepovers once a month?' Seb could hear the scathing scorn punctuating each of his words and Daisy paled, taking a nervous step away, her hand fumbling for the car handle.

'I haven't really thought that far ahead.'

Seb took another deep breath, doing his best to sound reasonable as he grabbed the slight advantage. 'You work what? Fifteen hours a day at weekends? Not just weekends. People get married every day of the week now. What are you going to do for childcare?'

'I'll work something out.' The words were defiant but her eyes were troubled as she twisted her hand around the handle, her knuckles white with tension.

He put as much conviction into his voice as possible. 'You don't need to. Marry me.'

Her eyes were wide with confusion. 'Why? Why on earth would you want to marry someone you barely know? Why would I agree to something so crazy?'

Seb gestured, a wide encompassing sweep of his arm taking in the lake, the woods and fields, the castle proudly overshadowing the landscape. 'Because that baby is my heir.'

Daisy stared at him. 'What?'

'The baby is my heir,' he repeated. 'Our baby. To Hawksley.'

'Don't be ridiculous. What has the castle got to do with the baby?'

'Not just the castle, the estate, the title, everything.'

'But—' she shook her head stubbornly '—you're the handyman, aren't you? You had a shovel and a fleece and that office.'

'The handyman?' He could see her point. If only his colleagues could see him now, it was all a long way from his quiet office tucked away in a corner of an Oxford college. 'In a way I guess I am—owner, handyman, manager, event-booker—running the estate is a hands-on job nowadays.'

'So that makes you what? A knight?'

'An earl. The Earl of Holgate.'

'An earl?' She laughed, slightly hysterically. 'Is this some kind of joke? Is there a camera recording this?' She twisted around, checking the fields behind them.

'My parents died six months ago. I inherited the castle then.' The castle and a huge amount of debt but there was no need to mention that right away. She was skittish enough as it was.

'You're being serious?' He could see realisation dawning, the understanding in her widened eyes even as she stubbornly shook her head. 'Titles don't mean anything, not any more.'

'They do to me, to the estate. Look, Daisy, you came here because you knew it was the right thing to do. Well, marrying me is the right thing to do. That baby could be the next Earl of Holgate. You want to deny him that right? Illegitimate children are barred from inheriting.'

'The baby could be a girl.' She wasn't giving in easily.

'It doesn't matter, with the royal line of succession no longer male primogeniture there's every chance the rest of the aristocracy will fall into line.' He held his hand out, coaxing. 'Daisy, come back inside, let's talk about this sensibly.'

She didn't answer for a long moment and he could sense her quivering, desperate need to run. He didn't move, just waited, hand held out towards her until she took a deep breath and nodded. 'I'll come inside. To talk about the baby. But I am not marrying you. I don't care whether you're an earl or a handyman. I don't know you.'

Seb took a deep breath, relief filling his lungs. All he needed was time. Time for her to hear him out, to give him a chance to convince her. 'Come on, then.'

Daisy pushed off the car and turned. Seb couldn't help taking a long appreciative look at her shapely rear as she bent slightly to relock the car. The tweed shorts fitted snugly, showing off her slender curves to perfection. He tore his eyes away, hurriedly focusing on the far hedge as she straightened and turned to join him, the blue eyes alight with curiosity.

'An earl,' she repeated. 'No wonder the gorgon was so reluctant to let me in.'

'Gorgon?' But he knew who she meant and his mouth quirked as she stared at him meaningfully. 'I don't think she's actually turned anyone to stone. Not yet. Mrs Suffolk's family have worked here for generations. She's a little protective.'

They reached the courtyard and Daisy started to make for the back door where Mrs Suffolk still stood guard, protecting the castle against day trippers and other invaders. Seb slipped a hand through Daisy's arm, guiding her round the side of the house and onto the sweeping driveway with its vista down to the wooded valley below.

'Front door and a fresh start,' he said as they reached the first step. 'Hello, I'm Sebastian Beresford, Earl of Holgate.'

'Sebastian Beresford?' Her eyes narrowed. 'I know that name. You're not an earl, you're that historian.'

'I'm both. Even earls have careers nowadays.' Although how he was going to continue his academic responsibilities with running Hawksley was a problem he had yet to solve.

He held out his hand. 'Welcome to my home.'

Daisy stared at his hand for a moment before placing her cool hand in his. 'Daisy Huntingdon-Cross, it's a pleasure to meet you.'

Who? There it was, that faint elusive memory sharpened into focus. 'Huntingdon-Cross? Rick Cross and Sherry Huntingdon's daughter?'

No wonder she looked familiar! Rock royalty on their father's side and pure county on their mother's, the Huntingdon-Cross sisters were as renowned for their blonde, leggy beauty as they were infamous for their lifestyle. Each of them had been splashed across the tabloids at some point in their varied careers—and their parents were legends; rich, talented and famously in love.

Seb's heart began to pound, painfully thumping against his chest, the breath knocked from his lungs in one blow. This was not the plan, the quiet, businesslike, private union he intended.

This was *trouble*.

If he married this girl then the tabloids would have a field day. A Beresford and a Huntingdon-Cross would be front-page fodder to rival anything his parents had managed to stir up in their wake. All the work he had done to remain out of the press would be undone faster than he could say, 'I do.'

But if he didn't marry her then he would be disinheriting the baby. He didn't have any choice.

Seb froze as he took her hand, recognition dawning in his eyes.

'Huntingdon-Cross,' he repeated and Daisy dropped his hand, recoiling from the horror in his voice.

For a moment she contemplated pretending she wasn't one of *those* Huntingdon-Crosses but a cousin, a far, far removed cousin. From the north. Of course, Seb didn't have to know that she didn't have any northern cousins.

But what was the point? He'd find out the truth soon enough and, besides, they might be wild and infuriating and infamous but they were hers. No matter how many titles or illustrious ancestors Seb had, he had no right to sneer at her family.

Daisy channelled her mother at her grandest, injecting as much froideur into her voice as she possibly could and tilting her chin haughtily. 'Yes. I'm the youngest. I believe the tabloids call me the former wild child if that helps.'

At this the green eyes softened and the corner of his mouth tilted; heat pooled in her stomach as her blood rushed in response. It was most unfair, the almost smile made him more human. More handsome.

More desirable.

'The one who got expelled from school?'

He had to bring that up. Daisy's face heated, the embarrassed flush spreading from her cheeks to her neck. He was an Oxford professor, he'd probably never met anyone who had been expelled before, let alone someone with barely an academic qualification to her name. 'I wasn't expelled exactly, they just asked me to leave.'

'Sounds like expulsion to me,' he murmured.

'It was ridiculously strict. It was almost impossible *not* to get expelled. Unless you were clever and studious like my sisters, that is.' Okay, it was eight years ago and Daisy had spent every minute of those eight years trying to prove her teachers wrong but it still rankled. Still hurt.

'The Mother Superior was always looking for a way to rid the school of the dullards like me. That way we didn't bring the exam average down.' She stared at him, daring him to react. He'd probably planned for the mother of his future children to have a batch of degrees to match his. His and her mortar boards.

'They expelled you for not being academic?'

'Well, not exactly. They expelled me for breaking bounds and going clubbing in London. But if I'd been predicted all As it would have been a slap on the wrist at the most. At least, probably,' she added, conscious she wasn't being entirely fair. 'There were pictures on the front page of *The Planet* and I think some of the parents were a little concerned.'

'A little?' Damn, the mouth was even more tilted now, the gleam intensifying in his eyes.

'I was sixteen. Most sixteen-year-old girls aren't locked away in stupid convent schools not even allowed to look at boys or wear anything but a hideous uniform. It isn't natural. But once front-page news, always front-page news. They hounded me for a bit until they realised how dull I really am. But I swear I could die at one hundred after a lifetime spent sewing smocks for orphaned lepers and my epitaph would read "Former wild child, Daisy, who was expelled from exclusive girls' school..."'

'Probably.' His voice was bleak again, the gleam gone as if it had never been there. 'Come on, let's go in. It's getting cold and one of us has unseasonably bare legs.'

Once the sun had started to set, the warmth quickly dissipated, the evening air tinted with a sharp breeze whipping around Daisy's legs. She shivered, the chill running up her arms and down her spine not entirely down to the cold. If she walked back into the castle everything would change.

But everything was changing anyway. Would it be easier if she didn't have to do this alone? It wasn't the proposal or the marriage of her dreams but maybe it was time to grow up. To accept that fairy tales were for children and that princes came in all shapes and sizes—as did earls.

Not that Seb's shape was an issue. She slid a glance over at him, allowing her eyes to run up his legs, the worn jeans clinging to his strong thighs and the slim hips, and up his torso, his lean muscled strength hidden by the shirt and fleece. But her body remembered the way he had picked her up without flinching, the play of his muscles under her hands.

No, his shape wasn't an issue.

But she had worked so hard to be independent. Not traded on her parents' names, not depended on their money.

Would marrying for support, albeit emotional not financial, be any different from accepting it from her family?

At least she knew they loved her. A marriage without love wasn't to be considered. Not for her. She needed to make that clear so that they could move on and decide what was best for the baby.

'Where's the cook? The faithful retainers? The maids' bobbing curtsies?' Daisy expected that they would return to the library but instead Seb had led her through the baize doors and back through the tangle of passages to the kitchen. She would need a ball of thread to find her way back.

The whole house was a restoration project waiting to happen and the kitchen no exception but Daisy quite liked the old wooden cabinets, the ancient Aga and Monty slumped in front of it with his tail beating a steady rhythm on the flagstone floor. It didn't take much imagination to see the ghosts of small scullery maids, scuttling out into the adjoining utility room, an apple-cheeked cook rolling out pastry on the marbled worktops. Automatically she framed it, her mind selecting the right filter and the focal point of the shot.

Any of Daisy's friends would strip out the cabinets, install islands and breakfast bars and folding doors opening out into the courtyard—undoubtedly creating something stunning. And yet the kitchen would lose its heart, its distinctive soul.

Seb gestured to a low chair by the Aga. 'Do you want to sit there? It's the warmest spot in the room. No, there's no one else, just me. A cleaner comes in daily but I live alone.' He had opened a door that led to a pantry bigger than Daisy's entire kitchen. 'Are you vegetarian?'

'For a term in Year Eleven.'

'Good. Anything you...erm...really want to eat?' He

sounded flustered and, as realisation dawned, her cheeks
heated in tandem with his. It was going to be uncomfortable if neither of them could mention the pregnancy without embarrassment.

'Oh! You mean cravings? No, at least, not yet. But if
I get a need for beetroot and coal risotto I'll make sure
you're the first to know.'

The green eyes flashed. 'You do that.'

Daisy didn't want to admit it, even to herself, but she
was tired. It had been a long week, excitement mixing with
shock, happiness with worry and sleep had been elusive. It
was soothing leaning back in the chair, the warmth from
the Aga penetrating her bones. Monty rested his head on
her feet as she watched Seb expertly chopping onions and
grilling steaks.

'From the estate farm,' he said as he heated the oil.
'I'm pretty much self-sufficient, well, thanks to the tenant farmers I am.'

Neither of them mentioned the elephant in the room
but the word was reverberating round and round her head.
Marriage.

Was this what it would be like? Cosy evenings in the
kitchen? Rocking in a chair by the fire while Seb cooked.
Maybe she should take up knitting.

'Did you mean what you said earlier, in the library?
That marriage is a business?'

He didn't turn round but she saw his shoulders set rigid,
the careless grace gone as he continued to sauté the vegetables.

'Absolutely. It's the only way it works.'

'Why?'

Seb stopped stirring and shot her a quick glance.

'What do you mean?'

Daisy was leaning back in the chair, her eyes half
closed. His eyes flickered over her. The bright waistcoat,

the hat and the lipstick were at odd with her pallor; she was pale, paler than he would have expected even at the end of a long, cold winter and the shadows under her eyes were a deep blue-grey. She looked exhausted. A primal protectiveness as unexpected as it was fierce rose up in him, almost overwhelming in its intensity. It wasn't what he wanted, the path he had chosen, but this was his responsibility; she was his responsibility.

She probably deserved better, deserved more than he could offer. But this was all he had.

'Why do you think that?'

Seb took a moment before answering, quickly plating up the steaks and tipping the sautéed vegetables into a dish and putting it onto the table. He added a loaf of bread and a pat of butter and grabbed two steak knives and forks.

'Come and sit at the table,' he said. 'We can talk afterwards.'

It was like being on a first date. Worse, a blind date. A blind date where you suddenly lost all sense of speech, thought and taste. Was this his future? Sitting at a table with this woman, struggling for things to say?

'My grandparents ate every meal in the dining hall, even when it was just the two of them,' he said after a long, excruciating pause. 'Grandfather at the head of the table, grandmother at the foot. Even with the leaves taken out the table seats thirty.'

She put down her fork and stared at him. 'Could they hear each other?'

'They both had penetrating voices, although I don't know if they were natural or whether they developed them after fifty years of yelling at each other across fifteen foot of polished mahogany.' He half smiled, remembering their stubborn determination to keep to the ritual formality of their youth as the world changed around them.

'And what about your parents? Did they dispense with the rules and eat in here or did they like the distance?'

'Ah, my parents. It appears my parents spent most of their lives living wildly beyond their means. If I can't find a way to make Hawksley pay for itself within the next five years…' His voice trailed off. He couldn't articulate his worst fears: that he would be the Beresford who lost Hawksley Castle.

'Hence the handyman gig?'

'Hence the handyman gig. And the leave of absence from the university and hiring the hall out for weddings. It's a drop in the ocean but it's a start.'

'You need my sisters. Rose is in New York but she's a PR whizz and Violet is the most managing person I have ever met. I bet they could come up with a plan to save Hawksley.'

He needed more than a plan. He needed a miracle. 'My grandparents followed the rules all their lives. They looked after the estate, the people who lived on it. Lived up to their responsibilities. My parents were the opposite. They didn't spend much time here. Unless they were throwing a party. They preferred London, or the Caribbean. Hawksley was a giant piggy bank, not a responsibility.'

Her eyes softened. 'What happened?'

'You must have read about them?' He pushed his half-empty plate away, suddenly sickened. 'If your parents are famous for their rock-solid marriage, mine were famous for their wildness— drugs, affairs, exotic holidays. They were always on the front pages. They divorced twice, remarried twice, each time in some ridiculous extravagant way. The first time they made me a pageboy. The second time I refused to attend.' He took a swig of water, his mouth dry.

It was awful, the resentment mixed with grief. When would it stop being so corrosive?

'Yes, now I remember. I'm so sorry. It was a plane crash, wasn't it?'

'They had been told it wasn't safe but the rules didn't apply to them. Or so they thought.'

Daisy pushed her seat back and stood up, collecting up the plates and waving away his offer of help. 'No, you cooked, I'll clear.'

He sat for a moment and watched as she competently piled the dishes and saucepans up by the side of the sink, rinsing the plates. He had to make it clear to her, make sure she knew exactly what he was offering. 'Marriage is a business.'

Daisy carried on rinsing, running hot water into the old ceramic sink. 'Once, perhaps...'

'I have to marry, have children, there are no other direct heirs and there's a danger the title will go extinct if I don't. But I don't want...' He squeezed his eyes shut for a brief moment, willing his pulse to stay calm. 'I won't have all the emotional craziness that comes with romantic expectations.'

She put the dishcloth down and turned, leaning against the sink as she regarded him. 'Seb, your parents, they weren't normal, you do know that? That level of drama isn't usual.'

He laughed. 'They were extreme, sure. But abnormal? They just didn't hide it the way the rest of the world does. I look at my friends, their parents. Sure, it's all hearts and flowers and nicknames at the beginning but I've lost count of how many relationships, how many marriages turn into resentment and betrayal and anger. No, maybe my ancestors knew what they were doing with a businesslike arrangement—compatibility, rules, peace.'

'My parents love each other even more than they did when they got married.' A wistful smile curved Daisy's lips. 'Sometimes it's like it's just the two of them even when we're all there. They just look at each other and you can tell that at that moment it's like there's no one else in the room.'

'And how do you feel at those moments?'

Her eyelashes fluttered down. 'It can be a little lonely but…'

Exactly! Strengthened by her concession he carried on, his voice as persuasive as he could manage. 'Look, Daisy. There's no point me promising you romance because I don't believe in it. I can promise you respect, hopefully affection. I can promise that if we do this, become parents together, then I will love the baby and do my utmost to be the best parent I can.'

'I hope you will. But we don't need to be married to co-parent.'

'No,' he conceded.

'I've worked really hard to be my own person, build up my own business.' The blue eyes hardened. 'I don't depend on anyone.'

'But it's not just going to be you any more, is it?'

'I'll cope, I'll make sure I do. And not wanting to marry you doesn't mean that I don't want you in the baby's life. I'm here, aren't I?'

Seb sat back, a little nonplussed. His title and the castle had always meant he had enjoyed interest from a certain type of woman—and with his academic qualifications and the bestselling history books he was becomingly increasingly well known for appealed to a different type. To be honest he hadn't expected he'd have to convince anyone to marry him—he had, admittedly a little arrogantly, just expected that he would make his choice and that would be it.

Apparently Daisy hadn't got that memo.

Not that there was a reason for her to; she hadn't been raised to run a home like Hawksley, nor was she an academic type looking to become a college power couple.

'If you won't marry me then the baby will be illegitimate—I know.' He raised his hand as she opened her mouth to interrupt. 'I know that doesn't mean anything any more. But for me that's serious. I need an heir—and if the baby isn't legitimate it doesn't inherit. How will he or she feel, Daisy, if I marry someone else and they see a younger sibling inherit?'

Her face whitened. 'You'd do that?'

'If I had a younger brother then, no. But I'm the last of my family. I don't have any choice.'

'What if I can't do it?' Daisy was twisting her hands together. 'What if it's not enough for me?' She turned and picked the dishcloth back up. Her back was a little hunched, as if she were trying to keep her emotions in.

'It's a lot to give up, Seb. I always wanted what my parents have, to meet someone who completes me, who I complete.' She huffed out a short laugh. 'I know it's sentimental but when you grow up seeing that...'

'Just give it a go.' Seb was surprised by how much he wanted, needed her to say yes—and not just because of the child she carried, not just because she could solve the whole heir issue and provide the stability he needed to turn the castle's fortunes around.

But they were the important reasons and Seb ruthlessly pushed aside the memory of that night, the urge to reach out and touch her, to run a finger along those long, bare legs. 'If it doesn't work out or if you're unhappy I won't stop you leaving.'

'Divorce?' Her voice caught on the word and her back seemed to shrink inwards.

'Leave that.' He stood up and took the dishcloth from her unresisting hand, tilting her chin until she looked up at him, her eyes cloudy. 'If you wanted then yes, an amicable, friendly divorce. I hope you'll give it a real try though, promise me five years at least.'

That was a respectable amount of time; the family name had been dragged through the mud enough.

'I don't know.' She stepped back, away from his touch, and he dropped his empty hand, the silk of her skin imprinted on his fingertips. 'Getting married with a get-out clause seems wrong.'

'All marriages have a get-out clause. Look.' Seb clenched his hands. He was losing her. In a way he was impressed; he thought the title and castle was inducement enough for most women.

It was time for the big guns.

'This isn't about us. It's about our child. His future. We owe it to him to be responsible, to do the right thing for him.'

'Or her.'

'Or her.'

Thoughts were whirling around in Daisy's brain, a giant tangled skein of them. She was so tired, her limbs heavy, her shoulders slumping under the decision she was faced with.

But she was going to be a mother. What did she think that meant? All pushing swings and ice creams on the beach? She hadn't thought beyond the birth, hadn't got round to figuring out childcare and working long days on sleepless nights. It would be good to have someone else involved. Not someone she was dependent on but someone who was as invested in the baby as she was.

And if he didn't marry her he would marry elsewhere. That should make it easier to turn him down. But it showed how committed he was.

What would she tell people? That she'd messed up again? She'd worked so hard to put her past behind her. The thought of confessing the truth to her family sent her stomach into complicated knots. How could she admit to her adoring parents and indulgent sisters that she was pregnant after a one-night stand—but don't worry, she was getting married?

It wasn't the whirlwind marriage part that would send her parents into a tailspin. After all, they had known each other for less than forty-eight hours when they had walked into that Las Vegas chapel. It was the businesslike arrangement that they would disapprove of.

But maybe they didn't have to know...

'How would it work?'

He didn't hesitate. 'Family first, Hawksley second. Discretion always. I'm a private person, no magazines invited in to coo over our lovely home, no scandalous headlines.'

That made sense. A welcome kind of sense. Publicity ran through her family's veins; it would be nice to step away from that.

But her main question was still unvoiced, still unanswered. She steeled herself.

'What about intimacy?'

Seb went perfectly still apart from one muscle, beating in his cheek, his eyes darkening. Daisy took another step back, reaching for the chair as support as an answering beat pounded through her body.

'Intimacy?' His voice was low, as if the word was forced from him. 'That's up to you, Daisy. We worked—' he paused '—well together. It would be nice to have a full marriage. But that's up to you.'

Worked *well*? *Nice*? She had been thinking *spectacular*. Could she really do this? Marry someone who substituted rules for love, discretion for affection and thought respect was the pinnacle of success?

But in the circumstances how could she not? It wasn't as if she had an alternative plan.

Daisy swallowed, hard, a lump the size of a Kardashian engagement ring forming in her throat. This was so far from her dreams, her hopes.

'I have a condition.' Was that her voice? So confident?

Seb's eyes snapped onto hers with unblinking focus. 'Name it.'

'We don't tell anyone why we're marrying like this. If we do this then we pretend. We pretend that we are head over heels ridiculously besotted. If you can do that then yes. We have a deal.'

CHAPTER THREE

'Hi.'

How did one greet one's fiancé when one was a) pregnant, b) entering a marriage of convenience and c) pretending to be in love?

It should be a kiss on the cheek. Daisy greeted everyone with a kiss on the cheek, from her mother to her clients, but her stomach tumbled at the thought of pressing her lips to that stubbled cheek, inhaling the scent of leather and outdoors and soap.

Instead she stood aside, holding the door half open, her knuckles white as she clung onto the door handle as if it anchored her to the safety of her old life. 'Come in, I'm nearly ready.'

Seb stepped through and then stopped still, his eyes narrowing as he looked around slowly.

A converted loft, all exposed brickwork and steel girders, one wall dominated by five floor-to-ceiling windows through which the midday sun came flooding in. A galley kitchen at one end, built-in shelves crammed with books, ornaments and knick-knacks running along the side wall and the rest of the ground-floor space bare except for an old blue velvet sofa, a small bistro table and chairs and the lamps she used to light her subjects. The bulk of her personal belongings were on the overhanging mezzanine, which doubled as her bedroom and relaxing space.

Daisy adored her light-filled spacious studio and yet, compared to Seb's home, steeped in history and stuffed with antiques, her flat felt sparse and achingly trendy.

'Nice.' Seb looked more at home than she had thought possible, maybe because he had ditched the fleece for a long-sleeved T-shirt in a soft grey cotton and newer, cleaner jeans. Maybe because he stood there confidently, unashamedly examining the room, looking at each one of the photos hung on every available bit of wall space. He turned, slowly, taking in every detail with that cool assessing gaze. 'Wedding photography must pay better than I realised.'

'It's not mine unfortunately. I rent it from a friend. An artist.' Daisy gestured over to the massive oil seascape dominating the far wall. 'I used to share with four other students on the floor above and it got a little cramped—physically *and* mentally, all those artistic temperaments in one open-plan space! It was such a relief when John decided to move to Cornwall and asked if I was interested in renting the studio from him.'

'Mates' rates?'

'Not quite.' Daisy tried to swallow back her defensiveness at the assumption. Her parents would have loved to set her up in style but she had been determined to go it alone, no matter how difficult it was to find a suitable yet affordable studio. John's offer had been the perfect solution. 'I do pay rent but John's turned into a bit of a hermit so I also handle all the London side of his business for him. It works well for us both.'

'Handy. Are you leaving all that?' He nodded towards the studio lights.

'I'll still use this as my workspace.' Daisy might have agreed to move in with Seb straight away but she wasn't ready to break her ties to her old life. Not yet, not until she knew how this new world would work out. 'It's only an hour's drive. I'm all packed up. It's over here.'

It wasn't much, less than her mother took for a week-end away. A case containing her favourite cameras and lenses. Her Mac. A couple of bags filled with clothes and cosmetics. If this worked out she could move the rest of her things later: the books, prints, artwork, favourite vases and bowls. Her hat collection. How they would look in the museum-like surroundings of Hawksley Castle she couldn't begin to imagine.

Seb cast a glance at the small pile. 'Are you sure this is all you want to take? I want you to feel at home. You can make any changes you want, redecorate, rearrange.'

'Even the library?'

His mouth quirked. 'As long as it stays warm.'

'Of course.' Daisy walked over to the hatstand at the foot of the mezzanine staircase and, after a moment's hesitation, picked up a dark pink cloche, accessorised with a diamanté brooch. It was one of her favourite hats, a car-boot-sale find. She settled it on top of her head and tugged it into place before turning to the mirror that hung behind it and coating her lips in a layer of her favourite red lipstick.

She was ready.

'First stop the registry office.' Seb had picked up both bags of clothes and Daisy swung her camera bag over her shoulder before picking up her laptop bag, her chest tight with apprehension.

She swivelled and looked back at the empty space. *You'll be back tomorrow*, she told herself, but stepping out of the front door still felt momentous, not just leaving her home but a huge step into the unknown.

Deep breath, don't cry and lock the door. Her stomach swooped as if it were dropping sixty storeys at the speed of light but she fought it, managing to stop her hand from trembling as she double-locked the door.

Did Seb have similar doubts? If so he hid them well; he was the epitome of calm as they exited the building and walked to the car. He had brought one of the estate Land Rovers ready to transport her stuff; it might be parked with the other North London four-by-fours but its mud-splattered bumpers and utilitarian inside proclaimed it country bumpkin. She doubted any of its gleaming, leather-interior neighbours ever saw anything but urban roads and motorways.

'Once we have registered we have to wait sixteen days. At least we don't have to worry about a venue. The Tudor hall is licensed and I don't allow weekday weddings so we can get married—' he pulled out his phone '—two weeks on Friday. Do you want to invite anyone?' He dropped his phone back into his pocket, opening the car door and hefting her bags into the boot.

Daisy was frozen, one arm protectively around her camera bag. How could he sound so matter-of-fact? They were talking about their wedding. About commitment and promises and joining together. Okay, they were practically strangers but it should still mean something.

'Can we make it three weeks? Just to make sure? Plus I want my parents and sisters there and I need to give Rose enough notice to get back from New York.'

'You want your whole family to come?' He held the door open for her, a faint look of surprise on his face.

Daisy put one foot on the step, hesitated and turned to face him. 'You promised we would at least pretend this was a real marriage. Of course my family needs to be there.' This was non-negotiable.

'Fine.'

Daisy's mouth had been open, ready to argue her point and she was taken aback at his one-word agreement, almost disappointed by his acquiescence. He was so calm about everything. What was going on underneath the surface? Maybe she'd never find out. She stood for a second, gaping, before closing her mouth with a snap and climbing into the passenger seat. Seb closed the door behind her and a moment later he swung himself into the driver's seat and started the engine.

Daisy wound her window down a little then leant back against the headrest watching as Seb navigated the narrow streets, taking her further and further from her home.

Married in just over three weeks. A whirlwind romance, that was what people would think; that was what she would tell them.

'That was a deep sigh.'

'Sorry, it's just…' She hesitated, pulling down the sun visor to check the angle of her hat, feeling oddly vulnerable at the thought of telling him something personal. 'I always knew exactly how I wanted my wedding to be. I know it's silly, that they were just daydreams…' With all the changes happening right now, mourning the loss of her ideal wedding seemed ridiculously self-indulgent.

'Beach at sunset? Swanky hotel? Westminster Abbey and Prince Harry in a dress uniform?'

'No, well, only sometimes.' She stole a glance at him. His eyes were focused on the road ahead and somehow the lack of eye contact made it easier to admit just how many plans she had made. She could picture it so clearly. 'My parents live just down the lane from the village church. I always thought I'd get married there, walk to my wedding surrounded by my family and then afterwards walk back hand in hand with my new husband and have a garden party. Nothing too fancy, although Dad's band would play, of course.'

'Of course.' But he was smiling.

Daisy bit her lip as the rest of her daydream slid through her mind like an internal movie. She would be in something lacy, straight, deceptively simple. The sun would shine casting a golden glow over the soft Cotswold stone. And she would be complete.

There had been a faint ache in her chest since the day before, a swelling as if her heart were bruised. As the familiar daydream slipped away the ache intensified, her heart hammering. She was doing the right thing. Wasn't she?

It's not just about you any more, she told herself as firmly as possible.

She just wished she had had a chance to talk her options over with someone else. But who?

Her sisters? They would immediately go into emergency-planning mode, try and take over, alternately scolding her and coddling her, reducing her back to a tiresome little girl in the process.

Her parents? But no, she still had her pride if nothing else. Daisy swallowed hard, wincing at the painful lump in her throat. She had worked so hard to make up for the mistakes of her past, worked so hard to be independent from her family, to show them that she was as capable as they were. How could she tell them that she was pregnant by a man she hardly knew?

Her parents would swing into damage-limitation mode. Want her to come back home, to buy her a house, to throw money at her as if that would make everything okay. And it would be so easy to let them.

Daisy sagged in her seat. She couldn't tell them, she wouldn't tell them, but all she wanted to hear was her dad's comforting drawl and step into her mother's embrace. She didn't allow herself that luxury very often.

'Actually, can we go to the registrar's tomorrow? I don't feel comfortable registering until we have told my parents. Would you mind if we visit them first?'

Daisy waited, her hands slippery with tense anticipation. It had been so long since she had consulted with someone else or needed consensus on any action.

'Of course.' Seb took his eyes from the road for one brief second, resting them appraisingly on her hands, twisting in her lap. 'But if we're going to tell your parents we're engaged we should probably stop at a jeweller's on the way. You need a ring.'

'Daisy! Darling, what a lovely surprise.'

It was strange being face to face with someone as familiar, as famous as Sherry Huntingdon: model, muse and sometime actress. Her tall willowy figure, as taut and slender at over fifty as it had been at twenty, the blonde hair sweeping down her back seemingly as natural as her daughter's.

'And who's this?' The famously sleepy blue eyes were turned onto Seb, an unexpectedly shrewdly appraising look in them. Maybe not that unexpected—you didn't stay at the top of your profession for over thirty years without brains as well as beauty.

'Sebastian Beresford.' He held his hand out and Daisy's mother took it, slanting a look at him from under long black lashes.

'What a treat.' Her voice was low, almost a purr. 'Daisy so seldom brings young men home. Come on in, the pair of you. Violet's around somewhere and Rick's in his studio— the Benefit Concert is creeping up on us again. Daisy, darling, you will be here to take some photos, won't you?'

'Wouldn't miss it.' Daisy linked her arm through her mother's as they walked along the meandering path that led from the driveway around the house. It was a beautiful ivy-covered house, large by any standards—unless one happened to live in a castle—dating back to William and Mary with two gracefully symmetrical wings flanking the three-storey main building.

Unlike Hawksley it had been sympathetically updated and restored and, as they rounded the corner, Seb could see tennis courts in the distance and a cluster of stable buildings and other outbuildings all evidently restored and in use.

An unexpected stab of nostalgic pain hit him. Hawksley should have been as well cared for but his grandfather had taken a perverse pride in the discomfort of the crumbling building—and as for Seb's father... He pushed the thought away, fists clenched with the unwanted anger that still flooded through him whenever he thought about his father's criminal negligence.

Sherry came to a stop as they reached a large paved terrace with steps leading upwards to the French doors at the back of the house. Comfortably padded wooden furniture was arranged to take the best advantage of the gorgeous views. 'I think it's warm enough to sit outside.' Sherry smiled at her daughter. 'I'll go get Rick. He'll be so happy to see you, Daisy. He was saying the other day we see more of Rose and she lives in New York. You two make yourselves at home. Then we can have a drink. Daisy, darling, let Vi know you're here, will you?'

'I'll text her.' Daisy perched on a bench as she pulled out her phone and, after a moment's hesitation, Seb joined her. Of course they would sit together. In fact, they should be holding hands. He looked at her long, slender fingers flying over the phone's surface and willed himself to casually reach over and slip his own fingers through hers.

Just one touch. And yet it felt more binding than the ring he had bought her and the vows he was prepared to make.

'That's Dad's studio.' Daisy slipped the phone back into her dress pocket and pointed at the largest of the outbuildings. 'The first thing he did was convert it into a soundproofed, state-of-the-art recording studio—we were never allowed in unsupervised but it didn't stop us trying to make our own records. They weren't very good. None of us are particularly musical, much to Dad's disgust. The room next to it is used as rehearsal space and we turned the orangery into a pool and gym, otherwise we pretty much left the house as it was. It hasn't changed much since it was built.'

But it had. The paintwork was fresh, the soft furnishings and wallpaper new, the furniture chosen with care. New money in an old building. It was what Hawksley needed, if only his great-great-grandfather had married an American heiress.

'Have you lived here long?'

'Mum grew up here, her uncle is a baronet and somewhere along the family tree we descend from William Fourth, although not through the legitimate line. So, you see—' Daisy threw him a provocative smile '—you're not marrying beneath you.'

'I didn't think I was.' Seb knew very well that his blood was as red as anyone else's. It wasn't Daisy's ancestry that worried him, it was her upbringing. If she had been brought up in a place as lavishly luxurious as Huntingdon Hall how would she cope with the draughty inconveniences of his grand and ancient home?

'Daisy? You *are* alive. Rose was trying to persuade me to break into your apartment and recover your dead body. A whole week with no word from you?'

'Vi!' Daisy jumped to her feet, sprinting up the stone steps and flinging her arms around the speaker. 'What do you mean? I texted you both! Every day.'

'Texts, anyone can send a text that says I'm fine, talk soon. But—' she eyed Seb coolly over Daisy's shoulder '—I can see you've been busy.'

Seb stood and held out his hand. 'You must be Violet.' A meaningful glare from Daisy reminded him of his role. 'Daisy has told me so much about you.' He walked forward and slipped an arm around Daisy, ignoring the electricity that snaked up his arm from the exact spot

where his fingers curled around her slender waist. Daisy
started, just a little, at his touch before inhaling and leaning into him, her body pliant, moulding into his side as if
she belonged there.

'Really? She hasn't mentioned you at all.' Violet took
his outstretched hand in her cool grasp for a moment. 'She
usually tells me everything.' Her eyes were narrowed as
she assessed him. It was more than a little disconcerting
to be so comprehensively overlooked even by such very
blue eyes.

The family resemblance was striking. Violet was a
little taller, a little curvier than her younger sister and her
heart-shaped face gave nothing away, unlike Daisy's all
too telling features, but she had the Huntingdon colour-
ing, the high cheekbones and the same mane of golden
hair.

That was as far as the resemblance went; Daisy was
wearing a monochrome print dress, the bodice tight fitting
and the skirt flaring out to just above her knees, a dark
pink short cardigan slung over her shoulders and the carefully positioned hat finishing off the outfit with a quirky
flourish. Violet, by contrast, was sensibly clad in jeans and
a white shirt, her hair held back from her face by a large
slide, her make-up understated and demure.

'Not everything.' Daisy flushed. 'I am twenty-four, you
know. I do have some secrets.'

'Daisy-Waisy, you never managed to keep a secret in
your whole life.' Violet grinned at her sister with obvious
affection. Her eyes cooled as she returned to assessing
Seb. 'And what is it that you do?'

For one, almost irresistible moment Seb had the urge
to emulate his grandfather, draw himself up to his full six
feet one, look down at Violet and drawl, 'Do? My good
woman, I don't *do*. I am. Earl of Holgate to be precise,'
just to shake her cool complacency. He didn't need Daisy's

warning pinch to resist. 'I manage a large estate. That's where we met. Daisy was working there.'

'He came to my rescue.' The face upturned to his was so glowing Seb nearly forgot they were acting. 'I was snowed in and he rescued me. It was super romantic, Vi.'

'Words no father wants to hear.' Seb started at the deep American drawl and hurriedly turned.

'Dad.' Daisy tugged Seb down the steps, almost running. She slipped out of Seb's grasp and threw her arms around the slight man on the terrace.

'Missed you, Daisy girl. How's that camera of yours?'

'Busy, I already promised Mum I would cover the Benefit Concert but if you want some promo shots doing beforehand just ask. Formal, informal, you choose.'

'I'll ask Rose. She makes all those kinds of decisions. So who is this romantic knight you've brought home?' Rick Cross turned to Seb with an appraising gaze.

For the third time in five minutes Seb stood still as he was examined by keen eyes. Lucky Daisy, having such a loving, protective family. She didn't need to marry him at all; they would close ranks and take care of her. If he wanted to raise his heir he'd better keep his side of their strange bargain.

'Sebastian Beresford. It's an honour to meet you, sir.' Seb managed, just, not to blurt out that Rick Cross had made one of the first CDs he had ever bought. A CD he had listened to over and over again.

Daisy's father was so familiar it seemed odd that he was a stranger; the craggy face, wild hair and skinny frame were timeless. Rick Cross had burst onto the music scene at twenty and never left. Age had definitely not withered him; he still toured, released and dominated the headlines although these days it was philanthropy not wild antics that kept him there.

'Beresford? I've read your books. Good to meet you.'

Daisy slipped an arm around Seb and he obediently held her close as she beamed at her family. 'We've got some news. Mum, Dad, Vi. Seb and I are engaged. We're going to get married!'

It was exhausting, pretending. Hanging on Seb's arm, smiling, showing off the admittedly beautiful but somewhat soulless solitaire on her third finger as her family crowded around with congratulations and calls for champagne.

A glass of champagne Daisy pretended to sip. If her parents suspected for one single second the real reason for her marriage they would be so disappointed. Not in her, for her.

And she absolutely couldn't bear that. To let them down again.

They knew how much she wanted to fall in love, to be loved.

Vi hung back a little, her eyes suspicious even as her mouth smiled. Her sister had been so badly burned, it was hard for her to trust. And Daisy was lying after all.

'I'll call the vicar right away.' Her mother had swung into action with alarming haste. 'You'll want spring naturally, Daisy darling, next year or the year after? I think next year. A long engagement is so dreadfully dreary.'

Daisy looked at Seb for help but he had been drawn into a conversation with her father about guitar chords. Did Seb know anything about guitars or chords? She had no idea.

No idea what his favourite food was, his favourite memory, band, song, poem, book, film, TV programme. If he played a musical instrument, liked to run, watched football, rugby or both…

'Daisy, stop daydreaming,' her mother scolded as she had so many times before. 'Next year, darling?'

Daisy tugged her hat back into place. 'Sorry.' She put on her widest smile and did her best to look as if her heart weren't shattering into ever smaller fragments with every word. 'We're not getting married here.'

The rest of her family fell silent and Daisy could feel three sets of eyes boring into her. 'Not getting married here?'

'It's all you have ever wanted.'

'Don't be silly, Daisy girl. Where else would you get married?'

'It's my fault, I'm afraid.' Seb had stepped behind her and Daisy leant back into the lean, hard body with a hastily concealed sob of relief. 'I, ah, I own a licensed property and we rather thought we would get married there. I hope you're not too disappointed.'

'A licensed venue?' Vi, of course. 'Like a pub?'

'No, well, actually yes, there is a pub in the village. It's a tied village, so technically it belongs to me but I don't run it.'

So much for Seb rescuing her, although Daisy would bet her favourite lens that Mr Darcy would quail faced with her entire family. If Rose were here as well to complete the interrogation then Seb would be running for the hills, his precious heir forgotten.

'Seb owns Hawksley Castle, we're getting married there and it won't be next spring.' It was time to act as she had never acted before. Daisy nuzzled in closer to Seb, one arm around his neck, and kissed him. Just a short, quick kiss, his mouth hard under hers.

Heat shimmered through her, low and intense and she quivered, grabbing for words to hide behind, hoping Seb hadn't noticed how he had affected her. 'We're getting married this month, in just over three weeks. Excited?'

'Why the rush?' Vi's eyes flickered over Daisy's belly and she resisted the urge to breathe in.

'Why not?' Keeping her voice as light and insouciant as possible, Daisy pressed even closer to Seb, his arm tight around her. It might just be for show but she was grateful for the support both physically and mentally. 'After all, Mum and Dad, what do you always say? When you know, you know. You only knew each other for a weekend before you got married.'

'But, Daisy, darling that was the late seventies and we were in Vegas.'

'It's true though, honey.' Rick Cross's voice had softened to the besotted tones he still used whenever he spoke to his wife, the intimate voice that excluded everyone else, even their three daughters. 'We only needed that weekend to know we were meant to be. Maybe Daisy girl has been as lucky as we were?'

The ever-present ache intensified. 'I am, Dad. Be happy for me?'

'Of course we are. Hawksley, eh? I met your father once. Remember, Sherry? On Mustique. Now that was a man who liked to party. Talking of which, we've finished the champagne. Let's go in and get some more and toast this thing properly. I might have some photos of that holiday, Seb.'

Her parents bore Seb off up the steps, both talking nineteen to the dozen. Daisy stood for a moment, watching. In nearly every way this was the image from her dreams: a handsome, eligible man, her parents' approval.

A man she barely knew. A man who didn't love her. A man who might have a comforting embrace and a mouth she melted against but who wanted a businesslike, emotion-free marriage.

'You don't have to rush into this. How long have you known him?' Vi had also stayed behind. Her arms were folded as she waited for Daisy to answer.

'Six weeks.' This at least wasn't a lie. 'And I'm not rushing into anything. I want to do this, Vi. Be happy for me.' She smiled coaxingly at her sister.

'I want to be.' Vi stared at her, worry in her eyes. 'It's just, I heard rumours. Daisy, Hawksley Castle is beautiful but it's expensive and his parents spent a lot. More than a lot. Are you sure he's not…?' She paused.

'Not what?' But she knew. 'After my fortune? I don't have a fortune, Vi!'

'No, but Daddy does and you know it drives him mad we won't live off him. He'd do anything for you, Daise, even prop up a money pit like Hawksley.'

If Daisy knew anything about Seb it was this: she could hand on heart acquit him of any interest in her father's money. The shock in his eyes when he'd found out who she was had been utterly genuine. But Vi was right to be suspicious; they were deceiving her.

And yet anger was simmering, slow, hot, intense. 'Seb does not need my non-existent fortune or Daddy to bail him out. He's working every waking hour to turn Hawksley around his way and he'll do it too. So butt out, Vi. And no running to Rose either. Let her make her own mind up.'

Where had that come from?

Vi looked at her searchingly. 'Okay, Daise, calm down. I won't say anything. Let's go in and I'll get to know your Seb properly. My little sister's marrying an earl. You always did like to show off.'

'I didn't know he was an earl when I met him!' But Vi just laughed and pulled her up the steps and into the vast kitchen diner that dominated the back of the house.

'There you are, darling. Three weeks! That's no time at all to plan. We need to get started right now. How many people can you seat? There will be rooms at the castle for the family, I suppose? Colour scheme yellow and white, of course.'

'Great!' Violet scowled. 'So I get lumbered with light purple and Rose gets almost any colour she wants.'

'I could have called you Marigold, just think about

that,' her mother said. 'We need to go shopping right away, Daisy. And discuss menus, and cakes and do you think Grandpa will come?'

'The thing is, Mum...' Daisy took a deep breath. 'I don't need any of those things. It's going to be very small. Just us, and Rose, of course, if she can come. So no colour scheme needed. We could have cake though.'

'No!' Daisy jumped at the autocratic note in her mother's voice. It wasn't a note she heard often; her parents were indulgent to the point of spoiling their girls. Rose always said that was why they had sent them to such a strict boarding school, so that someone else would do the hard parts and they could just enjoy their daughters.

'No, Daisy. Not this time.'

This time? Daisy stared at her mother in confusion. 'I...'

She didn't get a chance to continue. Sherry's voice rose higher. 'You wanted to leave home in your teens? Your father and I respected that. We were both working at eighteen after all. You won't allow us to pay your rent or buy you a car or help you in any way? I don't like it but I accept it. You visit once in a blue moon? I tell myself that at least you text us and I can follow you on Twitter.'

The heat burned high on Daisy's cheeks. It hadn't really occurred to her that her parents would interpret her need to go it alone as rejection. She held up a hand, whether in defence or supplication she didn't know.

It made no difference; her mother had hit her stride. 'You want to get married in less than a month? Fine. You want to get married away from home? No problem. But you will *not* have a tiny wedding. I know you, you've dreamt of a big, beautiful wedding since you were tiny and that, my girl, is exactly what you are going to have. You are going to let me pay for it and, young lady, nobody—' the blue eyes flashed '—*nobody* is going to stop me organising it for you.'

CHAPTER FOUR

'I'M SO SORRY.' Daisy hadn't said much as they drove the sixty miles back to Hawksley Castle but she straightened once Seb turned the Land Rover down the track that led to the castle. 'I should have planned the visit—gone on my own, maybe. I know you don't want any fuss.'

Seb slid a gaze her way. She was pale, the red lipstick bitten away. 'We could just say no.' We. It felt odd saying the word, like putting on somebody else's sock.

'We could.' Daisy slumped further down into the seat and sighed. 'But then they'd know something was up. I may have mentioned my dream wedding plans once or twice.'

He'd bet she had, he already knew far too many details about Daisy's Dream Wedding. Details imparted by eager parents and a grim-faced sister all determined that she should have her Big Day. 'Tell them I'm allergic to the thought. Cold sweats, clammy hands and hives. Or that small is more romantic and they're lucky we're not eloping.'

She didn't respond and at her silence an unwelcome thought crept into his mind; was he being presumptuous? Starting off this unconventional marriage by trampling over his prospective wife's wishes. Great start. 'Unless you want this?'

'I thought I did.' Her voice was wistful. 'But that was before...'

A stab of something that felt uncomfortably like guilt pierced him. She hadn't sought this out. His carelessness had thrust it upon her—the least he could do was allow her to have her way on this one small thing, even if the thought of all that attention did make his stomach churn, his hands clammy on the steering wheel.

Seb inhaled. To make this work meant compromise on both sides. He needed to start somewhere. 'We could rearrange. Your house, your church, garden party—the whole shebang if it means that much to you.'

'Really?' Her face brightened for one second and then it was gone, as if the spark had never been. 'No, thank you for offering, I do really appreciate it but it's fine. That wedding was a dream, a romance. It would feel—' she hesitated '—even more fake if I made you go along with my silly dreams. Here will be much more appropriate. But would you mind, if we did accommodate Mum a little and allow her to help? I'll keep it under control, I promise.'

'Of course. This is your wedding and your home.' The words slid out easily even as his chest constricted. How would this pampered butterfly manage in a place as unwieldy and stately as Hawksley? But what choice did he have? Did either of them have? They had made their bed…

He braked as he slid the car into the parking space and turned to face her. 'Look, Daisy, I really think this can work. If we're honest with each other, if we keep communicating.'

She was staring down at her hands, her lashes dark as they shadowed her eyes. 'You don't think we are rushing into it?'

Seb couldn't help the corner of his mouth curving up. 'Not at all. I believe several of my ancestors only met their spouse on their wedding day. We'll have had at least two months between meeting and wedding—a shocking amount of time.'

There was no responsive smile. 'I still think there would be no harm in waiting until after we've had a scan and know more. It's still such early days. I haven't even been to the doctor's yet. If we marry and I am just ten weeks along there's still a chance something could go wrong. We'd be trapped in a marriage neither of us want with no baby! What would we do then?'

She made sense, every word made sense and the sensible side of Seb acknowledged the truth of it, welcomed the truth of it—and yet something in him recoiled.

'There are no certainties anywhere. If it goes wrong then we mourn. We mourn and regroup. Daisy…' He reached over and took one of her hands; it lay unresisting in his, the long slender fingers cold. 'I can't see into the future and, yes, in some ways you are right. We can wait, for the scan, wait till sixteen weeks or even thirty weeks. Or we can take a leap of faith. That's what marriage is. Ours is just a bigger leap.'

He thought about it for a moment. 'Or a shorter one. Our eyes are open after all.'

She looked straight at him, her eyes wide and troubled. 'I'm only agreeing to an early marriage so my family doesn't find out I'm pregnant, so they don't try and talk me out of it. They know how important marriage is to me, how important love is. What about you? Why don't you want to wait?'

Seb squeezed his eyes shut. He could still hear them, his parents' vicious arguments, their exuberant reconciliations. He thought about brushing her off but if he wanted this to work then he needed to be honest. Needed her to understand what he was offering—and what he could never give her.

'My mother didn't want a baby. She didn't want to ruin her figure with pregnancy, didn't want to stop partying, didn't want to go through labour. But she did want to be a countess and an heir was part of the deal. She told me once, when she was drunk, how happy she had been when they said I was a boy so that she didn't have to go through it all again. That if it was up to her she would have remained childless.'

I had you because I had no choice. It was the worst year of my life.

'Luckily there were grandparents, schools, nannies. She could at least pretend to be child-free—except when it suited her. I don't want our child to think that, to feel like a burden. I want to welcome him or her into the world with open arms and make sure he or she knows that they were wanted. Because we may not have planned it but I do want it—and you do too. That's why it matters, that they are born with all the ridiculous privileges this title gives them. That's why it matters that we marry.'

She didn't say anything for a long moment but her fingers closed over his, strength in her cool grasp. 'Okay,' she said finally. 'Three weeks on Friday it is. Let's go and see the registrar tomorrow morning and get booked in. I guess I should register with a doctor nearby as well.'

'Good.' He returned the pressure, relieved. At her acquiescence. At her silent understanding. 'Are you tired or do you want the full guided tour of your new home?'

'Are you kidding? A personal guided tour from the hot prof himself? Show me everything.'

'So this is the Norman keep. Family legend has it that a knight, Sir William Belleforde, came over with the invasion in 1066 and was granted these lands. During the next few centuries the name was anglicised and corrupted to Beresford. He built the keep.'

'Cosy.' Daisy pivoted, looking about her at the dark grey walls built out of blocks of grey stone, the narrow window slits. She pulled her cardigan closer as the wind whistled through the tower. 'Was this it?'

'There was a wooden castle attached but this was the main defensive base and would have been quite roomy. There were three floors inside here—look, there's the old staircase. There was also a fortified wall around the rest of the castle. When you visit the village you'll see that many of the older houses are built with the stone from the walls.'

Daisy tilted her head back, trying to imagine one thousand years away. 'Walls, battlements, arrow slits. Nothing says home like defensive buildings. Were there many battles here?'

Seb shook his head. 'There was very little fighting here even during the Wars of the Roses and the Civil War. My ancestors were too canny to get involved.'

'No Cavalier ghosts trailing along with their heads under their arms?' Obviously this was a relief and yet didn't a house like this deserve a few ghosts?

'Not a one. We changed our religion to suit the Tudors and the colour of our roses for the Plantagenets. You'll be glad to hear that an impetuous younger son did go to France with Charles II and when he inherited the title he was made first Earl of Holgate. Although some say that was because his wife was one of the King's many mistresses—with her Lord's consent.'

'Good to know she was doing her bit for the family's advancement. Is that still a requirement for the countess? I'm not sure I'm up to it if so!'

He shot her a wry smile. 'I'm glad to hear it. No, I'm more than happy with the earldom, no favours for advancements required. Of course by then the keep was abandoned as a home. It was already unused by the late fourteenth century and the Great Hall was built around one hundred years later.'

He led her out of the chill stone building and swung

open the huge oak door that led into the Tudor part of the castle.

Daisy had spent an entire day in this part of the castle, photographing a wedding. It had felt completely different with long tables set out, the dais at the far end filled with a top table, the candle-like iron chandeliers blazing with light. 'I can see why they moved in here. It may be large but it's a lot warmer. Having a working roof is a definite advantage. A floor is helpful too.'

'Especially when you let the place out,' he agreed. 'Brides can be a bit precious about things like dirt floors and holes in the roof.'

'It's in incredible condition.' She had taken so many photos of the details: the carvings on the panelling, the way the huge beams curved.

'It has to be. We couldn't hold events here if not. It may look untouched since Elizabethan times but there is electricity throughout, working toilets and a fully kitted-out kitchen through that door. In fact, this is more up to date than parts of the main house. It's always been used as a ballroom, which made the decision to hire it out a little easier.' He winced. 'My grandfather thought we had a duty to share the castle with the wider world, but not for profit.'

'Hence the restrictive opening hours?'

'Absolutely. I don't know what he would say if he saw the weddings. They're not making enough of a difference though, even though I charge an obscene amount. I'm trying to work out how to make the castle self-funding and yet keep it as a home. Keep the heart of it intact. It's not easy.'

'You're planning to stay here, then, not live in Oxford?'

'Now it's mine? Yes. I can stay in college if I need to, although it will be strange, commuting in after all these years. It's like being pulled constantly in two different directions, between the demands of my career and the demands of my home—they both need all of my time or so it seems. But a place like this? It's a privilege to own it, to be the one taking care of it.'

His eyes lit up with enthusiasm, the rather severe features relaxing as he pointed out another interesting architectural feature and recounted yet another bit of family history that Daisy was convinced he made up on the spot. Nobody could have such a scandalous family tree—rakes and highwaymen and runaway brides in every generation.

'You really love it, don't you?'

'How could I not? Growing up here, it was like living in my own time machine. I could be anybody from Robin Hood to Dick Turpin.'

'Always the outlaw?'

'They seemed to have the most fun. Had the horses, the adoration, got the girls.'

'All the important things in life.'

'Exactly.' He grinned; it made him look more boyish. More desirable. Daisy's breath hitched in her throat, her mouth suddenly dry.

Their gazes caught, snagged, and they stood there for a long moment, neither moving. His eyes darkened to an impenetrable green, a hint of something dangerous flickering at their core and awareness shivered down Daisy's spine. She moved backwards, just a few centimetres, almost propelled by the sheer force of his gaze until her back hit the wooden panelling. She leant against it, thankful for the support, her legs weak.

She was still caught in his gaze, warmth spreading out from her abdomen, along her limbs, her skin buzzing where his eyes rested on her, the memory of his touch skittering along her nerves. Nervous, she licked her lips, the heat in her body intensifying as she watched his eyes move to her mouth, recognised the hungry expression in them.

He wanted a working marriage. A full marriage.

Right now, that seemed like the only thing that made sense in this whole tangled mess.

He took a step closer. And another. Daisy stayed still, almost paralysed by the purposeful intent in his face, her pulse hammering an insistent beat of need, of want at every pressure point in her body, pressure, a sweet, aching swelling in her chest.

'Seb?' It was almost a plea, almost a sob, a cry for something, an end to the yearning that so suddenly and so fiercely gripped her.

He paused, his eyes still on her and then one last step. So close and yet still, still not touching even though her body was crying out for contact, pulled towards him by the magnetism of sheer need. He leant, just a little, a hand on either side of her, braced against the wall.

He still hadn't touched her.

They remained perfectly still, separated by mere millimetres, their eyes locked, heat flickering between them, the wait stoking it higher and higher. He had to kiss her, had to or she would spontaneously combust. He had to press that hard mouth against hers, allow those skilled hands to roam, to know her again. To fulfil her again. He had to.

Daisy jumped as a tune blared out from her pocket, a jaunty folk cover of one of her father's greatest hits. Seb's hands dropped and he retreated just a few steps as she fumbled for it, half ready to sob with frustration, half relieved. She hadn't even moved in yet and she was what? Begging him to kiss her?

Very businesslike.

Hands damp, she pulled out the phone and stared at the screen, unable to focus. Pressing the button, she held it shakily to her ear. 'Hello?'

'Daisy? You *are* alive, then?'

'Rose!' Daisy smiled apologetically at Seb and turned

slightly, as if not seeing him would give her some privacy, her heart still hammering.

'Vi said I had to call you right now. Where have you been? Not cool to go offline with no warning, little sis, not cool at all.'

It was what, four o'clock in the afternoon? It felt later, as if several days, not just a few hours, had passed since she had woken up in her own bed, in her own flat for the last time. It would still be morning in New York. She pictured her sister, feet on the desk, a coffee by her hand, an incorrigible mixture of efficiency, impatience and effortless style.

'Things have been a bit crazy.' Daisy knew she sounded breathless, welcomed it. Hopefully her sister would put it down to girlish excitement not a mixture of frustration and embarrassment. 'Rose, I have some news. I'm engaged!'

There was a long silence at the end of the phone. Then: 'But you're not even dating anyone. It's not Edwin, is it? I thought you said he was dull.'

'No, of course it's not Edwin!' Daisy could feel her cheeks heating. 'We split up months ago, and he's not dull exactly,' she added loyally. 'Just a little precise. It's Seb, Sebastian Beresford, you know, Rose, he wrote that book on Charles II's illegitimate children you loved so much.'

'The hot professor? England's answer to Indiana Jones?' The shriek was so loud that Daisy was convinced Seb could hear it through the phone. 'How on earth did you meet him, Daisy? What kind of parties are you going to nowadays? Dinner parties? Academic soirées?' Rose laughed.

There it was, unspoken but insinuated. How could silly little Daisy with barely a qualification to her name have anything in common with a lauded academic?

'Through work,' she said a little stiffly. 'He owns Hawksley Castle.'

'Of course,' her sister breathed. 'Didn't he just inherit a title? What is he, a baron?'

'An earl.' It sounded ludicrous just saying the words. She could feel Seb's sardonic gaze on her and turned around so her back was entirely towards him, wishing she had gone outside to have this awkward conversation.

'An earl?' Rose went off into another peal of laughter. Daisy held the phone away from her ear, waiting for her sister to calm down. 'Seriously? This isn't you and Vi winding me up?'

Was it that implausible? Daisy didn't want to hear the answer.

'It's true.'

'Well, I suppose I had better meet him if you're going to marry him. I'll be over for the Benefit Concert in about four weeks. There's only so much I can do this side of the Atlantic. With the tour on top of everything else I am completely snowed under. I can't cope with one more thing at the moment.' Rose was in charge of all their parents' PR as well as organising the annual Benefit Concert their father did for charity. His decision to take the band back on tour had added even more to her sister's already heavy workload.

So she was going to love the last-minute changes to her plan. 'Actually you're going to meet him sooner than that. We're getting married in three weeks and you have to be my bridesmaid, Rose. You will be there, won't you?'

'What? When? But why, Daisy? What's the rush?'

'No rush,' she replied, hating that she was lying to her family. 'We don't want to wait, that's all.'

There was a deep sigh at the other end of the telephone. 'Daise, you know what you're like. You always go all in at first. You thought you'd found The One at sixteen for goodness' sake, and again when you were at St Martin's. Then there was Edwin—you told me you were soulmates.

Then you wake up one day and realise that they're actually frogs, not your prince. Nice frogs—but still frogs. What makes this one different? Apart from the amazing looks, the keen brain and the title, of course.'

Daisy wanted to slide down onto the floor and stay there. Her family had always teased her about her impetuous romantic nature. But to have it recited back to her like that. It made her sound so young. So stupid.

But Rose was wrong. This wasn't like the others. She was under no illusions that Seb was her soulmate. She wasn't in love.

'This is different and when you meet him you'll understand.' She hoped she sounded convincing—it was the truth after all.

'Okay.' Rose sighed. 'If you say it's different this time then I believe you.'

What Rose actually meant was that she would phone Vi and get her opinion and then the two of them could close ranks and sit in judgement on Daisy. Just as they always did.

'You will be there though, won't you, Rosy Posy?' Daisy wheedled using the old pet name her sister affected to despise. 'I can't get married without you.' Her breath hitched and she heard the break in her voice. Her sisters might be bossy and annoying and have spent most of their childhood telling her to leave them alone but they were hers. And she needed them.

'Of course I'll be there, silly. I'll make the rings, my gift to you both. Send me his finger size, okay?'

'Okay.' Daisy clung onto the phone, wishing her sister were there, wishing she could tell her the truth.

'I have to go. There are a million and one things to do. Talk soon. Call me if you need anything.'

'I will. Bye.'

Daisy clicked the phone shut, oddly bereft as the connection cut. Rose had been abroad for so long—and when she did come home she worked.

'That was my other sister.'

Seb was leaning against the wall, arms folded, one ankle crossed over the other. 'I guessed.'

'She makes rings, as a hobby although she's so good she should do it professionally. She's offered to make ours so I need to send your finger size over.'

She half expected him to say he wasn't going to wear a ring and relief filled her as he nodded acquiescence. 'Why doesn't she—do it professionally?'

It was a good question. Why didn't she? Daisy struggled to find the right words. 'She's good at PR. Mummy and Daddy have always relied on her, and on Vi, to help them. They're so incredibly busy and it's easier to keep it in the family, with people they trust.' Her loving, indulgent, generous but curiously childlike parents.

'What about you? What do you do?'

'Me? I take photos. That's all I'm good for. They don't need me for anything else.' She couldn't keep the bitterness out of her voice.

He looked her curiously. 'That's not the impression I got today. They were bowled over to see you, all fatted calves and tears of joy.'

'That's because I don't go home enough.' The guilt gnawed away at her. 'I don't involve them in my life. It drives my mum crazy as you can probably tell. She doesn't trust me not to mess up without her.'

'Why not?'

Daisy looked at him sharply but the question seemed genuine enough. She sighed. 'It always took me twice as long as my sisters to do anything,' she admitted. 'I was a late talker, walker, reader. My handwriting was atrocious, I hated maths—I was always in trouble at school for talking or messing around.'

'You and half the population.'

'But half the population don't have Rose and Violet as older sisters,' she pointed out. 'I don't think I had a single teacher who didn't ask me why I couldn't be more like my sisters. Why my work wasn't the same standard, my manners as good. By the time I was expelled that narrative was set in stone. I was like the family kitten—cute enough but you couldn't expect much from me. Of course actually being expelled didn't help.'

'It must have been difficult.'

'It was humiliating.' Looking back, that was what she remembered most clearly. How utterly embarrassed she had been. 'It was all over the papers. People were commiserating with my parents as if my life was finished. At sixteen! So Mum and Dad tried to do what they do best. Spend money on me and paper over the cracks. They offered to send me to finishing school, or for Mum to set me up with her modelling agency. I could be a socialite or a model. I wasn't fit for anything else.'

'But you're not either of those things.'

'I refused.' She swallowed. 'I think the worst part was that the whole family treated the whole incident like a joke. They didn't once ask me how I felt, what I wanted to do. To be. I heard Dad say to Mum that I was never going to pass any exams anyway so did it really matter.' She paused, trying not to let that painful memory wind her the way it usually did.

It had hurt knowing that even her own parents didn't have faith in her.

'I didn't want them to fix it. I wanted to fix it myself. So I went to the local college and then art school. I left home properly in my first term and never went back. I needed to prove to them, to me, that they don't have to take care of me.' She laughed but there was no humour in her voice. 'Look how well that's turned out.'

'I think you do just fine by yourself.'

'Pregnant after a one-night stand?' She shook her head. 'Maybe they're right.'

'Pregnant? Yes. But you faced up to it, came here and told me, which was pretty damn brave. You're sacrificing your own dreams for the baby. I think that makes you rather extraordinary.'

'Oh, well.' She shrugged, uncomfortable with the compliments. 'I do get to be a countess and sleep with a king for social advantage after all.'

'There is that.' His eyes had darkened again. 'Where were we, when your sister phoned and interrupted us?'

Daisy felt it again, that slow sensual tug towards him, the hyper awareness of his every move, the tilt of his mouth, the gleam of his eye, the play of muscle in his shoulders.

'You were telling me about wanting to be an outlaw.' She felt it but she wasn't going there. Not today, not when she was in such an emotional tumult.

'Coward.' The word was soft, silky, full of promise. Then he straightened, the intentness gone. 'So I was. Ready to see the rest of your home? Let's zoom forward to the eighteenth century and start exploring the Georgian part. I'll warn you, there's a lot of it. I think we'll stick to the ground and first floors today. The second floor is largely empty and the attics have been untouched for years.'

'Attics?' A frisson of excitement shivered through her. As a child she had adored roaming through the attics at home, exploring chests filled with family treasures. Only there was nothing to discover in the recently renovated, perfectly decorated house. Photos sorted into date order? Yes. Tiaras dripping with diamonds or secret love letters? No. But here, in a house that epitomised history, she could find anything.

'Would you mind if one day I had a look? In the attics?'

Seb walked towards the door and stopped, his hand on the huge iron bolt. 'One day? I think you'll need to put aside at least six months. My family were hoarders—I would love to catalogue it all, although I suspect much of it is junk, but there's too much to do elsewhere. The whole house could do with some updating. I don't know if your talents run in that direction but please, feel free to make any changes you want. As long as they're in keeping with a grade one listed building,' he added quickly.

'And there I was, thinking I could paint the whole outside pink and add a concrete extension.' But she was strangely cheered. A house with twenty bedrooms and as many reception rooms—if you included the various billiard rooms, studies and galleries—was no small project. But taking it in hand gave her a purpose, a role here. Maybe, just maybe, she could make Hawksley Castle into a home. Into her home.

CHAPTER FIVE

'MORNING. HUNGRY?'

Seb half turned as Daisy slipped into the kitchen, tiptoeing as if she didn't want to offend him with her presence.

'Starving. I keep waiting for the nausea to start.' She was almost apologetic, as if he would accuse her of being a fraud if she wasn't doubled over with sickness. It would be easier, he admitted, if she were ill. He was after all taking it on trust that she was even pregnant in the first place, although she had offered him plenty of chances to wait for confirmation.

'You may be lucky and escape it altogether. How did you sleep?'

'Good, thanks. Turns out five-hundred-year-old beds are surprisingly comfy.'

The problem of where to put Daisy had haunted him since she had agreed to move in. To make this work, to fulfil her criteria as far as he could, meant he couldn't treat her like a guest and yet he wasn't ready to share his space with anyone.

Even though part of him couldn't help wondering what it would be like lying next to those long, silky limbs.

Luckily Georgian houses were built with this kind of dilemma in mind. When he first took a leave of absence and returned to Hawksley six months ago to try and untangle the complicated mess his father had left, he'd moved into his grandparents' old rooms, not his own boyhood bedroom on the second floor.

There was a suite adjoining, the old countess' suite, a throwback to not so long ago when the married couple weren't expected to regularly share a bed, a room or a bathroom. The large bedroom, small study, dressing room and bathroom occupied a corner at the back of the house with views over the lake to the woods and fields beyond. The suite was rather faded, last decorated some time around the middle of the previous century and filled with furniture of much older heritage but charming for all that.

'There is a door here,' he had said, showing her a small door discreetly set into the wall near the bed. 'It leads into my room. You can lock it if you would rather, but I don't bother.'

The words had hung in the air. Were they an invitation? A warning? He wasn't entirely sure.

It was odd, he had never really noticed the door before yet last night it had loomed in his eyeline, the unwanted focal point of his own room. He had known she was on the other side, just one turn of the handle away. Seb's jaw tightened as he flipped the bacon. He could visualise it now as if it were set before him. Small, wooden, nondescript.

'Did you lock the door?'

'Bolted it.'

'Good, wouldn't want the ghost of a regency rake surprising you in the middle of the night.'

Daisy wandered over to the kettle and filled it. Such a normal everyday thing to do—and yet such a big step at the same time. 'I'm sure bolts are no barrier to any decent ghosts, not rakish-type ones anyway. Coffee?'

'All set, thanks.' He nodded at the large mug at his elbow. The scene was very domestic in a formal, polite kind of way.

Daisy sniffed the several herbal teas she had brought with her and pulled a face. 'I miss coffee. I don't mind giving up alcohol and I hate blue cheese anyway but waking up without a skinny latte is a cruel and unusual punishment.'

'We could get some decaf.' Seb grabbed two plates and spooned the eggs and bacon onto them.

'I think you're missing the whole point of coffee. I'll give liquorice a try.' She made the hot drink and carried the mug over to the table, eying up the heaped plate of food with much greater enthusiasm. 'This looks great, thanks.'

'I thought we might need sustenance for the day ahead. Registrar at ten and I booked you into the doctor's here for eleven. I hope that's okay. And then we'd better let the staff and volunteers know our news, begin to make some plans.'

'Fine.' A loud peal rang through the house causing a slight vibration, and Daisy jumped, the eggs piled up on her fork tumbling back onto the plate. 'What on earth is that?'

Seb pushed his chair back and tried not to look too longingly at his uneaten breakfast. It was a long way from the kitchen to the door, plenty of time for his breakfast to cool. 'Doorbell. It's a little dramatic admittedly but the house is so big it's the only way to know if there's a visitor—and it's less obtrusive than a butler. Cheaper too.'

'Is it the gorgon? If I get turned to stone I expect you to rescue me.'

He tried not to let his mouth quirk at the apt nickname. There was definitely a heart of gold buried deep somewhere underneath Mrs Suffolk's chilly exterior but it took a long time to find and appreciate it. 'The volunteers have a key for the back door—there's only two working doors between the offices and the main house and I lock them both at night.'

'Good to know. I don't fancy being petrified in my bed.'

Her words floated after him as he exited the kitchen and headed towards the front of the house.

Once, of course, the kitchen would have been part of the servants' quarters; it was still set discreetly behind a baize door, connected to the offices through a short passageway and one of the lockable doors that defined the partition between his personal space and the work space. But even his oh-so-formal grandparents had dispensed with live-in servants during the nineties and started to use the old kitchen themselves. For supper and breakfast at least.

His parents had brought their servants with them during the four years they had mismanaged Hawksley. Not that they had ever stayed at the castle for longer than a week.

The doorbell pealed again, the deep tone melodic.

'On my way.' Seb pulled back the three bolts and twisted the giant iron key, making a mental note to oil the creaking lock. He swung open the giant door to be confronted with the sight of his future mother-in-law, a huge and ominously full bag thrown over one shoulder, a newspaper in one hand and a bottle of champagne in the other.

Seb blinked. Then blinked again.

'Goodness, Seb, you look like you've seen a ghost.' She thrust the champagne and the newspaper at him, muttering cryptically, 'Page five, darling. Where is Daisy?'

'Good morning, Mrs Huntingdon...'

'Sherry.' She swept past him. '"Mrs" makes me feel so old. And we are going to be family after all.'

Family. Not something he knew huge amounts about but he was pretty sure the tall, glamorous woman opposite wasn't a typical mother-in-law. 'Right, yes. This way. She's just eating breakfast.'

He led the supermodel through the hallway, wincing as he noticed her assess every dusty cornice, every scrap of peeling paper. 'My grandparents rather let the place go.'

'It's like a museum. Apt for you in your job, I suppose.' It didn't sound like a compliment.

They reached the kitchen and Sherry swept by him to enfold a startled-looking Daisy in her arms. 'Bacon? Oh, Daisy darling, the chances of you fitting sample sizes were small anyway but you'll never do it if you eat fried food. No, none for me, thank you. I don't eat breakfast.'

'Mum? What are you doing here?'

Seb couldn't help smiling at Daisy's face. She looked exactly as he felt: surprise mixed with wariness and shock.

'Darling, we have a wedding to plan and no time at all. Where else would I be? Now hurry up and eat that. We'll get you some nice fruit while we're out. Page five, Seb.'

Seb glanced down at the tabloid newspaper Sherry had handed him and opened it slowly, his heart hammering. Surely not, not yet...

He dropped it on the table, a huge picture of Daisy and himself smiling up from the smudged newsprint. 'Hot Prof Earl and Wild Child to Wed' screamed the headline. He stepped back, horror churning in the pit of his stomach, his hands clammy.

'I knew it.' Daisy's outraged voice cut into his stupor. 'They mentioned the expulsion. Why not my first in photography or my successful business?'

'I expect they also mentioned my parents' divorces, remarriages, drinking, drug taking and untimely deaths.' He knew he sounded cold, bitter and inhaled, trying to calm the inner tumult.

'Yes.' Her voice sounded small and Seb breathed in again, trying to calm the swirling anger. It wasn't her fault.

Although if she wasn't who she was then would they be so interested?

'I'm sorry,' she added and he swallowed hard, forcing himself to lay a hand upon her shoulder.

'Don't be silly, Daisy, of course they're interested. Seb

is just as big a draw as you, more so probably.' Sherry's blue eyes were sharp, assessing.

'Yes,' he agreed tonelessly. 'We knew there would be publicity. I just thought we would have more time.'

If Daisy hadn't gone to Huntingdon Hall, hadn't involved her parents...

'The best thing to do is ignore it. Come along, darling. Show me the wedding venue. I don't have all day.'

Daisy sat for a moment, her head still bowed, cheeks pale. 'We have appointments at ten, Mum, so I only have half an hour. If you'd warned us you were coming I could have told you this morning was already booked up.'

'You two head off, I'll be fine here. There's plenty to do, just show me the venue.'

'Honestly, Mum. I can organise this quite easily. I really don't need you to do it.' There was a hint of desperation in Daisy's voice as she attempted to reason with her mother.

'I know very well that you prefer to do everything alone, Daisy. You make that quite clear.'

Daisy pushed her half-eaten breakfast away and, with an apologetic glance at Seb, took her mother's arm. 'Okay, you win. Seb, I put your breakfast back in the pan to keep warm. Come along, Mother. I don't think even you can fault the Tudor Hall.'

Seb watched them go before sliding his gaze back to the open newspaper. He focused on the picture. He was driving and Daisy was looking back, smiling. It must have been snapped as they left the hall. How hadn't he noticed the photographer?

Was this how their lives would be from now on? Every step, every conversation, every outing watched, scrutinised and reported on.

With one vicious movement he grabbed the paper and tore the article from it, screwing it into a ball and dropping it in the bin, his breath coming in fast pants. He wouldn't, couldn't be hounded. Cameras trained on him, crowds waiting outside the gate, microphones thrust into his face. He had been five the first time, as motorcycles and cars chased them down the country lanes.

His father had driven faster, recklessly. His mother had laughed.

The tantalising aroma of cooking bacon wafted through the air, breaking into his thoughts. Seb walked over to the stove, his movements slow and stiff. The frying pan was covered, the heat set to low and inside, warmed through to perfection, was his breakfast. Saved, put aside and kept for him.

When was the last time someone had done something, anything for him that they weren't paid to do?

It was just some breakfast, food he had actually cooked, put aside. So why did his chest ache as he spooned it back onto his plate?

Daisy had to work hard to stop from laughing at the look on Seb's face. He stood in the Great Hall, staring about him as if he had been kidnapped by aliens and transported to an alternate universe.

And in some ways, he had.

Her mother had wasted no time in making herself at home, somehow rounding up two bemused if bedazzled volunteers to help her set up office in the Great Hall. Three tables in a U-shape and several chairs were flanked by a white board and a pin board on trestles with several sticky notes already attached to each. A seamstress's dummy stood to attention behind the biggest chair, a wreath of flowers on its head.

A carafe of water, a glass and a vase of flowers had been procured from somewhere and set upon the table and Sherry had proceeded to empty her huge bag in a Mary Poppins manner setting out two phones, a lever arch file already divided into labelled sections, a stack of wedding magazines and—Daisy groaned in horror—her own scrapbooks and what looked like her own Pinterest mood boards printed out and laminated.

So she planned weddings online? She was a wedding photographer! It was her job to get ideas and inspiration.

If Sherry Huntingdon ever turned her formidable mind towards something other than fashion then who knew what she'd achieve? World peace? An end to poverty? Daisy winced. That wasn't entirely fair; both her parents did a huge amount for charity, most of it anonymously. The Benefit Concert might be the most high-profile event but it was just the tip of the iceberg.

'There you are, Seb.' Sherry was pacing around the Great Hall, looking at the panelling and the other period details with approval. 'Before you whisk Daisy away I need a bit of information.'

'Whatever you need.' His eyes flickered towards the arsenal of paper, pens and planning materials set out with precision on the tables and a muscle began to beat in his stubbled jaw as his hands slowly clenched. 'Good to see that you've made yourself at home.'

'I think it's helpful to be right in the centre of things,' Sherry agreed, missing—or ignoring—his sarcastic undertone. 'Your nice man on the gate tells me that there are weddings booked in both weekends so I can't leave everything set up but we'll have the hall to ourselves for the four days before the wedding so I can make sure everything is perfect.'

Daisy noticed Seb's tense stance, the rigidity in his shoulders, and interrupted. 'It won't take four days to set up for a few family and friends—and it's such short notice I'm sure most people will have plans already.'

'Don't be ridiculous, of course they'll come. It'll be the wedding of the year—rock aristocracy to real aristocracy? They'll cancel whatever other plans they have, you mark my words. Now, the nice young man tells me the hall will seat two hundred so I'll need your list as soon as possible, Seb.'

'List?' The muscle was still beating. Daisy couldn't take her eyes off it. She wanted to walk over there, lay a hand on the tense shoulder and soothe the stress out of it, run a hand across his firm jawline and kiss the muscle into quiet acquiescence. She curled her fingers into her palms, allowing her nails to bite into her flesh, the sharp sting reminding her not to cross the line. To remain businesslike.

'I already did you a list, Daisy.' Of course she had. Numbly Daisy took the sheet of neatly typed names her mother handed her and scanned it expecting to see the usual mixture of relatives, her parents' friends and business associates and the group of people her age that her parents liked to socialise with: a few actors, singers and other cool, media-friendly twenty-somethings she had absolutely nothing in common with.

And yet... Daisy swallowed, heat burning the backs of her eyes. The names she read through rapidly blurring eyes were exactly—almost exactly—those she would have written herself. It was like a *This Is Your Life* recap: school friends, college friends, work associates, London friends plus of course the usual relatives and some of the older villagers, people she had known her entire life.

'This is perfect. How did you know?' Blinking furiously, Daisy forced back the threatening tears; all her life she had felt like the odd one out, the funny little addition at the end of the family, more a pampered plaything than a card-carrying, fully paid-up adult member of the family, a person who really mattered.

A person who they knew, who they understood. Maybe they understood her better than she had ever realised.

'Vi helped me.' Her mother's voice was a little gruff and there was a telltale sheen in her eyes. 'Is it right?'

'Almost perfect.' There were just a few amendments. Daisy swiftly added several new names, recent friends her family had yet to meet.

Seb moved, just a small rustle but enough to bring her back to the present, to the reality that was this wedding. What was she thinking?

Her hand shook a little bit as she reread the top lines. These were exactly the people she would want to share her wedding day with. Only...

'The thing is we did agree on a small wedding.' She tried to keep all emotion out of her voice, not wanting her mother to hear her disappointment or Seb to feel cornered. 'If we invited all these it would be a huge affair. I'll take a look at it and single out the most important friends. What do you think? Immediate family and maybe five extra guests each?' She looked around at the long hall, the vast timbered ceiling rearing overhead. They would rattle around in here like a Chihuahua in a Great Dane's pen.

But it was still a substantially larger affair than Seb wanted. Daisy allowed the piece of paper to float down onto the desk as if the thought of striking out the majority of the names didn't make her throat tighten.

Seb had moved, so silently she hadn't noticed, reaching over her shoulder to deftly catch the paper mid-fall. 'The problem is I don't actually have any immediate family.'

Daisy automatically opened her mouth to say something inane, something to smooth over the chasm his words opened up. Then she closed it again. What good were platitudes? But understanding shivered over her. No wonder this marriage was important to him. The baby was more than a potential heir; it would be all that he had. Responsibility crushed down on her. She had been so naïve, so happy at the thought of having a person in her life who needed her, depended on her. But the baby wasn't just hers. It was theirs.

'There are school friends.' He was scribbling away on the back of the list, his handwriting sure and firm. 'Other academics, publishing colleagues, staff and volunteers here and villagers I have known all my life. I think I will need eighty places including the plus ones but, if you agree, I propose a hog roast in a marquee in the courtyard in the evening and invite the whole village. Noblesse oblige I know but it's a tied village and expected.'

'Do you have a marquee?' Thank goodness her mother was on the ball because Daisy couldn't have spoken if her life had depended on it. He didn't want this, she knew that. People, publicity, fuss, photos and the inevitable press. The only answer, the only possible reason was that he was doing this for her.

She slipped her hand into his without thought or plan and his fingers curled around hers.

Maybe, just maybe this could work after all.

'Weddings here are all run and catered for by The Blue Boar, that's the village pub, and yes, they have several marquees of all sizes. Paul—' he smiled slightly, that devastating half-lift of his mouth '—the helpful man on the gate, he can give you all the details you need.'

'That is wonderful.' Her mother was rapidly taking notes. 'That gives me a lot to be getting on with. Rose will be doing the rings of course and Violet the flowers. You know what, Daisy, I think somehow we are going to be able to pull this wedding off.'

'We're going all the way into London?'

When she had left the day before Daisy had felt, fully aware of her own inner melodrama, as if she were being taken away from her beloved city for ever even though she knew full well that she would be returning for a studio shoot later that week. But it still felt slightly anticlimactic to be returning just over twenty-four hours later.

Her mother looked mildly surprised. 'Of course, we have a wedding dress to buy.' Her voice grew wistful. 'It was such a shame that Seb vetoed a Tudor theme. I think he would have carried off a doublet really well. And such an eminent historian, you would have thought he would have jumped at the chance to really live in the past.'

'So short-sighted.' Daisy couldn't suppress the gurgle of laughter that bubbled up as she remembered the utter horror on Seb's face when her mother had greeted them with her brilliant idea. 'I would have preferred regency though.'

'The building is all wrong but you were made to wear one of those high-waisted gowns. And breeches are possibly even better than doublet and hose.'

'Infinitely better.' Daisy settled herself into a more comfortable position, allowing her hand to move softly across her abdomen. All had been confirmed. She was definitely pregnant, close to seven weeks. Just as she had expected but it had been a relief to hear another human say it out loud.

A relief to give Seb the definitive tidings; backing out of the wedding now would have been awkward for both of them. It wasn't that she was actually beginning to enjoy the planning process, enjoy having her mother's undivided attention or even enjoy seeing Seb pulled so far out of his comfort zone he could barely formulate a sentence.

Except when the Tudor theme was mooted. He had been more than able to turn that idea down flat.

Once she had established where they were going Daisy took little notice of the route. It wasn't often she spent time alone with her mother.

Maybe if she had allowed her mother in a little more then there would have been more occasions like this but the price had always seemed too high. Her mother did have a tendency to try and take over, the wedding a perfect case in point.

But it came from a place of love; maybe she should have respected that more.

Daisy leant across and kissed her mother's still smooth and unlined cheek.

'Thank you,' she said. 'For helping.' It almost hurt, saying the words, but she felt a sense of relief when they were out, as if she had been holding onto them for a long, long time.

Her mother's blue eyes widened. 'Of course I want to help. My baby, getting married. And there is so much to do. Hawksley may be grand but I've seen more up-to-date ruins.'

'Part of it is ruined.' Daisy was surprised at how protective she felt towards the stately building.

Her mother gave her a wry glance. 'I mean the house part. Really, darling, it's a major project. Some of the rooms have been untouched for years.'

'I just wish you had checked with Seb before organising the cleaners.' Only her mother could get an army of cleaners, decorators and handymen organised in under two hours. It had been a shock to arrive back from their morning appointments to find the car park full of various trade vans, the house overrun by ladders, buckets and pine scents.

'Most of the family will be staying in the house after all. Updating and decorating are your preserve, darling, but cleaning and touching up before the big day is very much mine. Consider it my wedding present to you both.'

Daisy tried not to sigh. Seb employed one cleaner who was responsible for the offices as well as the house and she barely made a dent in the few areas he used. It would be nice to see the main house brought up to hygienic standards: the paintwork fresh, the wood polished and the sash windows gleaming. At the same time it was so typical of her mother to wave her magic wand with extravagant generosity, to think that money would solve the problem regardless of how it made the recipients feel.

There had been a bleak look on Seb's face when he surveyed the workers. He had withdrawn into his study pleading work and Daisy hadn't felt able to follow him in there.

The car drew up outside the iconic golden stone building that housed Rafferty's, London's premier designer store.

'It's simply too late for a gown to be made for you. I am owed a lot of favours but even I can't work miracles. But then I remembered what a fabulous collection Nina keeps here at Rafferty's. She has promised that she can have any gown altered to fit you in the timescale. Luckily I had my pick of the new spring/summer collections in Fashion Week last year so there will be something suitable for me.' Her mother sounded vaguely put upon, as if she were being expected to put an outfit together from a duster and an old feather boa, not premier one of the several haute couture outfits that had been made specifically for her.

Daisy felt the old shiver of excitement as they exited the car and walked into the famous domed entrance hall. It was once said you could buy anything and become anybody at Rafferty's—as long as you had the money. Would she become the bride of her dreams?

They were met at the door and whisked upstairs to the bridal department, an impressive gallery decorated in Rafferty's distinctive art deco style. The entrance to the department, reached through an archway, was open to the public and sold an array of bridal accessories including lingerie, shoes, tiaras and some ready-to-wear bride and bridesmaids dresses. But it was the room beyond, tactfully hidden behind a second, curtained arch, where the real magic lay. This room was accessed by appointment only. Today, Daisy and her mother were the only customers.

It needed little decoration and the walls were painted a warm blush white, the floor a polished mahogany. The sparkle and glamour came from the dresses themselves; every conceivable length, every shade of white from ice through to deep cream, a few richer colours dotted around: a daring red, rich gold, vibrant silver, pinks and rich brocades.

Daisy was glad of the cosy-looking love seats and chaises scattered about. So much choice was making her head whirl.

'Champagne?' Nina, the department manager who had been dressing the city's brides for nearly forty years, came over with a bottle of Dom Perignon, chilled and opened.

'No, thanks.' Daisy thought rapidly. 'I want a clear head. There's so much choice.'

'A large glass for me, please.' Violet walked in, slightly out of breath. 'I sense it's going to be a long afternoon. Rose says hi, don't make her wear frills and definitely not shiny satin.'

'They're all so beautiful.' Their mother was already halfway down a glass of champagne, a wistful look in her eyes as she fingered the heavy silks, slippery satins and intricate laces. 'Obviously I wouldn't have changed my wedding to your father for the world. It was very romantic, just us, in a tiny chapel. I was barefoot with flowers in my hair. But I did miss out on all this…' Her gaze encompassed the room. 'Which is why, Daisy darling, I am determined that no matter how whirlwind your wedding, no matter how little time we have, you are going to have the day you always dreamed of.'

CHAPTER SIX

'YOU LOOK TERRIBLE. What's wrong?'

Daisy, Seb had discovered in the week they had been living together, was just like him—an early bird. She usually appeared in the kitchen just a few moments after he did, already dressed, ready to moan about the lack of caffeine in her day while hopefully trying yet another of the seemingly endless array of herbal teas she had brought with her, hoping to discover the one to replace her beloved lattes.

Today she was dressed as usual, if a little more demure, in a grey skater-style dress with an embroidered yellow hem, a yellow knitted cap pulled back over her head. But there was no exaggerated groaning when she saw his coffee, no diving on the toast as if she hadn't eaten in at least a month. Instead she pulled out a chair and collapsed into it with a moan.

'Why, why, why did I agree to start work at nine?' She looked at the clock on the wall and slid further down her seat. 'It's going to take me well over an hour to get there. I'll need to set off in ten minutes.'

'Toast?' Seb pushed the plate towards her but she pushed it back with an exaggerated shudder.

'No, it's far too early for food.'

She hadn't said that yesterday at a very similar time. Between them they had demolished an entire loaf of bread.

'Is that a new brand of coffee?' Daisy was looking at his cup of coffee as if he had filled it with slurry from the cow sheds, her nose wrinkled in disgust.

'Nope, the usual.'

'It smells vile.'

Seb took another look. She was unusually pale, the violet shadows under her eyes pronounced despite powder, the bright lipstick a startling contrast to her pallor. 'Didn't you sleep well?'

'I could have slept for ever.' She sniffed again and went even paler. 'Are you sure that's the usual brand? Have you made it extra strong?' She pressed her hand to her stomach and winced.

'You look really ill. I think you should go back to bed.'

'I can't.' The wail was plaintive. 'I have a wedding to photograph. I'm due at the bride's house at nine for the family breakfast followed by the arrival of the bridesmaids and getting ready. I need to be at the groom's at half eleven for best man and ushers then back to the bride's for final departures, church at one and then the reception.'

'With a blog up by midnight and the first pictures available the next day?' His mouth folded into a thin line. It was a ridiculous schedule.

'That's what they pay me for.'

'There is no way you are going to be able to manage an eighteen-hour day on no breakfast.'

Daisy pushed her chair back and swayed, putting a hand onto the table to steady herself. 'I don't have any choice. I work for myself, Seb. I can't just call in sick. Besides, I'm not ill, I'm pregnant. This is self-inflicted, like a hangover. I just have to deal with it.'

'It's nothing like a hangover.' He stopped as she winced, a hand to her head. 'You need an assistant.'

'Possibly, but unless you can produce one out of one of the trunks in the attic that's not going to help with today.'

Seb regarded her helplessly. He wanted to march her back upstairs, tuck her in and make her soup. He was responsible for the slight green tinge to her skin and the shadows under her eyes.

But she was right, if she cried off a wedding on the day her reputation would be shattered. 'Can anyone cover for you?'

'Seb, this is morning sickness not a twenty-four-hour bug.' Her voice rose in exasperation. 'It could last for days, or weeks, or even months. What about Monday's engagement shoot? Or next Saturday's wedding? Or the baby photos on Wednesday? I can't just walk away from all my responsibilities.'

'No, but you can plan ahead.'

'But none of this *was* planned. Don't treat me like I'm some fluffy little girl without a brain cell.'

Woah, where had that come from?

'I didn't mean to offend you.' He knew he sounded stiff but this: histrionics, overreacting, unreasonable responses to reasonable points. It was everything he didn't want in his life.

To his surprise Daisy let out a huge sigh and slumped. 'I'm sorry, I am just so tired. You're right, I do need to start planning how I am going to cover my commitments over the next year.'

It was over, just like that. No escalation, no screaming, no smashing of crockery. Just an apology.

'I could have phrased it better.' It wasn't as full an apology as hers but it was all he could manage in his shock.

'I have been meaning to talk to Sophie. She was on my course and specialises in portraits, personal commissions mostly although she's been beginning to get some magazine work. Her studio rent was just doubled and now I'm not living in mine I thought we might join forces and she could cover weddings for me in lieu of rent, or at least give me a hand. But that doesn't solve today.'

No. It didn't.

Daisy took one dragging step towards the door and then another. Her laptop case, camera case and tripod were neatly piled up, waiting. How she was going to carry them he had no idea.

And she really needed to eat something.

'I'll come with you and help.'

She half turned, the first flicker of a smile on her face. 'You? Do you know when to use a fifty-millimetre, an eighty-five-millimetre or switch to a wide-angled lens?'

'No, I can barely use the camera on my phone,' Seb admitted. 'But I can fetch, carry, set up, organise groups, make sure you eat.'

A flicker of hope passed over her face. 'Don't you have a million and one things to do here?'

'Always.' Seb grimaced as he remembered the unfinished grant applications, the paperwork that seemed to grow bigger the more he did. Not to mention his real work, the research that seemed more and more impossible every day. The looming deadline for a book still in note form. 'Promise me you'll chat to Sophie tomorrow and at least sort out a willing apprentice for next week and I'll come and help.'

She was tempted, he could see. 'You really don't mind?'

'No, not at all. On the condition I drive and you try and eat something in the car.' The grant applications could wait, the paperwork could wait. He'd be worrying all day if he allowed her to walk out of the door and start a gruelling day on her feet without someone to watch out for her.

The sooner she got an assistant or partner, the better.

There were times when Seb wondered if all that sassy style and confidence was only skin deep. When he thought he saw a flash of vulnerability in the blue eyes. But not here. Not today.

If Daisy still felt sick she was hiding it well. She was all quiet control and ease as she snapped: candid shots, posed shots, detailed close-ups. Always polite, always professional but in complete control, whether it was putting the nervy mother of the bride at her ease or settling the exuberant best man and ushers down enough to take a series of carefully choreographed shots.

She was everywhere and yet she was totally discreet. Focused on the job at hand. Seb followed her with bags and the box of ginger biscuits, completely out of place in this world of flowers and silks and tears.

Even the groom had had tears in his eyes as the bride had finally—an entire twenty minutes late—walked down the aisle.

As for the mother of the bride, five tissues hadn't been enough to staunch her sobs. The whole thing was a hysterical nightmare. Leaving the church had been a huge relief and he had gulped in air like a drowning man.

But the ordeal wasn't over.

'I don't understand what else there is for you to do.' Daisy had directed him towards a woodland nearby and Seb was following her down the chipping-strewn path. 'You must have taken at least three hundred pictures already. How many group shots outside the church? His family, her family, his friends, her friends, his colleagues, her colleagues. The neighbours, passers-by…'

'Far more than three hundred.' She threw him a mischievous smile. 'Bored?'

'It just takes so long. No photos at our wedding, Daisy. Not like this.'

'No.' The smile was gone. 'But ours is different. We don't need to document every moment.'

'Just the obvious ones.' Perversely he was annoyed

she wasn't trying to talk him round. 'It would seem odd otherwise.'

'If you want.' She chewed her bottom lip as she looked at him thoughtfully. 'I think I'm going to change the order a little bit as you are here. If I put you in charge of the photo booth then there is some entertainment for the guests while I do the couple's portraits in the woods. Is that okay?'

Seb blinked. He was here to carry bags, not perform. 'The what? Do I have to do anything?'

'Smile. Tell them to say cheese. Press a button, four times. Can you manage that?'

Possibly. 'What do you mean by photo booth? Like a passport photo? At a wedding?'

She shot him an amused look. 'In a way, you know, teenagers sit in a photo booth and take silly pictures—or at least they did before selfies became ubiquitous.'

He shook his head. 'No, never did it. I've never taken a selfie either.'

Her mouth tilted into a smile. 'That doesn't surprise me. But you know what I mean? This is the same, only with props. And not a booth, just me with a camera—or in this case you. They put on silly accessories and then stand in front of a frame and try different poses. I print them up as a long strip of four pictures.'

Seb stared at her incredulously. 'Why on earth do you do that?'

'Because it's fun.' She rolled her eyes at him. 'I'll set the tripod up. All you need to do is explain they have three seconds to change pose and press the button. Honestly, Seb, it's fine. A monkey could do it.'

'And where will you be?'

'Portrait time. Followed by more group shots. And then candid evening and reception shots. Having fun yet?'

'Absolutely. The thought of wandering around these woods for hours carrying your cases is my idea of a perfect day. Sure you know where you're going?' They seemed to be going further into the woodland with no building in sight.

'Yep, I did the engagement shoot here. Ah, here we go.' She stopped, a hand to her mouth. 'Oh, Seb. Look at it. Isn't it utterly perfect?'

Seb came to a halt and stared. Where was the hotel? Or barn? A barn would be nice and cosy. Cosier than open canvas at least. 'They must be crazy? An outdoor wedding in April?'

'It's not outdoors!'

'It's in a tent.'

'It's a tepee.'

'You say tent, I say tepee.'

Daisy ignored him as he hummed the words, a chill running through him as the next line of the song ran through his head.

There was no calling the whole thing off now, not easily. It had escalated far beyond his wildest imaginings: a guest list of over two hundred not including the evening guests, dresses, button holes, hog roasts, centrepieces, cravats— Sherry's determination and vision taking it to a level neither Seb nor Daisy had wanted or sanctioned.

Did he want to call it off? He still wanted to marry Daisy; it was still the most sensible solution. But this circus his life was becoming was out of control. His peaceful Oxford existence seemed further and further away.

Although that wasn't Daisy's fault. Running Hawksley was more than a full-time job and not one he was finding it easy to delegate no matter how much he missed his old life.

'Oh, that's perfect.' Daisy's voice broke in on his thoughts and he pushed them to one side. He couldn't change anything—including the wedding. He owed her that much.

Daisy was lost in a world of her own. It was fascinating to watch her pace, focus, move again as she looked at the scene before her, crouching down to check angles and squinting against the light. No insouciance, no hesitation, just quietly in control.

Seb moved with her, trying to see with her, picture what she pictured. The path opened out into a woodland glade, which had been decorated with cheerful bunting and swaying glass lanterns. In the middle of the glade the huge canvas tepee stood opened up on three sides to the elements—although Daisy promised there were covers ready to be fastened on if April proved true to its name and christened the wedding with showers.

A wooden floor had been laid and trestle tables and benches ran down the sides, the middle left bare for dancing. A stage held the tables covered with food for the buffet; later food would be switched for the band. Two smaller tents were pitched to one side, one holding the bar and the other a chill-out area complete with beanbags.

On the other side a gazebo was pitched, the table inside heaped with a variety of wigs, hats, waistcoats and other props. A large frame hung from the tree beside it. This was to be Seb's workspace for his first—and hopefully last—foray into professional photography.

He had never been to a wedding like this before and something about its raw honesty unsettled him; it was a little Bohemian, a touch homespun with its carefully carefree vibe.

'Look at these colours. Their friends and family supplied the food in lieu of presents. Don't you think that's lovely? Everyone made something.' Daisy was over at the buffet table, camera out, focusing on a rich-looking salad of vibrant green leaves, red pomegranate seeds and juicy oranges.

'It depends on their cooking skills.' If Seb asked his

friends and colleagues to bring a dish they would buy something from a local deli, not spend time and love creating it themselves. He looked at a plate of slightly lumpy cakes, the icing uneven, and a hollow feeling opened up in his chest.

Someone had lavished care and attention on those cakes, making up with enthusiasm for what they lacked in skill. That was worth more than clicking on an item on a wedding list or writing a cheque.

Daisy looked up at a rustle and relaxed again as a bird rose out of a tree. 'Tell me as soon as you hear anybody. I want to capture their faces as they walk in.' The guests were being brought to the woodland by coach via a drinks reception at the local pub, the place where the bride and groom had first met.

'Shouldn't you be sitting down and maybe eating something while there's a lull?' But she didn't hear him, lost in a world of her own.

'Look, Seb,' she said softly, and he did, trying to see what she saw as she zoomed in on the brightly patterned bunting that bedecked the inside of the tent as well as the glade.

'These are the touches that make this wedding so special. Did you know that Ella and her friends made the bunting during her hen party? And look at these.' The camera moved to focus in on one of the paintings propped up on the small easels that were the centrepiece on each table. 'Rufus painted these, a different tree for each table—oak, laurel, ash, apple, all native species. Aren't they gorgeous?'

Studying one of the confident line drawings, Seb had to admit that they were. 'He's very talented.'

'Even the wedding favours are home-made. Ella spent her first day off work making the fudge, and her gran embroidered the bags. Look, they all have a name on. One for each guest.'

'It must have taken months.' Seb kept pace with her as she wandered.

'It did. This wedding is a real labour of love. Even the venue belongs to one of their friends.'

The contrast with their impending nuptials couldn't be starker.

But theirs wasn't a labour of love. It was a convenient compromise. Mutually beneficial. Maybe it was better to have the glitz and the glamour so lovingly lavished upon them by Sherry Huntingdon. Anything as heartfelt as this wedding, any one of the myriad tiny, loving, personal touches would be completely out of place at his wedding. Would be a lie.

'Admit it, you had fun.' Daisy threw herself into her favourite rocking chair, grateful for the warmth and the cushion supporting her aching back. She crooned to Monty as he padded over to lay his head in her lap. He was already her most faithful friend much to Seb's much-voiced disgust, possibly because she was not averse to sneaking him titbits from her plate.

'I'm not sure fun is the right word.' Seb filled the kettle and stifled a yawn. 'I always said your schedule was crazy but it's more than that, it's downright gruelling.' But there was respect in his voice and it warmed her. She was well aware of his opinion about her job.

And he was right, it *was* gruelling, somehow even more so in a small intimate setting like today's woodland scene. Gruelling and odd, being part of someone's wedding, integral to it and yet not connected. A stranger. As the afternoon faded to evening and the guests drank more, ate more, danced and the mood shifted into party atmosphere the gap between the help and the guests widened. There were times it was almost voyeuristic watching the interactions from the sidelines. It had been nice to have company today.

She really should get an assistant and not just because of her pregnancy.

'I would normally be the first to suggest you rest but don't you have a blog to write? If it's not up before midnight the world shifts on its axis and Cupid dies?' He held up a ginger teabag for her approval. Daisy considered it without enthusiasm before pulling a face and agreeing.

She shifted in the chair, pulling her feet under her, and began to pull at Monty's long, soft ears. He gave a small throaty groan and moved closer. 'Did it in the car. It's amazing, home before midnight and job done, for today at least.'

She looked over at her bag, the cameras loaded with images. 'Tomorrow however is most definitely another day. I promised them thirty images before they go away on honeymoon. Still, I feel much better than I thought I would. I don't suppose you would consider a permanent career as bag carrier and chauffeur—and photo-booth operator?' She smiled, a sly note creeping into her voice. 'You were quite a hit. Some of the women went back to have their photo taken again and again.'

'How do you know? I still can't believe it took an hour and a half to take those woodland shots. I think you went for a nap somewhere leaving me to do all the work.'

'Oh, I was. Curled up in a pile of leaves like Hansel and Gretel while woodland birds sang me to sleep and squirrels brought me nuts. And I know because the sexy photographer was quite the topic of conversation—and I don't think they meant me!'

'Jealous?'

Daisy didn't answer for a moment, focusing all her attention on Monty as she scratched behind his ears, the spaniel leaning against her blissfully. 'A little, actually.'

She still couldn't look at him as she chose her next words carefully. 'There was a little bit of me that wanted to tell them that you weren't available, that you were mine.' She looked up.

Seb froze, his eyes fixed on her.

The blood was pounding hard in her ears, like a river in full flood. What had she said that for? Not even married and already she was pushing too hard, wanting too much. 'Which is silly because you're not,' she back-pedalled, desperately wanting to make light of the words. 'Maybe it's pregnancy hormones not wanting my baby's hunter gatherer to shack up in someone else's cave.' She made herself hold his gaze, made herself smile although it felt unnatural.

'I have no intention of shacking up in anyone's cave.' She winced at the horror in his voice and his face softened. 'I promised you, Daisy, I promised you that if you married me I would be in this completely.' He paused and she held her breath, waiting for the inevitable caveat. 'As much as I can be.' There it was. Known, expected. Yet it still hurt.

And she didn't want to dwell on why. Maybe she was beginning to believe their fantasy a little too much, fool that she was.

'But there will be nobody else, you have no reason to worry on that score.'

'Thank you.' She exhaled, a low painful breath. 'It's just difficult, the difference between the public and the private. I know I asked you to pretend but I admit I didn't realise it would be so hard.'

'Why?' He hadn't moved.

'Why what?'

'Why are we pretending? Why don't you want to be honest?'

Her eyes flickered back to Monty and she focused

on the fuzzy top of his head, drawing each ear lovingly through her hands, trying to think of a way to explain that wouldn't make her sound too pathetic. 'It's a bit of a family joke, that I'm always falling in and out of love, that I'm a hopeless romantic. Even when I was a little girl I knew that I wanted to get married, to have children. But I wanted more than just settling down. I wanted what Mum and Dad have.'

'They're one in a million, Daisy.' Ouch, there it was. Pity.

'Maybe, but I know it's possible. It's not that they wouldn't understand us marrying for the baby, wouldn't be supportive. But they'd know I was giving up on my dream. I don't want to do that to them.' She paused then looked straight at him. 'As well as to myself.

'All my parents want is for me to be happy. They don't ask for anything more than that. When I was photographed and expelled they were disappointed, of course they were, although they didn't yell or punish me—but they weren't surprised either. They knew I'd mess up, somehow. And now I've messed up again. I was so determined to do it right, to show them I could cope on my own.'

'I think you are being hard on yourself—and on them,' he added unexpectedly. 'They adore you. Do you know how lucky you are to have that? People who care about you? Who only want you to be happy?'

All Daisy could do was stare at him in shock. 'I…' she began but he cut her off.

'I agree, lying to your family is wrong and I wish I had never agreed—but do you know what I fear? That you're right, that if you tell them the truth then they will stop you, they will show you that with a family like yours there is no way in hell you have to shackle yourself to me, that you and the baby will be fine, that you won't need me.'

'No, you're the baby's father and nothing will change

that. Of course the baby will need you.' There was so much she didn't know, so much that she feared—but of this she was convinced.

She could need him too. If she allowed herself. Today had been almost perfect: help, support, wordless communication. But she knew it was a one-off. She had to train herself to enjoy these days when they came—and to never expect them.

'I hope so.' His smile was crooked. 'As for the rest, Daisy, you messed up at sixteen. Big deal. At least you learned from it, got on with your life, made something of yourself. You're not the only member of your family—or mine—to have dominated the headlines. Both your sisters spent their time on the front covers and they were older than you.'

'I know.' Could she admit it to him? The guilt she never allowed herself to articulate to anyone? Not even herself. 'But Violet was set up. Horribly and cruelly and callously set up and betrayed—and I don't think it is a coincidence that it wasn't long after everything that happened to me. I often wondered.' She paused. 'I think it was because of me. I had dropped out of the headlines so they went after my sister. And they destroyed her.'

'It's because of who your parents are, simple as that. You're all wealthy and beautiful.' A shiver went through her at the desire in his eyes as he said the last word. 'You're connected. People love that stuff. That's why we have to be careful, not a breath of scandal. Or they'll never leave us alone.'

Daisy knew how deadly publicity could be, had experienced the painful sting firsthand, watched one sister flee the country and the other hide herself away. Had done her best to stay under the parapet for the last eight years. But she didn't have the visceral fear Seb had.

He was right, they couldn't allow their child to grow

up under the same cloud. Which meant she had to stick to their agreement. A civilised, businesslike, emotion-free marriage. She had to grow up.

'What are you thinking, Daisy?' His voice was low and the green eyes so dark they were almost black.

'That you're right. That I can do this.'

His mouth quirked into that devastating half smile and Daisy's breath hitched. 'Marriage is going to be a lot easier than I imagined if you're going to keep on thinking I'm right.'

Her chin tilted. 'This is a one-off, not carte blanche.'

His slow grin was a challenge. 'Just how right am I?'

'What do you mean?' But she knew. She knew by the way it was suddenly hard to get her breath. She knew by the way his voice had thickened. She knew by the way his eyes were fixed on hers. She knew by the heat swirling in her stomach, the anticipation fizzing along her skin.

She knew because they had been here before.

The memory of that night was impressed on each and every nerve ending and they heated up in anticipation, the knowledge of every kiss, every touch imprinted there, wanting, needing a replay.

'How in are you, Daisy?' His meaning was unmistakeable.

The heat was swirling round her entire body, a haze of need making it hard to think. They were going to get married, were going to raise a child, make a life together. They had every right to take that final step. Every need.

So he didn't love her? That hadn't mattered before, had it? A mutual attraction combined with champagne and the bittersweet comedown she always experienced after a wedding had been enough.

And it wasn't as if she were foolish enough to go falling in love with someone after just one week, someone who made it very, very clear that love was always going to be a step too far.

He didn't love her. But he wanted her. The rigidity of his pose, his hands curled into loose fists, the intensity of his gaze told her that. Every instinct told her that.

And, oh, she wanted him. She had tried to fight it, hide it, but she did. The line of his jaw, the way he held his hands, the dark hair brushed carelessly back, the amused glint that lit up the green eyes and softened the austere features.

The way each accidental touch burned through her, every look shot through to her core.

And, dear God, his mouth. Her eyes moved there and lingered. Well cut, firm, capable. She wanted to lick her way along the jaw, kiss the pulse in his neck and move up to nibble her way along his lips. She wanted to taste him. For him to taste her. To consume her.

The heat intensified, burning as her breasts ached and the pull in her body made the distance, any distance unbearable.

There was nothing to stop her. They were going to be married. It was practically her right to touch him. To be touched.

It was definitely her right to kiss him.

And just because she had been fixated on romance in the past didn't mean she had to be in the future. After all, look how quickly she tumbled out of love, disillusioned and disappointed.

There was a lot to be said for a businesslike, respectful marriage. Especially marriage with benefits.

She swallowed, desperate for moisture.

'Daisy?' It was more of a command than a question and she was tired. Tired of fighting the attraction that burned between them, tired of being afraid to take it on.

She stood up, slowly, allowing her body to stretch out,

knowing how his eyes lingered on her legs, up her body, rested on her breasts sharply outlined by her stretch. She saw him swallow.

'I'm going to bed,' she said, turning towards the door. She paused, looked back. 'Joining me?'

CHAPTER SEVEN

THE CUP TILTED as Seb nudged Daisy's door open and he hastily righted it before the lurid green mixture slopped onto the threadbare but valuable nineteenth-century runner. The tea was supposed to be completely natural but he'd never seen anything that resembled that particular green in nature.

He didn't wait for an answer but opened the door. 'Daisy? Tea.'

Luckily the nausea of last week had yet to grow into anything more debilitating but Daisy still found the first hour of the day difficult. A cup of something hot helped although replacing her beloved caffeine was still proving problematic. She was going to run out of new flavours of herbal tea to try soon.

'I'm in the bath.' A splashing sound proved her words.

'I'll just leave it here.' Seb tried to put the image of long, bubble-covered limbs and bare, wet torsos out of his mind as he placed the tea onto the small table by her window. He didn't have time for distractions, especially naked ones.

He turned and took in the bedroom properly. He hadn't set foot in here since Daisy had moved in two weeks ago. It had been the first suite tackled by her mother and, although the nineteen-fifties chintz flowery wallpaper still covered the walls, the furniture was still the heavy, stately mahogany and the carpet as threadbare as the landing's, the paintwork was fresh and white and the room smelled of a fresh mixture of beeswax, fresh air and Daisy's own light floral scent.

It wasn't just the aesthetic changes though. Daisy had somehow taken the room and made it hers from the scarves draped over the bedposts to the hat stand, commandeered from the hallway and now filled with a growing selection of her collection. Every time she went back to her studio she brought a few more. There were times when Seb feared the entire castle would be overtaken by hats.

Pictures of her parents and sisters were on one bedside table, a tower of stacked-up paperbacks on the second. A brief perusal showed an eclectic mix of nineteen-thirties detective novels, romances, two of last year's Booker Prize shortlist and a popular history book on Prince Rupert by one of Seb's colleagues and rivals.

Jealousy, as unwanted as it was sharp, shot through him. She did read history, just not his books it seemed.

'Get over yourself, Beresford,' he muttered, half amused, half alarmed by the instant reaction. It was professional jealousy sure, but still unwarranted. Unwanted.

A brief peek into the dressing room showed a similar colonisation. The dressing table bestrewn with pots and tubes, photos of herself and her sisters and friends he had yet to meet tucked into the mirror. The study was a little more austere, her laptop set up at the desk, her diary, open and filled with her scrawling handwriting, next to it.

Hawksley Castle had a new mistress.

Only the bed looked unrumpled. Daisy might bathe, dress and work in her rooms but she slept in his. Much as her nineteenth-century counterpart might have done she arrived in his bed cleansed, moisturised and already in the silky shorts and vest tops she liked to sleep in. Not a single personal item had migrated through the connecting door.

A buzz in his pocket signalled a message or a voice-mail. It was almost impossible to get a decent mobile signal this side of the castle. Seb quite liked not being wired in twenty-four hours a day.

He pulled his phone out and listened to the message, wincing as he did so.

'Problems?' Daisy appeared at the bathroom door clad in nothing but a towel.

'My agent.' He stuffed the phone back into his pocket, glancing at Daisy as he did so.

He drew in a long, deep breath. It was impossible to ignore the twinge of desire evoked by her creamy shoulders, the outline of her body swathed in the long creamy towel.

The towels were another of Sherry's luxurious little additions to the house. By the date of the wedding Hawksley would resemble a five-star hotel more than a run-down if stately family home.

There were fresh flowers, renewed every other day, in all the repainted, cleaned bedrooms as well as in the bigger salons and hallways. Every bathroom, cloakroom and loo was ornamented with expensive soaps, hand creams and bath salts. In one way the luxurious touches hid the signs of elegant decay, but Seb couldn't help calculate how the price of the flowers alone could be better spent on plumbing, on the roof, on the myriad neglected maintenance jobs that multiplied daily.

No matter. Seb would give Sherry her head until the wedding but after that, no more. He wouldn't accept a penny, not even from his bride-to-be's indulgent and very wealthy parents. Hawksley was his inheritance, his responsibility, his burden.

'What did she want on a Saturday?' Daisy sat herself at her dressing table and began to brush out her hair. Seb's eyes followed the brush as it fought its way through the tangled locks leaving smooth tresses in its wake.

'Just to finalise arrangements for this afternoon.' And to try and start another conversation about a television deal. He would shut that down pretty fast although the numbers must be good to make her this persistent.

'This afternoon?'

'I'm lecturing. Didn't I mention it? Talking of which…' He looked at his watch, blinking as he caught the time. 'What are you still doing sat in a towel? Shouldn't you be capturing a bride's breakfast? Or is this one a late-rising bride?'

She shook her head, the newly brushed hair lifting with the movement. 'I have the whole weekend off. Sophie's covering today's wedding for me as a trial. They didn't have the full engagement-shot package so I don't have a personal relationship with them. It seemed like a good place for her to try and see how it works. I do have a few interviews tomorrow with possible assistants but today I am completely free.' She pulled a face. 'That can't be right, can it? Whatever will I do?'

Seb looked at her critically. She still looked drawn and tired. 'You could do with a day off. Between wedding planning and work you never seem to stop.'

'Says the man who put in sixteen hours on the estate yesterday and still wanted to do research when he came home.'

'Technically I am on a research year, not an estate management year.' The ever-present fear crowded in. Could he do both? What if he had to give up his professorship? Swap academia for farming? He pushed it aside. That was a worry for another day.

'Besides, I'm not turning greener than that drink of yours every morning and growing another human being.

Why don't you book yourself into a spa or have a day shopping?'

She wrinkled her nose. 'Are those the only relaxing pursuits you can think of? I can't do most spa treatments and the last thing I want to do is shop, not after motherzilla of the bride's efforts.'

Sherry had been keeping Daisy hard at it. Seb had barely seen her all week. She was either holed up in the Great Hall creating wedding favours, shopping for last-minute essential details or back in her studio, working.

Things would be much easier if she had a studio here. Would she want that? Moving her hats across was one thing, moving her professional persona another. Seb adored his library but there were times when he missed his college rooms with an almost physical pain. The peace, the lack of responsibility beyond his work, his students,

'My lecture's in Oxford. I doubt that would be relaxing or interesting. But maybe you could walk around some of the colleges, have lunch there.' His eyes flickered over to the book by her bed. 'Or you could come to the lecture.'

The blurring of professional and private had to happen at some point.

'What's the lecture on?'

'The history of England as reflected in a house like Hawksley.' His mouth twisted. 'It's the subject of my next book, luckily. It's hard enough finding time to work as it is, at least I'm on site. It's a paid popular lecture so not too highbrow. You might enjoy it.'

He could have kicked himself as soon as he uttered the words. Her face was emotionless but her eyes clouded. 'Not too highbrow? So even dullards like me have a chance of understanding it?'

'Daisy, there's nothing dull about you. Will you come? I'll take you out for dinner afterwards.'

There it was, more blurring. But he had promised respect and friendship. That was all this was.

'Well, if there's food.' But her eyes were still clouded, her face gave nothing away. 'What time do you want to leave? I'll meet you downstairs.'

'What an incredible place. I've never looked around the colleges before.' Daisy focused the lens onto the green rectangle of lawn, the golden columns framing it like a picture.

'Maybe it's because I knew I had no chance of actually coming here.' She clicked and then again, capturing the sun slanting through the columns, lighting up the soft stone in an unearthly glow.

'But you wouldn't have wanted to come here. You went to one of the best art colleges in the country. I doubt that they would have even let me through the door.' Daisy bit back a giggle. She had seen Seb's attempts to draw just once, when he was trying to show Sherry how the marquee connected to the hall. It was good to know there were some areas where she had him beat.

'You could pretend you were creating some kind of post-modern deconstruction of the creative process.' She followed the quadrangle round with her viewfinder. 'This place is ridiculously photogenic. I bet it would make a superb backdrop for wedding photos.'

'It's always about weddings with you, isn't it?' Seb slid a curious glance her way and she tried to keep her face blank. His scrutiny unnerved her. He always made her feel so exposed, as if he could see beyond the lipstick and the hats, beyond the carefully chosen outfits. She hoped not. She wasn't entirely sure that there was any substance underneath her style.

'It's my job.' She kept her voice light. 'You must walk in here and see the history in each and every stone. It's no different.'

He was still studying her intently and she tried not to squirm, swinging the camera around to focus on him. 'Smile!'

But his expression didn't change. It was as if he was trying to see through her, into the heart of her. She took a photo, and then another, playing with the focus and the light.

'Why photography? I would have thought you would have had enough of being on the other side of the lens?'

It was the million-dollar question. She lowered the camera and leant against one of the stone columns. Despite the sunlight dancing on it the stone was cold, the chill travelling through her dress. 'Truth is I didn't mind the attention as a kid,' she admitted, fiddling with her camera strap so she didn't have to look up and see judgement or pity in his eyes. 'We felt special. Mum and Dad were so adored, and there was no scandal, so all the publicity tended to be positive—glamorous red carpets at premieres or at-home photo shoots for charities. It wasn't until I was sixteen that I realised the press could bite as easily as it flattered.'

'Lucky you.' His voice was bleak. 'I was five when I was first bitten.'

She stole a look at him but his gaze was fixed unseeingly elsewhere. Poor little boy, a pawn in his parents' destructive lives. 'It was such a shock when it happened, seeing myself on the front pages. I felt so exposed. I know it wasn't clever.' She traced the brand name on her camera case, remembering, the need for freedom, the urge for excitement, the thrill of the illicit. 'But most sixteen-year-olds play hooky just once, try and get a drink underage somehow just once. They just don't do it under the public's condemning gaze.'

One set of photos, one drunken night, one kiss—the kind of intense kiss that only a sixteen-year-old falling in love could manage—and her reputation had been created, set in stone and destroyed.

'You couldn't have stuck to the local pub?'

He was so practical! She grinned, able to laugh at her youthful self now. 'Looking back, that was the flaw in my plan. But honestly, we were so naive we couldn't think where to go. The village landlord at home would have phoned Dad as soon as I stepped up to the bar. The pubs nearest school seemed to have some kind of convent schoolgirl sensor. We all knew there was no point trying there. Tana and I decided the only way we could be truly anonymous was in the middle of the city. We were spectacularly wrong.'

'Tana?'

'My best friend from school. I was going out with her brother and she was going out with his best mate. Teenage hormones, a bottle of vodka, an on-the-ball paparazzi and the rest is history. I don't even like vodka.'

'So as the camera flashes followed you down the street you thought, I know, I'd like to be on the other side?'

'At least I'm in control when I'm the one taking the photos.' The words hung in the air and she sucked in a breath. That hadn't been what she had intended to say—no matter that it was true.

She shifted her weight and carried on hurriedly. 'After school kicked me out I had no qualifications so I went to the local college where, as long as I took English and maths, I could amuse myself. So I did. I took all the art and craft classes I could. But it was photography I loved the most. I stayed on to do the art foundation course and then applied to St Martin's. When they accepted me it felt as if I had found my place at last.'

That moment when she looked through the viewfinder and focused and the whole world fell away. The clarity when the perfect shot happened after hours of waiting. The happiness she evoked with her pictures, when she took a special moment and documented it for eternity.

A chill ran through her and it wasn't just from the stone. She felt exposed, as if she had allowed him to see, to hear parts of her even her family were locked out of. She pushed off the column, covering her discomfort with brisk movements. 'What about you?' She turned the tables on her interrogator. 'When did you decide you wanted to stand in a lecture theatre and wear tweed?'

'I only wear tweed on special occasions.' That quirk of the mouth of his. It shocked her every time how one small muscle movement could speed her heart up, cause her pulse to start pounding. 'And my cap and gown, of course.'

'Of course.' Daisy tried not to dwell on the disparity in their education. Sure she had a degree, a degree she had worked very hard for, was very proud of. But it was in photography. Her academic qualifications were a little more lacking. She barely had any GCSEs although she had managed to scrape a pass in maths, something a little more respectable in English.

The man next to her had MAs and PhDs and honorary degrees. He had written books that both sold well and were acclaimed for their scholarship. He had students hanging on his every word, colleagues who respected him.

Daisy? She took photos. How could they ever be equal? How could she attend professional events at his side? Make conversation with academics? She would be an embarrassment.

'I don't think anyone grows up wanting to be a lecturer. I thought we already established that I wanted to be an outlaw when I was a child, preferably a highwayman.'

'Of course.' She kicked herself mentally at the repetition. Say something intelligent, at least something different.

'But growing up somewhere like Hawksley, surrounded

by history with literally every step, it was hard not to be enthused. I wanted to take those stories I heard growing up and make them resonate for other people the way they resonated with me. That's what inspires me. The story behind every stone, every picture, every artefact. My period is late medieval. That's where my research lies and what I teach but my books are far more wide ranging.'

'Like the one about Charles II's illegitimate children?' She had actually read his book a couple of years ago on Rose's recommendation. In fact, she'd also read his book on Richard III and his exposé of the myths surrounding Anne Boleyn, the book that had catapulted him into the bestseller lists. But she couldn't think how to tell him without exposing herself. What if he asked for her opinion and her answers exposed just how ignorant she really was?

Or what if he didn't think her capable of forming any opinion at all…?

'Exactly! Those children are actually utterly pivotal to our history. We all know about Henry VIII's desperate search for an heir and how that impacted on the country but Charles' story is much less well known beyond the plague and the fire and Nell Gwyn.' He was pacing now, lit up with enthusiasm. Several tourists stopped to watch, their faces captivated as they listened to him speak.

Daisy snapped him again. Gone was the slightly severe Seb, the stressed, tired Seb. This was a man in total control, a man utterly at home with himself.

'He actually fathered at least seventeen illegitimate children but not one single legitimate child. If he had the whole course of British History might have changed, no Hanoverians, no William of Orange. And of course the influence and wealth still wielded by the descendants of many of those children still permeate British society to this day.'

'Says the earl.'

It was a full-on smile this time, and her stomach tumbled. How had she forgotten the dimple at the corner of his mouth? 'I am fully aware of the irony.'

'Is it personal, your interest? Any chance your own line is descended through the compliant countess?'

'Officially, no. Unofficially, well, there is some familial dispute as to whether we can trace our descendants back to the Norman invasion or whether we are Stuarts. Obviously I always thought the latter, far more of an exciting story for an impressionable boy, the long-lost heir to the throne.'

He began walking along the quad and she followed him, brain whirling. 'A potential Stuart! You could be DNA tested? Although that might throw up some odd results. I wonder how many blue-blooded households actually trace their heritage back to a red-blooded stable boy?'

The glimmer in his eye matched hers. 'Now that would make an interesting piece of research. Not sure I'd get many willing participants though. Maybe the book after this, if I ever get this one finished.'

A book about Hawksley. Such a vivid setting. 'It would make a great TV show.'

'What? Live DNA testing of all the hereditary peers? You have an evil streak.'

'No.' She paused as he turned into a small passageway and began to climb a narrow winding staircase. Daisy looked about her in fascination, at the lead-paned windows and the heavy wooden doors leading off at each landing.

They reached the third landing and he stopped at a door, pulling a key out of his pocket. The discreet sign simply said Beresford. This was his world, even more foreign to her than a castle and a grand estate. Academia, ancient traditions, learning and study and words.

Daisy's breath hitched as he gestured for her to precede him into the room, a rectangular space with huge windows, every available piece of wall space taken up with book-shelves. A comfy and well-loved-looking leather chesterfield sofa was pulled up opposite the hearth and a dining table and six chairs occupied the centre of the room. His surprisingly tidy desk looked out over the quad.

She felt inadequate just standing in here. Out of place. Numb, she tried to grasp for something to say, something other than: 'Have you read all those books?' Or 'Doesn't your desk look tidy?'

She returned gratefully to their interrupted conversation. 'I was talking about Hawksley, of course. It's the answer to all your problems. Just think of the visitor numbers, although you'd have to rethink the ridiculous weekends only between Whitsun and August Bank Holiday opening times.'

'What's the answer?' His face had shuttered as if he knew what she was going to say and was already barricading himself off from it.

'Your book about Hawksley, how you can see England's history in it.'

He walked over to his desk and picked up the pile of letters and small parcels and began leafing through. 'The book I haven't actually written yet.' His tone was dismissive but she rushed on regardless.

'You should do it as a TV series. You would be an amazing presenter. Why aren't you? You're clever, photogenic, interesting. I'm amazed they haven't snapped you up.'

'Good God, Daisy.' There was no mistaking the look in his eyes now. Disgust, horror, revulsion. 'Despite everything you've been through that's your solution...' He paused and then resumed, his voice cutting. 'I suppose once a celebrity offspring, always a celebrity offspring. You don't think they've offered? That I haven't had a chance to sign myself and my life over? Do you know what it would mean, if I went on TV?'

She shook her head, too hurt by his response to speak.

'I'd be open game. For every paparazzi or blogger or

tabloid journalist. They could rake over my life with absolute impunity—and now your life too! Why would I want that? Why would you want that?'

Daisy could feel tears battling to escape and blinked them back. No emotion, that was the deal. And that included hurt. She wouldn't give him the satisfaction of seeing how much his contempt stung. But nor would she let him dismiss her. 'You need to make Hawksley pay and you said yourself land subsidies and a wedding every weekend won't do it. Besides, you write books—popular history books, not dull academic tomes. You don't mind the publicity for those.'

He paused and ran his hands through his hair. 'That's different.'

'Why?'

The question hung there.

She pressed on. 'Your books win prizes, have posters advertising them in bookshops, I've even seen adverts on bus shelters and billboards! You read in public, sign in public, give public lectures. How is that different from a TV series?'

At first she had sounded diffident, unsure of her argument but as she spoke Seb could hear the conviction in her voice. And he had to admit she was making sense. Unwelcome sense but still.

He fixed his eyes on her face, trying to read her. Every day he found out more about her; every day she surprised him. He had thought she was utterly transparent; sweet, a little flaky maybe, desirable sure but not a challenge. But there were hidden depths to Daisy Huntingdon-Cross. Depths he was only just beginning to discover.

'My books are educational.' He cringed inwardly at the pompous words.

She wasn't giving in. 'So is television, done right. More so, you would reach a far bigger audience, teach far more people, inspire more people. I'm not suggesting you pimp yourself on social media—though some historians do and they do it brilliantly. I'm not suggesting reality TV or magazine photoshoots. I'm talking about you, doing what you do anyway.'

Reach more people. Wasn't that his goal? He sighed. 'I didn't plan this.' Seb put down the pile of still-unopened post and wandered over to the window, staring out. 'I didn't think I'd write anything but articles for obscure journals and the kind of books only my peers would read. That's how I started. That's how academic reputations are made.'

'So what changed?'

'I got offered a book deal. It was luck really, an ex-student of mine went into publishing and the editor she was working for wanted a new popular history series. Stacey thought of me and set up a meeting.'

'She wouldn't have thought of you if you hadn't been an inspiring teacher. Not so much luck, more serendipity.' Daisy walked across the room and stood next to him. Without conscious intention he put his hand out and took hers, drawing her in close. Her hand was warm and yielding.

'Maybe.'

'It's just a suggestion, Seb. I know how you feel about courting publicity, I really do. But Dad always says that if you keep your head down and your life clean they'll lose interest. And he's right—just look at my parents. They were wild in their youth, real headline creators just like yours were. The difference is they settled down. They don't sleep around or take drugs or act like divas. They work hard and live quietly—in a crazy, luxurious bubble admittedly! But that's what we've agreed, isn't it? Quiet, discreet lives. If we live like that then there really is nothing to fear.'

Seb inhaled slowly, taking in her calm, reasonable words. Slowly he moved behind her, slipping an arm around her waist to rest on her still-flat stomach. 'They came after you though.' His voice was hoarse.

'We'll just teach the baby not to go out and get drunk in the middle of London when he or she is sixteen. And if it gets my beauty and your brains we should be okay as far as schooling goes.'

'The other way round works just as well. Stop putting yourself down, Daisy. Academic qualifications are meaningless. I think you might be one of the smartest people I know.'

Her hand came down to cover his, a slight tremor in the fingers grasping his. 'That's the nicest thing anyone has ever said to me.'

'I mean it.' The air around them had thickened, the usual smells he associated with his office, paper, leather and old stone, replaced by her light floral scent: sweet with richer undertones just like its wearer. Desire flooded him and he moved his other hand to her waist, caressing the subtle curve as he followed the line down to her hip.

Seb had no idea how this marriage was going to work in many ways but this he had no qualms about. They had been brought together by attraction and so far it continued to burn hot and deep. He leant forward, inhaling her as he ran a tongue over her soft earlobe, biting down gently as she moaned.

The hand covering his tightened and he could feel her breathing speed up. Reluctantly he left her hip, bringing his hand up to push the heavy fall of hair away from her neck so the creamy nape was exposed. She trembled as he moved in close to press a light kiss on her neck, then another, working his way around to the slim shoulder as his hand slid round to her ribs, splaying out until he felt the full underside of her breast underneath his thumb.

Her breaths were coming quicker as she leant against him, arching into his touch, into his kiss, holding on as she turned round to find his mouth with hers. Warm, inviting, intoxicating. 'Are we allowed to do this here?' she murmured against his mouth as he found the zip at the back of her dress and eased it down the line of her back. Her own hands were tugging at his shirt, moving up his back in a teasing, light caress.

'No one will come in,' he promised, slipping the dress from her shoulders, holding in a groan as one hand continued to tease his back, the other sliding round to his chest. 'We have over an hour before the lecture. Of course, I had promised you lunch…'

'Lunch is overrated.' She pressed a kiss to his throat, her tongue darting out to mark the most sensitive spot as her fingers worked on his shirt buttons.

'In that case, my lady—' he held onto her as she undid the final button, pushing his shirt off him with a triumphant smile '—desk, sofa or table?'

Daisy looked up at him, her eyes luminous with desire. 'Over an hour? Let's try for all three.'

Seb swung her warm, pliant body up. 'I was hoping you'd say that. Let's start over here. I think I need to do some very intensive research…'

CHAPTER EIGHT

'You wouldn't think you were publicity-shy, looking at those. My mother would kill to have that kind of exposure—and she doesn't get in front of a camera for less than twenty thousand a day.'

There were five large posters arrayed along the front of the lecture hall, each featuring the same black and white headshot of Seb. Daisy came to a halt and studied them, her head tilted critically. 'Not bad. Did they ask you to convey serious academic with a hint of smoking hot?'

'That was exactly the brief. Why, do you think I look like a serious academic?'

'I think you look smoking hot and—' she eyed the gaggle of giggling girls posing for selfies alongside the furthest poster '—so do they.'

Seb glanced towards the group and quickly turned away so his back was towards them. 'Just because they are a little dressed up doesn't mean they're not interested in the subject matter. They could be going out afterwards.'

'Sure they could.' Daisy patted his arm. 'And when I went to the very dull lectures on Greek vase painting it was because I thought knowing about classical figures on urns would be very helpful to my future career and not because I had a serious crush on the lecturer.'

She sighed. 'Six weeks of just sitting and staring into

those dark brown eyes and visualising our future children. Time very well spent. Of course he was happily married and never even looked twice at me.'

'This is Oxford, Daisy. People come here to learn.'

There was a reproving tone in his voice that hit her harder than she liked, a reminder that this was his world, not hers. 'I didn't say I didn't learn anything. You want to know anything about classical art, I'm your girl.'

'Seb!' Daisy breathed a sigh of relief as a smartly dressed woman came out of the stage door and headed straight for them, breaking up the suddenly fraught conversation. The woman greeted Seb with a kiss on both cheeks. 'I've been looking for you. You're late. How are you?'

Seb returned the embrace then put an arm around Daisy, propelling her forward. 'This is my fiancée, Daisy Huntingdon-Cross. I assume you've got the wedding invite? Daisy, this is Clarissa Winteringham, my agent.'

'So this is your mystery fiancée?' Daisy was aware that she was being well and truly sized up by a pair of shrewd brown eyes. 'Invite received and accepted with thanks. It's nice to meet you, Daisy.'

'Likewise.' Daisy held out her hand and it was folded into a tight grip, the other woman still looking at her intently.

'And what do you do, Daisy?'

Most people would probably have started with *congratulations*. Daisy smiled tightly. 'I'm a photographer.'

'Have you ever thought of writing a book?' The grip was still tight on her hand as Daisy shook her head. 'A photographer who gets propelled into the limelight as a model? Could work well for a young adult audience?'

'I don't think so.' Daisy managed to retrieve her hand. 'Thank you though.'

'I'm sure we could find someone else to write it. You would just need to collaborate on plot and lend your name to it. With *your* parents I'm sure I could get you a good deal.'

Of course Clarissa knew exactly who Daisy was, she wouldn't be much of an agent if she didn't, but it still felt uncomfortable, being so quickly and brutally summed up for her commercial value. 'Seb's the writer in the family and I don't think books about models are really his thing.'

'Shame, cheekbones like yours are wasted behind a camera. We could have done a nice tie-in, maybe a reality TV show. Get in touch if you change your mind. Now, Seb, they're waiting for you inside. Have *you* changed your mind about the BBC offer? You really should call me back when I leave messages.'

So she hadn't been the first person to mention TV? Seb didn't react with the same vehemence he'd shown Daisy earlier when she had made a similar suggestion, just shook his head, smiling, as Clarissa bore him off leaving Daisy to trail behind.

The lecture hall was crammed to capacity, an incongruous mixture of eager-looking students, serious intellectual types and several more groups of girls waving cameras and copies of Seb's latest books; pop culture meeting academia.

Daisy managed to find a seat at the end of a row next to an elderly man who commented loudly to his companion throughout the lecture but, despite the disruptions, the odd camera flashes and the over-enthusiastic laughter from Seb's youthful admirers every time he made any kind of joke, Daisy found that she enjoyed the lecture. Seb's enthusiasm for his subject and engaging manner were infectious.

It was funny how the sometimes diffident man, the private man, came alive in front of an audience, how he held them in the palm of his hand as he took them on a dizzying thousand-year tour of English history using his own family home as a guide. The hour-long talk was over far too quickly.

'He knows his stuff.' The old man turned to Daisy as the hall began to empty. Daisy had been planning to go straight to Seb, but he was surrounded immediately by a congratulatory crowd, including the girls she had seen earlier, all pressing in close, books in hand waiting to be signed.

Seb didn't look as if he minded at all. Hated publicity indeed!

'Yes, he was fascinating, wasn't he?' She'd seen her father perform in front of thousands, seen her mother's face blown up on a giant billboard but had never felt so full of awe. 'He's a great speaker.'

'Interesting theory as well. Do you subscribe to his school of thought on ornamental moats?'

Did she what? About what?

'I...'

'Of course the traditional Marxist interpretation would agree with him, but I wonder if that's too simplistic.'

'Yes, a little.' Daisy's hands were damp; she could feel her hair stick to the back of her neck with fear. *Please don't ask me to do anything but agree with you*, she prayed silently.

'Nevertheless he's a clever man, Beresford. I wonder what he'll do after this sabbatical.'

'Do? Isn't he planning to return here?' Seb hadn't discussed his future plans with her at all; he was far too focused on the castle.

'He says so but I think Harvard might snap him up. It would be a shame to lose him but these young academics can be so impatient, always moving on.'

Daisy sat immobile as the elderly man moved past her, her brain whirling with his words. *Harvard?* Okay, they hadn't discussed much in terms of the future, but surely if Seb was considering moving overseas he'd have mentioned it? She got to her feet, dimly aware that the large hall was emptying rapidly and that Seb was nowhere to be seen.

'There you are, Daisy.' Clarissa glided towards her accompanied by a tall man in his late fifties. 'This is Giles Buchanan, Seb's publisher. Giles, Daisy is Seb's mysterious fiancée. She's a photographer.'

'Creative type, eh? Landscapes or fashion?'

Daisy blinked. 'Er…neither, I photograph weddings.'

'Weddings?' Obviously not the kind of job he expected from Seb's fiancée judging by the look of surprise on his face. Daisy filled in the blanks: too commercial, not intellectual enough.

She'd wanted a chance to look inside Seb's world but now she was here she felt like Alice: too big or too small but either way not right. She stepped out onto the stairs. 'Excuse me, I need some air.'

How on earth was she going to fit in? Say the right things, do the right things, be the right kind of wife? She'd thought being a countess was crazy enough—being the wife of an academic looked like being infinitely worse.

Right now it didn't feel as if there was any chance at all. The gap between them was too wide and she had no idea if she even wanted to bridge it—let alone work out *how* to do it.

'Table decorations, seating plans, favours, flowers, outfits. We've done it all, Vi. There can't be anything left to plan.' Daisy tucked the phone between her ear and her chin as she continued to browse on her laptop. The wedding was feeling less and less real as it got nearer. It was one day, that was all.

And it felt increasingly irrelevant. The real issue was how the marriage was going to work, not whether Great-aunt Beryl was speaking to Great-uncle Stanley or what to feed the vegetarians during the hog roast.

Seb was right. The marriage was the thing. Not that she was going to tell him that, of course.

Less than a week to go. This was it. Was she prepared to spend the foreseeable part of her future with a man who was still in so many ways a complete stranger?

It wasn't that the nights weren't wonderful. Incredible actually. But was sex enough to base a marriage on?

But it wasn't just sex, was it? There was the baby too. The sex was a bonus and she needed to remember that. *Stop being greedy, stop wanting more.*

Seb definitely found her desirable. Had promised to respect her. That was a hell of a lot more than many women had at the start of their marriages. So she wasn't sure where she fitted in his professional life or at Hawksley? They didn't have to live in each other's pockets after all.

She was completely and utterly lucky—and that was before you factored in the fact she would be living in a castle and, improbable as it seemed, would be a countess. She just had to start feeling it and stop clinging onto the shattered remnants of her romantic dreams. Start carving out a place for herself at Hawksley, turn it into a home. Into her home.

If only she could help Seb work out how to make it pay. Other estates managed it, even without an eminent historian occupying the master bedroom...

Her sister's exasperated voice broke in on her thoughts. 'Daisy, Rose isn't getting here until the day of the wedding itself so as the only bridesmaid on the same continent it's down to me. I've hinted, Mum's hinted and you have been no help so I am asking you outright. Hen night. What are you wanting?'

Daisy straightened, the phone nearly falling out of her hand as she registered her sister's words. 'I forgot all about the hen night.'

'Sure you did.' Vi sounded sceptical. 'I've seen your scrapbooks, Daise, remember? And lived through twenty-four years of your birthday treats. You've left it too late for the Barcelona weekend or the spa in Ischia. So spa day near here? Night out clubbing in London? We could manage a night in Paris if we book today. You're cutting it awfully fine though. We should have gone yesterday.'

Daisy managed to interrupt her sister. 'Nothing, honestly, Vi. I'm not expecting anything.'

'Nothing?'

'Nope.'

'This isn't a test?' Vi sounded suspicious. 'Like the time you said you didn't want a birthday treat but we were supposed to know that you wanted us to surprise you with tickets to see Busted?'

'I was twelve!' Violet had to wheel that one out.

'Seriously, Daisy. Mum will be so disappointed. She's planned matching tracksuits with our names spelled out in diamanté.'

'Mother wouldn't be seen dead in matching tracksuits!'

'But she will be disappointed. You'll be telling me you're not going on some exotic honeymoon next!'

Daisy stopped dead. Honeymoon? She hadn't even thought about what would happen after the wedding and Seb hadn't mentioned it.

The Maldives, Venice, a small secluded island in the Caribbean, a chateau in the south of France; the destinations of the brides and grooms she had photographed over the last couple of years floated through her mind.

They all sounded perfect—for a couple in love.

It was probably a good thing they had forgotten all about it. A week or two holed up together would be excruciating. Wouldn't it? 'It's all been so quick, we haven't actually thought about a honeymoon yet.'

There was an incredulous pause. 'No hen night, no honeymoon. Daisy, what's going on?'

Daisy thought rapidly. She couldn't have a hen night. She couldn't be around her friends and family pretending to be crazy in love, she couldn't drink and her abstinence might have escaped their sharp eyes so far but nobody was going to believe that she wasn't going to indulge in at least one glass of champagne on her own hen night.

Her eyes fell on the copy of Seb's birth certificate lying on her desk; she'd put it in her bag after their visit to the register office and forgotten to return it to him. Name: Sebastian Adolphus Charles Beresford. How on earth had the Adolphus slipped past her attention? She hoped it wasn't a family name he'd want for their son.

Her eyes flickered on. Date of birth. April twentieth. Hang on...

Why hadn't he mentioned it? Right now she wasn't going to think about that. Not when salvation was lying right in front of her.

'The problem is, Vi, tomorrow's Seb's birthday and I've planned a surprise. And then it's just a few days before the wedding and I don't want a big night out before then. Besides,' she added with an element of truth, 'it wouldn't feel right without Rose. We can do something afterwards.'

'Wednesday night.' Vi wasn't giving up. 'That gives you two days before the wedding and we can do something small. Just you, me and Mum and Skype Rose in. Films and face masks and manicures at your studio?'

That sounded blissful. Dangerous but blissful. 'Okay. But low-key—and I won't be drinking. I'm on a pre wedding detox. For my skin.' That sounded plausible.

'Done. I'll source the girliest films and organise nibbles. Wholesome, vitamin filled, organic nibbles.'

'Thanks, Vi.' She meant it. An evening in with her mother and sister would be lovely. As long as she kept her guard up.

Meanwhile there was the small matter of Seb's birthday and the surprise she was supposed to be organising. Once she had decided just what the surprise actually was.

* * *

Something was up.

Daisy was going around with a suppressed air of excitement as if she were holding a huge balloon inside that was going to burst any second.

It should have been annoying. Actually it was a little bit endearing.

Seb stretched out in his old leather wingchair, the vibrant red of the curtains catching his eye. Sherry had not received the Keep Out of My Library vibe and his sanctuary was looking as polished and fresh as the rest of the house. It was actually quite nice not to sneeze every time he pulled out a book although he had preferred the curtains unlaundered. They had been less glaringly bright then.

It wasn't just Sherry. Daisy was quietly but firmly making changes as well: painting the kitchen, opening up the morning room and turning it into a cosy sitting room despite using little more than new curtains and cushions and replacing the rather macabre paintings of dead pheasants with some watercolour landscapes she had rescued from the attics. Although they still lived mainly in the kitchen or library, they had begun to spend their evenings in there reading, watching television or playing a long-running but vicious game of Monopoly.

It was almost homely.

But even as the castle began to take shape he was all too aware there still weren't enough hours in the day. It would be much easier if he brought in a professional to manage the estate, leaving Seb to his teaching and research.

It wasn't the Beresford way though. His grandfather had been very clear on that. A good owner managed his land, his people, his family and his home no matter what the sacrifice. And there had been many throughout the long centuries. There were times when Seb wondered if he would ever be able to return to Oxford and his real work.

Yet at the same time the pull of his ancestral home was so strong. He couldn't carry on juggling both the estate and academia but making a final decision was unthinkable.

He looked up at the sound of a soft tap on the door, relieved to take his eyes off the blank laptop screen. He had barely achieved anything yet again, he noted wryly. Worries and thoughts circling round and round; even his research wasn't distracting him the way it usually did. Money, Daisy, the baby, Hawksley, the book. In less than six months his whole life had turned upside down.

Although if he hadn't allowed himself to be so distracted by his career maybe Hawksley at least wouldn't be in such a state. He had his own culpability here.

The door opened and Daisy appeared bearing one of the massive silver tea trays. One mobile brow flew up as she looked at him. 'That's a terrifying scowl. Am I interrupting a crucial moment?'

'You're interrupting nothing but mental flailing and flagellation.' He tried to smile. 'Sorry if I scared you.'

'Mental flagellation? Sounds painful. Anything I can help with?' She carried the tray over to the table in the opposite corner and set it down with an audible thud.

'Not unless you have a time machine.'

Seb regretted the words as soon as he uttered them; he didn't need the flash of hurt to cross her face to show him how ill-judged they were. 'Not you, not the baby.' Not entirely. 'Goodness knows, Daisy, out of all the crazy tangled mess my life has become the baby is the one bright spot. No, I was just thinking if I'd acted sooner then things would be a hell of a lot easier now.'

'How so?'

He pushed his laptop away and sat back in the chair trying to straighten out his skein of thoughts and regrets. 'Kids are selfish, aren't they? I spent my holidays here, school and university—unless my mother was suffering one of her occasional fits of maternal solicitude, but I was so wrapped up in the past I never took an interest in the present. Never saw how Grandfather was struggling, never tried to help.' He suppressed a deep sigh of regret.

'History is all well and good but it's not very practical, is it? Grandfather suggested I go to the local agricultural college and do estate management, come and work here. I brushed him off, convinced I was destined for higher things.'

'You were right.' She was perched on the arm of the old leather chair, legs crossed, and his eyes ran appreciably up the long bare limbs. She was wearing the black tweed shorts, this time teamed with a bright floral shirt and her trademark hat was a cap pulled low over her forehead.

'Was I?' He had been sure then, sure throughout his glittering career. But the past few months had shown just how flawed his ambition had been. 'Hawksley needed new blood, Grandfather was struggling and my father was never going to step in. My grandfather was too proud to ask me directly and I was too busy to notice. But maybe I could have helped him turn things around—and been on the ground to stop my father's gross negligence.'

It was more than negligence. His father's wilful use of estate capital had been criminal.

'How could you have stopped it?'

'The money funding his extravagant lifestyle came from a family trust. It was never intended for private use, certainly not on his scale. Just one look at the accounts would have alerted me.' And he could have stepped in.

'I was far too busy chasing my own kind of fame.' The taste in his mouth was bitter.

She swung her legs down and hopped to her feet. 'Just because he suggested estate management doesn't mean he was desperate for you to live and work here. He was proud of you no matter which path you chose.'

'I wish I believed that.' His mouth twisted. 'I guess we'll never know.'

'I know.' She went over to one of the shelves, pulling a hardback book out. 'This is yours, isn't it? The first one? Look how well read it is, the spine is almost broken. So unless you spend your evenings reading your own words I think your grandparents must have read it. Several times.'

He took the book from her outstretched hands. He had given it to them, signed it and handed it over unsure if they would ever read it. The hardback was battered, corners turned, the pages well thumbed. A swell of pride rose inside him. Maybe they had been proud of his chosen career. He looked over at Daisy. 'Thank you.'

'I knew this library was all for show. If you ever looked at a book you'd have seen it for yourself,' but her eyes were bright and the corners of her full mouth upturned.

'Anyway—' she walked back to the tray '—I have a small bone to pick with you, my Lord. Why didn't you tell me it was your birthday?'

Seb gaped at her in shock. 'How did you know?'

'Incredible detective skills and a handy copy of your birth certificate. In my family birthdays are a very big deal.' She turned with a shy smile, her hands behind her back. 'And I must warn you I have very high expectations for mine, just ask my sisters, so if we are going to be a family—' the colour rose high on her cheeks and her eyes lowered as she said the words '—then your birthday has to be a big deal as well. So. Happy Birthday.'

With a flourish she pulled her arms from behind her back. One held a plate complete with a large cupcake, a lit candle on the top, the other a shiny silver envelope.

He stood, paralysed with surprise. 'What's this?'

'It's a card and cake. These are usual on birthdays.' Her colour was still high but her voice was light. 'You're supposed to blow the candle out.'

He just stood there, unable to move a muscle, to process what she was saying. 'I haven't had a birthday cake since I was ten. I was always at school, you see.'

Her eyes softened. 'The procedure hasn't changed. You blow, the flame goes out, I clap and then we eat it. Simple.'

He made a huge effort to reach out and took the plate of cake, holding it gingerly as if it were a bomb about to explode. The small flame danced before his eyes. He didn't want to blow it out; he wanted to watch it twist and turn for ever. 'And the card?'

'That you open. And then we get changed. I have a surprise for you. And I am quite convinced it is going to blow your socks off.'

CHAPTER NINE

'How did you know that this is my favourite band?' Seb, Daisy was learning, was not a huge one for words. If someone arranged a surprise for Daisy she found it hard to sit back and wait; instead she would be peppering them with questions, trying to guess where they were going, slightly anxious it wasn't going to live up to her own fevered imaginings.

Seb had just looked bemused, as if the concept of a surprise trip was completely alien to him. Which was ridiculous. He might not want high emotions or romance but he'd had girlfriends before—had none of them ever organised a day out? To a special library or a site of special historical significance?

But even his slightly annoying calm and collected manner had disappeared when the taxi pulled into the concert venue.

'Seriously, Daisy. You must be some kind of witch.' His hand sought hers and squeezed, his touch tingling. For a brief moment she allowed herself to fantasise that this was real, that she was on a night out with someone she was mad about, with someone who was mad about her.

'Yes, I am. My spells include listening to the music that people play and reading the labels on CD collections.' She couldn't help it, music had been such a huge part of her childhood she subconsciously noticed whatever music was playing although she didn't play an instrument herself and rarely listened to music for pleasure, preferring silence as she worked.

But Seb liked background noise whether in the kitchen, his study or driving around and when she had been searching the internet, trying to find something to do tonight, the name had jumped out at her—it had been the CD he was playing that very first night. One call to her father later and VIP seats had been procured.

But it had evidently been the perfect gift. Daisy was torn between shame that all she had managed was a last-minute, hastily organised event and a sneaking fear that maybe she knew him better than she had realised, than she wanted to admit.

Knew exactly what would make him happy. That would involve caring. Was that part of their deal?

Seb was evidently not having any deep thoughts or misgivings. It was fun to see him enjoying every moment like a child set free in a toy shop as they were led through the plush VIP area. 'A box? Seriously?'

'You may have the title but I am rock aristocracy and this is how we experience concerts,' she told him as they took their seats. 'If you would prefer to stand on the beer-covered floor with all the other sweaty people then you can. Your wristband allows you access.'

She could tell he was tempted. Daisy had never understood the allure of the mosh pit herself.

'Maybe later. You wouldn't mind?'

She shook her head. 'Knock yourself out.'

He looked around in fascination and Daisy tried to see it through his eyes, not her own jaded viewpoint. They were the only occupants of a box directly opposite the stage. Behind them was a private room complete with bar and cloakroom. The entire row was taken up with similar boxes for celebrities and friends and family of the band; corporates were restricted to the row above. Access to their coveted seats was strictly controlled.

'This is crazy.' Seb was staring at the aging rock star and his much-younger girlfriend enthusiastically making out in the next-door box. Daisy sat back; she hoped the rock star hadn't seen her. She'd been flower girl at his third wedding—and his new girlfriend looked younger than Daisy herself. 'I've been to plenty of events, literary events, historical conferences, Oxford balls but never anything like this.

'But I would have been just as happy on the beer-soaked floor with the other sweaty people,' he said. He meant it too.

'I'm spoiled,' she admitted. 'Dad gets tickets to everything and always took us along. I'd been to more concerts than films by the time I was ten. He drew the line at boy bands though. That's probably why they remain my own guilty pleasure. But I haven't done anything like this for ages.'

'Why not? If I had free access to gigs I'd go to everything!'

He wouldn't. Not with the high price tag. 'I don't usually like to ask for favours. Mum can get me anything, the new must-have bag or coat or dress—but the deal is you get photographed wearing it. If, like me, you want a quiet life then the price for a freebie is far too high. But tickets for this sold out months ago so it was best seats in the house or nothing!'

Daisy crossed her fingers, hoping that they weren't papped while they were here. There were far more gossip-worthy couples out in force; hopefully the spotlight would be far from them.

'Well, if we must sit in luxury while free drinks and

food are pressed on us then I suppose we must. Seriously, Daisy. Thank you. This is incredibly thoughtful.'

Daisy shifted uncomfortably, guilt clamping her stomach. Not so much thoughtful as expedient. She hurriedly changed the subject. 'I'm going to spend Wednesday night at the studio. Vi was insistent that I have some kind of hen night. Obviously I didn't want anything big so it's going to be a family-only films and pampering night. I've told her I'm not drinking for the sake of my skin. I must be more of a demanding bride than I realised. She completely bought it. I might stay there Thursday night too. It's meant to be bad luck to spend the night before together.'

'I guess we need all the luck we can get.' His voice was dry.

'Are you going to have a stag night?'

The shock on his face was almost comical. 'It hadn't even occurred to me! Maybe I should go to the local pub for a couple of drinks—just to add convincing detail to the wedding.'

'What a method actor you are.' But the rest of her conversation with Violet was running through her mind. 'Vi also asked about the honeymoon.'

Seb froze; she could see his knuckles turn white and hurried on. 'I said that we were planning something later on and were too busy right now. I don't think she's wholly convinced but when I tell them about the baby I'm sure they'll forget all about whether we did or did not go away.'

'Do you want a honeymoon?'

To her horror Daisy felt her mouth quiver. She gulped down an unexpected sob as it tried to force its way out. She had told herself so many times that she was at peace with her decision, that she was almost happy with her situation—and then she'd be derailed and have to start convincing herself all over again. 'Of course not.' She could hear the shakiness of her voice. 'I think we're doing brilliantly under the circumstances but a honeymoon might be a bit too much pressure.'

'Are you sure?'

She nodded, hoping he wasn't looking too closely. That he didn't see the suspicious shine in her eyes as she blinked back tears. 'Besides, I'm pregnant. No cocktails on the beach or exotic climates for me.'

'Is that what you would want?'

Yes. Of course it was. That was what people did, wasn't it? Flew to beautiful islands and drank rum and snorkelled in the sun, making love all night in a tangle of white sheets on mahogany beds.

Lovely in theory. Would the reality live up? 'Actually, I think I would want something a little less clichéd. Amazing scenery I could photograph, good food. History. The Alps maybe, Greece, the Italian coast.'

'A friend of mine has a villa on Lake Garda, right on the water's edge. I could see if it's free?'

For one moment she wavered. The Italian lakes. A private villa overlooking the lake sounded sublime. But they would still be pretending and without their work, without the routine of their everyday lives, how would they manage? 'No.' Her voice was stronger. 'Honestly. I'm absolutely fine.'

To her relief as she said the words the lights went down and Seb leaned forward, all his attention on the stage in front, leaving Daisy free to imagine a different kind of honeymoon. One where both parties wanted to be there, were so wrapped up in each other that they didn't need anyone or anything else. The kind of honeymoon she had always dreamed of and now knew she would never have.

It just wasn't adding up.

The Georgian part of the castle needed a new roof, ideally rewiring and, with the baby due before Christmas,

Seb really should sort out some of the ancient plumbing problems as well.

The work he had been doing on the estate land was already paying dividends and the farms and forests were looking healthy. It was just the castle.

Just. Just one thousand years of history, family pride and heritage. No big deal.

Seb tried to avoid his grandfather's eye, staring balefully out of a portrait on the far wall. He knew how much his grandfather had hated the idea of using the castle for profit—but surely he would have hated it falling around his ears much more.

But how far could Seb go? He was allowing a location agency to put the castle on their books, ready to hire it out for films and TV sets. It felt like a momentous step.

But not a big enough one.

Meanwhile there was the book to finish researching— and he was already halfway through his sabbatical. Just returning to Oxford for a day had reminded him how time consuming his teaching and administrative duties were.

Something was going to have to give and soon. It wasn't an easy decision.

'Seb, darling?' Sherry had materialised by his side. How on earth was the woman so dammed soft-footed? It was most unnerving.

Seb gripped the edge of his desk and took a deep breath, trying not to show his irritation. There were still three days to go until the wedding and he hadn't had ten uninterrupted minutes since breakfast. 'I have no idea, ask Daisy.' Whatever the question she was bound to know the answer.

'I haven't seen Daisy all morning.' Sherry frowned. 'Really, Seb. It would be helpful if one of you took an interest. These details may seem unimportant but they matter. A high bow at the top of the chair can be smart but rather showy. A lower one is classier maybe but can be lost. Especially with the pale yellow you've chosen.'

He'd chosen? Things might have changed at an alarming speed but there was one thing Seb knew for sure—he had had nothing whatsoever to do with choosing the colour of ribbons for the backs of chairs.

'Let's go for classy.' He rubbed his eyes. If anyone had suggested a month ago that he would be sitting in his library discussing bows with a supermodel he would have poured them a stiff brandy and suggested a lie-down. Yet here he was—and this particular supermodel wasn't going anywhere until he gave her the answer she wanted.

'You're probably right.' She reached over and ruffled his hair in a maternal way, incongrous coming from the glamorous Sherry Huntingdon. 'Classy is always best. Less is more, as I told the girls when they were growing up.'

'Wise advice.' But something she had said earlier was nagging at him. 'Where's Daisy gone?'

'I have no idea. She said she was tired after last night and wandered off. She did look peaky. There's a lovely picture of you two on the *Chronicle Online*. You do scrub up nicely, Seb. It's good to see you make an effort. There's no need to take the absent-minded-academic thing quite so seriously, you know.' Sherry gave his old worn shirt a pointed look.

'Hmm?' But he had already reached for the phone she was holding out, stomach lurching as he scrolled through the *Chronicle*'s long list of celebrity sightings and pictures. There they were entering the concert venue last night: Daisy long-legged in black shorts and a red T-shirt, her lipstick as bright as her top and her favourite trilby pushed back on her head. Seb had been unsure what to wear and had plumped for black trousers and a charcoal-grey shirt. Daisy's arm was linked through his and she was laughing.

To a casual observer—and to the headline writer—they looked very much the happy couple.

He thrust the phone back at Sherry. 'Why are they even interested? So we go to a concert, what's the big deal?'

'You have to admit it's a fairy-tale romance, rock star's daughter marrying an earl after just a few weeks.' Her voice was calm but the sharp gleam in her eyes showed her own curiosity. 'Of course they're interested. It'll die down.'

'Will it?' He could hear the bitter note in his voice and made an effort to speak more normally. 'I hope so.'

With in-laws like the ones he would shortly be acquiring, any chance of anonymity seemed very far away.

Sherry drifted away, her long list wafting from one elegant hand, and Seb tried to turn his attention back to his laptop. But once again his attention wandered. Where *was* Daisy?

She had slept in her own room last night citing tiredness. His own bed had seemed so huge, empty. Cold. At one point he had rolled over, ready to pull her into his arms—only she hadn't been there. It was odd how her absence had loomed through the long, almost sleepless night.

Odd how quickly he had grown accustomed to her presence; the low, even breathing, the warmth of her. The way she woke up spooned into him, the long hair spread over both pillows.

Odd how right it felt.

She hadn't shown up for breakfast either. Seb drummed his fingers on the desktop, the leather soft under his persistent touch. She had looked so vibrant in the photo but at some point in the evening her usual exuberance had dimmed and she had hardly said a word on the way back to Hawksley.

He cast his mind back, trying to remember the conversation of the night before. What had they talked about?

Had it been the mention of the honeymoon? The honeymoon she didn't want.

The honeymoon she didn't want to take with him.

Maybe she was wrong. Maybe they needed this, time away from the pressures of work and family, time away from putting on their best manners and working hard to fit their lives together—maybe it was time to find out how they operated as a couple. He would discuss it again with her.

Only… His fingers drummed a little harder as he thought. She had surprised him last night and it had been one of the most thoughtful things anyone had ever done for him. Maybe it was time for Seb to return the favour.

He pulled the laptop towards him, not allowing himself time to think things through and change his mind, quickly typing in Gianni's email address. Subject heading 'Lake Garda'.

He might not be her dream fiancé but Daisy deserved the perfect honeymoon and he was going to make sure she had it. It was the least he could do.

He had expected to find her in the kitchen. Daisy had been forbidden from doing any of the actual sanding herself. Seb was pretty sure all the dust wasn't good for the baby, but it didn't stop her superintending every job. Under her instructions the walls had been repainted a creamy white, the sanded and restored cupboards, cabinets and dresser a pale grey. He'd been sceptical about the colour but, walking into the warm, soothing space, he had to admit she was right.

The estate joiner had been hard at work planing and oiling wood from one of the old oaks that had fallen in the winter storms, creating counter tops from the venerable old tree. It seemed fitting that a tree that had stood sentry in the grounds for so many generations should be brought inside and used for the changing of the guard.

Daisy had found an old clothes rack in one of the out-buildings and had arranged for it to be suspended from the ceiling, hanging the old copper saucepans from it. She had unearthed his great-grandmother's tea set from the attic and arranged it on the shelves, the old-fashioned forget-me-not pattern blending timelessly with the creams and greys. The overall effect was of useful comfort. A warm, family kitchen, a place for work and conversation. For sweet smells and savoury concoctions, for taking stock of the day while planning the next.

The kitchen had been changing day by day and yet he hadn't really taken in the scale of her efforts. It wasn't just that the kitchen was freshly restored, nor that it was scrupulously clean. It wasn't just the new details like the pictures on the wall, old landscapes of the grounds and the castle, the newly installed sofa by the Aga and the warm rug Monty had claimed for his own. It was the feeling. Of care, of love.

The same feeling that hit him when he walked into her rooms, cluttered, sweet-smelling and alive. The same feeling she had created in the morning room and in the library where she had removed some of the heavier furniture and covered the backs of his chairs with warm, bright throws, heaped the window seats high with cushions.

His home was metamorphosing under his eyes and yet he'd barely noticed.

He should tell her he liked the changes.

Seb poured himself a glass of water and sat at the table, thinking of all the places she could have disappeared to. He didn't blame her for wanting some breathing space before the wedding; but if even Sherry couldn't run her to earth Daisy must have chosen her hiding space with care.

Neatly piled on the tabletop were some of the old scrapbooks and pictures Sherry had printed out from Daisy's website and internet pin boards. Seb reached out curiously and began to leaf through them. He expected to see a little girl's fantasy, all meringues and Cinderella coaches.

Instead he was confronted by details: a single flower bound in ribbon, a close-up of an intricate piece of lace, an embellished candle. Simple, thoughtful yet with a quirky twist. Like Daisy herself.

A piece of paper fell out and he picked it up. It was a printed-out picture of a ring: twisted pieces of fine gold wire embellished with fiery stones. A million miles away from the classic solitaire he had presented her with.

A solitaire she rarely wore. She was worried she'd lose it, she said. But it wasn't just that; he could see it in her eyes.

He hadn't known her at all when he'd bought it for her. Picked out a generic ring, expensive, sure, flawless—but nothing special, nothing unique. He could have given that ring to anyone.

And Daisy was definitely not just anyone.

Seb leant back, the picture in his hand. He really should show her just how much he appreciated all that she had done.

She was so busy trying to fit in with him, to turn his old house into a home. It was time he gave something back. The wedding of her dreams, the honeymoon of her dreams.

The ring of her dreams.

It wasn't the full package, he was all too aware of that. But it was all he had, wasn't it? It would have to do.

He just hoped it would be enough.

CHAPTER TEN

THERE IT WAS. Daisy sucked in a long breath, forcing herself to stay low and remain still, remain quiet despite every nerve fizzing with excitement. Slowly, carefully, she focused the zoom lens.

Click.

The otter didn't know it was being photographed—much like Daisy herself last night. Would the otter feel as violated, as sick to its stomach if she published the shot on her website?

Had Seb seen it? Each time a photo of them appeared in the press he got a little colder, a little more withdrawn and she could feel herself wither with each snap too.

Was it the intrusion itself she minded—or the image portrayed in the pictures? They looked so happy last night, hands clasped, heads turned towards each other, as if they were wrapped up in their own world, totally complete together.

And they said the camera never lied…

Daisy shook off the thought, allowing her own camera to follow the sleek mammal as it swam up the river, turning giddy somersaults in the water, playing some game she longed to understand. Was it lonely, swimming all by itself? Maybe by the summer it would have cubs to play with. She hoped so.

Her mind drifted down to the new life inside her. Still so small, only perceptible by the swelling in her breasts and sensitivity to certain smells and yet strong, growing, alive. 'Will I be less lonely when you're here?' she whispered.

It was a terrible burden to put on a baby. Happiness and self-fulfilment. Daisy focused again on the gliding otter. She had her camera, her work, her family. That was enough. It had to be enough.

Only. What if it wasn't? She was trying so hard. Trying to be calm and sensible and fit in with the slow and steady pace of life at Hawksley she glimpsed between wedding preparations: Seb with his research, Seb out in the fields, talking to tenants, the weekend tourists herded around the small areas open to the public. It was as distant from her busy London life as the otter's life was from an urban fox's streetwise existence.

She was making a list of the most immediate refurbishments needed in the house and was happily delving deep into the crammed attics. But despite everything Seb said she didn't feel as if she had a right to start making changes; it felt as if she were playing at being the lady of the house. She was still a visitor, just a momentary imprint in the house's long history.

And although Seb hadn't gone into great detail she knew that money was tight, the trust set up to keep the castle depleted, ransacked in return for a jet-set existence. Seb had to wait for probate before he could start to sell off all the luxury items his parents had lavished their money on. Until they were sold it was impossible to know just how much she could draw on. Right now she was doing her best with things scavenged from the attic, materials she could turn into cushions or curtains, pictures that just needed a polish.

Hawksley needed far more work than easy cosmetic

fixes. How could she plan the renovations it needed when she knew full well the cost would be exorbitant?

It was hard to grasp how life would be afterwards. The wedding overshadowed everything, created buzz and fuss and work and life. Once Sherry left for good, the vows were said and the marquee tidied away what would be left for her? Would she find herself desperate to shout out loud, to stand in the middle of the courtyard and scream, to tear the calm curtain of civility open? To get some reaction somehow.

The wedding was just a day. She had the rest of her life here to navigate.

And there was nobody to discuss it with. Seb didn't want emotions in his life and she had agreed to respect that. This fear of loneliness, emotions stretching to breaking point, was exactly the kind of thing he abhorred.

And of course, where there wasn't emotion there couldn't be love. Could there?

Daisy got slowly to her feet, careful not to disturb the still-basking otter. Love? Where had that come from? She knew full well that love wasn't on offer in this pact of theirs. It was just...

There was passion behind that serious, intellectual face. She had known it that very first night. Had seen it again time after time. Not just in bed but in his work, his attachment to his home. And passion was emotion...

Seb might not think that he did emotion but he did. His books were bestsellers because they brought the past alive. No one could write with such sensual sensitivity about the lusts of the Stuart court without feeling the hunger himself.

There were times when the almost glacial green eyes heated up, darkened with need. Times when the measured voice grew deeper, huskier. Times when sense was tossed aside for immediacy. Seb desired her, she knew that. Desire was an emotion.

Of course he was capable of love! Just not for her. Maybe, if she hadn't interrupted the steady pace of his life, he would have met somebody suitable. Someone who shared his love for the past, who would have known how to overcome his fears, helped to heal his hurts.

He'd been robbed of his chance for love just as she had. They were in this together.

And so she wouldn't dwell on the way her stomach lurched every time he looked directly at her, on the way her skin fizzed at every causal touch. She wouldn't allow herself to think about how he made her feel smart as well as sexy. As if she counted.

Because that way lay madness and regret. That way led to revelations she wasn't ready to face. That way led to emotions and maybe Seb was right. Maybe emotions were too high a price to pay. Maybe stability was what mattered.

'Where have you been?' Daisy started as she heard the slightly irritable voice. She bit back a near hysterical giggle. Think of the devil and he will come.

'I've been looking everywhere. Your mother is worried. Says she hasn't seen you all morning and that you look tired.' His gaze was intent, as if he were searching out every shadow in her face. In her soul.

'I just couldn't face any more in-depth discussions about whether as Violet's best friend Will should count as her date, or if Vi and Rose should have the same hairstyle so I came out for some air.' It wasn't a total lie. The nearer the wedding got, the more she wanted to run. Funny to think that once she had planned for this, thought all these tiny details mattered.

Now she just wanted it over and done with.

'Some air?' Seb bit back a smile. 'You're almost at the edge of the estate. I couldn't believe it when Paul said he'd seen you walk this way.'

'I like it down here. It's peaceful.' The river wound

around the bottom of the wooded valley, Hawksley invisible on the other side of the hill. Here she was alone, away from the fears and the worries and the nerves.

'It used to be one of my favourite places when I was younger. There's a swimming spot just around that bend.'

'Shh! Look!' Daisy grabbed his arm and pointed. 'There's another one. Do you think they're mates? Do otters live in pairs?' She dropped his arm to pull her camera back up, focusing and clicking over and over.

'Not European otters.' Seb spoke in a low even tone as they watched the pair duck and dive, their sinewy bodies weaving round each other in an underwater dance. 'They're very territorial so I think we might be lucky enough to see a mating pair—in two months' time there could be cubs. They actually mate underwater.'

'It looks like she's trying to get away.'

'The dog otters often have to chase the females until she agrees.'

'Typical males!'

They stood there for a few minutes more, almost unable to breathe trying not to alert the couple to their presence until, at last, the female otter took off around the bend in the river doggedly pursued by the male and the pair were lost from sight.

'That was incredible.' Daisy turned to Seb. His eyes reflected her own awe and wonderment, the same incredulous excitement. 'I can't believe we were lucky enough to witness that.'

'Do you think he's caught her?'

She tossed her head. 'Only if she wants him to. But I hope she did. What a project that would make—documenting the mating dance right through to the cubs maturing.'

'I didn't know you were into nature photography?'

His words brought back the look of utter incomprehension on his publisher's face. Nature photography, high fashion, art—they were intellectual pursuits, worthy. Weddings, romance? They just didn't cut it.

'I'm into anything wonderful, anything beautiful.' She turned away, a mixture of vulnerability and anger replacing the excitement, then turned back again to face him, to challenge him. 'What, you thought I was too shallow to appreciate nature?'

He gripped her shoulders, turning her to face him, eyes sparkling with anger of his own. 'Don't put words into my mouth, Daisy.'

'But that's what you meant, wasn't it?' She twisted away from his touch, acidic rage, corrosive and damaging, churning her stomach. 'A nature photographer wife would be so much more fitting for you than a wedding photographer. So much more intellectual than silly, frivolous romance.'

'How on earth did you reach that crazy conclusion? This has nothing to do with me.' Seb dropped his hands, stepped back, mouth open in disbelief. 'It's to do with you. Why do you always do this? Assume everyone else thinks the worst of you? The only person who puts you down, Daisy Huntingdon-Cross, is you. Photograph babies or weddings or cats or otters. I don't care. But don't take all your insecurities and fasten them on me. I won't play.'

'Why? Because that would mean getting involved?' Daisy knew she was making no sense, knew she was stirring up emotions and feelings that didn't need to be disturbed. That she was almost creating conflict for the sake of it. But she couldn't stop. 'God forbid that the high and mighty Earl of Holgate actually feel something. Have an opinion on another person.'

Seb took another step back, his mouth set firm, his eyes hard. 'I won't do this, Daisy. Not here, not now, not ever. I told you, this is not how I will live. If you want to fight, go pick a quarrel with your mother but don't try and pick one with me.'

Daisy trembled, the effort of holding the words in almost too much. But through the tumult and silent rage another emotion churned. Shame. Because Seb was right. She was trying to pick a quarrel, trying to see if she could get him to react.

And he was right about something else. She was fastening her own insecurities on him. He was very upfront about her job; he mocked it, laughed at it but he *had* supported her when she'd needed it. And he might think weddings frivolous but he had commented on some of her photos, praised the composition.

'I was being unfair.' The words were so soft she wasn't sure if she had actually said them aloud. 'I don't know if it's the stress of the wedding or pregnancy hormones or lack of sleep. But I'm sorry. For trying to provoke you.'

He froze, a wary look on his face. 'You are?'

Her mouth curved into a half smile. 'I grew up with two sisters, you know. This is how we operated—attack first.'

'Sounds deadly.' But the hard look in his eyes had softened. 'Are you ready to walk back? If you're very lucky I'll show you where I used to build my den.'

Daisy recognised the conciliatory note for what it was and accepted the tacit peace offering. 'That sounds cool. We had treehouses but they were constructed for us, no makeshift dens for us.'

'I can imagine.' His tone was dry. Whatever he was imagining probably wouldn't be too far from the truth. They had each had their own, ornate balconied structures constructed around some of the grand old oaks in Huntingdon Hall's parkland.

They strode along, Seb pointing out objects of interest as Daisy zoomed in on some of the early signs of spring budding through the waking woodland. The conversation was calm, non-consequential, neither of them alluding to the brief altercation.

And yet, Daisy couldn't help thinking, he had been the first to react. Immediate and unmistakeable anger. In his eyes, in his voice, in the grip on her shoulders, in his words. She had got to him whether he admitted it or not. Was that a good thing? A breakthrough?

She had no idea. But it was proof that he felt something. What that actually was remained to be seen but right now she would take whatever she could get.

Because it meant hope.

'These are really good, Daisy.'

'Mmm.' But she sounded critical as she continued to swipe through the files. Seb had no idea why. Whether the pictures were colour or black and white she had completely captured the otters' essence. Watching the photos in their natural order was like being told a story.

She obviously felt about her photos the way he felt about his words—no matter how you tinkered and played and edited they could always be better.

Daisy pulled a face and deleted a close-up that looked perfect to him. 'What I need down there is a proper hide. Preferably one with cushions and a loo.'

It would be the perfect spot. 'I did consider putting in a nature trail, but it means more people coming onto the land.'

'And that's a problem, why?' She looked up from the laptop, her gaze questioning.

He bit back the surge of irritation, trying to keep his voice even. 'This is my home, Daisy. How would you like people traipsing all over Huntingdon Hall at all times of the day?'

She leant back, the blue eyes still fixed on him. 'We often open up the hall. Mum and Dad host charity galas and traditionally the hall is the venue for the village fete plus whatever else the village wants to celebrate—and there's always something. Besides, yes, they do own some parkland and the gardens are huge by nearly anyone else's standards but it doesn't even begin to compare to Hawksley. Don't you think you're a bit selfish keeping it locked up?'

Selfish? Words were Seb's trade—and right now he had lost his tools. All he could do was stare at her, utterly nonplussed. 'I let people look around the castle.'

She wrinkled her nose and quoted: '"Restricted areas of the house are available to members of the public from eleven a.m. until three p.m., weekends only between Whitsun and September the first."'

Okay, the hours were a *little* restrictive. 'I hire out the Great Hall.'

'Saturdays only. And you don't allow anyone else onto the estate apart from the villagers and your tenants.'

His defensive hackles rose as she continued. It was as if she had looked into all his worries and was gradually exhuming each one. 'That's how we've always done things.' An inadequate response, he knew, but until he made some difficult decisions it was all he had.

'I know.' She looked as if she wanted to continue but instead closed her mouth with a snap, continuing to flick through the photos.

'But?' he prompted.

'But things are different now. You need to start running the estate as a commercial enterprise, not as a gentleman's hobby.'

Ouch. 'What do you think I've been doing these last few months?' he demanded. 'Research? I have barely touched my book. I've been doing my damnedest to try and get all the farming grants I can…'

'That's not going to be enough.' She bit her lip and

looked down at her screen, clearly thinking hard about something. 'I didn't want to show you this until I had done more work on it. It's not ready yet.'

'Show me what?' Wariness skittered down his spine.

She clicked on the screen and swivelled the laptop round so he could see the screen.

Seb had expected a photo. Instead a formatted slide complete with bullet points faced him. He raised an eyebrow. 'PowerPoint?'

Daisy coloured. 'I know it's a little OTT but I couldn't think how else to order it.'

'Go on, then. Amaze me.' He knew he sounded dismissive but, honestly, what on earth could a wedding photographer who was expelled from school at sixteen contribute to the ongoing Hawksley struggle that he hadn't considered? But, he conceded, if this was going to be her home he should at least listen to whatever crackpot ideas she had dreamed up.

She chewed on her lip for a moment, looking at him doubtfully before taking a deep breath and pointing one slim finger at the screen.

'Okay.' She slid him a nervy glance. 'I want you to have an open mind, okay?'

He nodded curtly even as he felt his barriers go up.

'This is Chesterfield Manor. The house, grounds and estate are a similar size to Hawksley. Chesterfield Manor has been open to the public for the last fifteen years. They specialise in outdoor trails and natural play.' She sounded self-conscious, as if she were reading from a script.

'An insurance nightmare.'

'This one…' The slide showed a magnificent Tudor house. 'This is known for productions of plays, especially Shakespeare and they also do themed medieval banquets.'

'In costume? Tell me you aren't serious!'

Daisy didn't reply, just carried on showing him slide

after slide of stately homes spread throughout the UK rang-ing from a perfectly preserved Norman Castle to a nine-teenth-century gothic folly, her manner relaxing as she settled into the presentation, pointing out all the various ways they attracted paying visitors.

Seb's heart picked up speed as he looked at each slide, hammering so hard it rivalled the tick of the old grandfa-ther clock in the hallway.

Everything she was showing him he had considered. Every conclusion she had drawn he had already drawn—and rejected. Too risky, not in keeping. A betrayal of his grandfather's already squandered legacy.

Risks and spending money without thought of the con-sequences had almost broken Hawksley once.

Allowing the cameras into their home had just fuelled his parents' narcissism, and greed.

He couldn't go down that road. Didn't she understand that?

He had thought she understood.

He had obviously been very wrong...

Seb took in a deep breath, stilling his escalating pulse, and sat back and folded his arms. 'So people like stately homes.'

'Hawksley has two things none of these have.' She waited expectantly.

He sighed. 'Which are?'

'Its utterly unique appearance—and you. An eminent historian in situ right here. Look, I've been talking to Paul...'

His eyes narrowed. 'You have been busy.'

She lifted her chin. 'The farms pay for themselves, the village pays for itself—but the castle is in deficit. You can apply for as many grants as you like but that's not going to fix the roof and certainly won't replace the money your fa-ther squandered. The income from the trust used to pay for all the castle's bills and living expenses for the earl and his family—right now you'd find it hard to replace the toaster.'

It was an exaggeration but his gut tightened at her words. Did she think he didn't know this? Didn't lie awake night after night thinking of every which way he could solve it?

'But, Seb, there are so many ways we could use the castle to generate the income it needs. Start using the keep, as well as the hall, for weddings and parties too—erect a wooden and canvas inner structure inside the walls just like they did at Bexley. Hold plays, open all week Easter to September and weekends out of season. Have a Christmas open house.' She hesitated. 'Allow tours of the main house.'

Seb's chest tightened at the very thought of strangers wandering around his house. 'No!'

She hurried on. 'I don't mean open access but "pay in advance and reserve your place" tours. Put in a farm shop and nature trails and play parks. We could convert some of the outbuildings into holiday cottages and bridal accommodation.'

'With what?'

'There's some capital left.'

He stared. 'You want me to gamble what's left, finish what my father started?'

'Not gamble, invest.'

'Meanwhile I'm what? A performing earl, the public face of Hawksley, like some medieval lord of the manor...'

'You are the lord of the manor.'

'It's all about publicity with you, isn't it? You say you don't want it but you can't see any way but the obvious—photos and newspapers and the public.'

'No.' She was on her feet. 'But with a place like Hawksley the right kind of publicity is a blessing.'

'There is no such thing as the right publicity.'

She stared at him. 'Come on, Seb, you know that's not true. Look at your books!'

'They're work, this is my home.' His voice was tight.

Daisy bit her lip, her eyes troubled. 'You can't see past your fears. You are so determined to do things your way you won't even consider any alternatives!'

His mouth curled in disgust. 'Is this about those damned TV lectures?'

'They would be a great start.'

Bitterness coated his mouth. 'I thought you understood.'

'I do. But you want me to marry you, to give you an heir. An heir to what? To worry? To debt? To fear? Or to a thriving business and a home with history—and a roof that doesn't leak?'

He pushed his chair back and stumbled to his feet. 'Hawksley is mine, Daisy. Mine! I will sort this out and make it right.'

Her eyes were huge. 'I don't get any say?'

That wasn't what he meant and she knew it. 'Stop twisting my words and stop creating drama.'

But she wasn't backing down. He didn't know her eyes could burn so brightly. 'You can't just shut me down, Seb, every time we have a difference of opinion. That's not how life works, not how marriage works.'

'I'm not shutting you down.' He just didn't want to argue. What was wrong with that?

'You are! If we are going to do this then we have to be partners. I have to be able to contribute without you accusing me of picking fights. I have to be involved in your decisions and your life.'

He couldn't answer, didn't know what to say. He hadn't expected her to push him like this. He had underestimated her, that was clear. What had he expected? A compliant partner, someone to warm his bed and agree with him?

He could feel his heart speeding up, his palms slick

with sweat. He had obviously overestimated himself just as much. Pompous ass that he was.

'That's not what you want, is it?' Her voice was just a whisper. 'You're happy for me to redecorate some rooms but you don't want my input, not where it matters.' Her voice broke. 'You're right, what does a romantically in-clined girl with no qualifications know anyway?'

'That's not what I said.'

'It's what you think though.'

He couldn't deny it.

The blue eyes were swimming. 'I know I said I could do this, Seb, but I'm not sure I'm the kind of woman who can warm your bed and raise your children and not be needed in your life.'

She could read him like a book. He wanted to say that he did need her but the words wouldn't come. 'You prom-ised to try.'

'I have tried.' Her cry sounded torn from the heart. Half of him wanted to step forward and enfold her in his arms, promise her that it would be okay—the other half of him recoiled from the sheer emotion.

'So what are you saying? The wedding is off?'

She swallowed. 'I don't know. I know how important getting married is for the baby's sake but I have to think about me as well. I need some time, Seb. Some time on my own to figure things out. I'm sorry.'

And while he was still searching for the right words, the right sentiments, a way to make her stay she slipped out of the room and he knew that he'd lost her.

And he had no idea how to find her again.

CHAPTER ELEVEN

SHE'D LEFT HER favourite camera at Hawksley. She'd also left her favourite laptop and half of her hats but right now it was her camera she needed.

If she wasn't going to expose herself to her own merciless gaze then she needed to turn that gaze elsewhere. She needed to find a subject and lose herself in it.

Daisy stared mindlessly out of the windscreen. She had other cameras at her studio but returning there, right now, felt like a retreat. Worse, it felt like an admission of failure.

But she had failed, hadn't she?

She'd tried to change the rules.

They hadn't even managed the shotgun marriage part before she had started interfering. Demanding responses, pushing him, putting together PowerPoint presentations. Daisy leaned forward until her forehead knocked against the steering wheel.

She was a fool.

And yet…

Slowly Daisy straightened, her hands pressing tighter on the wheel. And yet she had felt more right than she had in a long, long time. As if she had finally burst out of her chrysalis.

She didn't know if she could willingly shut herself back in. She'd enjoyed the research, enjoyed finding conclusions—she'd even enjoyed figuring out PowerPoint in the end after she had emerged victorious after the first few scuffles. She'd never put together any kind of business plan before, never pushed herself.

Never allowed herself to broaden her horizons, to think she might be capable of achieving more. Hidden behind her camera just as Seb hid behind his qualifications.

She'd wanted to help him. Had seen how much he was struggling, torn between his career and his home, the expectations of his past and the worries of the present.

But he didn't want her help. Didn't need her.

Without conscious thought, just following her instinct, Daisy began to drive, following the road signs on autopilot until she turned down the long lane that led to her childhood home. She pulled the small car to a stop and turned off the engine, relief seeping through her bones. This was where she needed to be, right now.

It had been a long time since she had run home with her problems.

It was only a short walk along the lane and through the gates that led to the hall but with each step Daisy's burden lightened, just a little. Maybe asking for help wasn't a sign of weakness.

Maybe it was maturity.

Huntingdon Hall glowed a soft gold in the late afternoon light. Daisy paused, taking in its graceful lines, the long rows of windows, the perfectly symmetrical wings, the well-maintained and prosperous air of the house. It wasn't just smaller than Hawksley, newer than half of Hawksley—it was a family home. Loved, well cared for and welcoming.

But it wasn't her home any more, hadn't been for a long time. She shut her eyes for a moment, visualising the way the sun lit up the Norman keep, the thousand-year-old tower reflected in the water. When had Hawksley begun to feel like *her* home?

The kitchen doors stood ajar and she ran up the steps, inhaling gratefully the familiar scent of fresh flowers, beeswax and the spicy vanilla scent her mother favoured. Inside the kitchen was as immaculate as always, a huge open-plan cooking, eating and relaxing space, the back wall floor-to-ceiling glass doors bringing the outside inside no matter what the weather.

She'd walked away from all this comfort, luxury and love at eighteen so convinced she wouldn't be able to find herself here, convinced she was the family joke, the family outcast. Tears burned the backs of her eyes as she looked at the vast array of photographs hung on the walls; not her father's record covers or her mother's most famous shoots but the girls from bald, red-faced babies, through gap-toothed childhood to now. Interspersed and lovingly framed were some of Daisy's own photos including her degree shoot prints.

What must it have cost them to let her go? To allow her the freedom to make her own mistakes?

'Hey, Daisy girl.' Her father's rich American drawl remained unchanged despite three decades living in the UK. 'Is your mother with you?' He looked round for his wife, hope and affection lighting up his face. What must it be like, Daisy wondered with a wistful envy, to love someone else so much that your first thought was always of them?

'Nope, she's still browbeating the caterers and obsessing over hairstyles.' She leant gratefully into her father's skinny frame as he pulled her into a cuddle. How long was it since she had allowed herself to be held like this? For too long she had stopped after a peck and a squeeze of the shoulders. 'Hi, Dad.'

'It's good to see you, Daisy girl.' He pulled back to look

her over, a frown furrowing the famously craggy face. 'You look exhausted. Your mother working you too hard?'

'I think you and Mum had the right idea running away.' Daisy tried not to wriggle away from his scrutiny.

'It saved a lot of bother,' he agreed, but the keen eyes were full of concern. 'Drink?'

'Just water, please.' She accepted the ice-cold glass gratefully, carrying it over to the comfortable cluster of sofas grouped around the windows, sinking onto one with a sigh of relief.

She had begun to recreate this feeling in the kitchen at Hawksley, sanding back the old kitchen cupboards so that they could be repainted a soft grey and bringing in one of the better sofas from an unused salon to curl up on by the Aga. Slowly, step by step turning the few rooms she and Seb used into warm, comfortable places. Into a family home.

'I feel like I should be coming to you with words of advice and wisdom.' Rick sat down on the sofa opposite, a bottle of beer in one hand. 'After three daughters and three decades of marriage you'd think I'd know something. But all I know is don't go to bed angry, wake up counting your blessings and always try and see the other person's point of view. If you can manage that—' he raised his bottle to her '—then you should be okay.'

'Funny.' She smiled at him. 'Mum said something very similar,'

Rick took a swig of his beer. 'Well, your mother's a wise woman.'

Daisy swung her legs up onto the sofa, reclining against the solid arm and letting the cushions enfold her. She half closed her eyes, allowing the sounds and smells of her childhood home to comfort her. After a few moments Rick got up and she could hear him clattering about in the food preparation part of the kitchen. Her eyelids fluttered shut and she allowed herself to fall into a doze, feeling safe for the first time in a long while.

'Here you go.' She roused as a plate was set before her. 'I know it's fashionable for brides to waste away before their wedding but if you get any thinner, Daisy girl, I'll be having to hold you down as we walk down that aisle.'

'My favourite.' The all-too-ready tears pricked her eyelids as Daisy looked at the plate holding a grilled cheese and tomato sandwich and a bowl of tomato soup. Her childhood comfort food—not coincidentally also the limit of Rick Cross's cooking skills. 'Thanks, Dad.'

Her father didn't say another word while she ate; instead he picked up one of the seemingly endless supplies of guitars that lay in every room of the house and began to strum some chords. It had used to drive Daisy mad, his inability to stay quiet and still, but now she appreciated it for what it was. A safety blanket, just like her camera.

As always the slightly stodgy mix of white bread, melted cheese and sweet tomatoes slipped down easily and a full stomach made her feel infinitely better. Rick continued to strum as Daisy carried her empty dishes to the sink, the chords turning into a well-known marching song.

Rick began to croon the lyrics in the throaty tones that had made him a star. He looked up at his daughter, a twinkle in his eyes. 'Thought I might sing this instead of making a speech.'

She couldn't do it, couldn't lie to him a single moment longer. So she would slip back into being the problem daughter, the mistake-making disaster zone. Maybe she deserved it.

She could take it. She had to take it.

She was tired of doing it all alone. Tired of shutting her family out. Tired of always being strong, of putting her need to be independent before her family.

Maybe *this* was what being a grown-up meant. Not shutting yourself away but knowing when it was okay to accept help. When it was okay to lean on someone else. The day Seb had come to help her with the wedding had been one of the best days of her adult life. She'd come so close to relying on him.

Tension twisted her stomach as she fought to find the right words. But there were no right words. Just the facts.

Daisy turned, looked him straight in the eyes and readied herself. 'I'm pregnant. Dad, I'm pregnant and I don't know what to do.'

Her father didn't react straight away. His fingers fell off the guitar and he carefully put the instrument to one side, his face shuttered. Slowly he got to his feet, walking over to Daisy before pulling her in close, holding her as if he meant to never let her go.

The skinny shoulders were stronger than they looked. Daisy allowed herself to lean against them, to let her father bear her weight and finally, finally stopped fighting the tears she had swallowed back for so long, shudders shaking her whole body as the sobs tore out of her.

'It's okay, Daisy girl,' her father crooned, stroking her hair as if she were still his little girl. 'It's okay.'

But she couldn't stop, not yet, even though the great gusty sobs had turned into hiccups and the tears had soaked her father's shirt right through. The relief of finally not having to put on a brave face was too much and it was several minutes before her father could escort her back to the sofa, setting another glass of water and several tissues in front of her.

'Hold on,' he said. 'If living with a pack of women has taught me anything it's that there's a surefire remedy for this kind of situation.' He walked, with the catlike grace that made him such a hypnotic stage performer, to the fridge and, opening the freezer door, extracted a pint of ice cream. 'Here you go, Daisy girl,' he said, setting it down in front of her and handing her a spoon. 'Dig in.'

He didn't say anything for a while. Just sat there as Daisy scooped the creamy cold chocolatey goodness out of the carton, allowing it to melt on her tongue. She couldn't manage more than a couple of mouthfuls, the gesture of far more comfort than the actual ice cream.

'I take it this wasn't planned?' His voice was calm, completely non-judgemental.

Daisy shook her head. 'No.'

'How long have you known?'

She could feel the colour creeping over her cheeks, couldn't meet her father's eye. 'A month. I told Seb three weeks ago.'

'This is why you're getting married?'

Daisy nodded. 'It's because of Hawksley, and the title. If the baby isn't legitimate...' Her voice trailed off.

'Crazy Brits.' Her dad sat back. 'Do you love him, Daisy girl?'

Did she what? She liked him—sometimes. Desired him for sure. The way his hair fell over his forehead, a little too long and messy for fashion. The clear green of his eyes, the way they darkened with emotion. The lean strength of him, unexpected in an academic. The way he listened to her, asked her questions, respected her, made her feel that maybe she had something to contribute—until today.

She understood him, knew why he strived so hard to excel in everything he did, tried to keep himself aloof, the fear of being judged.

Her father's gaze intensified. 'It's not that hard a question, Daisy girl. When you know, you know.'

'Yes.' The knowledge hit her hard, almost winding her. 'Yes, I do. But he doesn't love me and that's why I don't know if I can do it. I don't know if I can marry him. If I can say those words to someone who doesn't want to hear

them, for him to say them to me and not mean them.' That
was it, she realised with a sharp clarity. She had been prepared to lie to everyone but she couldn't bear for him to
lie to her. To make promises he didn't mean.

'Love means that much to you?' Her father's eyes were
kind, knowing.

Daisy put her hand down to cradle her still-flat stomach. She wanted the baby; she already loved it. Which
love meant more? Pulled at her more? What was worse?
Depriving her baby of its heritage or bringing it up in an
unequal, unhappy household?

'With your example before me? Of course it does. I
want a husband who looks at me the way you look at Mum.
That's what I've always wanted. But it's not just about me,
not any more. Oh, Dad, what am I going to do?'

Her father put an arm around her and she sank into
his embrace wishing for one moment that she were a little girl again and that there was nothing her dad couldn't
fix. 'That's up to you, Daisy girl. Only you can decide.
But we're all here for you, whatever happens. Remember
that, darling. I know how independent you are but we're
here. You're not alone.'

Loneliness had been such a constant friend for so many
years he had barely noticed it leave.

Yet now it had returned it felt heavier than ever.

The primroses carpeted the woodland floor, their pale
beauty a vivid reminder of the colour overtaking his home.
Sherry liked a theme and had incorporated the yellow-
and-white colour scheme into everything from the guest
towels to the bunting already hung in the marquee. It was
like living in a giant egg.

Apart from the rooms Daisy had been working on. She
had kept her mother out of those, keeping them private,
personal.

Creating a family space.

His throat closed tight. *Their* family space.

Normally Seb loved this time of year, watching the world bud, shaking off the sleepy austerity of winter. It wasn't as obvious in Oxford as it was here at Hawksley where every day signalled something new.

Oxford. It had been his focus for so long, his sole goal. To excel in his field. He had almost made it.

But suddenly it didn't seem that important, more like a remembered dream than a passion. His research? Yes. Digging into the past, feeling it come alive, transcribing it for a modern audience, that he missed. But college politics, hungover undergraduates, teaching, tourist-filled streets, the buzz of the city?

Seb breathed in the revelation. He didn't miss it at all.

He was home. This was where he belonged.

But not alone. He had been alone long enough.

Seb retraced his steps, anticipating the moment his steps would lead him out of the wood and over the hill, that first glimpse of Hawksley Castle standing, majestic, by the lake edge. The Norman keep, grey, watchful, looking out over the water flanked by the white plaster and timbered Tudor hall, picturesque with the light reflected off the lead-paned windows. Finally the house itself, a perfect example of neoclassical Georgian architecture.

Daisy was right: it would make a wonderful setting for a TV series.

Seb's heart twisted. Painfully.

What if she didn't come back? How would he explain her absence to her mother? The guests already beginning to arrive in the village and in neighbouring hotels? If the wedding was called off the resulting publicity would be incredible, every detail of his own parents' doomed marriage exhumed and re-examined over and over.

The usual nausea swirled, sweat beading at his fore-

head, but it wasn't at the prospect of the screaming headlines and taunting comments. No, Seb realised. It was at
the thought of the wedding being called off.

Slowly he wandered back towards the castle barely noticing the spring sunshine warming his shoulders. No wedding. It wasn't as if he had wanted this grand, showy affair
anyway. It was a compromise he had had to make for the
baby, wasn't it?

Or was it?

The truth was he hadn't hesitated. He'd taken one
look at Daisy's face as she'd read through that long list
of names and known he couldn't deny her the wedding
of her dreams.

Truth was he couldn't deny her anything.

He wanted to give her everything—not that she'd take
it, absurdly proud as she was.

She was hardworking, earnest and underestimated herself so much she allowed everybody else to underestimate
her too, hiding behind her red lipstick, her quirky style
and her camera.

He knew how she put herself down, made light of her
own perceived failures, preempting the judgement she was
sure would come. What must it have taken to put that presentation together, to show him her work—and yet he had
thrown all her enthusiasm, all her help back in her face.

Shame washed over him, hot and tight. He hadn't
wanted to listen, to accept that a fresh pair of eyes could
ever see anything in Hawksley that he couldn't see. Hadn't
wanted to accept that he was stuck on the wrong path.

He had spent so long ensuring he was nothing like his
spoilt, immoral parents he had turned himself into his
grandfather: upstanding sure, also rigid, a relic from a time
long dead, refusing to accept the world had changed even
as his staff and income shrank and his bills multiplied.

It seemed a long way back to the castle, weighted down

with guilt and shame. The truth was Daisy was right: he did need to make some changes and fast.

Starting with the estate. Much as he wanted to jump in his car, find her, beg her forgiveness he had to make the much-needed changes first. That way he could show her.

Show her that he had listened, show her that her work had value.

That he valued her.

Seb stood still, feeling his heart beat impossibly hard, impossibly loud.

Was this valuing her? This nausea, this knot of worry, this urge to do whatever it took to show her?

Or was it something more? Was it love?

It was messy and painful, just as he had feared, but it was more than that.

It was miraculous.

She made him a better person. It was up to him to repay that gift, even though it would take him the rest of his life.

The estate office was, as usual, a mess, cold and cluttered, an unattractive tangle of paperwork, old furniture, tools and filing cabinets. It felt unloved, impermanent. Seb sank down into the creaking old office chair and looked about at the utilitarian shelves, filled with broken bits of machinery and rusting tools. This was no way to run a place the size of Hawksley.

He picked up a notebook and flipped it open to a fresh white page. It mocked him with the unwritten possibilities and he sat for a moment, paralysed by how much he had to do, how sweeping the changes ahead.

But this wasn't about him, not any more. It was about his child, about his heritage, about the man he was—and the man he should be.

It was about his future wife.

The first thing he needed to do was admit he needed

some help, he couldn't do it all on his own no matter how much he wanted to.

He uncapped his fountain pen and began to write.

1. Resign from college

Seb sat back and looked at the words, waited to feel sad, resentful, to feel the weight of failure. He still had so much more to achieve; the visiting professorship at Harvard for one. Was he ready to give up his academic career? He could produce another ten bestselling books but without his college credentials they would mean nothing, not to his colleagues.

But the expected emotions didn't materialise; instead the burden on his shoulders lessened.

He leant forward again.

2. Employ a professional estate manager

Daisy was right, damn her. What use was he to anyone, sitting up late, scrutinising crop-rotation plans and cattle lists? He had done his best but he still knew less than an apprentice cattle man. If he put in an estate manager he could free his time up for writing—and for the house itself. Which led to the third thing. Admitting that Hawksley wasn't just his family home, it was a living legacy and he needed to start treating it as such.

3. Tidy and redecorate the offices to a professional standard

So that he could then…

4. Employ an events planner

5. Talk to the solicitor about breaking into the trust and investing in the estate

What was it Daisy had suggested? An internal structure in the Norman keep. That could work, maintain the integrity of the historical ruins while making it both safe and comfortable for weddings and parties. Seb winced. It looked as if the medieval-themed banquets might be unavoidable after all. As long as he wasn't expected to wear tights and a jerkin...

What else? Holiday cottages, nature trails... He thought back. It had only been this morning. How was it possible that so few hours had passed? She had left her laptop behind. He needed to take a look, see what other ideas he had dismissed. But there was definitely one more thing to add to the list.

6. Tell my agent I am willing to consider TV ideas

Her room looked just as it always did, with no inkling that its mistress had fled. The usual jumble of scarves, the ever-increasing collection of hats. Seb stood at the door and inhaled the faint floral scent she always wore.

When had he begun to associate that smell with home?

He didn't want her hidden away behind the discreet door, not any more. He wanted her with him; hats, scarves and whatever else she needed to make herself at home. Her rooms would make an incredible nursery.

If she would just come back.

He stepped past the neatly made bed and into the small chamber Daisy used as an office. Her laptop still stood open and, when he tentatively touched a key, it lit up, her PowerPoint presentation still on the screen. Seb took it back to the beginning and began to read.

Shame flared again. Searing as he flicked through the

slides. She had put a lot of time into this. For him. She had only looked at comparable estates in terms of size and had got as much useful information as she could including entrance prices, numbers of staff, opening hours and affiliations to member organisations. It was invaluable data, the beginnings of a business plan right here.

He closed the file down and sat back, his chest tight. How could he make it up to her?

Seb was about to switch the laptop off when a file caught his eye. Saved to her desktop, it was simply titled Hawksley. Was it more research? Curious, he double clicked.

More photos. Of course. A smile curved his mouth as he looked at his beloved home from Daisy's perspective: panoramic views, detailed close-ups, the volunteers at work, the farms. All the myriad details that made up Hawksley chronicled. She understood it as much as he did—possibly even more. She was so much more than the mother of his child, more than a fitting mistress for this huge, complicated and much-loved house.

She was perfect.

Another photo flashed up, black and white, grainy, an almost-sepia filter. It was Seb, sitting at his desk. His first instinct was to recoil, the way he always did when faced with a candid shot, the familiar churn of horror, of violation.

But then he looked again. He was reading, his forehead furrowed; he looked tired, a little stressed. It completely encapsulated the past few months, the toil they had taken on him.

Another image, Seb again, this one in full colour. He was outside, leaning against a tractor chatting to one of the tenant farmers. This time he looked relaxed, happy.

Another—Seb in Oxford, mid flow, gesticulating, eyes shining as he spoke. Another, another, another…

It wasn't just Hawksley she understood, had got to the heart of. It was Seb himself.

He closed the laptop lid and sat back, images whirling about his brain. Not the ones she had captured but those images firmly stuck in his memory. The tall, earnest girl stuck in the snow, desperate to fulfil her promise to a couple she didn't even know. That same girl later that night, eyes half closed in ecstasy, her long limbs wrapped around him.

The look in her eyes when she told him she was pregnant. Her reaction to his proposal. Her desperate plea for him to pretend he loved her. Her need to be loved. Wanted. Appreciated.

Did he love her enough? Want her enough? Appreciate her enough?

Did he deserve her?

Seb's hands curled into fists. He liked having her here. He liked waking up next to her, liked listening to her take on life, liked the way she brought fresh air and life into his ancient home.

He liked the way she used her camera as a shield, he liked how hard she worked, how seriously she took each and every wedding. He liked the way she focused in on the tiniest detail and made it special.

How she made him feel special.

He liked her dress sense, the vivid shade of red lipstick. He liked how long it took her to choose the hat of the day, how that hat evoked her mood. He liked her first thing in the morning, rosy-cheeked, make-up free, hair tousled.

He liked pretty much everything about her. He loved her.

They were supposed to be getting married in just a few days. Married. For him a business arrangement sealed with a soulless diamond solitaire. He was a fool.

He flipped open her laptop again, clicking onto her

email. He needed her sister Rose's email address. Maybe, just maybe, he could put this right. It might not be too late for him after all.

And then he would bring her home.

CHAPTER TWELVE

'Hi.'

It seemed such an inadequate word. Daisy's breath hitched as Seb came to a stop and looked at her. He was pale, his eyes looked bruised as if he hadn't slept at all and a small, shameful thrill of victory throbbed through her.

Only to ebb with the realisation that it probably wasn't Daisy herself he had spent the night tossing and turning over. The publicity that calling the wedding off would cause? Probably. Losing a legitimate heir? Most definitely.

'Hello.'

He took a step forward and stopped, as if she were a wild animal who might bolt.

It was chillier today and Daisy wrapped her arms around herself, inadequate protection against the sharp breeze blowing across the lawn.

'How did you know I was here?' Had her father called him?

'I didn't. I tried the studio first.'

That meant what? Three hours of driving? A small, unwanted shot of hope pulsed through her. 'I'm sorry for just taking off. I know how much you hate emotional scenes but I really needed some space.'

'I understand.' He swallowed, and her eyes were drawn to the strong lines of his throat. 'I've been thinking myself.'

'About what?'

'Us. Hawksley. My parents. My job. Everything really.'

'That's a lot of thinking.'

'Yes.' His mouth quirked. Daisy tried to look away but she couldn't, her eyes drawn to the firm lines of his jaw, the shape of his mouth.

'Does my mother know why I left?' Sherry had been sleeping at the castle the past week, dedicating every hour to her daughter's wedding. How could Daisy tell her it was all for nothing?

'No. I just said you needed some space,' His eyes were fixed on her with a painful intensity; she was stripped under his gaze. 'She and Violet have gone to your studio to decorate.'

'To what?' What day was it? Her stomach dropped at the realisation. 'Oh, no, the hen night. It's supposed to be low-key.'

'I got the sense that things may have evolved a little. Violet was very excited about buying in some special straws?'

'Straws?'

'Shaped straws…anatomically shaped straws.'

'Oh. Oh! Really? Vi has?'

'I didn't want to tell them they may not be needed, not until I'd spoken to you.' His mouth curved into the familiar half smile and Daisy had to curl her fingers into a fist to stop herself from reaching out to trace its line. 'And, well, it's always good to have a stock of penis straws in.'

'I'll bear that in mind.'

All the things she had planned to say to him had gone clear out of her mind. Daisy had been rehearsing speeches all night but in the end it was her father's words that echoed round and round in her mind. *When you know, you know.*

She knew she loved him. Just one look at him and she was weakening, wanted to hold him, feel his arms around her, allow him to kiss away her fears. But he wouldn't do that, would he? No. Kisses were strictly for the bedroom.

And wonderfully, toe-curlingly delicious as they were, that wasn't enough.

'Seb,' she began.

Another step and he was right before her. 'No hat.' His hand reached out and smoothed down her hair. 'No lipstick.' He ran it down the side of her cheek, drawing one finger along her bottom lip. Daisy's mouth parted at the caress, the tingle of his touch shivering through her.

'I didn't bring anything with me.' She had raided Violet's wardrobe first thing: jeans, a long-sleeved T-shirt. Ordinary, sensible clothes. She felt naked in them; there was nothing to hide behind.

'You're beautiful whatever you wear.' His voice was husky and her knees weakened as she looked up and saw the heat in his eyes.

Her mouth dried. All she wanted to do was press her mouth to his, forget herself, forget the wedding, the baby, her doubts in the surety of his kiss. 'I can't.' She put a hand out, warding him off.

'Daisy.' He swallowed and she steeled herself. Steeled herself against any entreaty. Steeled herself against the knowledge that whatever he told her, however he tried to convince her there were words he would never say no matter how much she yearned to hear them.

And steeled herself not to yield regardless.

'Will you come back with me? No—' As she began to shake her head. 'I don't mean for good. I mean now. There's something I want to show you.'

So much for all her good intentions. But she had to return at some point didn't she? To collect her things. To help dismantle the wedding her mother had spent three weeks lovingly putting together.

To start forgetting the jolt her heart gave as the car pulled over the hill and she saw Hawksley, proud in the distance.

Or to make up her mind to make the best of it, to keep her word, to put their baby first. Trouble was she still didn't know which way to turn.

To be true to her own heart or to be true to her child?

And in the end weren't they the same thing?

Daisy started walking, no destination in mind; she just had to keep moving. Seb fell into step beside her, not touching her, the inches between them a chasm as she rounded the corner past the stables.

'I was thinking that this end stable would make a great studio. They're not listed so you could do whatever you wanted for light—glass walls, anything. I know you want to carry on photographing weddings and that's fine but if you did want to exhibit your other work we could even add a gallery.'

Was this what he wanted to show her? A way of making her career more acceptable? Her heart plummeted. 'A gallery?'

'Only if you wanted to. I know how much you love weddings, but your other work is amazing too. It's up to you.'

'It would make a great space, it's just…' She faltered, unable to find the words.

'It's just an idea. This is your home too, Daisy. I just want you to know that I can support you too, whatever you need. The way you support me.' He sounded sincere enough.

Yesterday those words might even have been enough.

Her heart was so heavy it felt as if it had fallen out of her chest, shrivelled into a stone in the pit of her stomach. She had to keep moving, had to try and figure out the right thing to say. The right thing to do.

The marquee had been set up at the far end of the court-yard and curiosity pulled her there; she hadn't seen inside since it had been decorated.

'Wow.' Swathes of yellow and silk covered the ceiling, creating an exotic canopy over the hardwood dance floor. Buffet tables were set up at one end, covered in yellow cloths, and benches were set around the edges.

Daisy swivelled and walked back through the tent, trying to envision it full, to see it as it would be in just forty-eight hours filled with laughter and dancing—or would it be taken down unused?

A canvas canopy connected the marquee with the door to the Great Hall, a precaution against a rainy day. The heavy oak doors were open and she stepped through them, Seb still at her side. 'Oh,' she said softly as she looked around. 'Oh, it's beautiful.'

Daisy had seen the Great Hall in several guises. Empty save for the weight of history in each of the carved panels, the huge old oak beams. Set up for another wedding ceremony and, later, a busy party venue. Her mother's work-space complete with whiteboards, elaborate floorplans and forelock-tugging minions.

But she had never seen it look as it did today.

The dais at the far end was simply furnished with a white desk and chairs for the registrar, flanked on both sides by tall white urns filled with Violet's unmistakeable flower arrangements: classy, elegant yet with a uniquely modern twist. A heavy tapestry hung from the back wall: Seb's coat of arms.

Facing the dais were rows of chairs, all covered in white, hand-sewn fabric daisy chains wound around their legs and backs.

A yellow carpet lay along the aisle ready for her to walk up, and more of the intricate woven daisy chains hung from the great beams.

'Mum has worked so hard,' she breathed.

'The poor staff have done three dummy runs to make sure they can get the tables set up perfectly in the hour and a half your mother has allowed for drinks, canapés and photographs—on the lawn if dry and warm enough, in the marquee if not. Everything is stacked in the back in perfect order—linens, table decorations, place settings, crockery. Your mother should really run the country,' Seb added, his mouth twisting into a half smile. 'Her organisational skills and, ah, persuasive skills are extraordinary.'

'We've always said that.' Daisy stared at the room perfectly set up for the perfect wedding. For her perfect wedding.

This was what she had always wanted—she had just never known who would be standing by her side. She had certainly never imagined a tall, slightly scruffy academic with penetrating green eyes, too-long dark hair and a title dating back four centuries.

Could she imagine it now? Standing up there making promises to Seb? Images swirled round and round, memories of the last three weeks: tender moments, passionate moments—and that remote, curt aloofness of his. Nausea rose as a stabbing pain shot through her temples; she swayed and he leapt forward, one arm around her shoulders, guiding her to a chair.

Daisy rubbed her head, willing the pain away. 'I'm okay. I forgot to eat breakfast.'

'Come with me, there's some croissants in the kitchen. And there's something I want to show you.'

The knot in her stomach was too big, too tight, food an impossibility until she spoke to him. But would a few more minutes of pretending that all this could be hers hurt?

'I told you I had been doing a lot of thinking,' he said as they stepped back into the courtyard. The wind was still sharp but the sun had come out, slanting through the grey clouds, shining onto the golden stone of the main house. Seb had a glimpse of a future, of children running in and out of the door, games in the courtyard, dens in the wood.

If he could just convince her to stay.

'I've resigned from the university.'

She came to an abrupt stop. 'You've what?'

'Resigned. I'll still write, of course. In fact, without my academic commitments I'll have more time to write, more time to explore other periods, other stories.'

'Why?'

'I'm needed here.' But that wasn't all of it. 'I love delving into the past, you know that. And I loved academia too. Because it was safe, there were rules. When I was a boy—' he inhaled, steady against the rush of memories '—I just wanted to keep my head down, to do the right thing. At school, as long as you worked hard, played hard and didn't tell tales then life was easy. I liked that. It was safe compared to the turbulence of my parents' existence. In a way I guess I never left school. Straight to university and then on an academic path. Everything was clear, easy. I knew exactly what I had to do, what was expected of me—until I inherited Hawksley.

'Until I met you.'

A quiver passed through her but she didn't speak as they walked around the house and in through the main door, towards the library, their steps in harmony. He pushed the library door open and stood there, in the entrance.

'I've made some other decisions too. I've spoken to my agent and asked her to investigate TV work, I've got an agency looking for suitable candidates to take over the estate management and kick-start an events programme and I've asked three architects to submit plans for converting the outbuildings.'

She did speak then, her voice soft. 'You've been very busy.'

'No.' He shook his head. 'I've been at a standstill. You were the one who was busy, busy looking into the future. I've just taken your ideas and made the next step. But I don't want to do it alone.'

She shook her head, tears swimming in her eyes. Tears were good, right? They meant she felt something. Meant she cared.

He needed to throw everything he had at her. Strip away the diffidence and fear and lay it all out. No matter how much it cost him to do it, the alternative was much worse.

'Daisy, I do need you. Not just physically, although my bed has been so empty the last two nights I couldn't sleep. But I need you to challenge me, to push me, to make me take my head out of the sand and face the future.'

'You'd have got there on your own, eventually.'

Would he? He doubted it.

'Seb, I can't live in fear. I don't like being in the papers but I accept it may happen. I can't hide just in case some bored person snaps me. And I can't not say what I think because you don't like emotional outbursts. Life isn't that tidy.'

'I thought it could be,' he admitted. 'I didn't see a middle way between the hysterical ups and downs of my parents' life and the formality of my grandparents. If it was a choice between sitting at opposite sides of a fifteen-foot table and making polite conversation or throwing plates and screaming then give me cold soup and a hoarse voice any day.'

'Most families aren't so extreme…'

'No. No, they're not. And I don't want either of those for the baby. I want it to grow up like you did, part of a happy, stable family. With two parents who love each other.'

Her eyes fell but not before he saw the hurt blaze in them. 'You don't have to say that. I don't want you to lie to make me feel better.'

'The only person I've been lying to was myself.' Seb took her chin and tilted it, trying to make her see the sincerity in his eyes.

'Love, it's complicated. It's messy and emotional and difficult. I wasn't ready for it. But then you came sauntering in with your hats and that mouth—' his eyes dropped to her mouth, lush and full even without its usual coating of slick red '—your camera and your absolute belief in love. Your belief in me and in Hawksley and you turned my world upside down. And not just because of the baby.'

Her eyes blazed blue with hope. 'Really?'

'I hadn't been able to stop thinking of you since that first night,' he told her frankly. It was all or nothing time. 'I asked the groom who you were the next morning and he sent me a link to your website. I must have clicked onto the contact me button a dozen times. But I was afraid. Nobody had ever got under my skin like that before. And then you came back…'

She laughed softly. 'You looked like you'd seen a ghost.'

Seb smiled back down at her, the warmth creeping back into her voice giving him a jolt of hope. 'I couldn't believe my luck. But I was terrified too. Of how you made me feel. How much I wanted you. There was nothing sensible about that. And the more I got to know you, Daisy, the more terrified I was.'

'I'm that scary?' A light had begun to shine in her eyes, the full mouth quivering.

'You are quite frankly the most terrifying woman I have ever met—and I am including your mother in that. And if you ever begin to believe in yourself, Daisy Huntingdon-Cross, then I don't think there is anything you won't achieve. Because—' he moved in slightly closer, emboldened by the curve of her smile '—you are definitely the smartest out of the two of us. It took you leaving for me to acknowledge how I felt about you. But now that I have I want to tell you every day. Every hour of every day. I love you, Daisy, and I really, really hope that you will marry me in two days.'

With those words the load he had been carrying for so long, the fear, the shame, finally broke free. Whatever her answer he would always be grateful to her for that—even if he had to spend the rest of his life proving the truth of his words to her.

'You love me? You think I'm smart?' Her voice broke and he dropped her chin to encircle her waist, pulling her in close. He inhaled the soft floral scent of her hair. It was like coming home.

'Ridiculously so.' Reluctantly he let her go, backing into the half-open door and pushing it open, taking her hand and pulling her inside.

'You're not the only one to see that the house needs changing, needs making into a home. I can't begin to match what you've achieved but I'm trying to make a start.'

Daisy stood stock-still, staring at the wall. Gone was the line of stern portraits; no more bewigged gentleman with terrifying eyebrows or stern Victorians with bristling moustaches. Even Seb's grandfather had been removed to a more fitting place in the long gallery.

Instead two huge canvas prints hung on the wall, surrounded by smaller black-and-white prints of Hawksley: the castle, the woods, the gardens. Her photos.

She looked up at the photos, eyes widening as she took in the photo of Seb. It was the one she'd taken of him in Oxford, the light behind him. It felt hubristic having such a large picture of himself on his own wall.

But it wasn't just his wall now.

Flanking him was another black-and-white photo, this time of Daisy—also at work. The trees framed her as she held the camera up to her face, her profile intent, her focus absolute.

'Where...?' She gaped up at the picture. 'Where on earth did you get that?'

'I took it.' Seb tried and failed to keep the pride out of his voice. 'I had a moment in between those photobooth shots and I turned around—and there you were. Lost in the moment. So I snapped it. I saved it onto my computer, thought you might want it for your website or something.'

'It's actually pretty good, nice composition.'

'Total and utter fluke,' he admitted. 'Daisy—' he took her hands in his '—I want the castle, every room, every decision we make to be about us. About you, me and the baby. I want to help you turn Hawksley into a family home. Into a house full of love and laughter. I asked you to marry me three weeks ago for all sorts of sensible reasons. I told you marriage was a business. I was a fool.

'I want to marry you because I love you and I hope you love me. Because I actually don't think I can live without you—and I know I can't survive without you. So, Daisy.' Seb let go of her hands and took out the ring. The ring that had miraculously arrived by overnight courier, the ring that Daisy's sister had somehow known to have ready.

Slowly, looking up into her face, he lowered himself onto one knee.

'Daisy Huntingdon-Cross. Will you please, please marry me?'

'Get up!' Daisy pulled him up, snaking her arms around his neck, smiling up at him, her eyes full of joy. 'Well, the guests *are* already invited.'

'They are.'

'It would be a shame to waste my mother's hard work.'

'A real shame.'

'And the chance to see my mother with a penis straw is not one to be passed up.'

Seb grimaced. 'I can personally live without that image, my love. But knock yourself out.'

'Say that again.'

'Knock yourself out?'

'No, the name you called me.'

'My love.' Seb's heart felt as if it might explode from his chest as he bent his head, ready to capture her mouth with his. 'My love.'

EPILOGUE

'READY, DAISY GIRL?'

Daisy pulled at the waist of her dress with nervous fingers before smiling up at her father.

'Ready, Dad.'

'Well, I'm not.' Rick Cross's eyes were suspiciously damp. 'I don't think I will ever be ready to walk you down that aisle and hand you over to another man.'

Violet rolled her eyes. 'It's the twenty-first century, Dad. Nobody gets handed over.'

'If anyone is in charge in this house, I'm sorry, I mean in this castle, it's Daisy. I've only been here a few hours and even I can see she's got that poor earl right under her thumb.'

Daisy stuck her tongue out at Rose. 'How I wish I had made you wear frills.'

Her sisters looked stunning in the simple silk dresses she had chosen. The sweetheart necklines and ruched bodices were white, flaring out into yellow knee-length skirts. Her dress had a similar bodice although instead of bare shoulders, hers were covered with a sheer lace and her floor-length skirt fell straight from the bust in a sweep of white silk to the floor.

'And I wish I had made that ring too large.' Rose nodded at the band made of twisted yellow gold, white gold petals alternating with small diamonds that adorned Daisy's left hand.

Daisy smiled down at the ring. 'I don't think you've ever made anything more lovely, Rose. I don't know how you knew to make it but thank you.'

'It goes better with your wedding ring,' Rose said, but her eyes, so like Daisy's own, were sparkling with pride. 'You look beautiful, Daisy.'

'Will Seb recognise you without a hat?' Violet tucked an errant curl behind Daisy's ear and tweaked the flowers that held her twist of hair back into place. 'There, perfect.'

'You picked a good dress.' Rose was looking her up and down. 'Your boobs are a little bit bigger but otherwise you don't look pregnant.'

'I'm not showing yet!' Daisy still couldn't mention the pregnancy without blushing. She'd told her mother and sisters during her hen night while Rose Skyped in; they had all been delighted. Especially as she hadn't needed to lie to them—they weren't just getting married because of the baby. They were getting married because they belonged together.

It was as simple and as wonderful as that.

Seb had expected to feel nervous. He was used to standing in front of large crowds, used to speaking in public. But when he taught or lectured he put on a persona. This was him, raw and exposed, in tails and a yellow cravat, ready to pledge his troth to the woman he loved.

He bit back a wry smile. He was even using her terminology now.

Sherry sat at the front, resplendent in something very structured and rigid. Seb knew very little about fashion but he was aware she was wearing something very expensive that mere mortals would never be able to carry off.

The buzz of voices came to a sudden stop as the band

struck up one of Rick's most famous tunes, a song he had composed soon after Daisy's birth. The familiar chords sounded even more poignant than ever as a violin picked up the vocal lines, soaring up into the beams as one of the twins, Seb had no idea which one, solemnly began to walk down the central aisle followed by the other.

And then his heart stopped as Daisy appeared. All in white except for her red lipstick and the bouquet of daisies, her eyes shining and a trembling smile on her lips. His fiancée, his bride, the mother of his baby.

Two months ago he was struggling on alone. Now he had a family, hope, joy. He had a future.

He smiled as a camera flashed from the back of the hall. Let them take photos, let them publish them everywhere and anywhere. He was the luckiest man alive and he was happy for the whole world to know.

* * * * *

CONVENIENTLY WED TO THE GREEK

KANDY SHEPHERD

To Catherine and Keith,
with thanks for introducing me
to the beauty of the Ionian Islands.

CHAPTER ONE

ADELE HUDSON WAS too busy concentrating on the yoga teacher's instructions to take much notice of the late-comer who took a place to her left and unrolled his mat. From the corner of her eye she registered that he was tall, black-haired, and with the lean, athletic body she would expect from a man who did yoga. *Nice.* But that was as far as her interest went.

Until she attempted to balance on one leg, with the other tucked up against her upper inner thigh, in the *vrksasana* or 'tree' pose. It seemed impossible for a beginner. Why had she thought this class was a good idea?

Dell risked a glance to see if the guy next to her was doing any better. He held the pose effortlessly, broad shoulders, narrow hips, tanned muscular arms in perfect alignment. But the shock of recognition as he came into focus made her wobble so badly she had to flail her arms to stay upright.

Alexios Mikhalis. It couldn't be him. Not here in this far-flung spa retreat on the south coast of New South Wales where she had come to find peace. Not now when she so desperately needed to regroup and rethink her suddenly turned upside down life. But a second quick glimpse confirmed his identity, although he looked very different from the last time she had seen him three years ago pummelling her reputation in court. This man had done everything in his power to destroy her career. And very nearly succeeded.

A shiver of dread ran through her—threatening her balance in more ways than one. He was the last person on earth she wanted to encounter. She had more than enough on her mind without having to shore up her defences against him. Quickly Dell looked away, praying her nemesis hadn't recognised her. Tragedy had visited him since they'd last met, but she doubted he would be any less ruthless. Not when it came to her.

'Lengthen up through the crown of your head,' the yoga teacher intoned in her breathy Zen-like voice.

But it was no use. Dell's concentration was shot. *Why was he here?* The more she tried to balance on one shaky leg, the more impossible the pose seemed. How the heck did you lengthen through the crown of your head anyway? In spite of all efforts to stay upright, she tilted sideward, heading for a humiliating yoga wipe-out.

A strong, masculine hand gripped her elbow to steady her. *Him.* 'Whoa there,' came the deep voice others might find attractive but she had only found intimidating and arrogant.

'Th…thank you,' she said, her chin down and her eyes anywhere but at him, pretending to be invisible. But to no avail.

His grip on her arm tightened. *'You,'* he said, drawing out the word so it sounded like an insult.

Dell turned her head to meet his hawk-like glare, those eyes so dark they were nearly black. She tilted her chin upwards and tried without success to keep the quiver from her voice. 'Yes, *me*.'

Her final encounter with him burned in her memory. Outside the courthouse he had stood on the step above her using his superior height to underline the threat in his words. *'The judge might have ruled in your favour but you won't get away with this. I'll make sure of that.'*

In spite of his loss since then, she had no doubt he still meant every word.

'What are you doing here?' His famously handsome face contorted into a frown.

'Apart from attempting to learn yoga?' she asked with the nervous laugh that insisted on popping out when she felt under pressure. 'Resting, relaxing, those things you do when you come to a health spa.' She didn't dare add *reviewing this new resort*.

This was the tycoon hotelier who had chosen to do battle with her. She was the food critic who had dared to publish a critical review of the most established restaurant in his empire. He'd sued the newspaper that had employed her for an insane amount of money and lost.

Alex Mikhalis had not liked losing. That he was a winner was part of the ethos he'd built up around him—the hospitality mogul who launched nightclubs and restaurants that instantly became Sydney's go-to venues, wiped out his competitors and made him multiple millions. *'Playboy Tycoon with the Magic Touch'*—her own newspaper had headlined a profile on him not long before her disputed review.

After the scene on the courtroom steps, she'd been careful to stay out of his way. Then he'd disappeared from the social scene that had been his playground.

Even the most intrepid of her journalist colleagues hadn't been able to find him. *And here he was.*

'You've hunted me down,' he said.

'I did no such thing,' she said. 'Why would I—?'

'Please, *silence.*' The yoga instructor's tone was now not so Zen-like.

'Let's take this outside,' he said in a deep undertone, maintaining his grip on her elbow.

Dell would have liked to shake off his hand, then place her hands on his chest and shove him away from her. But she was a guest at the spa—here at the owner's invitation—and she didn't want to cause any kind of disruption.

'Sorry,' she mouthed to the instructor as she let herself be led out of the room, grateful in a way not to have to try any more of those ridiculously difficult poses.

With the door to the yoga room shut behind them, Dell took the lead to one of the small guest lounges scattered through the resort. Simple white leather chairs were grouped around a low table. It faced full-length glass windows that looked east to a view of the Pacific Ocean, dazzling blue in the autumn morning sun filtered through graceful Australian eucalypts.

Now she did shake off his arm. 'What was that all about?'

'My right to privacy,' he said, tight-lipped.

Dell was struck again by how different the tycoon looked. No wonder she hadn't immediately recognised him. Back then he'd been a style leader, designer clothes, a fashionable short beard, hair tied into a man bun—though not in court—flamboyant in an intensely masculine way. She'd often wondered what his image had masked. Now he was more boot camp than boutique—strong jaw clean shaven, thick dark hair cropped short, pumped muscles emphasised by grey sweat pants and a white singlet. Stripped bare. And even more compelling. Just her type in fact—if he had been anyone but him.

'And I impinged on your privacy how?' she asked. 'By taking a yoga class that you happened to join? I had no idea you were here.'

'Your newspaper sent you to track me down.' It was a statement, not a question.

'No. It didn't.' The fact she no longer worked for the paper was none of his concern. 'I'm a food writer, not an investigative journalist.'

His mouth twisted. 'Does that matter? To the media I make good copy. No matter how hard I've worked to keep off the radar since…since…'

He seemed unable to choke out the words. She noticed tight lines around his mouth, a few silver hairs in the dark black of his hair near his temples. He was thirty-two, three years older than her, yet there was something immeasurably weary etched on his face.

Another shiver ran up Dell's spine. How did she deal with this? This wealthy, powerful man had been her adversary. *He had threatened her with revenge.* She was convinced his attack on her newspaper had led in part to her losing her job. But how could she hold a grudge after what he had endured?

'I know,' she said, aware her words were completely inadequate. Just a few months after his unsuccessful court case against her, his fiancée had been taken hostage by a crazed gunman in one of his city restaurants. She hadn't come out alive. His grief, his anger, his pain had been front-page news. Until he had disappeared.

Wordlessly, he nodded.

'I'm so sorry,' she said. 'I…wanted to let you know that when…when it happened. But we weren't exactly friends. So I didn't. I've always regretted it.'

He made some inarticulate sound and brushed her words away. But she was glad she had finally been able to express her condolences.

She was surprised at the rush of compassion she felt for him at the bleak emptiness of his expression. *He had lost everything.* She didn't know where he had been, why he was back. His colourful and tragic history made him eminently newsworthy. But she wouldn't make a scoop of his secret by selling the story of her encounter with him. In spite of the fact such a story would bring her much-needed dollars.

'Be assured I won't be the one to reveal your whereabouts,' she said. 'Not to my press contacts. Not on my blog. I'm here for the rest of the week. I'll stay right out of your way.'

She left him looking moodily out to the waters of Big Ray beach and had to slow her pace to something less than a scurry. No way did she want this man to think she was running away from him.

In theory, Alex should not have seen Adele Hudson again. The Bay Breeze spa was designed for tranquil contemplation as well as holistic treatments. In the resort's airy white spaces there was room for personal space and privacy.

But only hours after the yoga class he encountered her in the guest lounge, still in her yoga pants and tank top, contemplating the range of herbal teas and chatting animatedly to an older grey-haired woman who was doing the same. He was on the hunt for caffeine so did not back away. Not that he was in the habit of backing away. He'd always thrived on confrontation.

Alex had always regarded the sassy food critic as an adversary—an enemy, even. Back then he had been implacable in protecting every aspect of his business—an attack on it was an attack on *him*. He certainly hadn't registered anything physical about the person he'd seen as intent on undermining his success with her viperish review of his flagship restaurant. Yet now, observing her, he was forced to concede she was an attractive woman. Very attractive. And in spite of their past vendetta, he had seen compassion and understanding in her eyes. Not the pity he loathed.

She wasn't anything like the type of woman he'd used to date—blonde and willowy models or television celebrities who'd looked good on his arm for publicity purposes. Mia had been tall and blonde too. He swallowed hard against the wave of regret and recrimination that hit him as it always did when he thought about his late fiancée and forced himself to focus on the present.

Adele was average height, curvier than any model, with thick auburn hair she'd worn tied back in the yoga class but which now tumbled around her shoulders. She wasn't conventionally pretty—her mouth was too wide, her jaw line rather too assertive for 'pretty'—but she was head turning in her own, vibrant way. It was her smile he was noticing now—she'd never had cause to smile in his presence. In fact he remembered she'd been rather effective with a snarl when it had come to interacting with him.

Her mouth was wide and generous and she had perfect teeth. When she laughed at something the other woman said her whole face lit up; her eyes laughed too. What colour were they? Green? Hazel? Somewhere in between? The other woman was charmed by that smile. Alex could tell that from where he stood.

Yet when Adele looked up and caught him observing her the smile faded and her face set in cool, polite lines. Her shoulders hunched as if to protect herself from him and her eyes darted past him and to the doorway. Who could blame her for her dislike of him? He wished he could make up to her for the way he'd behaved towards her. As he'd tried to make amends to others he'd damaged by his ruthless, self-centred pursuit of success. Make amends to them because he could never make amends to Mia. Her death hung heavily on his conscience. *His fault.*

He headed towards Adele. She smiled at him. But it was a poor, forced shadow of the smile he'd seen dazzling her companion just seconds before—more a polite stretching of her lips. He found himself wanting to be warmed by the real deal. But not only did he not deserve it from this person he had so relentlessly hounded, it would be pointless.

There was something frozen inside his soul that even the most heartfelt of smiles from a lovely woman could never melt. Something that had started to shut down the day he'd got a phone call from the police to say a psycho had his city restaurant in lockdown and was holding his fiancée hostage with a gun to her head. Something that had formed cold and rock solid when Mia had lost her own life trying to save another's.

'Hello there,' Dell said very politely. Then turned to the woman beside her and gestured towards him. 'We met in the yoga class,' she explained, not mentioning his name by way of introduction.

So she intended to keep her word about maintaining his privacy. He was grateful for that. Alex nodded to the older woman. He did not feel obliged to share anything about himself with strangers—even his name.

He turned to the artful display of teas in small wooden chests. 'This is a fine selection,' he said with genuine interest. He was here to glean information for his new project. A hotel completely different from anything he'd created before. He'd been isolated from the hospitality business in the past years and needed to be on top of the trends. He knew all about partying and decadence—what he sought now was restraint and calm. A different way of doing business. A different *life*.

'Tea has become very fashionable,' Adele said in what seemed a purposely neutral voice, more for the benefit of the other woman rather than any conscious desire to engage in conversation with *him*. 'Not any old teas, naturally. Herbal teas, healing tisanes, special blends. I highly recommend the parsnip, ginger and turmeric blend—organic and vegan, which is a good thing.'

Alex gagged at the thought of it.

But if that was what people wanted at a place like this, it would be up to him to give it to them. Of course Adele would know about what was fashionable in foods and beverages. Her *Dell Dishes* blog attracted an extraordinary number of visitors. Or it had three years ago when he had instructed his lawyers to delve deep into her life with particular reference to her income.

At one stage he had thought about suing her personally as well as via the publishing company that had employed her as a food critic and editor of its restaurant guide. Back then, scrutinising *Dell Dishes*, he hadn't thought she had done enough to monetise her site, to take advantage of the potential appeal to advertisers. Needless to say he hadn't offered her any advice—he'd wanted to bring her down, not help her soar.

'I'll pass on the parsnip tea, thank you,' he said, suppressing a grimace. 'What I want is coffee—strong and black.' He couldn't keep the yearning from his voice.

'No such thing here, I'm afraid,' she said, with a wry expression that he couldn't help but find cute. *Cute.* It was incomprehensible that he should find Adele Hudson *cute.*

He groaned. 'No coffee at all?'

She shook her head. 'Not part of the "clean food" ethos of the spa. You'll have to sneak out to the Bay Bites café. They serve Dolphin Bay's finest coffee. I can personally vouch for it.'

'I might follow up on that.'

His friends the Morgan brothers, Ben and Jesse, had made the once sleepy beachside town of Dolphin Bay into quite a destination with the critically acclaimed Hotel Harbourside, Bay Bites, Bay Books and now the eco-friendly Bay Breeze spa in which Alex had invested in the early stages. It would not be long before he saw a return on his investment.

The new resort was still in its debut phase but had been an immediate success. It had been booked out for Easter a few weeks back. The Morgans had read the market well. In just one day Alex had picked aspects he liked about the operation and ones he didn't think would translate to his new venture. What worked in Australia might not necessarily work in Greece.

'Escaping for coffee is hardly in the spirit of eating clean food.' Adele sounded stern but there was an unexpected gleam of fun in her eyes. Eyes that were green like the olives growing on the island in the Ionian Sea that had once belonged to his ancestors and that he had bought so it once more was owned by a Mikhalis.

He couldn't help his snort of disgust at her comment. 'So does "clean food" mean that all other food is "dirty"? I don't like the idea of that. Especially the traditional Greek foods I grew up on.'

'I think that term is debatable too,' she said. 'I wonder if—?'

Adele's grey-haired companion chose that moment to pick up her cup of herbal tea and make to move away. 'I want to say again how much I love your blog,' she enthused. 'My daughter told me about it. Even my granddaughter is a fan, and she's still at school.'

Adele flushed and looked pleased. As she should—it was no mean feat to have her site appeal to three generations. 'Thank you. I hope I can keep on bringing you more of what you enjoy.'

'You'll do that, I'm sure,' the other woman said. 'In the meantime, I'll leave you two to chat.' She departed but not without a speculative look from Alex to Adele and back to him again.

Alex groaned inwardly. He recognised that gleam in her narrowed eyes. The same matchmaking gleam he'd seen often in the women of his extended Greek family. This particular lady had got completely the wrong end of the stick. He had no romantic interest whatsoever in Adele Hudson. In fact he had no interest in any kind of permanent relationship with any woman—in spite of the pressure from his family to settle down. Not now. Not ever. Not after what he'd endured. Not after what he had *done*.

Besides, Adele was married. Or she had been three years ago. He glanced down at her left hand. *No ring.* So maybe she was no longer married. Not that her marital state was of any interest to him.

Adele had obviously not missed that matchmaking gleam either. When she looked back at him, the undisguised horror in her eyes told him exactly what she thought of the idea of anyone pairing her with *him*.

Alex had taken worse insults in his time. So why did that feel like a kick to the gut? He decided not to linger any longer at the tea station. Or to admit even to himself that he would like lovely Adele Hudson to look at him with something other than extreme distaste.

CHAPTER TWO

THE NEXT TIME Alex saw Adele Hudson he'd beaten her to their mutual destination—the dolphin-themed Bay Bites café that overlooked the picturesque harbour of Dolphin Bay. The café was buzzing with the hum of conversation, the aromas of fresh baking— and that indefinable feeling of a successful business. Alex missed being 'hands on' in his own restaurants so much it ached. That world was what had driven him since he'd been a teenager. Even before that. As a child he'd spent some of his happiest hours in his grandfather's restaurant.

Here he could sense the goodwill of the customers, the seamless teamwork of the staff. All was as he liked it to be in his own establishments. And Adele had been right, the café did have excellent coffee. He was sitting at a table near the window, savouring his second espresso, when he looked up to see her heading his way, pedalling one of the bicycles Bay Breeze provided for guests.

She cycled energetically, a woman on a mission to get somewhere quickly. Her face was flushed from exertion as she got off and slid the bike onto a rack outside the café. She took off her bike helmet and shook out her auburn hair with a gesture of unconscious grace. Her hair glinted with copper highlights in the morning sunlight, dazzling him.

This woman was nothing to him but an old adversary. Yet Alex found it difficult to look away from her fresh beauty. Since he'd been living in Greece, getting back to basics with his family there, he felt as if he were seeing life through new eyes. He was certainly seeing something different in Adele Hudson. Or maybe it had always been there and he'd been so intent on revenge he hadn't noticed. There was something vibrant and uncontrived about her, dressed in white shorts and a simple white top, white sneakers and with a small multicoloured backpack. She radiated energy and good health, her face open and welcome to new experience.

Alex didn't alert her to his presence; she'd notice him soon enough. When she did, her first reaction on catching sight of him was out-and-out dismay, quickly covered up by another forced smile. Again he felt that kick in the gut—quite unjustifiably considering how he'd treated her in the past.

She stopped by his table and he got up to greet her, glad she hadn't just walked by with a cursory nod. 'So you took my advice,' she said. Her flushed cheeks made her eyes seem even greener. Her hair was tousled around her face.

'Yes,' he said. 'I become a raging beast without my coffee.'

It was a bad choice of words. The look that flashed across her eyes told him she found the *beast* label only too appropriate. And that not only did she dislike him, but it seemed she also might fear him.

A jolt of remorse hit him. That was not the reaction

he ever wanted from a woman. He thought back to the court case. There'd been some kind of confrontation outside on the day the judge had handed down his decision—although surely nothing to make her frightened of him.

'I'm not partial to raging beasts,' she said. *Beasts like you* were the words she left unspoken but he understand as well as if she had shouted them.

Against all his own legal advice he'd gone after her and the major Sydney newspaper that had published her review. He'd been furious at her criticism of Athina, his first important restaurant—the one that had launched him as a serious contender on the competitive Sydney market. He'd had a lot to prove when he'd closed his grandfather's original traditional Greek restaurant and reopened with something cutting-edge fashionable. The risk had paid off—and success after success had followed. And then she'd published a bad review of Athina, detailing how the prices had gone up and the quality gone down, along with the levels of service. It had seemed like a personal assault.

So much had happened to him since then. His fury at her review now seemed disproportionate—a major overreaction to what the court had found to be fair comment. In light of what had happened during the hostage scenario and its aftermath it seemed insignificant. She had nothing to fear from him. Not now.

He looked directly at her. 'I told you this beast has been tamed,' he said gruffly. It was as much an explanation as he felt able to give her. He didn't share with anyone how he'd had to claw his way out of the abyss.

But her brow furrowed. 'Tamed by the coffee?'

She didn't get what he meant. But he had no intention of spelling out the bigger picture for her. How devastated he'd been by Mia's death. The train wreck his life had become. He'd been a broken man, unable to deal with the public spotlight on him—the spotlight he'd once courted. There had only been the pain, the loss, the unrelenting guilt.

His father had intervened, packed him up and sent him back to the Greek village his grandfather had left long ago to emigrate to Australia. At first, Alex had deeply resented his exile. But the distance and the return to his family's roots had given him a painfully gained new perspective and self-knowledge. He'd discovered he hadn't much liked the man he'd become in Sydney.

The presence of Adele Hudson was like an arrow piercing his armour, reminding him of how invincible he'd thought himself to be back then when he'd been flying so high, how agonising his crash into the shadows. He forced his voice to sound steady and impartial. 'The magical powers of caffeine,' he said. 'Can I order you a coffee?'

Adele gave him a look through narrowed eyes that let him know she realised there was something more to his words that she hadn't grasped. But didn't care to pursue. She peered towards the back of the café to the door that led to the kitchen. 'No, thank you. I've popped in to see Lizzie.'

'Lizzie Dumont?'

Jesse's wife was a chef and the driving force behind the exemplary standards of the Morgan eateries. Alex had tried to poach her to work for him on a start-up in Sydney, a traditional French bistro. That was before he'd realised she'd been engaged to Jesse Morgan. That had stopped him. Back then he'd let nothing stop his quest for success—except loyalty to friends and family. That had never been negotiable.

'She's Lizzie Morgan now, well and truly married to Jesse,' Adele said. 'They have a beautiful baby boy, a brother for her daughter Amy.'

'Yes,' he said.

Lizzie had a child from her first marriage. Alex had admired Jesse for taking on a stepchild. Had admired him the more because it wasn't something Alex himself could ever do. His feeling for family and heritage was too deeply ingrained to ever take on another man's child. He would never date a woman who came encumbered.

'Here she is.' Adele waved at a tall woman with curly, pale blonde hair who had pushed her way through the doors from the kitchen.

'Dell! It's so good to see you.' Alex watched as Lizzie swept Adele up in a hug. 'It's been too long. We've got so much to catch up on.'

'We certainly do,' said Adele, giving Lizzie the full benefit of her dazzling smile. Politely, she turned to include him in the conversation. *No smile for him.* 'Lizzie, I think you know Alex Mik—'

'Of course I do,' Lizzie said. She greeted him with a hug and kisses on both cheeks. 'He's a good friend of Jesse's. When we heard he was going to be in Sydney we invited him down to Bay Breeze. Long time, no see, Alex.' Her smile dimmed and her voice softened. 'Are you okay?'

He nodded. 'As okay as I can be,' he said. 'I've appreciated the support from you and Jesse. It means a lot.' He didn't want to talk about his loss any further.

Displaying vulnerability clashed with all the ideals of manhood that had been imbued in him by his family. 'I didn't know you two knew each other,' he said. How much did Lizzie know of his history with Adele? No doubt he'd been painted as an ogre of the first order. *A beast.*

Lizzie beamed. 'Dell was one of our first customers. Her glowing reviews of Bay Bites helped put us on the map. The bonus was we became friends. Though we don't see each other as much as we'd like.'

Adele studiously avoided his eyes, obviously uncomfortable at the mention of her good reviews when she'd given Athina such a stinker. The court case had ensured she'd never reviewed his newer ventures, never put them 'on the map'.

'I've always loved this part of the world,' she said. 'And Bay Breeze is the icing on the cake. I love what you guys have done with it, Lizzie. The building, the fit-out, the food. The timing is perfect. Stress and burnout are endemic today. Offering this kind of retreat in such an awesome natural setting is just what a particular lucrative market is looking for.'

Had she read his mind? She could have been quoting him on the pitch for his new luxury boutique resort.

As she chatted with Lizzie, Alex was surprised at how much Adele knew about the hospitality business. She was both perceptive and canny. She understood how success came from meeting people's needs but also about anticipating them. Giving them what they didn't know they wanted until it was offered to them, all new and shiny. Knowing your customer through and through. Being open to change and nimble enough to adapt to it.

The strength of Bay Breeze she had pinpointed was on track with what he wanted for his new venue. It wasn't often he met someone who was so in tune with how he thought about the business. Although that was perhaps not such a surprise when in the past he'd surrounded himself with too many 'yes' men.

'So what are your plans for life after the newspaper?' Lizzie asked her.

Adele frowned at Lizzie with what was obviously a warning. Alex realised she didn't want him to hear that. Which made him determined not to miss a word.

'What do you mean?' he asked.

Lizzie sounded outraged. 'That darn newspaper fired Dell. Booted her out with a cheque in lieu of notice.'

Adele glared at her friend for spilling the beans.

'Is that true?' he asked Adele. 'You've lost your job?'

She shrugged. But he could see it was an effort for her to sound casual about such a blow. Especially in front of him. 'Budget cuts, they said. It…it was a shock.'

'Because of the court case?' Regret churned in him. How much damage had he caused for something that now seemed unimportant?

She didn't meet his eye. 'No. That was three years ago. Although I was never popular with management afterwards. Being sued wasn't regarded as a highlight of my résumé.'

He frowned. 'What will you do?' He felt a shaft of shame at what he had put her through. Although he had felt totally in the right at the time.

Alex expected a snarl and a rejoinder to mind his own business. But she couldn't mask the panic in her eyes. 'I don't know yet. They only gave me the boot a week ago. But I've got options.'

'Of course you have,' said loyal Lizzie. 'Publicity and marketing among them. That would be a logical move for you.'

Adele nodded to her friend. 'Yes, I've thought of that,' she said. 'And I can freelance. It will also allow me to give my blog more attention.'

Alex doubted she could make enough to live on from that blog, in spite of the number of readers it attracted. Unless she'd made big strides with attracting advertising since he'd last looked at *Dell Dishes*.

'Your husband?' he asked after some hesitation. He was sure there'd been a husband.

Her mouth twisted. 'Divorced.' Her chin tilted upward. 'In any case, I don't depend on a man to support me.'

He wouldn't have expected any other response from the feisty food critic. 'Do you have children?'

Something he couldn't read darkened her eyes. She shook her head.

'Then come and work for me.' The words escaped his mouth before he'd had time to think about them. But some of his best decisions had been made on impulse.

Dell looked up at Alex Mikhalis, the man she regarded as the devil incarnate. He towered over her, darkly formidable in black jeans and a black T-shirt that made no secret of his strength, his impressive muscles.

'Did you just offer me a job?' She couldn't keep the disbelief from her voice. From behind her, she heard Lizzie gasp.

'I did,' he said gruffly.

'Why would you do that?'

'You need a job. I need help with a new venture. Your understanding of hospitality is impressive. You have skills in PR and publicity.'

Entitled and arrogant, he so obviously expected an instant 'yes'. But it would not be forthcoming from her. She sympathised with his personal loss. That didn't mean she wanted to work with him. Especially not to be under his control as an employee.

She couldn't think of anything worse.

'I appreciate the offer,' she said. 'But I can't possibly accept. I suspect you know why.'

His legal team had undermined her credibility at every opportunity. Even though her newspaper had won the case, she had come out of it bruised and battered with her reputation intact but shredded around the edges. Even three years later she felt it had influenced her employer into 'letting her go'. And that was apart from the stress it had put on her marriage.

He scowled. 'I want to make amends.'

Alex Mikhalis make amends? To her? She frowned. 'Is this some kind of trick?'

'No tricks,' he said. His voice was deep, assured, confident. Yet did nothing to reassure her.

'I find that difficult to believe. You…you threatened me. Told me you would get even.' He made her so nervous it was difficult to get her words out. She had heard the rumours of how effectively he had brought down his business opponents. But she would not let him sense her fear.

'That was a different time and place. There is no threat.'

'Why should I trust you?' Memories of his intimidation on the courtroom steps flooded back.

Dell became aware that she and the tall, broad-shouldered man were the focus of interest among the customers of the café. She moved closer to him so she could lower her voice. He moved closer as well. *Too close.* She felt as if he were taking up all the air, making her heart race, her breath come short.

'I'm a different man,' he said, his expression intent, dark eyes unreadable as he searched her face.

He *looked* different, that was for sure. Stripped of designer trappings to a raw masculinity that, in spite of her dislike of him, she could not help but appreciate. As for his nature? Leopards didn't change their spots. And there had always been something predatory about him.

She couldn't help the snort of disbelief that escaped her. 'Huh! You? As if I believe—'

A flash of pain contorted his features but was gone so quickly she might have imagined it if it hadn't made such an impression on her that it stopped her words short. For a long moment she stared up at him. It had been three years since she had faced him on the courtroom steps. He had been through trauma like she couldn't imagine. Who knew how that might have affected him? Maybe he was telling the truth.

She felt a gentle tap on her arm and turned, dazed, to see Lizzie. 'Perhaps you should consider this offer,' her friend said quietly. Her eyes gave her a silent message. *You have debts.*

Dell was only too aware of the debts she had run up during her marriage and that had become her responsibility. Lizzie always gave her wise counsel. Her friend would be horrified if she knew the decision she had made just the week before she had lost her job. If it paid off, she might need a job more than ever. And with so many people reviewing restaurants online for free, she felt the newspaper editor had been telling the truth when he'd told her that her role was redundant. Job offers weren't exactly flooding her inbox. She forced herself to take a deep, calming breath.

Then turned back to face Alex. 'Why do you want to make amends?' she said. 'And what makes you think we could work together? I'm a writer, not a restaurateur.'

'I'll answer both your questions with one reply,' he said. 'Every criticism you made about my restaurant Athina was true. My manager was systematically defrauding me. Your judgement was spot on. I should have taken your review as a warning instead of taking you to court.'

'Oh,' was all she was able to choke out. Alex Mikhalis admitting he was *wrong*?

A ghost of a smile lifted the corners of his mouth. She was more used to seeing him glare and scowl at her. The effect was disconcerting. A devil undoubtedly. But a fiendishly handsome devil. For the first time she saw a hint of the legendary charisma that had propelled him to such heights in a people-pleasing business.

'I've shocked you speechless,' he said.

'I admit it. I'm stunned. After all that…that angst. When did you find out?'

'When I slipped back into Sydney for the review of the police handling of the siege,' he said, now without any trace of a smile.

Dell nodded, unable to find the words to say anything about what must have been such a terrible time in his life. The saga had made headlines in the media for weeks. 'From my memory, the manager was your friend,' she said instead.

'Yes,' he said simply.

How betrayed he must have felt on top of everything else he'd had to endure.

'Perhaps if I had been an investigative reporter I might have discovered that,' she said.

'I wouldn't have believed you. Everything in your review pointed that way. I just didn't see it.'

'Didn't *want* to see it, perhaps,' she said.

He paused, then the words came slowly. 'I… I'm sorry, Adele.'

Alex Mikhalis *apologising*? After all this man had put her through?

She thought again about all *he* had been through since. Realised she was intrigued at the thought of what project he might be working on now. And that it wasn't healthy to hold a grudge or wise to refuse an apparently sincere apology. Especially when she really needed a job. Lizzie was right. She should consider this.

'Dell,' she said. 'Please call me Dell. Adele is my newspaper byline, the name on my birth certificate.' She looked up at him. 'Tell me more about this job.'

CHAPTER THREE

ALEX DIDN'T KNOW why it had suddenly become so important that Adele Hudson—Dell—accept his impromptu job offer. But he didn't question it. Much of his success in business had come from following his instinct and he'd learned not to ignore its prompts.

Dell could be just the person he needed to help him launch his new project. The project he needed to get him back on track with life.

Mentally, he checked off the skills she brought to the table. Without a doubt she was good with words— a huge asset for launching into a new market. Another strength was she saw the hospitality industry through the eyes of the customer while at the same understanding how the business side operated. Her blog gave her an international view with access to readers all around the world. On top of that, she was smart and perceptive.

Her review of Athina had raised red flags he should have heeded. His traitorous so-called friend had been doing illicit deals with suppliers and siphoning off funds to a private bank account. He would have saved himself a good deal of money if he hadn't let pride and anger blind him to the truth of what she had observed.

Since he'd been back living in the land of his ancestors he had thought a lot about the Ancient Greek concept of fate. Was it his selfishness or fate that had put Mia in his city restaurant when a sociopath had decided to make a deadly statement? Could it be that fate had brought Dell back into his life? Right at the time when he needed help to launch something different and she was in need of a job? At a time when he was growing weary of punishing himself for something that had been out of his control.

Dell looked up at him, her green eyes direct. 'What exactly does the job entail?' she asked.

Fact was, there wasn't a job vacancy as such. He would create a role for her.

Alex looked around the café, filling up now as lunchtime approached. Lizzie had left them to return to the kitchen. 'We need to go somewhere more private where we can talk.'

Dell nodded with immediate understanding. 'What about the harbour front?' she said.

He put cash on the table to cover both his coffee and a very generous tip. 'Good idea.'

He followed her out of the café. She looked good in shorts with her slender legs and shapely behind. In fact she was downright sexy. How had he not noticed that sensuous sway before? Alex forced his gaze away. *This was about business.*

He walked with her past the adjoining bookstore towards a lookout with a view across the stone-walled harbour with its array of fishing and pleasure craft. The scene was in some ways reminiscent of the fishing village his Greek ancestors came from, in others completely different.

He'd been born and grown up in Australia and

thought of himself as Australian. But his Greek heritage was calling to him. He was back here just for a quick visit to help celebrate his father's sixtieth birthday and to take a look at Bay Breeze. Greece was where he wanted to be right now. He didn't think he could ever live back in Sydney again. Not with the memories and regrets that assaulted him at every turn.

'No one will overhear us here,' Dell said when they reached the lookout. 'Fire away.'

He looked around to be sure. His success hadn't come about by sharing his strategies. 'I would usually require you to sign a confidentiality agreement before discussing a new project.'

She shrugged. 'I'm good with that. Just tell me where to sign.'

Through his dealings with her as an adversary he'd also come to a grudging admiration of her honesty. According to the judge, her review had been scrupulously within the boundary of fair comment. And his lawyers had been unable to dig up even a skerrick of dirt on her.

'I wasn't expecting this, so I don't have an agreement with me,' he said.

'You can trust me,' she said. 'I'm good at keeping secrets.'

He had been accused of being a ruthless and cynical businessman—never taking anyone on trust. Yet instinct told him he could talk to this woman without his plans being broadcast where they shouldn't.

Still…he hadn't changed *that* much. 'I'll email a document to you when I'm back at the resort.'

'Of course,' she said with a tinge of impatience. 'I'll sign it straight away. But right now I'm dying of curiosity about the role you have in mind for me.'

Alex leaned back against the railing. 'I'm not at Bay Breeze for the yoga and the parsnip tea,' he said.

Dell's green eyes danced with amusement. 'I kind of got that,' she said.

'I'm a stakeholder and I wanted to see what my investment has got me. The more I'm involved, the more I like the well-being concept. It seems right for the times.' And for *his* time.

'You want to start a similar kind of resort?'

He nodded. 'It's already under way. On a private island. Upscale. Exclusive. To appeal to the top end of the market. But my experience is all in restaurants and nightclubs. A resort is something different and challenging. I need some help.' Alex had to force out the final words. He never found it easy to admit he needed help in anything. Had always seen it as a weakness.

'That's where I come in?'

He nodded. 'But I don't have a job description for the role. I wasn't expecting someone like you to come along at this stage.'

'You mean you're making the job up as you go along?'

She was direct. There was another thing he'd found interesting about Dell during their legal stoush. He added another, less tangible asset to the list of her attributes. *He would enjoy working with her.*

'Yeah. I am. Which is good for you as I can shape the role to your talents. I have input from top designers and consultants for the building and fit-out. I've got my key hospitality staff on contract. But I want someone to work with me on fine-tuning the offer to guests and with the publicity. Establishing an exclusive well-being resort on a private island is something different for me.'

'That is quite a challenge,' she said.

'Yes,' he said. And a much-needed distraction. He'd go crazy if he didn't throw himself into a big, all-consuming project.

He'd thought he could walk away from his business. The business he blamed for Mia's death. She'd been a chef in one of his restaurants when he'd met her. There had been a strict company rule against fraternising between staff in his businesses. He'd instigated it and he'd broken it when he'd become beguiled by Mia. They'd been living together—her pushing for marriage, he putting it off—when the chef at his busiest city lunchtime venue had been injured in an accident on the way to work. Mia was having a rostered day off. Alex had pulled rank and insisted she go into work that day to replace the chef. He could not take that memory out again, to pick and prod at it, a wound that would never heal.

Since he'd been away, he'd discreetly sold off his Sydney venues one by one. All except Athina. He couldn't bear to let his inheritance from his grandfather go. Financially he never needed to work again. But he *had* to work. He hadn't realised how much his work had defined him until he hadn't had it to occupy himself day after lonely day.

Dell's auburn brows drew together in a frown. 'Why me? There must be more experienced people around who would jump at the chance to work with you on such a project.'

He didn't want to mention fate or kismet or whatever it was that had sent her here. The hunch that made him think she was what he needed right now. 'But it's you I want. And you need a job.'

'The role does interest me,' she said cautiously. 'Although I'd want to keep my blog. It's important to me.'

'I see your blog as an asset, complementary to your work with me,' he said. 'You could utilise it for soft publicity, along with social media.'

She nodded. 'I'll consider that.'

'I'm thinking the title of Publicity Director,' he said. He named a handsome salary.

She blinked. 'That definitely interests me,' she said.

'I pay well and expect utmost commitment in return.'

'I have no issue with that,' she said. 'I've been described more than once as a workaholic.'

Her mouth set in a rigid line and he wondered if it was the ex-husband who had criticised her. He remembered wondering why he hadn't been at court to support his wife during the case. 'Truth is, if I get really involved, the line between work and interest blurs,' she said.

As it always had with him. 'I think you'll find this interesting,' he said. 'The project is under way but the best is yet to come. You'd be coming on board at an exciting time. I want to open in June.'

Her eyes widened. 'It's already April. Isn't that leaving it late?'

'Agree. It's cutting it fine. I won't expect full occupancy until next year.'

'When would you want me to start?' she asked. He could sense her simmering excitement. 'Because I'm firing with ideas already.'

'A week. Two weeks max.'

She smiled. 'I could do that.' That big embracing smile was finally aimed at him. For a moment, he had to close his eyes against its dazzle. 'I love the idea of an exclusive private island. Where is it? North of Sydney? Queensland? South Australia?'

He shook his head. 'Greece.'

'*Greece?* I… I wasn't expecting that.'

Alex had expected her to react with excitement. Not a clouding of her eyes and a disappointed turn down of her mouth. He frowned.

'My island of Kosmima is in northern Greece where my ancestors come from. Where I've been living with my Greek family since I left Australia. The most beautiful private island in the Ionian Sea. I'm sure you would love it.'

Of course she would love it.

Dell had always wanted to visit Greece. It had held a fascination for her since she'd studied ancient history at school. The mythology. The history. The ancient buildings. She wanted to climb the Acropolis in Athens to see the Parthenon. To visit the picturesque islands with their whitewashed buildings and blue roofs. There was nowhere in the world she wanted to visit more than Greece.

But travel had long been off the cards. She'd committed young to her high-school boyfriend and been caught up in mortgages and marriage to a man who hadn't had an ounce of wanderlust in him. She'd travelled some with her parents and longed to travel more. Even to live abroad one day.

But there was something else she'd wanted more.

Wanted so desperately she'd put all her other dreams on hold to pursue it.

'I…assumed the job was in Australia,' she said.

He shook his head. 'No new venues in Australia for the foreseeable future. Europe is where I want to be. But I'd like a fellow Australian on board with me. Someone who knows about my businesses here, understands how things operate. In other words, you.'

So this was how it felt when big dreams collided.

Dell swallowed hard against the pain of her disappointment. 'I'm very sorry, but I'm going to have to say no to your job offer. I can't possibly go to Greece.'

His dark eyebrows rose in disbelief. She had knocked back what anyone might term a dream job. *Her* dream job. She suspected Alex wasn't used to people saying no to him. But there was disappointment too in those black eyes. He had created a role just for her, tailored to her skills. She was grateful for the confidence he had put in her ability.

But she couldn't tell him why she had to turn down the most enticing offer she was ever likely to get. Why she couldn't be far away from home. That there was a chance she might be pregnant.

CHAPTER FOUR

WHEN DELL HAD been a little girl and people asked her what she wanted to be when she grew up, she had always replied she wanted to be a mummy. They had laughed and asked what else, but she had stubbornly stood her ground.

She didn't know why, as heaven knew her mother hadn't been particularly maternal. And her father had verged on the indifferent. Both her parents had been—still were—research scientists for multinational pharmaceutical companies. She suspected they would have been happy to stop at the one child, her older brother, and when she'd come along when he'd been five she'd been more of an inconvenience than a joy. Her brother was of a scientific bent like her parents. She, while as intelligent, had broader interests they didn't share or understand.

As a child, Dell had loved her dolls, her kitten, her books and food. Her mother was a haphazard cook and by the time she was twelve Dell had been cooking for the family. It became a passion.

At the insistence of her parents, she had completed a degree in food science. A future in the laboratory of a major grocery manufacturer beckoned. Instead, to the horror of her parents, after graduation she went straight to work as an editorial assistant on a suburban newspaper. She showed a flair for restaurant reviewing and articles about food and lifestyle and her career went on from there.

At twenty-two, she married Neil, her high-school boyfriend. He supported her in her desire to become a mother. That was when her plans derailed. In spite of their most energetic efforts, pregnancy didn't happen. At age twenty-seven they started IVF. The procedure was painful and disruptive. The hormone treatments sent her emotions soaring and plunging. The joy went out of her love-life. But three expensive IVF procedures didn't result in pregnancy. Just debt.

Then Neil had walked out on her.

Growing up, Dell had often felt like a fluffy, colourful changeling of a chick popped into the nest of sleek, clever hawks who had never got over their surprise in finding her there. She had become adept at putting on a happy face when she'd felt misunderstood and unhappy.

The end of her marriage had come from left field and she'd been devastated. She'd loved Neil and had thought she'd be married for ever. She shared her tears with a few close friends but presented that smiling, fluffy-chick face to the world.

Being suddenly single came as a shock. She'd been part of a couple for so long she didn't know how to deal with dating. After a series of disastrous encounters she'd given up on the idea of meeting another man. Work became her solace as she tried to deal with the death of her big dream. Accepted that, if IVF hadn't worked, she wasn't likely to ever be a mother.

Then just weeks ago the fertility clinic had called

to ask what she wanted them to do with the remaining embryo she had stored with them.

Dell knew she should have told them she was divorced. That her ex-husband was in another relationship. But they didn't ask and she didn't tell. She'd undergone the fourth procedure the week before she'd been fired. All her other attempts at IVF had failed. She hadn't held out any real hope for this time. But she'd felt compelled to grab at that one final chance.

Now, the day after her meeting with Alex Mikhalis, Dell lay back on her cool white bed at Bay Breeze racked by the cramps that had always heralded failure. She took in a great, gasping sob then stayed absolutely still, desperately willing that implant to stay put. Her baby. But a visit to the bathroom confirmed blood. She'd failed again.

She would never be a mother.

Dell stood at the window for a long time staring sightlessly out to the view of the sea. Her hand rested on her flat, flat stomach. There was nothing for her here. No job. No man. No close family. Just parents who, if she left the country, would wave her goodbye without thinking to ask why she was going. Her friends were starting families and moving into a life cycle she couldn't share. She hadn't told anyone about this last desperate effort to conceive so there was no one to share her grief. But she did have all her cyber friends on her blog. She had to put on her fluffy-chick face and move on.

Without thinking any further, she picked up the house phone and called through to Alex Mikhalis's room. She braced herself to leave a message and was shocked when he answered. Somehow she found the words to ask could she have a meeting with him. His tone was abrupt as he told her to be quick—he was packing to head back to Sydney.

Dell had no chance to change. Or apply make-up. Just pushed her hair into place in front of the mirror and slicked on some lip gloss. Yoga pants were *de rigueur* in a place like this anyway. He wouldn't expect to see her in a business suit and heels.

He answered the door to his room. 'Yes?' he said, his voice deep and gruff and more than a touch forbidding.

For a long moment Dell hesitated on the threshold. He towered over her, in black trousers and a charcoal-grey shirt looking every inch the formidable tycoon. Half of the buttons on his shirt were left open, as if he'd been fastening them when she'd sounded the buzzer on his door. It left bare a triangle of olive skin and a hint of dark chest hair on an impressively muscled chest.

Her heart started to beat double-quick time and she felt so shaky at the knees she had to clutch at the doorframe for support. Not because she was nervous about approaching him. Or feared what kind of a boss he might be. No. It was because her long-dormant libido had flared suddenly back into life at the sight of him—those dark eyes, the proud nose, the strong jaw newly shaven but already shadowing with growth. *He was hot.*

Dell swallowed against a suddenly dry mouth. This unwelcome surge of sensual awareness could complicate things. She was beginning to rethink his devil incarnate status. But who knew if he was sincere about having changed? After all, she'd seen him at his intimidating worst on those courtroom steps. She had to take him on trust but be cautious. That did not mean fancying the pants off him.

Eyes off the gorgeous man, Dell.

He stepped back and she could see his bag half packed on his bed. Perhaps he was headed to Greece and she would never see him again. This could be her only chance.

She forced her lips into a smile, the wobble at the edge betraying her attempt to be both nonchalant and professional. And not let him guess the turmoil of her senses evoked by his half-dressed state. 'Your job offer?' she said.

He nodded.

'Can…can a person change her mind?'

Alex stared at Dell. What had happened? Thinly disguised anguish showed in the set of her jaw, the pallor of her face, her red-rimmed eyes. The expression in her eyes was sad rather than sparkling. But as she met his gaze, her cheeks flushed pink high on her cheekbones, her chin rose resolutely and he wondered if he'd imagined it.

'I'd like to accept the job.' She hesitated. There was an edge to her voice that made him believe he had not imagined her distress. 'That is, if the position is still on offer.'

Alex had been gutted when she'd turned him down. Disappointed out of all proportion. And stunned that he'd been so shaken. Because of course she'd been right. Whisper a word in a recruitment agent's ear and he'd be inundated with qualified people ready to take up the job with him. Why Dell Hudson? Because it was her and only her he'd wanted. He'd had no intention of taking her 'no' as final. In fact he'd been planning strategies aimed at getting a 'yes' from her.

Once he'd made up his mind about something it was difficult to budge him. It was a trait he had inherited from his stubborn grandfather. No one else would do but *her*. Was it his tried and tested gut feel telling him that? Or something else? It was nothing to do with the fact he found her attractive. That was totally beside the point. He did not date employees. Never, ever after what had happened with Mia.

'Why did you change your mind?' he asked Dell.

She took a deep breath, which emphasised the curve of her breasts outlined by her tight-fitting tank top. How had he never noticed how sexy she was? He forced his eyes upward to catch the nuances of her expression rather than the curves of her shapely body.

'A…sudden change of circumstances,' she said. 'Something…something personal.'

'Problems with a guy?' he asked. Over the years he'd learned to deal with the personal dramas of female staff. Not that it ever got easier.

She shook her head and again he caught that glimpse of sadness in her eyes. 'No. I'm one hundred per cent single. And intending to stay that way. I'm free to devote my time entirely to my work with you.'

'Good,' he said. He didn't want to hear the details of her marriage breakup. Or any bust-ups that came afterwards. That was none of his concern. This was about a job. Nothing more.

Although he found it very difficult to believe she was single by choice.

'I don't let my personal life impinge on my work,' she said. 'I want your job and I want to go to Greece.'

'You're sure about that? You're not going to change your mind again?'

She took another distracting deep breath. 'I'm very sure.'

He allowed himself a smile, knowing that it was tinged with triumph. Reached out to shake her hand. 'When can you be ready to fly to Athens?'

CHAPTER FIVE

SHE WAS IN GREECE, working for Alex Mikhalis!

It had all happened so fast Dell still felt a little dizzy that, just two weeks after her wobbly encounter with him in the yoga room, the man who had been her adversary—the man she had loathed—was her boss.

So far so good. It had been a long, tedious trip to get here even in the comfort of the business-class seats he had booked for her—twenty-three hours to Athens alone. Then another short flight to the small airport at Preveza in north-western Greece.

Too excited to be jet-lagged, she staggered out into the sunshine expecting to find a sign with her name on it held up by a taxi driver. But her new boss was there to meet her. Tall and imposing, he stood out among the people waiting for passengers. He waved to get her attention.

Dell's breath caught and her heart started hammering. It was the first time she'd seen Alex since that meeting in his room at Bay Breeze. For a moment she was too stunned to say anything. Not just because her reawakened senses jumped to alert at how Greek-god-handsome he looked in stone linen trousers and a collarless white linen shirt. But because she wasn't sure what rules applied to their changed status. It was quite a leap for her to take from enemy to employee.

'Good flight?' he asked.

'Very good, thank you,' she said, uncertain of what to call him. He was her employer now but they had history of a kind. 'Er…thank you, Mr Mikhalis.'

His dark eyes widened as if she'd said something ridiculous, then he laughed. 'That's my father's name,' he said. 'Alex will do. You're not working for a corporation here. Just me.'

He held out his hand to take hers in a firm, warm grip. 'Welcome on board.' His handshake was professional, his tone friendly but impersonal. She would take her cue from that. And totally repress that little shiver of awareness that rippled through her at his touch.

'Thank you,' she said. *That was her third 'thank you'*. Their status might have changed but she wondered if she would ever be able to relax around him.

He went to take her luggage and made a mock groan. 'What on earth have you got in here?'

Her suitcase was stuffed to the limit—she'd had no real idea of what she'd be facing and had packed for any occasion. 'Just clothes and…er…shoes.'

'Enough to shoe a centipede by the weight of it,' he said. But he smiled and she felt some of the tension leave her shoulders.

'There's snorkelling equipment there too,' she said a tad defensively. She knew this wouldn't be a regular nine-to-five job but she hoped there'd be leisure time too.

'The waters around the island are perfect for snorkelling,' he said. 'But the water temperature is still too

cold to swim without a wetsuit. It warms up towards
the end of May. I'll swim every day then.'

A vision came from nowhere of him spearing
through aqua waters, his hair slicked dark to his head,
his body lean and strong and muscular, his skin gilded
by shafts of sunlight falling through the water. *This was
all kinds of crazy.* She forced the too personal thoughts
away and thought sensible work-type thoughts. The
only kind of thoughts she could allow herself to have
about him.

What kind of boss would he be?

He'd had a reputation for being somewhat of a tyrant
in Sydney. There were rumours of banks of CCTVs in
his most popular venues to ensure he could monitor
the staff at all times. Spying on them, according to dis-
gruntled employees. Alex's explanation had been the
surveillance was there to ensure drinks weren't being
spiked with date rape drugs. She hadn't known who
to believe at the time.

She followed him to his car. In Sydney at the time of
the trial, he had driven the latest model Italian sports
car, as befitted his wealthy, playboy image. Now she
was surprised to see a somewhat battered four-by-four.
Effortlessly he swung her heavy luggage in the back.

'Next stop is Lefkada,' he said. 'You'll be staying
at a villa in the port of Nidri and coming over daily by
boat to Kosmima.'

Dell already knew that Kosmima was the small private island he owned and the site of his new resort. 'I
can't wait to see it,' she said, avid for more information.

As soon as she was settled in the front seat, she
launched into a string of questions. She listened as he
explained the size of the island—about one thousand

metres by one and a half thousand metres. That it was largely untamed vegetation of cypress and oak and a cultivated olive grove. Past owners had turned old donkey trails into accessible roads. The most recent had put in a helipad.

But his deep sonorous voce had a hypnotic effect. Dell was interested—intensely interested—but she had been awake for more than thirty hours. She only kept her eyes open long enough to leave the airport behind and to cross the causeway that connected Lefkada to the mainland.

She woke up, drowsy, to find the car stationary. For a moment she didn't know where she was. An unfamiliar car. An unfamiliar view through the window. *An unfamiliar man.*

Dell froze, suddenly wide awake. In her sleep she had leaned across from her seat and was snuggled up to Alex Mikhalis's shoulder. Mortified, she snapped her eyes shut again before he realised she was awake. *What to do?* She was aware of a strong, warm body, a spicy masculine scent, his breath stirring her hair— and that she liked it very much. She liked it too much. *He was her boss.*

She pretended to wake with a gasp and scooted across the seat away from him as fast as her bottom would take her. 'I'm so sorry,' she said, aware of the sudden flush staining her cheeks. That short, nervous laugh she was forever trying to control forced its way out. 'How unprofessional of me.'

His eyes met hers, dark, inscrutable, as he searched her face. She swore her heart stopped with the impact of his nearness. *He was gorgeous.* But she could not let herself acknowledge that. This inconvenient attraction had to be stomped on from the start. She needed this job and could not let anything jeopardise it.

He shrugged broad shoulders. 'Jet lag. It happens to the best of us.' But not everyone used their boss's shoulder as a pillow. 'Don't worry about it,' he said as if he'd scarcely noticed her presence. As if it happened all the time.

No doubt he'd been used to women flinging themselves at him. That was, of course, before he'd lost his fiancée, the lovely chef who had worked for him. The story of their tragic romance had been repeated by the press over and over after she'd died. Everywhere he'd looked he must have seen her face. Such an intensity of loss. No wonder he'd escaped the country.

She realised she was doing the same thing. Running from loss of a different kind but painful just the same. Every month she'd been just a day late she'd hoped she was pregnant. Before each IVF procedure she had allowed herself to dream about the baby she would hold in her arms, imagined how he or she would look, thought about names. Then grieved those lost babies who had seemed so real to her. Two pairs of tiny knitted booties, one pink and one blue, had been hidden in a drawer to be taken out and held against her cheek while she dreamed. But not this last failed attempt at IVF. Packing up her possessions to move out of her small rented apartment, she had found the booties and packed them with the clothes she gave away to charity.

'Thank you,' she said. Again. Were *thank you* and *sorry* going to be the key words of this working relationship? *Toughen up, Dell.*

They were parked near a busy harbour. The marina was packed with a flotilla of tall-masted yachts, motor cruisers and smaller craft of all kinds. The waterfront was lined with colourful cafés and restaurants, each fronted by signs proclaiming their specialities. 'This is the port of Nidri,' Alex said.

Dell noticed charter boats and ferries and signs in English and Greek—of which she couldn't understand a word—to the islands of Corfu and Ithaca and Cephalonia. Excitement started to bubble. She really was in Greece. That dream, at least, had come true.

'This is the town where I'm staying?' she said.

'In a villa complex owned by my aunt and uncle. You'll be comfortable there. There are shops, restaurants, lots of night life. My cousin will take you to and from Kosmima by boat.'

'Do you live there too?' she asked. He didn't wear any rings. She hadn't given thought to whether or not he was still single. He could be married for all she knew, he'd done so well to keep out of the gossip columns where he used to be a regular item. A man like him wouldn't be alone—unless by choice.

'I live on Kosmima, by myself,' he said. His tone told her not to ask any more questions.

She might not be an investigative journalist—she came under the category of lifestyle writer—but Dell was consumed with curiosity about how the nightclub prince of Sydney came to be living in this place. How he had kept his whereabouts so secret when he had disappeared from Sydney.

'I'll take you to the villa,' he said. 'We'll have lunch there then you can settle in and get some sleep before you start work tomorrow.'

Dell wanted to protest that she was ready to start work right now but of course that would be ridicu-

lous. Her impromptu nap in his car had proved that.
She needed to get out of the jeans she'd worn on the
plane, shower and then sleep before she could be of
any use to Alex.

She'd been expecting bare cliffs and blinding white
buildings accented in bright blue. But Alex explained
that landscape was typical of the southern Greek islands. This part of Greece had green, vegetated islands
with homes that blended more into the landscape. The
Greek blue was there all right but in a more subtle way.

The one-bedroom apartment she was to make her
home was in a small complex of attractive white-
painted villas with terracotta roofs set around a swimming pool. Tubs of lavender and sweet-scented herbs
were placed at every turn. Sad memories would have
a hard time following her here.

Her compact apartment was white and breezy with
a tiled floor. Dell looked around her in delight. She
would be more than comfortable. Even better, her accommodation was part of her salary package. With the
generous remuneration Alex had offered her, she hoped
she might be able to make a dent in the debt left to her
from the IVF. As she showered and then changed into
a simple linen dress, she found herself humming and
wishing she knew some Greek songs.

New start?

Bring it on.

As soon as Alex's Aunt Penelope and Uncle Stavros
had heard he was picking up his new staff member
from Australia from the airport, they had insisted he
bring her to share a meal with them. The elderly couple
lived on site and managed the villas they let out over

the summer, one of which he had secured as Dell's accommodation.

They were actually his great aunt and uncle, Penelope being the youngest sister of his grandfather, but no one in the family bothered with that kind of distinction. He hadn't tried to keep track of all the familial layers. It was just enough that his Greek family had welcomed him without judgement when he had arrived, the high flyer from Australia who'd crashed in spectacular manner. Like Icarus of Greek myth he'd melted his wings by flying too high—in Icarus's case to the sun, in his case too much hard living and stress followed by the tragedy with Mia had led to burnout. He'd come here to heal but wasn't sure how he'd ever get his wings back. He hoped the new venture might lead to the growth of new feathers. Because he couldn't stay grounded for ever.

Dell had instantly charmed his aunt and uncle with her winning smile and chatty manner. She seemed to have a gift for making people feel at ease in a natural, unselfconscious way. Even in repose her face looked as if she was on the verge of smiling. Who could help but want to smile back in response? Yet he'd seen her snarl too and knew she could be tough when required. He felt some of the tension relax from his shoulders. It had been the right decision to bring her here. Dell Hudson on his side could be a very good thing.

The table was set up under a pergola that supported a grape vine, its bright new leaves casting welcome shade. Dell's hair flashed bright in the filtered light, her simple blue and white striped dress perfectly appropriate.

It was a typically Greek scene and he marvelled, as

he had many times since he'd got here, how quickly he'd felt at home. During school vacations there had been visits with his parents and two sisters. But once he'd taken over Athina, he hadn't had time to make the obligatory trek to Greece, despite the admonishments of his parents.

'*Family is everything,*' his grandfather had used to say. But it was only now that Alex really appreciated what he had meant. It wasn't that he didn't value his heritage. Or that he didn't love his family back home. But as he was the much-longed-for son after two daughters, too much pressure and expectation had been put on him. His subsequent rebellion had caused ructions that were only now healing. He felt he'd at last made his peace with his father on his recent visit to Sydney.

Now he tucked into his aunt's splendid cooking— sardines wrapped in vine leaves and herbs; lemon and garlic potatoes; and a sublime eggplant salad. The food was reminiscent of his grandfather's old Athina, not surprising when the recipes had probably been handed down from the same source. Dell chatted and laughed with his aunt and uncle over lunch, as if they were already friends.

'I'm asking your Thia Penelope if I can interview her about her cooking for my blog,' Dell said.

'I am teaching her Greek,' his aunt interjected.

'I'm keen to learn.' Dell smiled at the older lady. 'I've never tasted eggplant cooked as deliciously as this. It's a revelation. That is, if I'm allowed to tell my readers that I'm living in Greece.'

'Why not?' he said, bemused by the fact his aunt

had taken it upon herself to teach his newest employee the language. 'Just don't mention the new venture yet.'

'Sure, this will be a subtle way of leading into it,' she said. 'When the time is right it will be fun to reveal exactly what I'm doing here. Right now I'll say I'm on vacation.'

His aunt beamed, her black eyes almost disappearing into the wrinkles around her eyes. 'She's a clever girl, this one,' she said. As she said it she looked from him to Dell and back again.

There it was again—that matchmaking gleam. Just because he was single and his aunt had ascertained that Dell was single. Even though his aunt knew the story of how Mia had died. How responsible he felt for her death. How he did not want—did not deserve—to have love in his life again.

Dell blushed and looked down at her plate. The speculation must be annoying for her too.

'That she is, Auntie,' he said. 'Which is why I've employed her to work with me on the hotel.' He had to make it clear to his family that his relationship with Dell was strictly a working one. He had to keep reminding himself too.

On the drive from the airport she had got drowsier and drowsier as she'd tried to keep up the conversation through her jet lag. Her responses had dwindled to the odd word in answer to something he'd said minutes before and quite out of context. If he knew her better, he'd tease her about it.

But he would not tease her about the way, when she'd fallen fully asleep, she'd slid across her seat to rest her head on his shoulder. Because instead of pushing her away, as she'd murmured something unintelligible in her sleep he'd smiled and without thinking dropped a light kiss on her head. He'd been without a woman for too long. It was the only explanation for his lapse.

That could not happen again.

CHAPTER SIX

THE NEXT MORNING Dell stood on the expansive front balcony of Alex's new resort building on the private island of Kosmima and looked around her in awe. There wasn't another building in sight—just the jetty that belonged to the island.

Below her, the waters of the Ionian Sea sparkled in myriad tones of turquoise as they lapped on the white sands of the bay. She breathed in air tinged with salt and the scent of wild herbs. The bay was bounded by pale limestone cliffs and hills covered in lush vegetation. The sky was a perfect blue with only the odd cloud scudding across the horizon. She felt almost overcome by the natural beauty of the site as she felt the tension and angst of the last weeks start to melt away.

Her new boss stood beside her—waiting, she suspected, with a degree of impatience for her verdict. She turned to him. 'It's every bit as perfect as you said. Magical.'

Alex nodded slowly. 'I think so too. It makes me believe that people have been feeling the magic for hundreds of years. Thousands, perhaps.'

They stood in silence for a long moment, looking out to sea. Was he, like her, imagining the pageant of history that must have been played out on and near these islands?

'Do you know anything about the history of this island?' she asked. 'Any chance it was the site of an ancient Greek temple? That would be useful for publicity.'

'It could also mean Kosmima could be declared as a site of archaeological significance and business prohibited. So I don't think we'll go there,' he said.

'I hadn't thought of that,' she said. 'Maybe we should stick to the de-stressing and well-being angle. Just taking in this view is making me feel relaxed. Although not too relaxed to start work, of course. Tell me what you need me to do. I'm raring to start.'

'First thing is to inspect the site.'

Dell turned and looked back at the magnificent white building that sat stepped back into the side of the hill. It was modern in its simplicity but paid homage to traditional architecture. 'I expected something only half constructed but you must be nearly ready to open.'

'On first sight you might think so, but there's still a way to go before we welcome the first guests in June. This main building was initially built as a private residence. It was very large, but needed alteration and additions to make it fit for the purpose.'

The building was light and airy, luxurious in pale stone with bleached timber woodwork and marble floors. Expansive windows took full advantage of the view, to be shuttered in the colder months. From the back of the building she could hear the construction crew who had been here since early morning.

The last thing she wanted to do was remind Alex of the car journey from the airport. But she couldn't pretend to know important details she had missed while snoozing. 'In the car yesterday you were telling me about the background of this place. But I… I'm afraid I didn't hear it all.'

'Really?' he said, dark brows raised. 'You don't recall anything?'

'Er… I remember the geographical details.'

'Before you fell asleep, you mean?'

'Yes,' she admitted, unable to meet his eyes.

'Was I so boring?' he said.

'No! Not boring at all.' In fact, she'd never met a man less boring. Who would have thought she might be actually growing to like the man who had been so vile during the court case? A man she'd considered an entitled, arrogant playboy who in the short time she'd known him seemed anything but that.

Now she did look up to find his black eyes gleaming with amusement. 'I soon realised you were drowsing off.'

And falling all over him.

How utterly mortifying. But she would not say the sorry word again. 'I do recall something about a billionaire,' she said. 'I promise I'm over the jet lag and wide awake and listening.'

She followed him into the high-ceilinged living space destined to be the 'silent' room where guests could meditate or just be quiet with their thoughts without interruption. Their voices echoed in the unlived silence.

'There was an older, traditional house on this site when the island was owned by a very wealthy Greek industrialist,' he said. 'He and his family used it as a summer retreat. Some members of my family were tenant farmers on the island. Others were employed as gardeners and caretakers.'

'So there's a personal connection?' She was still looking for angles for publicity.

'Yes,' he said. 'The owner was a benevolent landlord who, for all the opulence, never forgot his peasant roots. There were many good years for my family.' He paused. 'I've only found out all this since I've been living in Greece.'

'I guess it wasn't relevant when you were building your empire in Sydney.'

'Correct,' he said. 'I hardly knew this side of my family. Just my grandfather, my father's father, emigrated. The rest of the family stayed here. I only visited a few times back with my parents, the last when I was a teenager.'

'So how did you come to buy the island?'

'The Greek owner died and it was left to a nephew in Athens who had no use for it. He sold it to a Russian billionaire who demolished the house to build this summer palace.'

The tone of his voice told her that the transfer of ownership might not have been good news. 'What happened to your family?'

'They were evicted. The new owner wanted utter privacy. The only staff to live on the island were the ones he brought with him. The island is only accessed by sea. He installed a heliport, and armed guards patrolled the coastline. The construction crews were escorted on and off the island. Every delivery was scrutinised.'

'That's scary stuff. Was there any real threat?' She

wasn't quite sure how she could work that into a press release.

He shrugged. 'Who knows? The locals were pragmatic. They got used to it. The development brought employment—much needed in Greece as you probably know. The good thing is the guy was passionate about sustainability and brought those organic principals to the new build. That was good for me when I took over.'

'So how did you end up owning the island?'

'The owner decamped with the mega-residence unfinished. No one ever found out why, although as you can imagine there were all sorts of rumours. Then the island went up for sale again.'

'What made you buy it?'

'Impulse.'

'You bought an entire island on *impulse*?'

Of course, he'd been a multimillionaire while he was still in his twenties. Why wouldn't he? And if his past history had anything to do with it, the impulse would pay off in return on investment.

'I've always operated on instinct. It seemed the right thing to do.'

There was an edge to his voice but Dell wasn't sure how deep she should dig into his motives. Escape. Retreat. Heal. Even giving back to the land of his ancestors at a time when investment was desperately needed.

But once they started to generate publicity for his new venue, it would be inevitable his personal tragedy would come to the fore. She would carefully suggest they work with it rather than hope it would stay buried. Perhaps a few carefully negotiated exclusives might be the way to go.

The story of the crazed gunman holding Alex's

lovely fiancée and a number of customers hostage in a robbery gone wrong had travelled around the world. That the handsome hotelier had sought refuge from his grief in the islands of his ancestors and built a resort there would generate good publicity. But she didn't feel ready to raise it with him just yet. She would have to learn to read him first.

As Alex continued his tour Dell continued to be impressed by everything she saw—kitchen, spa treatment areas, guestrooms, an office area with Wi-Fi and computers. When he asked her opinion she gave it honestly. Better to have areas of potential weakness sorted now rather than after the retreat opened. His venues in Sydney had won design awards. This one would no doubt be clocking up some wins too.

'You certainly know your stuff,' she said. 'I realise you've got a ton of experience in Sydney, but it must be very different doing remodelling and a fit-out in a different country. Where did you find the architects and interior designers?'

'That's where having an extended Greek family helps. My cousins in Athens were able to point me to the right people.'

'And furnishings?' Many of the rooms were still bare.

'In the hands of the designers. Most of it is being made to measure and exclusive to this resort. I need to go to Athens next week. I'd like you to come with me.'

'I would be pleased to,' she said. A ripple of excitement ran through her. 'Just one thing. Would it be possible to time it before I have a day off? I'd love to stay in Athens overnight so I could climb the Acropolis and see the Parthenon. It's something I've always wanted to do. Then I'd like to spend some time in the Acropolis Museum. I've heard it's wonderful.'

'It is spectacular,' he said. 'I'm not what you'd call a museum kind of guy. But when you're seeing all the antiquities and then look up to see the Parthenon through the windows it's quite something.'

Alex spoke with pride of the museum. He looked Greek, spoke like an Australian. Yesterday he'd been too well-mannered to speak more than a few words of Greek to his aunt and uncle in front of her. But he had sounded fluent. She wondered what country he now identified with. Again she felt it was too personal for her to ask him. His grief must run very deep to have left everything familiar behind.

The tour ended outside with a beautiful aquamarine swimming pool, landscaped around with palm trees and bougainvillea. 'Was the pool already here?' she asked.

'Yes. It's big for a private residence but not outstanding for a hotel. I considered extending it but—'

'Why bother when you have the sea on the doorstep?' she said.

'Exactly.' He met her eyes and they both smiled at the same time. It wasn't the first time today that they'd finished each other's words. She felt she was in tune with his vision and it gave her confidence that she would be able to do a good job for him. She held his gaze for a moment too long before she hastily switched her focus.

Set well back from the pool and completely private was an elegant pavilion, the design of which, with its columns and pediments, gave more than a nod to classical Greek architecture. 'Was the pool house here, too?'

He nodded. 'It's a self-contained apartment and where I'm living.'

'It looks fabulous.'

Dell wondered if he would show her around his personal residence. She ached with curiosity to see inside where he spent his private time.

But he took her around to the southern side of the building where there were substantial kitchen gardens and a greenhouse full of early tomatoes. Mature fig, pomegranate, fruit and nut trees were planted behind— spring blossom surrendering to new leaves so green they seemed fluorescent. From their size, she assumed the trees had been there since the days of the Greek owner. Maybe longer.

'How wonderful,' she breathed.

'I've employed the gardeners who used to work here. We intend to grow as much fresh produce as possible,' he said.

'I couldn't think of anything better,' she said. 'It's early days for me planning the food, but I really think the core of the food offering should be based on the Mediterranean diet. I mean mainly plant-based from this garden, olive oil from your grove, fish from these waters, white cheese and yogurt—could you keep goats here, chickens?—with lots of fruit. Food like your aunt's baked eggplant based on traditional recipes handed down in your family. Maybe some of the daring new twists to old favourites that you served at Athina. Greek dishes interpreted in an Australian way, which would be a point of difference. Of course you'll also have to cater for allergies and intolerances as well as whatever faddy ways of eating are in fashion. The juice bar is essential, and the fancy teas.' She indicated the vegetable garden with an enthusiastic wave. 'But the heart of it starts here. The locavore movement at its best. It checks the boxes for locally grown and "clean", whatever you like to call it. This resort will be an organic part of this island, not *on* it but *of* it.'

Dell faltered to a halt as she realised she'd held the floor for too long, having scarcely paused for breath. 'Er…that is if you think so too…'

He stood watching her, dark eyes enigmatic, before he broke into a slow smile. 'That's exactly what I think,' he said.

Dell felt as breathless as if she'd run a long race. It seemed she'd passed a test of some sort. After all, he'd acquired her on an impulse too. She kept up to date with food trends. She had a degree in food science, which had covered commercial food preparation. She had critiqued a spectrum of restaurants and resorts in Sydney. But that wouldn't have mattered a flying fig if she hadn't proved herself to be on the same wavelength as Alex when it came to his project.

'That's a relief,' she said. 'I do tend to go on when I'm…passionate about something.'

He smiled again, teeth white against his olive skin, eyes warm. His shirt was open at the neck, rolled up to show tanned forearms. Had a man ever looked better in a white shirt? It would be only too easy to get passionate about *him*.

'Don't ever hold back,' he said. 'I like your enthusiasm. It energises me.'

Passion, energy, his eyes focused on her, his hands— *She couldn't go there.*

She took a deep, steadying breath. 'One more thing,' she asked. 'Have you decided on a name for the resort?'

'Pevezzo Athina,' he said without hesitation. '*Pevezzo* in the local dialect means "safe haven". That's what I want it to be: a haven from life's stresses for our guests.'

And for you too, Dell thought.

'Why the name Athina again?' she said. 'In homage to your restaurant in Sydney?' She felt uncomfortable mentioning it, considering their history.

'That restaurant was named by my grandfather after the *taverna* on the adjoining island, Prasinos, which was run by his parents. It's still there. Pappouli left his home for a better life in Australia. The seas here were becoming over-fished and he found it difficult to make a living as a fisherman. He wanted more. I'm named after that grandfather, in the Greek way.'

Dell took up the story. 'So he started Athina restaurant in the city, serving traditional Greek food. It was a great success. First with other migrants like himself and then the Australian business people caught on to how good the food was and it became an institution.'

'You know a lot about it. Of course you do. Because of the—'

'The court case,' she said. No point in avoiding the elephant lurking in the garden.

'What you did not realise—what no one outside our family knew—was how important Athina was to me personally.'

'You defended it so…so fiercely.'

'You mean irrationally?'

'I didn't say that,' she said, her voice dwindling away. But she meant it and he knew it.

'My grandfather came to Australia with nothing, unable to speak more than a few words of English. He ended up successful and prosperous. His kids became professionals—my father is an orthopaedic surgeon, his sister a dermatologist. All thanks to Athina. As a kid, I spent happy times with my *pappouli* and my *yia-yia* at the restaurant. I'd get underfoot in the kitchens, annoy the chefs with questions. Helped out as a waiter as soon as I was old enough.'

'So that's where your interest in restaurants started.' An image of what a dear little boy he must have been flashed into her mind. But she pushed it away. Neil had been dark-haired and dark-eyed—the image of Alex as a child came way too close to what her longed-for babies might have looked like. She had to put that dream behind her.

'I didn't want to be a chef. I wanted to be the boss.' He smiled, an ironic twist of his mouth. 'That's what comes of being the only son in a Greek family. But the pressure was on for me to be a doctor, to keep the migrant dream alive of being upwardly socially mobile. I enrolled in medicine. Loved the social life at uni, the classes were not where I wanted to be. My parents were not happy, to say the least.'

'And your grandfather?'

'Pappouli wasn't happy either. He left Greece and his extended family to better himself. Everyone saw me as going backwards when I dropped out of uni and started work behind a bar. It didn't count that it was at the most fashionable nightclub in Sydney at the time. No one thought it was worth applauding when I became the club's youngest ever manager. I continued to be a great disappointment.'

She knew some of this story. But not the personal insights about his family. Not how his spur to success was proving himself to them. 'If I remember, your grandfather became ill.'

'He had a stroke. I insisted on running the restaurant for him while he was in hospital. Straight away I could see Athina's time was past. It was now in the wrong end of town for a traditional Greek restaurant. The older people who had come for the nostalgia were dying off. The younger punters had moved on. I saw what could be done with it, but of course my hands were tied.'

'Until…' Dell found she couldn't say the words.

'Until my grandfather died and left the restaurant to me. You know the rest.'

Not quite all the rest—much as she ached to know it. But Alex was her boss. Knowing this was relevant to the naming of the resort. His private life continued to be none of her business. 'I see why you want to honour your grandfather. Thank you for sharing that with me.'

She'd believed she and Alex were poles apart. Perhaps they had more in common than she could have dreamed. Both brought up by parents who wanted to impose their ambitions and expectations on their kids. She'd fought those expectations to get where she was. As a result, she remained a disappointment to her parents too. Alex's arrogance and ruthlessness seemed more understandable now. But it seemed he'd paid a price.

She had to fight an impulse to hug him.

'Now I better understand your attitude in court,' she said. Not that she was condoning it.

He sighed. 'It seems a long time ago in a different place. I'm a different person.'

Was he truly? Was she? She remembered how she'd

wondered if he'd worn his public image like a mask. Was she now seeing glimpses of the man behind the mask? Because she liked what she saw.

'I'd rather put it right behind me if we're to work in harmony together,' she said. *In harmony.* She was already using the language that would define this place.

'I've apologised and I hope you have forgiven me,' he said, a little stiffly. 'One day I'll take you to my family's Taverna Athina and you can see where it all started.'

'I'd like that very much.' She realised she was hungry to find out as much as possible about this man who was beginning to take up way too much time in her thoughts.

CHAPTER SEVEN

TWO WEEKS INTO her new job and Dell was loving every minute of it. She and Alex worked so well together she found herself musing that if they had met under different circumstances they might be friends. *More than friends,* her insistent libido reminded her with inconvenient frequency.

Often when she was with him, from nowhere would come a flash of awareness of how heart-thuddingly handsome she found him. When he laughed—and he seemed to laugh more often these days—he threw back his head and there was a hollow in his tanned neck that she felt an insane urge to press her lips against. When they were going through a document or a set of plans, she'd become mesmerised by his hands, imagining how his long, strong fingers might feel on her bare skin.

She treasured the day he'd taken her to Athens for work. The music he'd played in the car on the way to the airport had been the same music she liked. They'd operated with the designers and suppliers like a team— so much so the people thought they'd been working together for years. But on the journey home, when she'd felt overwhelmed by sudden tiredness, she'd been very careful to stay on her side of the car. She didn't trust herself. Sometimes she'd awoken from dreams of him—dreams filled with erotic fantasy.

Every time she realised the way her thoughts were taking her, her redhead's skin would flush. She prayed he didn't notice, because she never saw anything in his reactions to her to indicate *he* might feel in any way the same about *her*.

Although he had never mentioned Mia—not once— she got the impression she'd been the love of his life and no other woman would ever measure up to her.

According to his aunt Penelope, her landlady, there was no woman in his life. Not that Dell had indulged in gossip with her about her nephew, in spite of her curiosity. There was no guarantee it wouldn't reach Alex and she doubted he'd be happy about her speculating on his love life—or lack of it—with his family. Then there was the annoying fact that Aunt Penelope appeared convinced that she and Alex were more than boss and employee. The older woman seemed to think that the more often she subtly mentioned her suspicions, the more likely Dell would cave in and admit it through the course of the conversation.

But no matter how Dell denied it, she could no longer deny the truth to herself—*she was developing a crush on her boss.*

What a cliché—and not one she had thought she would ever find herself caught up in. The anticipation of seeing him brought a frisson of unexpected pleasure to her working day. She found herself taking greater care with the way she dressed. If Alex happened to compliment her on her dress, she would hug the knowledge to herself and make sure she wore something similar the next day. He'd mentioned he liked her perfume—and she had to fight the temptation to douse herself in it. But her secret crush was harmless, she told herself. He would never know.

There was only one flaw in her new life in this Greek paradise—a new susceptibility to seasickness. It was most inconvenient when she was working on an island accessible only by boat.

Every day, Alex's cousin Cristos took her and some of the tradespeople across and back to Kosmimo in his blue-painted converted wooden fishing boat. At first she'd looked forward to it. She'd always been fine on the water, whether sailing on Sydney Harbour with friends or a cruise to Fiji with her parents.

Yet this small boat chugging across calm, clear waters had her gagging with nausea all the way. She'd sat by turns at the front and back of the boat but it was no use. In desperation, she'd got up earlier to catch the construction company's much bigger boat, but it was no different. She had to deal with a niggling nausea until mid-morning. By mid-afternoon she was dreading the return trip for another dose.

It was getting worse. This morning she'd managed to get up the steps from the jetty to the lower levels of the building and into the bathroom just in time. She'd tried eating a bigger breakfast, a smaller breakfast, no breakfast at all, but the outcome was the same.

Afterwards, she splashed cold water on her face. Fixed her make-up to try and conceal the unflattering tinge of green of her skin and brushed back her lank hair from her face. She gripped the edge of the hand basin and practised her fluffy-chick smile in the mirror. The last thing she wanted was for Alex to notice all was not well.

She loved working here with him. However she was aware it was early days yet. Theoretically, she was still on probation although he had told her several times how pleased he was with her job performance. But how could she continue in a job on an island only accessible by boat if she was going to feel like this every day?

Alex finished going through some plans with the plumber who was installing the fittings in the guest bathrooms. A smile of anticipation tugged at the edges of his mouth as he headed back to the office that would become the hotel's administration centre but right now served just for him and Dell. She should be at her desk by now.

He realised the day didn't really start for him until she smiled a 'good morning' greeting. Her warm presence was like the dark Greek coffee that kick-started his day. How had he managed without her?

But as he got to the office he stopped, alarmed. She was leaning on her elbows on the desk, her head resting in her hands in a pose of utter exhaustion. Had she been out last night partying late in the nightclubs of Nidri? Somehow he didn't think so. She wouldn't be so unprofessional to come to work with a hangover.

'Dell, are you okay?'

She looked up, her splayed hands still holding onto her head. 'Alex. I thought you were out the back with the builders,' she said in a voice so shaky it hardly sounded like her. Her face was so pale a smattering of freckles stood out across the bridge of her nose. Make-up was smeared around her eyes. Her wavering smile seemed forced.

'What's wrong?' he asked, fear stabbing him.

He'd become accustomed to her presence in his day. Her smile, her energy, her awesome attitude to work, the way he could fire ideas off her and she'd come back with ideas to counter or complement his own. Whatever he'd directed her to do she'd taken a step further. He'd found himself thanking whatever lucky star had made him turn around to see her in that yoga class. She couldn't be ill. Especially with so much still to do before the hotel would be ready to open. He depended on her. He couldn't imagine his days on the island without his right-hand person. Fate had delivered her to him at just the right time.

He could see what an effort it was for her to force out the words. 'I feel dreadful. The boat. I'm getting seasick. I don't know why as I don't usually suffer from it.'

He frowned. 'But the sea is so calm.'

'I know. The first few days I was fine. But since then it's getting worse.'

'Is Cristos showing off and speeding around? That would make anyone sick.' He'd have words with his cousin if that was the case.

'Not at all, he's very good and taking extra care since I told him I wasn't feeling well.'

Maybe it was her time of the month. Alex knew enough not to suggest it. Two older sisters had trained him well in that regard. Not that he wanted to press for details. 'Are you sure it's the boat? You're living in a new country. It could be the water. Or the food. Maybe you're allergic to something. Eggplant perhaps. You told me you're on a mission to try all the different Greek ways of cooking it and put them on your blog. You could be eating too much.'

'I suppose it could be that.' She looked doubtful.

'Or a stomach flu?'

'I don't think so. But I guess it's a possibility.'

'Then I suggest you go see a doctor as soon as you can. Perhaps you need to get medication for motion sickness. At least until you get more used to the boat. Aunt Penelope will be able to help find an English-speaking doctor in Nidri. I'll take you back in my boat now.' The sooner she sorted this out, the better.

She groaned and put up her hand in protest. 'Thank you but no. I couldn't face getting back into a boat right now. I'll feel better as the day goes on and go back with Cristos this evening as usual.'

'See a doctor tomorrow. I insist. Call and make an appointment this morning. Don't come in to work until you find out what's wrong. If it's serious and you have to take time off work let me know. Whatever the result let me know.'

It was on the tip of his tongue to ask her would she like him to come with her. But that would be overstepping the mark as her employer. It would be appropriate as a friend, and he realised he already thought of her as a friend. The informal nature of their work arrangement had seen a kind of intimacy develop very quickly between them.

If he was honest with himself, he would admit he didn't view her in just a platonic way. He found her very attractive. Not his tall and blonde type, but alluring just the same. Curvy and auburn-haired was growing on him in a major way. He reacted to the sway of her hips in a tight pencil skirt, the tantalising hint of cleavage when she was shoulder to shoulder with him discussing a plan, the wide curves of her mouth. And he delighted in that smile. Always her warm, embracing smile that made him feel better than any other stimulant ever had.

But he forced himself to turn away, to switch off his feelings. He was not ready for another woman in his life. Was not certain he would *ever* be ready. And it was never a good idea to have an affair with a member of his staff.

Next morning, Dell stared across the desk at the doctor, too shocked to comprehend what she was saying. It wasn't the doctor's lightly accented English that was incomprehensible, it was her words. 'You are pregnant, Ms Hudson.'

'You are pregnant.' The three words she had longed almost beyond reason to hear reverberated through her head but the doctor might as well have said them in Greek for all the sense they made. The middle-aged woman had insisted on Dell taking a pregnancy test, routine in cases of unexplained nausea she had said. Dell had muttered to herself about what a waste of time it was. To her utter shock, the test had proved positive. Then the doctor had examined her to confirm the diagnosis.

'But it's impossible for me to be pregnant,' Dell protested. As she explained her history, the doctor took notes.

'I would say that your IVF has been successful,' the doctor said. 'Bleeding in pregnancy is not uncommon. What you experienced could have been caused by implantation or any number of reasons. Have you had other symptoms?'

How Dell had prayed for the symptoms of pregnancy throughout all those years of hoping. Now she was so deeply immersed in her new life she hadn't actually recognised them. The 'seasickness' that was actually morning sickness. The sensitivity of her breasts she'd put down to the havoc IVF had played with her hormones. The tiredness she'd attributed to the long hours in her new job.

'I believe so,' she said slowly, then explained her symptoms to the doctor.

'I'm sure a blood test will confirm your pregnancy,' the doctor said. 'Congratulations.'

Dell's head was reeling. It was too much to take in. This was the best and the worst of news. *A baby at last.* But pregnant by IVF to her ex-husband while she was living in a different country on the other side of the world from home and with a halfway serious crush on another man?

Through a haze of disbelief, she made a further appointment with the doctor. Then walked blindly out into the street.

Nidri was more a boisterous, overgrown village than a town. Dell tripped on the uneven pavement and gave a hysterical little laugh that had a well-dressed woman turn and look at her askance. She steadied herself against the wall of a beauty salon that specialised in tiny fish nibbling the dead skin from people's feet. Moved on to a *fournos* with a tempting display of the most delicious local cookies and pastries. In her shocked, nauseated state the scent of baking did not appeal.

She was struggling to find a foothold in the suddenly turned upside down landscape of her own life. She would have to take step by dazed step to try to negotiate the uncharted new territory. Not at all certain where it would lead her.

Alex. How would she tell him? What would this mean? Almost certainly the end of her dream job. The end of the already remote chance that they could ever be more than friends. She wrapped her arms tightly around herself against the shivers that shuddered through her, even though the warm spring sun shone down on her shoulders.

CHAPTER EIGHT

ALL NIGHT ALEX had been plagued by a nagging concern for Dell. He'd become so concerned that next morning he decided to take his boat across to Nidri so he could check on her. Her ailment had sounded like something more than seasickness. What if she was seriously ill?

His gut clenched at the thought. Dell had become his responsibility. He had talked her into moving to Greece to work with him even though she had been initially reluctant. Now it was up to him to look out for her. He was all she had here. The job had kept her way too busy for her to get out and make friends. He hoped the doctor's diagnosis would be something easily fixed. That *he* could fix for her.

His aunt Penelope had pointed him in the direction to where Dell was seeing the doctor. He stood across the road and waited for her to come out of her appointment. It wasn't a long wait. He caught sight of her immediately, in the short pencil skirt he liked so much and a crisp striped shirt—she had obviously intended to head to work afterwards. Cristos was on call to take her over.

But as he watched her walk away from the doctor's

rooms, Alex wished he'd been somewhere closer. *What the hell was wrong?* She seemed to lurch as if in a daze, tripping on the uneven pavement, righting herself without seeming to realise what she was doing. Finally she stood out of the way in the doorway of a closed souvenir shop and hugged her arms tightly around herself. Her hair shone bright in a shaft of sunlight. Had she been prescribed medication? Was she suffering from a fever? Been given bad news? *She should not be on her own.*

He broke into a run to get to her. Cursing the traffic, he ducked in and out of cars and buses. The delivery guy on a bicycle balancing an enormous flower arrangement shouted at him but he scarcely heard him. *He had to reach her.* 'Dell!'

She looked up, seemed to have trouble focusing, her eyes huge in her wan face, her lovely mouth trembling. Alex was struck by how vulnerable and alone she seemed. How suddenly *frail*.

He felt swept by an almighty urge to protect her, to make her safe. An urge that went beyond the concern of an employer for a member of staff. *He cared for her.* Alex didn't know when or how it had happened, but somehow she had snuck under his defences. All he knew was he wanted to fold her into his arms and tell her everything would be all right because he was there for her.

'Alex,' she said. 'Wh…what are you doing here?' Her eyes darted every which way. As if she'd rather be anywhere but with him right at this moment. As if she was looking for an escape route, not a pair of comforting arms. Especially not *his*.

Alex shoved his hands into his pockets. He forced

his voice to calm, boss-like concern. 'To see if you're all right. Which you're obviously not. What news from the doctor?'

Emotions that he couldn't read flickered across her face. *Secrets she didn't want to share.* People shouldered past them on the narrow pavement. An English couple standing outside a shop loudly discussed the benefits of olive wood salad servers. Motor scooters in dire need of adjustment to their exhaust systems puttered by. 'Can we maybe go somewhere more private?' she said, her voice so low he could scarcely catch it.

'There's a coffee shop just up there,' he said, indicating it with a wave of his arm. 'You look like you could do with Greek coffee, hot and strong.' If it weren't only mid-morning he'd suggest brandy.

She shuddered and swallowed hard. 'Some orange juice, I think.'

'Sure,' he said. 'Whatever you need.' He put his arm around her shoulder to shepherd her in the right direction. Initially she stiffened against his touch, then the rigidity of her body melted. Her curves felt soft and warm against him. Alex tightened his hold to keep her close, liking the feeling he could keep her safe. But as soon as they reached the coffee shop she broke away from him.

He sat her down at a table in a quiet corner. Pushed the juice towards her. Once she'd taken a few sips, she seemed to revive somewhat, although there was still a worrying pallor to her face.

'Thank you,' she said. Her hands cradled around the glass in an effort, he realised, to stop their trembling.

'So what's wrong? Eggplant allergy?'

A hint of a smile—perhaps ten per cent of its full

incandescent power—hovered around the corners of her mouth. 'Not quite,' she said. She met his gaze directly. 'There's no easy way to say this. Turns out the seasickness wasn't that at all. I… I'm pregnant.' She sounded as though she didn't quite believe it, was just trying on the words for size.

Alex reeled back in his chair, too stunned to say anything. Shock at her words mingled with his own disbelief and disappointment. And a sudden bolt of jealousy that she had a man in her life. A man she had denied. 'Did you know about this when you accepted the job with me?'

The words spilled out from her. As if she was trying to explain the situation to herself as well as to him. 'No. It came as a complete shock. I… I thought—hoped— there was a chance, which is why I said no to your offer in the first place. Then…well, then it seemed I wasn't pregnant. But…the evidence that led me to think I wasn't pregnant and could accept your job turned out to be a false alarm. Turns out, though, I am pregnant.'

'You said you didn't have a man in your life. "One hundred per cent single," if I remember correctly.'

'I don't. There hasn't been anyone for a long time.'

He drummed his fingers on the metal top of the table. 'That doesn't make sense.'

'I realise that. It…it's complicated.'

Cynicism welled up and spouted into his words. 'What's complicated about getting a woman pregnant?' He didn't know why his reaction to her news was so sour. Perhaps because he'd started to think of Dell as *his*. Her news made it very clear she had another man in her life. *The father of her child.*

'We all know how it happens.' Had she met a man

since she'd been in Greece? One of his family? His cousin? She'd remarked on several occasions how good-looking Cristos was. He had no right to be furious if that was the case, he had no claim on her, but a black rage consumed him at the thought.

She bit her lower lip. 'In this case, not quite the way you think,' she said with a dull edge to her voice.

'Perhaps you'd better explain.' He made no effort to keep his disillusionment from his voice. One of the things he'd liked most about her was her open face, her apparent honesty. It appeared he'd read her incorrectly.

Dell quailed against Alex's grim expression. He hadn't been able to hide his shock at her revelation. Of course he'd be annoyed, angry even that his newly contracted employee was pregnant. It had been an incredible shock to her, too. But her joy in finally seeing her dream of motherhood in sight overrode everything.

There was no point in telling him anything other than the unembellished truth. She took a steadying breath. 'This baby was conceived by IVF. I'd been undergoing treatment during my marriage.'

Alex's dark brows pulled into an even deeper frown. 'But you're divorced now.'

'Yes,' she said. 'Legally divorced. The marriage is done and dusted.'

'So who is the father?'

'My ex-husband.'

He pushed back in his chair. Slanted his shoulders away from her. It hurt to see him distancing himself. 'I don't get it,' he said.

Dell caught a half-sob in her throat. She'd known this wouldn't be easy. But she hadn't expected it would be this difficult. 'The IVF procedures I had when I was married to Neil didn't work. It was one of the reasons we broke up. Well, not broke up strictly speaking. He left me. I hadn't been expecting it. But he wanted out. He blamed my obsession with having a baby and…and for neglecting him as a husband.'

Alex's eyes narrowed. 'And was that the reason?'

'Looking back, I see it did put the marriage under stress. I always thought having a baby was what we both wanted. But maybe…maybe it was more about me. I'd always wanted to have kids, felt a failure that I couldn't fall pregnant when everyone around me seemed to do it so easily. My life became a roller coaster of alternate anticipation then despair. And with some hormone crazy happening too. Maybe there were cracks in the marriage I just didn't want to see. That it wasn't strong enough to survive the pressure.'

She looked down at her hands, realised abstractedly that the dent from where she'd worn her wedding ring for so long had finally disappeared.

Alex shifted in his chair, obviously uncomfortable. She appreciated this was an awkwardly personal conversation for a boss with his employee. 'That still doesn't enlighten me to how you're pregnant to your ex-husband.'

'It took me a while to pick myself up from the aftermath of my marriage. We'd been dating since high school and—'

'So you'd been with the same guy since high school?' Alex sounded incredulous. She remembered his reputation as a player and a man about town before he'd met the lovely Mia. How tame her own life had been in comparison. But she hadn't wanted it any other way.

She nodded. 'He was nice. Steady. I thought he'd be a good husband and father.'

There hadn't been a lot of fireworks to start and what there had been had eventually fizzled out. But then it hadn't been sizzling sensuality she'd been after. She'd seen Neil as steady and secure and a family man totally unlike her distant father. Had it been enough? For the first time she wondered if sex had become the effort for Neil that it had for her. It had become all about making babies, not making love. She thought about the thrill she felt just being in the same room as Alex. Had she ever felt that way about her ex-husband?

'But he didn't turn out so nice,' Alex said.

Slowly she shook her head. 'To be fair, there must have been wrong on both sides for the marriage to have ended.'

'So how did you manage on your own?'

She shrugged. 'Okay.' Of course it hadn't been okay but she didn't want to admit that to Alex. Of how Neil had screwed her out of her fair share of their assets. How she'd been left with the considerable IVF expense as he'd convinced her it was what she'd wanted, not him. She hadn't been able to understand how he'd turned so nasty until she'd discovered he'd met someone else while they were still married and had moved in with her straight away.

Alex's dark eyes were perceptive. 'Really okay?'

'Not really.' An awkward silence fell between them. But she had no desire to discuss her dating disasters with Alex. That was something she could laugh at with her girlfriends. Not with the only man who had attracted her since—well, pretty well ever.

Alex was the one to break the silence. 'So…back to your pregnancy.'

'The fertility clinic got in touch, asked me what I wanted to do with our last stored embryo.' She implored him with her eyes to understand. 'I'd wanted a baby for so long. Desperately. I saw this as my last chance. At twenty-nine I was running out of time to meet a guy who wanted to get married and have kids. Start again. I told the clinic I wanted to try.'

'What did your ex say?'

Dell found it difficult to meet Alex's eyes. Concentrated instead on the pattern of olives printed on the café placemat. 'Here's where it gets complicated. I didn't tell him.'

'What?' His voice made no bones about his disapproval. 'You didn't tell the guy who fathered it?'

She looked up at him again. There was no point in dissembling. 'I know. It was probably wrong. Even immoral.' She leaned over the table towards him. 'But you don't understand what baby hunger feels like. A constant ache. Torture every time you see someone else's baby. When you have to congratulate a friend who's pregnant and all the time you're screaming inside *why not me?'*

'No. I don't understand that,' he said shortly.

'Don't judge me, Alex. I did what I did because I had to grab that one, final chance of achieving the dream of holding my baby in my arms. I didn't hold out any hopes as no attempt had ever worked before. But when the chance was offered to me I had no choice but to take it.'

'Is that why you initially turned down my job offer?'

'Yes. I didn't want to be away from home if by some miracle the treatment worked. It never had before but I kept alive that tiny beam of hope. Until…until it appeared I had failed again. Evidence that it turns out was false.'

'So what does your ex think of this?'

'What? Me being pregnant? I only just found out myself. He doesn't know.'

'When do you intend to tell him?' It was ironic, she thought, that she had told Alex, her boss, before the biological father.

'Not…not yet. The pregnancy is still in its early stages. I… I…may still lose it. I wouldn't want to tell him until I'm more sure. Why go through all that for nothing?'

'You obviously don't anticipate a happy reaction.' Alex's fingers drummed on the table top. Dell resisted the temptation to reach over and still them with her own.

'He's moved on. Married already to the woman he left me for.' Swift, brutal, her ex had put their years together behind him as if they'd never happened.

She'd made the decision to take the embryo without really thinking about Neil. Possibly she'd even justified it by remembering how he'd said she wanted the IVF so much, she could pay the bills for it. Didn't that make the baby hers and hers alone? In her heart she knew that thinking was wrong. Not so much for Neil's sake—though she knew he had a right to know he was going to be a father—but for the baby's sake. Her child deserved to know about his or her other parent. The idea of a baby had seemed so abstract. Now it was beginning to feel real. A little person she hoped she would be bringing into the world. And for whom she bore the entire responsibility. It was both terrifying and exhilarating.

'What do you intend to do?'

'Give you my resignation, along with my sincere apology, if that's what you want. I certainly don't blame you if you do.'

He leaned forward across the table. 'Is that what you want? Legally, I can't fire an employee for being pregnant.' For a moment she saw a flash of her old adversary in the set of his jaw.

'It wouldn't come to that,' she said. 'I... I...' She was going to say *I love working with you* but somehow she couldn't utter the word *love* to him under any circumstance. Not with the knowledge of her secret crush on him throbbing away in her heart. 'I really enjoy working with you and would like to continue. The baby isn't due until after Christmas. I would like to stay here and help you with the launch, then return to Australia at the end of summer, say late August. I need to be back there for the birth.'

He leaned back against the chair. Templed his fingers. 'You're sure you want to do that?'

'Yes. I really want to continue working with you. To...to be part of your awesome project.' *To stay part of his life.*

His expression didn't give away anything. She had no idea what his decision would be. She would accept it either way. But she just hoped he would agree to keep her on.

'With all the hospitality staff I've employed over

the years, I've worked with pregnant women. There's no reason not to keep you on.'

Hope bubbled through her. 'You mean I've still got a job?'

'Yes,' he said.

'You're not just saying that because you'd be breaking some employment code if you asked me to go?'

'No,' he said gruffly. 'I want you to stay. I consider you an…an indispensable part of my team.'

She wanted to fling her arms around his neck to thank him, but knew it would be totally inappropriate. Especially now considering her condition.

'Thank you,' she said. 'I promise I won't let you down.'

'What about your motion sickness?'

'The doctor has given me some strategies to cope with that,' she said. 'No medication, of course.'

'What about the boat ride to and from the island every day? You looked very shaken by it yesterday.'

Her chin tilted up. She wouldn't give him any excuse to renege on his decision. 'I'll just have to grit my teeth and bear it, won't I?' she said. 'This job is really important to me, Alex.' *You are important to me, but I'll never be able to let you know that now.*

'I think there's a better way. You should move onto the island.'

'But…but none of the rooms are ready for occupation,' she said.

'There are two self-contained suites in the pavilion,' he said. 'You'll have to share it with me.'

CHAPTER NINE

How DID SHE deal with this new development?

Sharing an apartment with Alex would be quite the challenge, Dell realised. That afternoon, she followed him as he carried her suitcase across the marble floor of the pavilion into the sumptuous bedroom that was to be hers. She noted that, as he had said, the bedrooms and bathrooms were completely separate—thank heaven.

Growing up, she had shared a bathroom with her brother. And of course she had shared a bathroom with her ex. But she could not even imagine having to share a bathroom with Alex. Not in a room where the occupants spent most of their time naked. Not when her imagination would go crazy thinking about him naked in the same space where *she* was naked. Standing where he stood to shower that tall, broad-shouldered body, twisting to soap his powerful chest and lean, six-pack belly. At least, she assumed he'd have a six-pack belly. He did in those dreams that came to taunt and tantalise her—where he was wearing considerably fewer clothes than he did in real life. She shook her head to clear her thoughts. *Enough.*

She had to stop this crazy fantasising about Alex. It

was never going to happen. She was pregnant and he was *not* okay with it, no matter how much he quoted his employer code of practice. Her pregnancy was an inconvenience to him. There'd never before been a sign he was interested in her as anything other than an employee; there certainly wouldn't be now she was pregnant. She had a thrilling new life ahead of her—mother to her miracle baby—and that life would not include Alex. Once she went back to Australia she doubted he would be anything more than a name on her résumé, her boss on a particularly exciting project.

That new life was not quite the way she had envisaged it for all those years—having the child's father around had been the plan. But she had not the slightest regret about her rash visit to the clinic. In fact the more she thought about it, the happier she became that she had made that reckless choice. *Her baby.* Now she needed to concentrate on doing the best possible job she could do so Alex would not regret keeping her on in a job she still sorely needed. She needed to earn to both pay off her debts and start saving for the baby. Indulging in fantasies about her handsome boss was a time-wasting distraction.

'This bedroom is magnificent,' she said, looking around her at the restful, white room straight out of a glossy interiors magazine. The furniture was sleek and modern, the huge bed piled with expensive linens and pillows. A few carefully chosen paintings hung on the walls, contemporary works she recognised as being by the artist she had visited in Athens with Alex. He had commissioned a series of arresting scenes of the islands for the resort. Nature also provided its own artworks, the windows framed a view of the green hills behind. Tasteful. Private. Peaceful. Well, as peaceful as it could be with *him* in a room just across a corridor. 'It's incredibly luxurious for a pool house,' she said.

'I understand the previous owner lived in it when he flew in to check on the construction of the main house.'

'That makes sense,' she said. 'Is your room the same as this one?'

Why did she say that? She didn't want him to show her his bedroom. To see his bed and imagine him there, his tanned, olive skin against the pale linen sheets, as he sprawled across— She flushed that tell-tale flush but thankfully he still had his back to her. Why was her libido leading her on such a dance? Pregnancy hormones? Or *him*? She didn't need to think about the answer. Fight the unwelcome feeling as she might, she had never felt so attracted to a man.

'Yeah, it's the same,' he said. 'A slightly different colour scheme.' He was more subdued than she'd seen him, closed off, communicating only what he needed to. Possibly he was regretting his offer for her to share the pavilion with him.

What would he think if he could see the scenarios playing in her head, where he played a starring role? Again she flushed, this time with mortification.

She forced herself back to the real world. He was her boss. She was nothing more to him than an employee—valued, she knew, but an underling just the same. Now she felt she had to work even harder, to prove herself to him all over again. Prove that being pregnant was no barrier to performance. She would do well to keep reminding herself of that.

'Thank you, Alex, for this. I think I feel better already knowing I don't have to face that boat trip twice a day. As soon as the sickness abates I can go back to the villa.'

'When you're ready,' he said. 'You can stay here as long as you need to.'

Dell followed him through to the spacious living area and kitchen. Despite her good working relationship with Alex, she felt awkward at the subtle shift between them that being roommates would inevitably bring. She knew she was intruding but at the same time she was very grateful for the offer of such wonderful accommodation on the island. She was happy at the villa but this apartment was the ultimate in opulence. Once the resort was up and going, the pavilion would become exclusive, highly priced accommodation for well-heeled guests. What a treat to stay here in the meantime. She could never afford this level of luxury on her own dime.

'So how do we handle this?' she asked him. 'I'm aware I'm invading your privacy and I'll stay out of your way as much as possible. What do you do about food? Do you cook for yourself or—?' She actually knew a daily housekeeper came over on the construction crew boat every day to cook and clean for him. But she didn't want to admit she'd been snooping into his life.

He told her what she already knew and she pretended it was news to her. 'The housekeeper can leave meals for you, too, if you like,' he said. 'Or you can order what you need to cook your own meals. Just co-ordinate with her when you're likely to need to use the kitchen. There's breakfast stuff in the pantry. Again, order what you need.'

So no shared meals, then. No intimate evenings over

the elegant table set in the loggia overlooking the pool.
Not that she'd expected that. Alex made it very clear
he put her in the same category as the housekeeper—
mere staff.

'I'll leave you to unpack and settle in,' he said. 'Then
you can join me in the office. That is, if you feel up
to it.' He was bending over backwards to be consid-
erate when she knew he must be cursing the break in
their timetable.

'I'm feeling better by the minute, just knowing I
don't have to get back into a boat every day.'

He paused. 'I need to go to Athens again day after
tomorrow. Will you be able to come?'

'I'll manage,' she said. 'I don't want to miss out.' If
she had to nibble on dry crackers and swig lemonade
all day to keep the nausea at bay she'd be there.

'We'll have a very full day. Pack for a night away,'
he said. 'If you want to see the Acropolis, it might be
a good opportunity to get up early and do it before we
fly back. I don't know how you'll feel about all the
walking and steps involved in getting up to the Parthenon once you're further into your pregnancy. It will
get too hot as well.'

'That's very thoughtful of you. I'd love to.' *Why was
he being so nice?*

'Good.' He turned on his heel. 'I'll see you in the
office. I've got work to catch up on.' The implication
being he had lost valuable time attending to her. Dell
felt bad about that. She had hours to make up too.
She'd work later that evening. Which would make any
awkward encounters in the pool house less likely. She
would be careful to schedule her meals around his so
she did not intrude.

He started to stride away. 'Alex. Before you go. One more thing.'

He turned back to face her.

'Your aunt Penelope…'

'Yes?'

'I got to like her while I was staying in the villa. She's teaching me Greek, you know. And sharing her traditional recipes. My blog fans are loving them.'

'Very nice,' he said dismissively. But Dell felt she had to plough on.

'As I got to know her, I realised that she…well, your aunt Penelope is the disseminator of information to your extended family.'

'Which is your kind way of saying she's an outrageous gossip.'

Dell laughed. 'I wouldn't quite say it like that, but yes.'

Alex laughed too and Dell felt a relaxing of the thread of tension that had become so taut between them since she'd dropped her bombshell back at the café in Nidri.

He might not be so relaxed when he heard what she had to say next. 'Er…with that in mind, do you realise your aunt thinks I'm moving in to the pool house to be with you? I mean, not to share like a roommate, to actually live with you. She's convinced we're lovers.'

'What?' Alex exploded. 'Where the hell did she get that idea from?' His eyes narrowed. 'What did you say to give her that opinion?'

'Nothing. Not a word, I promise you. As far as I'm concerned you're the boss and I'm the employee. You're helping me out because I'm suffering so much from motion sickness it's affecting my efficiency in my job. That's all I told her.'

His face set granite hard. 'It needs to be perfectly clear that there is nothing else whatsoever between us and never could be.' Dell tried not to react to the shard of pain that speared her at his words. She knew that to be the case, but hearing it so vehemently expressed hurt.

'Promnestria.' He spat the Greek word.

'What does that mean?' Dell asked. 'It…er…doesn't sound very pleasant.'

'It means "matchmaker", and I'm using it as a short-cut to express how annoyed I am at the interference from my family—well-meaning as they are. My aunt, and some of the other women, know very well I don't intend ever to marry. Yet they continue to speculate about me and every halfway eligible female who comes my way. And even the entirely unsuitable ones.'

Like me, thought Dell, the shard of pain stabbing deeper.

He cursed some more under his breath. This time she didn't ask for a translation.

'I'm afraid there's more,' she said.

He rolled his eyes heavenward. 'I'm so fond of my aunt but—'

'She also suspects I'm pregnant. I think she recognised the signs I never saw myself. At her age I guess she's seen it all before. I have a feeling she's crowing with delight because she thinks my baby is…is, well, yours.'

The normally eloquent Alex seemed completely lost for words. Dell squirmed in an agony of expectation

of his reaction. Suddenly her job didn't seem so secure after all.

When he finally found his voice, it was ominously
calm. 'How on earth would she think that?'

Dell shrugged. 'I guess she thought we knew each
other in Australia. Put two and two together and came
up with completely the wrong answer.'

'What have you told her?' Again she caught a
glimpse of her old adversary. Alex seemed as though
he was looking for her to slip up in her evidence. Had
he really changed? She so wanted to believe he had.

She willed him to believe she was telling the truth.
'Nothing, I assure you. Not about the court case, nothing. I'm here to work, Alex, not to gossip with your
family. I mean it.' It was a trap she'd been determined
not to fall into, beguiling as Aunt Penelope could be.

'Good,' he said abruptly. But his taut look relaxed
and she felt like she was off the witness stand.

'It won't be long before it becomes obvious that I'm
pregnant. Should I tell your aunt? And that the baby
isn't yours?'

He shook his head. 'My publicity director's personal
life is none of their concern. Although in one way you
telling them would quell some of the speculation about
the reason you've moved in here. People close to me
know I would never get involved with a woman carrying another man's child.'

His eyes didn't meet hers as he said that. Dell was
relieved. It gave her valuable seconds to hide her surprise. Was that a message for her? She didn't need it
spelled out.

'On balance,' he continued, 'your pregnancy is your

business. My family can stay out of it.' Not for one moment would he think she might not want him along.

'I shall hereby resist all hints, innuendos and subtly worded questions,' she said, holding up her hand as if swearing an oath.

'Thank you,' he said. He stilled, his shoulders tensed, his stance braced. 'I can't bear to be the subject of gossip—my private life bandied around as if it's some game. Not after…not after everything that happened. When I couldn't turn around without seeing a paparazzi shot of myself with some journalist analysing my expression and suggesting what I was feeling. Photos of her and me together before…before…' His words faltered to an end in a tortured groan.

Again Dell felt a great rush of compassion for him. She couldn't begin to imagine how she would have dealt with what he had been through, the horror and loss, the immeasurable pain. She ached to put her arms around him and comfort him. But he was her boss and she his employee and he had drawn the line between them. She kept her distance.

'I promise I will not encourage your aunt in any speculation about my personal life or yours. Not that I will be seeing much of her while I'm staying on the island. There's a lot to be done here. I'm going to concentrate my efforts on that.'

'As far as my family is concerned, I suggest we present a united front—your role in helping me with the launch of Pevezzo Athina is why we spend time together,' he said. 'There is nothing else of interest to great-aunts, aunts, cousins and whoever else seems determined to see something else that simply isn't there.'

His tone was businesslike in the extreme, in complete denial of the informal, friendly tone she had become used to. As he spoke, she noticed the shift in the angle of his shoulders away from her, distancing her, re-establishing boundaries.

'Of course,' she said, swallowing against the lump of disappointment that threatened to choke her.

He turned on his heel to head out of the pavilion and towards the main building.

Dell watched him, his stride both powerful and graceful as he walked away, each footstep seeming to determine a new distance between them.

Some of the magic of this special place where she had been so happy seemed to spiral away above him to dissipate in the cloudless blue sky.

CHAPTER TEN

TWO DAYS LATER Alex gritted his teeth as he walked by Dell's bedroom suite. From behind the closed door he could hear the faint splashing of her shower. He could plug his ears to the sound. But he couldn't block his imagination. Images bombarded him of her in there, naked, the water flowing over the creamy skin of her shoulders, her breasts and downwards over the curves of her hips. Was she slowly soaping her body? Did she have her face tilted up towards the jets of water as if she was preparing to receive a kiss?

His kiss.

His wild imaginings were torture. Living with Dell in such close proximity was torture. Even a glass left on the sink with the lipstick outline of her lips on the rim drove him into a frenzy of fantasising about that mouth on his. It was crazy. And totally unlike him.

He'd always been confident with women. To be frank, he'd never had to chase them. From the age of fourteen they'd chased him. And he'd been only too happy to be caught. He'd never gone through that stage of stuttering awkwardness in the presence of a beautiful woman. Until now.

The pressure of denying his attraction to his lovely

employee, totally out of bounds because she was pregnant to another man, was telling on him. To his immense frustration, conversation with her about anything other than work had become awkward, stilted. *Because of him.*

He could tell she was puzzled at his often abrupt tone, at his silences. She made the effort to be her usual friendly self, but with an edge of uncertainty as she became unsure of his reaction. But he seemed incapable of returning to that comfortable working relationship, that easy camaraderie and repartee. Not when he couldn't get her out of his thoughts. Not as a trusted workmate. Or a person he thought could be a friend. But a smart, sensual, very appealing woman. A woman he *desired*.

He wasn't looking for this. He didn't want it. Not when her pregnancy complicated everything. But the feeling wouldn't go away. No matter how many times he plunged into the chilly water of the pool and swam laps until he was exhausted.

When she'd lived at the villa, he could escape to the pavilion. Now her warm presence had invaded his man cave, where he'd been able to retreat with his dark thoughts and memories. In just days, it had become stamped with her personality, even when she wasn't actually there. The sound of her laughter seemed to linger on the empty stillness, tantalising hints of her perfume wafted to greet him, there was Dell food in the fridge.

The enforced intimacy was making him yearn for something more, needs and feelings he had long denied himself because of the guilt that tore him apart over Mia's death. Sharing a house with a woman—if

only in the roommate sense—was bringing back painful memories of his late fiancée.

He had been happy dating Mia but she had pressed
for more commitment. In fact she had delivered an ul-
timatum—get engaged or she walked. He had agreed
to the engagement, she had agreed to move in. But
then it had stalled with his ambivalence about setting
a date for the wedding. As their relationship had gone
on, he hadn't been certain they had enough in common
to build a life together, the kind of committed family
life he'd had growing up with his parents and grandparents. Under his playboy, party prince exterior that
was what he'd known he'd wanted one day. He still
hadn't been certain Mia was the one when he'd sent
her to her death.

Dell was so different, in looks, personality, everything. Put both women together and Dell would be
overshadowed by Mia's tall, model-perfect looks. He
couldn't, *wouldn't* compare them. Yet in his mind he
could almost see Dell looking up at the other woman
with a wry smile, unleashing her own vibrant beauty in
acknowledging Mia's statuesque Scandinavian looks.
And Mia would smile back. Mia would have liked her,
and Dell would have liked Mia. Polar opposites they
might be, but they were both warm, kind people.

Mia had connected with his wild, party animal side.
Together they had worked hard and played hard. Dell…
Dell was something altogether different. There was a
connection with her he had never felt before, a sense
of certainty, of continuity. They thought in the same
way. He kept coming back to that concept of fate. It
was almost as if she'd been sent to him to help redeem
and heal him.

And yet it was impossible. He could not get around the fact she was pregnant to another man. Okay, so it was a 'test-tube baby'. He didn't have to torture himself with images of her making love with her ex. Of the baby being a product of an intimate union rather than a laboratory procedure.

But being in Greece only intensified an even deeper connection—the connection to his family and heritage. In a traditional Greek family like he came from, blood was everything. Even generations down the track and in Australia, thousands of miles away from the land of his ancestors, that hadn't changed. His family had liked Mia, but he knew they would have been a whole lot happier if she too had come from a Greek migrant family.

That deeply ingrained sense of family made the concept of taking on another man's child seem alien to him. His attitude was something he couldn't change—it was as much of him as the proud Mikhalis nose that went back through generations of males in his family. He had admired Jesse Morgan for accepting Lizzie's daughter when he had married her. Jesse adored little Amy, had an amicable relationship with the little girl's French father. But taking on another man's child was something Alex could never see himself doing.

He was so lost in his thoughts he started when the door to her room opened and Dell stood in the doorway. He had to force himself not to stare. She was wrapped in a white towelling bathrobe, her hair in damp tendrils around her face, cheeks flushed from the warmth of the shower. The neckline of the robe had fallen open to reveal a hint of cleavage and the smooth top curve of her breasts. Her legs were bare. *Was she naked under there?* He balled his hands by his sides.

'Is everything okay?' she said. 'I'm not late, am I? I got up in plenty of time so we'd get the plane to Athens.'

'It's okay,' he said gruffly, looking at her feet rather than letting his gaze centre on her chest. She had small, well-shaped feet with pink-painted toenails. Lovely from top to toe, came the thought from nowhere.

She frowned. 'It's just I heard you pacing up and down and wondered if—'

'I wasn't pacing,' he said.

'You needed to see me,' she said at the same time, with a small, perplexed frown.

'No,' he said.

'You could have knocked on the door if you did,' she said. 'I'm always there if…if you need me.' Her voice faltered away.

For a long moment their gazes met. For the first time he saw something in her green eyes that kick-started his heart into a violent thudding. An aware-ness, an unspoken acknowledgement that he was not alone in his feelings. That if he were to pull her into his arms and slide that robe down her shoulders, she would not object.

He took a step backward. Broke that connection with an abrupt turning away from her. 'I'll be out by the pool. Meet me there when you're ready. We've got a lot to get done in Athens.'

The next morning, Dell looked at the computer-gen-erated images on the screen with immense interest. She and Alex were in the architect's studio in the old centre of Athens in a street behind Syntagma Square. From the get-go, Alex had involved her in every aspect of the resort, not just the food, which was her primary area of expertise, and she was fascinated by how the plans had developed.

The designer was showing them on screen realistic images of how the interiors of Pevezzo Athina would look when everything was finished and ready for guests. The images were so detailed Dell could imagine herself walking through the rooms, furnished right down to the flower arrangements on the tables and the towels in the bathrooms.

'Every detail and change we discussed last meeting is there, looking perfect.' *We.* How easily she slipped into referring to herself and Alex as *we.* 'It makes it seem so real, so close to completion.'

She straightened up and in doing so caught Alex's eye. They shared a quick smile of complicity and triumph. They were a team and their team was firing on all cylinders.

Dell felt an overwhelming sense of relief. She'd mourned the loss of the easy feeling between them back at the island. Tortured herself with the thought that maybe he'd become aware of her crush on him and had backed off in discomfort. Perhaps moving in to the pavilion had been a mistake. Living in such close proximity was only making it more difficult—she had to be continually on alert.

She thought she'd kept her feelings carefully hidden, effectively masked. Then there had been a moment yesterday morning at that post-shower encounter when she'd sworn a recognition of mutual want had flashed between them. But the shutters had come down leaving just his inscrutable expression. Had she given herself away? Had she imagined his response?

He'd hardly spoken afterwards. On the journey she had been too busy keeping the nausea at bay to be concerned at the paucity of conversation, the silences that had been anything but comfortable.

But from the first meeting the day before, things had started to ease. Perhaps it was because at their meetings the designers and suppliers treated them as a team they started to behave like one again. She used the word *team* loosely. For all the politeness, for all the acknowledgement of her role as his assistant, the deference was very much to Alex as the boss. He was the person with the money and the authority and the power—the man who owned a private island and was spending a fortune on the services these talented people were providing. While they spoke mainly in English there were times they needed to break into Greek. She listened carefully but could only identify the odd word here and there. Still, that was better than when she'd first arrived, thanks to Aunt Penelope.

'Any other thoughts on the interior design?' Alex asked her now, indicating the CGI.

She shook her head. 'If you're happy, I reckon you can sign off on it.'

'Done,' he said and they again shared a smile.

That smile warmed her. Leaving the island to fly to Athens had been a good move. It marked, she hoped, a return to the working relationship that had bonded them in the first place. In her deepest heart she longed for the impossible, but was content to have their work camaraderie back.

Hands were shaken all round, congratulations and

thanks expressed. Then she and Alex were back out of the office and into the mid-morning busy street. She looked around her avidly trying to soak in as much detail as possible—the historical buildings guarded by soldiers in fabulous traditional uniforms, the shop-fronts, what people were wearing, the buzz of it all. One day she would love to spend more time here. Again that feeling of excitement swept through her that she was actually living in Greece. She needed to make the most of it before she went home to Australia. She pushed aside the feelings of sadness that looming return evoked in her. When big dreams collided there was ultimately a casualty.

'That was the last meeting for today,' Alex said. 'Time well spent. Thank you for your contribution.'

He really was a wonderful boss, certainly not the tyrant some had painted him in Sydney. Had his reputation sprung from a resentment of his high standards, envy even? Or had he really changed as he claimed to have done?

'Back to the hotel?' she asked.

After a jam-packed afternoon of meetings, they had spent the previous night in a luxurious hotel not far from Plaka, the oldest and most historical part of Athens. Separate rooms, of course, but on the same floor.

Alex had gone out to a fashionable bar and restaurant in Syntagma with one of his cousins. To her surprise, he had invited her too, though she suspected it was more from good manners than any real desire to have her along. Her presence would only fuel the rumours in his family that she was more than an employee.

But she'd been too exhausted to accept. She did not

want to admit to her bone-deep tiredness as she didn't want to remind him of her pregnancy, or that it could affect her capacity to work. Rather she'd had dinner in her room, looked for a long time at the amazing view of ancient ruins lit up from below and gone to bed very early.

Now he looked at her trim business suit and medium-heeled shoes; her stilettos had been put away until after the baby was born. 'You might want to change before you climb the Acropolis.'

'There's still time before we have to leave for the airport?' The meeting had run a little late.

'Your expedition was built into the schedule.'

'I don't quite understand why you did that, but thank you,' she said, looking up at him.

He didn't meet her eyes. 'It pleases me that you like Greece so much, are learning the language. Visiting one of our most significant historical sites is to be encouraged.'

Dell thought there was rather more to it than that. Remembered he had said he wanted to make amends for the past. But she didn't want to bring up the court case again. It seemed a lifetime ago that they had been enemies.

'I can't wait,' she said. 'I've wanted to see the Parthenon since I was a kid.'

'I chose the hotel for its easy access,' he said. 'We'll make our way through Plaka up onto the Acropolis, right up to the Parthenon and the Temple of Athena.'

It took a moment for the significance of what he'd said to sink in. *'We?'* she asked, her heart suddenly pounding. 'Are you—?'

'Coming with you? Of course.' He spoke with the confident assuredness she found so appealing.

'There's no need, you know. I'm perfectly okay by myself,' she said. Her fingers were mentally crossed that he would not agree.

'I want to come with you, Dell,' he said. His tone, to her delight, brooked no disagreement.

She knew her pleasure at the prospect of his company was beaming from her eyes but she didn't care. For just this few hours she was going to pretend there were no barriers between them and enjoy every second of her time alone with him.

CHAPTER ELEVEN

ALEX WAS GLAD he had booked a late flight back to Preveza. This was to be no cursory trip up to the Acropolis so Dell could check off a tourist 'must-see'. She stopped to examine and exclaim at everything on the walk up the rocky outcrop that towered over the city of Athens, the ancient citadel of the Acropolis that dated back to the fifth century BC. She was the one who filled him in on the dates and facts. Her knowledge of ancient Greek history was impressive, though when he complimented her, she demurred saying it was snippets she remembered from high school. Oh, and a little brushing up on the Internet.

First of the ancient structures to catch her attention was the Herodes open-air amphitheatre, with its semi-circular rows of marble seating built in tiers from the stage, built in 161 AD. 'Can you imagine how many people must have been entertained here over the centuries?' she said as, after a long pause for thoughtful contemplation, she snapped photos with her smartphone.

'And continue to do so,' he said. 'There are plays and concerts staged here throughout the summer.'

Her face lit up. 'Really? I would love to attend one. I wouldn't care what it was, just to be here would be the most amazing experience. Please, Alex, can you help me book a performance before I go home?'

Alex paused for a moment too long and the silence fell awkwardly between them. He knew she would have to go back to Sydney for the birth of her baby, but didn't want to think about the gap her loss would leave in his life. Almost as if he didn't acknowledge it, it wouldn't happen. 'Of course,' he said eventually, forcing himself not to sound glum.

As they continued the climb, glimpses of the immense marble columns of the Parthenon above them beckoned. 'There it is!' Dell paused, gawking above her, and tripped over the uneven paving on the pathway. 'I wondered if I would ever get to see it.'

'Careful,' Alex said as he took her elbow to steady her. He intended to keep a grip on her but she flushed and he loosened his hold.

'I'm okay,' she said.

'A woman in your condition isn't supposed to fall,' he said.

'Condition?' she said with a quirk of her auburn brows. 'You make it sound like something medical. Being pregnant is something natural for a woman. Something wonderful.'

'But you've been so ill,' he said, remembering the day he'd seen her in Nidri, how her haggard appearance had shocked him.

'That's just the hormones, the doctor told me. All part of the process of pregnancy. Some women suffer more than others. I don't need to be wrapped in cotton wool.' She looked up at him with a sweet curving of her lips. 'Although I do appreciate your concern. It's very chivalrous of you.'

'So long as you're okay.' Chivalrous? Alex didn't think he'd ever been called that before. Selfish. Inconsiderate. Arrogant. That was what he'd been used to in his past. He tried on the feel of *chivalrous* and liked it, though he really was only doing what came naturally when he was around Dell.

'I'm actually more than okay.' She breathed deeply as she looked around her, at the steep hill wooded in parts with cypress and olive. If you looked closely there were spring flowers in the undergrowth and Alex pointed them out to her. She took a few snaps with her smartphone.

'Thank you,' she said. 'I don't know anything about the plants here. And you never know what can make an interesting blog post.'

'The ten minutes you spent reading the poster on "Vegetation and Flora of the Acropolis" must surely have helped,' he said with a smile.

'Did I spend that long?' she said. 'I'm sorry. I'm fascinated with everything about this place.'

'I like that,' he said. He was learning that Dell was never satisfied with skimming the surface, she had to dig deep, to learn. It was one of the reasons she made such a good employee and why he valued her more each day.

'Being on this ancient ground, I can't help thinking of all the people who have been here before us, all the people who are to come,' she said. 'I'm bearing a new life. It makes me feel connected, part of something much greater.'

A new life? Alex had not thought of her pregnancy in that way, perhaps he hadn't wanted to. He had seen it as an inconvenience, limiting the months she could work for him, blocking the possibility of pursuing his attraction to her. Not as the growth of a new little person who would make Dell a mother. She would be a good mother, he thought. But what about the father? What role would he play in her life? He felt a stab of discomfort at the thought of her ex. He refused to consider it could be jealousy.

Dell placed her hand on her stomach. She was wearing a wearing a white dress of soft cotton that flowed around her body. He realised with a shock that she was probably wearing it because it was looser than what she usually wore. It tied under her breasts with a blue woven tie. He noticed a new curve to her belly. Were her breasts bigger too? A quick glance said they were. Her new curves made her even lovelier.

She must have noticed the direction of his gaze. She smiled. 'I've started to show. Now I'm letting myself really believe I'm having a baby. Did you notice me tugging at my skirt during the meetings today? I tried not to make it obvious, but it's getting very tight.'

'You're happy about that?' he said.

'Really happy,' she said without hesitation. Alex could see from the glow of her face and the joy in her eyes that she meant it. 'The timing isn't the most convenient, I acknowledge that. But I've wanted a baby for so long and this is probably my only chance.'

'What will you do when you go back to Sydney?' he asked.

A little of the glow faded. 'I'll have to fling myself on the mercy of my parents.'

He frowned. 'Wouldn't they be delighted they were going to be grandparents? My sisters both have children. Nothing makes my parents happier than their grandbabies.'

He wondered if they'd given up hope for any grandchildren from him. He had been so busy turning partying into a multimillion-dollar business he hadn't actually thought much about children. He'd always wanted to have kids but it had been filed in the 'one day' category—even with Mia, who had also thought of babies as something for the future.

'From what I've heard about your family, that doesn't surprise me,' she said. 'My parents are very different. They're not really family orientated. We're not close. They'll be shocked at what I've done. I'm just hoping they won't disapprove so much they won't help me.'

'Can't you live on your own? Don't you have your own apartment in Sydney?'

She shook her head. 'I came off the worst in the spoils of divorce. He got the apartment, I got the debts.' Her attempt to sound flippant failed miserably.

'Can you expect support from your ex?'

'No way. I…er… I'm not sure I'll even tell him. He's married again, has a new life. We're not in touch.'

He frowned. 'Doesn't he have a right to know he's going to be a father?'

'I'm not sure that he does,' she said, tight-lipped. Alex could read the *don't go there* signals flashing from her eyes. But the little she gave away made him believe she had reason to be wary of the ex. The guy sounded like a jerk.

'So you'll be going back to Sydney to nothing?'

'That's not quite true. My parents have a large house. Even if simply out of duty I'm sure they'll find

room for me and the baby until I get on my feet again.
Though to tell you the truth, I'm not looking forward
to telling them my news.'

'Your parents don't know you're pregnant?'

'No one does but you, and my doctor in Nidri, of
course.' She looked up at him, her eyes huge. 'I've been
disappointed so many times. I'm waiting until I'm further down the track before I tell anyone. Just in case.'

Pain shadowed her eyes and he realised how desperately she wanted this pregnancy, how vulnerable
it made her and how alone she seemed in the world.
He felt angry her parents sounded so distant, that they
wouldn't want to help her at such a time. As for the
ex, Alex's fists clenched beside him. Again that fierce
desire to protect her swept over him. He couldn't bear
to think of her struggling on her own. Life could be
tough for a lone parent. He knew that from the juggling some of his single-mother staff had had to do to
keep an income coming in. How would Dell manage?

This was not his baby. Not his business. But *she*
was his business. He had brought her to Greece and
she had proved herself tuned to the same wavelength
as he was when it came to the business. The plans for
the hotel would not be moving along so quickly or so
efficiently without her help. He'd have to find a way to
give her a substantial bonus before she left his employment. Otherwise, he didn't know how he could help her.

But there was one way he could help her now. He
took her hand in his. 'Come on, let's get up to the top.
But I'm going to make sure you don't stumble again.
You're stuck with my chivalry.'

This time she smiled and didn't pull away. He folded
her much smaller hand in his; the answering pressure

made him feel inordinately pleased. When they reached a smoother part of the path he didn't let go of her hand.

With each step forward up the hill Dell silently chanted a *what if?* inside her head. What if Alex was holding her hand because he wanted to, not just out of consideration of her pregnant condition? What if they were a genuine couple, linking hands as they always did when they walked together out on a date? What if she were pregnant to a man like him—she couldn't go so far as to fantasise she was actually pregnant to *him*. Then there was the biggest *what if* of them all, one she scarcely dared breathe for fear of jinxing herself: what if she weren't pregnant and she were free to explore her attraction to Alex, to flirt a little, let him know how she felt, act upon it? *What if he felt the same?*

He kept hold of her hand as they reached the top and at last the Parthenon towered above her. The ground was rough, broken stone and marble caused by ongoing repairs and the tramping of thousands—possibly millions—of feet across the ancient land over the centuries. She had to be careful she didn't go over on her ankle.

'Wow, just wow,' she breathed as she gazed up the iconic structure, which no photo or painting could do justice. Built around 432 BC as a temple to worship the Goddess Athena, it had been scarred by attacks and battle over the centuries. Yet its remaining pillars and sculptures still stood overlooking Athens, an imposing edifice to an ancient civilisation.

'You're so lucky to have this as your heritage,' she said with awe.

'It's the world's heritage,' he said, his voice edged with pride.

Dell had long realised how important his Greekness was to Alex. Would he ever go back to Australia? Would she ever see him again after she went back?

For a long time she stood gazing in wonder at the magnificence of the ancient building with its massive columns and pediments achingly beautiful against a clear blue sky. It made it poignant that she was sharing it with Alex—boss, friend, man she longed to be so more than that if things were different.

She looked up at him, so tall and broad-shouldered, handsome in light linen trousers and white shirt, his dark hair longer now than when she'd first seen him at Bay Breeze, curling around his temples. Her heart seemed to flip over. 'Thank you, Alex. I'll never forget this moment, here with you in the land of your ancestors.'

He looked back down at her for a long moment. She could tell by the deepened intensity of his dark eyes that he was going to kiss her and a tremor of anticipation rippled through her. At that moment, it was what she wanted more than anything in the world. She swayed towards him, not breaking the connection of their eyes, her lips parting in expectation of his mouth on hers. And then he was kissing her.

His mouth was firm and warm, a gentle respectful touch asking a question that she answered by tilting her head to better kiss him back. *Bliss.* This was one small dream that was coming true. Dell realised she had closed her eyes and she opened them again, not wanting to miss anything of this—touch, taste, his scent, the sight of his face. She found his eyes intent on hers and she smiled. He smiled back and then kissed her again. They exchanged a series of short, sweet kisses that escalated with a subtle sensuality that left her breathless.

She was dimly aware that they were still standing with the Parthenon behind them, in one of the most public arenas in Athens. But when he pulled her closer into a longer, more intense embrace she forgot where she was. All she was aware of was Alex—the feel of his arms holding her close, her arms twined around his neck, his mouth, his tongue, the fierce strength of his body. Every kiss she'd ever had faded into insignificance. *This.* Alex.

'Bravo!' Good-natured catcalls and cheering broke into the bliss and she realised they had an audience. She doubted anyone knew who Alex was, but there were a lot of smartphones around. Everyone was a potential *paparazzo* these days.

She broke away from the kiss although she couldn't keep the smile from her voice. 'That was probably not a good idea,' she murmured. On one level she meant kissing in public. On another, she meant shifting their relationship to something more personal wasn't either. If, indeed, that was what this had signalled.

'Yes, it wasn't,' he said with rather too much vehemence. The shutters came down over his eyes again, leaving them black and unreadable. He took an abrupt step back and tripped on the uneven ground. Dell had to catch his arm and hold him steady. But she didn't care about his less than romantic reaction. This day could end right now and she would be happy. Alex had kissed her and she would treasure the moment for ever. No matter what might or might not follow.

'Thank you,' he said. Then, his voice hoarse, 'Thank you for rescuing me.'

'All I did was help you keep your balance,' she said.

'You've done that all right,' he said and she realised they were speaking at a deeper level. 'But you've done so much more.' He reached down to trace a line from her cheekbone to the edge of her mouth. His touch sent a shiver of pleasure through her. 'I didn't think I could be attracted to another woman after...after Mia. But you've proved me wrong.'

'Was...was kissing me some kind of experiment?' She tried to mask the hurt in her voice with a light-hearted tone.

His face darkened. 'No. How could you think that? You looked so lovely, so warm and vibrant with laughter in your eyes, I simply couldn't resist you.'

Warmth flooded through her heart, only to chill at his next words. 'Even though I know I should not have done so. Dell, I—'

Her spirits plummeted to somewhere around her shoes. She put a hand up to halt him. 'Please, we still have an audience.'

He glared at the people watching them and they hastily dispersed.

Dell looked around her. 'It's getting hot. Can we find somewhere with some shade?'

Shade was in short supply on the Acropolis. But they managed to find a patch as they headed across to the Temple of Diana. Dell forced a laugh as they seated themselves on one of the large chunks of marble lying around the site. 'Is this marble a part of the Parthenon and an archaeological treasure, or destined to be used in the restoration? I can't believe there's so much marble scattered around the place.'

'The latter I suspect,' Alex said, obviously not interested in talking about marble, perhaps aware she was using it as a stalling tactic. He spoke bluntly. 'Dell, I meant what I said before. I find you very attractive in every way but you're pregnant to another man and that puts you out of bounds.'

'I… I see,' she said, thinking back to her list of *what ifs*. She took a deep steadying breath against a twisting stab of disappointment. 'I appreciate your honesty, understand where you're coming from. A lot of men would probably feel the same way, I imagine. That doesn't stop me from being delighted I'm pregnant.' Her eyes dropped, so did her voice. 'What it does make me feel is regret…regret that maybe we didn't meet at a different time or place.' She looked up at him again. 'For the record, I find you very attractive. I… I like you too, which is a surprise as I used to loathe you.'

His laugh was broken and rough. 'I can't imagine how I could ever have considered you an enemy,' he said.

He went to kiss her again but Dell put her finger across his lips to stop him. 'No. That last kiss—that *first* kiss was perfect. Let's not override it with a kiss of regret and…what might have been.'

She took his hand in hers. 'But please, hold my hand for the rest of the day, because I couldn't bear it if you didn't.'

'As you wish, although I would kiss you with no regret.' He folded her hand into his much bigger one.

She took a deep breath to keep her voice steady. 'When we get back to Kosmimo, I suggest we pretend this never happened. That we agree you're my boss and I'm your assistant. We go back to the status quo, as it can never be anything more than that between us. I… I couldn't bear working with you, sharing the pavilion with you, if it was any other way.' If ever there was a time for her fluffy-chick face, this was it.

But when in defiance of her feeble ban he lifted her hand to his lips and pressed a kiss into the sensitive centre of her palm, she did not object. She could not let a betraying quiver in her voice let him guess she was crying deep down inside her heart.

CHAPTER TWELVE

TRUE TO HER WORD, Dell didn't refer again to their trip to the Acropolis. Alex wasn't sure if he was surprised or relieved at the way she had totally wiped from their agenda their kiss in front of the columns of the Parthenon.

During the week they'd been back, she deftly changed the subject if anything regarding that day threatened to sneak into the conversation. He had even looked on her *Dell Dishes* blog to see what she had posted about her trip to Athens.

She wrote about her climb of the Acropolis and shared food images from the Athens restaurants where they had eaten together. But without a mention of him. *'My companion,'* she referred to when describing her climb. Her neuter-general companion was what he had been relegated to. Common sense told him that was perfectly appropriate. He should appreciate her discretion. It was insane to feel excluded. Not when he was the one who had called the shots.

At the office she was bright, efficient and as totally professional as she should be. As if she had never murmured her pleasure at his kiss with a sweet little hitch to her voice.

It was he who felt unsatisfied. Grumpy. Frustrated. Because just that taste of her lips had awakened a hunger for her. A need. If he could take her to bed and make love to her before she showed any further signs of pregnancy, pretend she wasn't expecting another man's baby, he would. Only he knew it would be the wrong thing to do. For him, for *her*. Because he liked her enough not to want to hurt her. And sex without commitment, whether she was pregnant or not, was not something that Dell would welcome. He sensed that, *knew* that.

Yet how ironic that the further she got into her pregnancy, the more she bloomed and the more beautiful she appeared. He had heard the word *blooming* used to describe expectant women but had never had an idea what it meant. She was still barely showing but she was curvier in the right places, her hair appeared thicker and glossier, her skin glowed and her eyes seemed a brighter shade of green.

On occasion her complexion was greener too. But her morning sickness seemed to be easing. Soon she might be able to handle the daily crossing between Nidri and Kosmima and go back to stay in Aunt Penelope's villa. But she didn't mention it and neither did he.

Alex liked having her in the pavilion, even though she studiously avoided any potential moments of intimacy. Even though it was frustrating knowing she was in the bedroom next to him—each of them all alone in those super-sized beds. Because her presence—her light, quick footsteps on the marble floor, snatches of her voice as she hummed a Greek song his aunt had taught her as she moved around the kitchen—was comforting.

He realised for the first time in a long time he didn't feel lonely. The nightmares about Mia in the clutches of the gunman had abated. Thanks to Dell. He dreaded how empty the rooms would seem when she went back to Australia to have her baby.

He felt like humming himself—although he never did anything so unmanly—as he checked the latest reports from the architects and designers. They were well on track; in fact some of the rooms in the hotel were already just about ready for occupancy. It was pleasing.

Dell had still been in the pavilion earlier this morning as he had headed over to the main building and their shared office. He hadn't enquired about her estimated time to start work. It was likely she wasn't well. Not that she'd let her morning sickness interfere in any way with her work. That added another notch to his admiration of her; he knew how difficult it must be.

This morning he was impatient for her to get to her desk. He wanted to share his exultation that things were going so well. Because she had contributed to it with her keen eye and smart observations. Not to mention her meticulous record-keeping. Another thing that pleased him was her handling of publicity. Her careful drip-feeding of snippets about the launch, her forward-planning of interviews and media site visits were beginning to create the low-level buzz he had hoped for. He had every reason to pay her that bonus—sooner rather than later perhaps.

He looked up from his desk as he heard her footsteps approach, dragging rather than tip-tapping on the marble. Alarmed, he leapt to his feet. Was she ill again?

But when she entered the room Dell looked more distressed than sick. Her face was flushed, high on her cheekbones, her eyes glittered, and her hands were balled into fists. 'Sorry I'm late,' she said, tight-lipped.

'Dell, what's going on?'

'Nothing,' she said.

'That's obviously not true.'

She gave a great sigh that wrenched at him. 'I don't want to bring my personal problems to work.'

'Where else can you take them right now?'

That forced a glimmer of a smile from her. 'Are you sure you want to hear this?'

If it had been anyone other than Dell, he would have beat a hasty retreat. Girl problems were something to be avoided. But she really didn't have anyone else with whom to share her obvious angst. 'Fire away,' he said.

She stood by her desk, feet braced as if steeling herself. 'I just had a horrible, abusive call from my ex-husband, Neil. He's found out that I'm pregnant.'

'How? You said no one else knows but me and your doctor.'

Alex swore he could hear her teeth grinding. 'The stupidest of mix-ups. The fertility clinic sent a letter to me at his address—which was my old address. Seemed they'd sent it to me at my rented apartment and it had been returned, even though I paid for a redirection order on my mail. So they sent it to the previous address they had for me. Needless to say I'm furious at them. And at the darn post office.'

'Your ex opened a letter that was addressed to you?'

'That would be typical—he always thought my business was his business. I… I used to think his controlling ways were because he cared. Boy, did I get to know better towards the end.'

Alex hated to see the bitter twist of her mouth. The

more he heard about her ex, the less he liked him. 'You said he was abusive?'

'Furious. Shouting. Making threats. Said he refused to have anything to do with the baby. That…that the embryo should have been destroyed. That I…that I had no right to take it. That… I was utterly selfish to have done what I did. That I… I wasn't thinking of anyone else but myself.'

'I'm so sorry, Dell. If there's anything I can do—'

'Thank you but, despite how vile he's being, he did have some right to be angry. I don't regret undertaking the procedure but I knew it probably wasn't the right thing to do. We weren't married any more. Circumstances were entirely different.'

Alex wanted to draw her into a hug but he knew it would not be welcome. In spite of all his business expertise he honestly didn't know how he could help her make the best of the complex and unusual situation she found herself in. But his thoughts were racing. He knew a lot of people in Sydney. People who could track down this guy. Keep an eye on Dell's ex. Report back to Alex so he could make sure Dell wasn't under any threat. He worried about her going back to Sydney on her own.

'What else did he have to say?'

'Again and again that he would deny paternity. That being a sperm donor didn't make him a father.'

'Good point. And why would you want him as the father?'

She made a gesture of despair with her hands. 'I guess he has good genes. He's handsome. Intelligent. Good at sport. I used to think he was kind.'

'What does the guy do for a living?'

'He's a civil engineer.'

Alex groaned.

'What was that for?' Dell asked.

'You should have added boring to his list of genetic attributes.'

That elicited a watery smile from Dell. 'I guess I should. He always was a tad on the dull side. But I traded that for security. How did I put up with it for so long?'

'Because you really wanted a kid and you thought he'd be a safe bet?'

'Something like that, I guess,' she said. 'There I was married and living in the suburbs at age twenty-two while you were building up your fortune.'

'Partying was a far less boring profession,' he said. 'But back then you wouldn't have looked at me, would you?'

'Probably not. I was far too prim.'

'Were you really? I find that very difficult to believe. I suspect you're a very passionate woman. When I kissed you I—'

'That's a no-go zone, Alex,' she warned. 'Can we change the subject?'

'Back to your boring, bad-tempered husband?'

That brought another smile. 'If you put it that way. Actually, I think I'll think of him that way from now on—Neil the BBTH.'

'The Boring Bad-Tempered *Ex*-Husband, you mean,' he said.

She giggled. 'Okay, the BBT Ex-H.' He was glad he could make her laugh. The phone call must have been traumatic.

'It's a mouthful. Why not settle on BX, *boring ex*,

for short?' he said. He could think of much worse
things he could call her odious former husband. 'Boring is worse than bad-tempered. We all have our bad-
tempered moments.'

'BX he shall be from now on.' She sobered. 'Deep
down I guess I hoped he might want to have some kind
of contact—for the baby's sake, not mine. Back then he
wanted a child as much as I did. But perhaps he didn't.
Perhaps he's right. Am I being selfish in having this
child on my own? Maybe it's always been about my
need to have a baby.'

'Isn't that how most people decide to have children?
Because they want them?' he asked. 'Not that I know
a lot about it.'

'Perhaps. But that's all beside the point, isn't it? I'm
going to love this baby enough for two parents. There
are worse ways to come into the world than being utterly loved, aren't there?' She sounded in need of reassurance.

'Indeed,' he said. 'Your baby will be lucky to have
a mother like you.'

But a child needed a father. Alex had had his dif-
ferences with his father, but he'd always been there
loving and supporting him. Dell's child would grow
up without that constant male presence. Of course,
she might marry again, meet someone like Jesse Morgan who would be a father to her child. He pulled the
'off' switch on that train of thought. He couldn't bear
to think of Dell with another man. He'd been called
selfish too.

'One last thing the BX told me was that his new wife
was pregnant. Therefore all the problems we had were
my fault.' Her voice broke. 'There was nothing wrong

with him—no, siree—it was *me* who was the failure.
Me who put him through all that. And if I insisted on
going ahead with this pregnancy I'd better get myself
checked out to see if I was actually capable of carrying
a child.' Her last words came out so choked he could
hardly hear them.

Alex could feel a bad-tempered moment of mammoth proportions threatening to erupt. Was there a
hitman among all those contacts in Sydney? He ran
through all the swear words he knew in both English
and Greek. None was strong enough to express his
contempt for Dell's ex-husband.

He gritted his teeth. 'Lucky he's not here because
if he was I'd—'

'Whatever you'd do I'd do worse.'

'Dell, you're better off without that…that jerk. So
is your child.'

'You're absolutely right. In some ways the encounter with him is a relief. I don't have to worry about the
BX ever again.' Dell spat out the initials so they came
out sounding like the worst kind of swear words. She
took a deep, heaving breath. 'I was so worried about
him, now I won't have to worry. If he denies paternity,
that's good too. It might make it easier for me to get
help if that's the case.'

'What do you mean?'

'Back home in Sydney, if I have to apply for a supporting mothers' benefit, I will have to name the father
and try to get support from him—something I never
intended to do, by the way. If I put "father unknown"
it might not make me look very good but I could get
help for a while if needed.'

Anguish that this spirited, warm, intelligent woman

should be in that position tore through him. 'Dell, don't go back to Sydney. Have the baby here. You're entitled to maternity leave. Your job would still be waiting for you. You wouldn't have to beg for help from your parents or the government or anyone else.'

Tears glistened in her green eyes and she scrubbed them away with her finger. It left a smear of black make-up that made her look more woebegone. 'Thank you, Alex. That's incredibly kind of you. I love it here but…but I don't want to give birth to my baby surrounded by strangers. I have to go home, no matter what I might face.'

Alex stared at her for a long moment. *A stranger.* That was all he was to her. *That was all he'd let himself be.* The realisation felt like another giant kick to his gut.

He had to pull himself together, not let her know how her words had affected him. 'The offer is still there,' he said.

'Thank you,' she said again. 'I truly appreciate it.' She squared her shoulders. 'But we have work to do.' She didn't seem to realise she was wringing her hands together. 'Now that we've got personal, it might be time for me to ask you about Mia. I have to know how to spin your story before the media goes off on their own wild tangents. I'm going to fix my face. When I get back I need to talk to you.'

Mia. When would he ever be able to talk about his guilt over what had happened? But if there was anyone he could open up to, it would be Dell.

CHAPTER THIRTEEN

DELL HAD BEEN trying to bring up the story of Alex's late fiancée for some time but she'd never quite found the courage to do so. The stricken look on his face told her no time would be the right time.

'I… I'm sorry if I sounded blunt,' she said. 'But you know the launch of the resort will mean you coming back into the spotlight. As soon as that happens all the stories of the siege and…and Mia's death will be re-suscitated. The personal story will always override the business one. I don't need to remind you that the anniversary of the siege is coming up. Let's give the media a story before they go burrowing for one.'

Alex slid both hands through his hair to cradle his head with such an abject look it tore at her heart. 'I knew this was coming,' he said. 'I suppose I can't put it off for longer?'

Dell shook her head. She felt mean forcing him to talk. But this was about helping launch his new venture. 'If we could give an exclusive interview to, say, one of the weekend newspaper magazines we might be able to control it to some degree.'

Alex looked barely capable of standing. 'Why don't

we sit over on the chairs so I can take notes?' she suggested tactfully.

'Sure,' he said.

Once they were seated—him opposite her, so close she had to slant her legs to avoid their knees touching—she decided to conduct this as if it were an interview.

'Alex, I know how difficult this is for you. Well, I don't really have any idea but I'm trying to imagine the unimaginable. I'm aware that Mia was the love of your life and what a tremendous blow it must have been to have lost her under such shocking and public circumstances. After she…she died you disappeared from Sydney. What people will want to know is where you went, why you did so, and how it led to the development of Pevezzo Athina. Try to answer me so we can work out what we tell the media.'

He was silent for a long time. Dell became very aware she might be overstepping the mark. But this was her job, why he had brought her to Greece. She wasn't interviewing Alex her boss, her friend, the man she was in serious danger of falling in love with. This was Alexios Mikhalis, multimillionaire tycoon, ruthless businessman, man who'd led a charmed life until that terrible moment a maniac had walked into his restaurant brandishing a gun and had grabbed Alex's beautiful fiancée as hostage.

The silence was getting uncomfortable before he finally spoke, his words slow and measured. 'As far as the media is concerned, I was so devastated by the tragic loss of my fiancée I decided to get as far away from Sydney as possible. It made sense that I went to Greece, to the place my grandfather came from, where I still had extended family and could remain anonymous. I stayed with my relatives, worked with them on their fishing boats and in their olive groves, even waited tables in the family *taverna*.'

'Getting your hands dirty? Grounding yourself?'

'That's a good way to put it,' he said. 'You could say I found peace in the glorious surroundings and wanted to share it with others. I came up with the concept of a holistic resort where our guests could also find peace.'

Dell scribbled on her notepad, not wanting to meet his eyes, too scared of what she might see there. 'Have you found peace, Alex?'

'I'm still seeking it. I think you know that.'

She looked up. 'Can I say guests can come to heal?' she asked tentatively. 'Like you healed?'

'You can say that,' he said.

Could the scars he bore ever really heal? For the press release she had to take his words at surface value.

'And you bought a private island? The media will be very interested in that.'

'That is a matter of public record, so yes, I should certainly talk about Kosmimo. Not, however, about the most recent owner.'

'What about the island's link to your family?'

'Many years ago, Kosmimo was owned by my ancestors. Circumstances conspired to allow me to buy it back. I will never let the island get out of my family's hands again.'

Dell turned a new page of her notebook. 'Sounds like the perfect sound bite. That will make an excellent story. Especially back in Sydney with the city's obsession with real estate.'

He cracked a half-smile at that. She braced herself

for the next question, knowing it would vanquish his smile. 'Alex, I have to ask about your private life.'

As predicted, his smile tightened into a grim line. 'I have no private life,' he said. 'The media will find nothing titillating about me and other women.'

Unless someone recognised him kissing his assistant on the Acropolis, Dell thought.

'Because you could never find a woman to live up to Mia?'

'You can tell that to the media,' he said. 'But the truth is quite different.' He leaned forward with his hands on his knees so his face was only inches from her. She breathed in the already familiar scent of him. The scent that made her feel giddy with the hopelessness of her crush on him, made even deeper by those kisses on the Acropolis. Kisses she revisited every night in her dreams.

'The truth is only for your ears,' he continued. 'I meant what I said on the Acropolis that day.'

She held her breath not daring to say anything, realising how important this was to him. And perhaps significant to her.

'The truth is I feel so damn guilty I sent Mia to her death that I will never be able to commit to another woman.' His eyes were shadowed with immeasurable sorrow.

Dell gasped. 'But you didn't send her to her death. How could you possibly believe that? The gunman chose your restaurant at random. It was sheer bad luck Mia was there at the time. It could have been any of your staff. It could have been *you*.'

His face darkened in a grimace, his voice was grave

and low. 'You don't know how many times I wished it had been me…'

Dell swallowed hard. She didn't know that she was capable of replying the right way to such a statement. But out of compassion—and her regard for him—she would try. 'Alex, you can't mean that. You cannot punish yourself for something that was completely out of your hands.'

He spoke through gritted teeth. 'It was my fault Mia was there that day. It should have been her day off.'

Dell frowned. 'I don't get it.'

'Here's something you wouldn't have read in the press. I insisted she go in to work when the head chef was injured in an accident. Mia and I argued about that. One argument led to another. Until it ended up where it always ended up. My tardiness in setting a date for the wedding. We hadn't resolved it when she stormed out. Mia went to her death worrying that I didn't really love her. That's what I can't live with.'

Dell realised she had been holding her breath. She let it out in a long sigh. 'Oh, Alex. I'm so sorry.' She reached out and laid her hand on top of his. 'But you were engaged to be married. She would have known you loved her.'

He choked out the words. 'Or suspected that I didn't love her enough.'

'I can't believe that's true.'

He got up from the chair. Started to pace the room. Dell got up too, stood anchored by the edge of her desk. She had long stopped taking notes. These revelations were strictly off the record.

'You have to understand the place I was in at the time I met Mia. Settling down with one woman hadn't been on the agenda. I was growing the business at a relentless pace. One new venture after the other.'

'To prove you could do it, to prove to your family that you'd made the right choices for yourself.'

He stopped his pacing. 'That's perceptive of you. I'd never thought of it that way, but you're right.'

'It left no time for dating?' She knew about the string of glamorous blonde women he had been seen with on any social occasion where a photographer had been present.

'I made it very clear to the women I dated that I was not interested in commitment. I didn't have the time, or the inclination.'

'Then you met Mia.' Their love story had been re-hashed over and over again in the media.

'Mia…she made me change my mind.'

'She was beautiful.' It hurt Dell to talk about the woman who had won his heart and met such a tragic end. But she wanted to understand him. And not just because she needed to for her job. That was the craziness of a crush on a man who wanted nothing to do with you. You wanted to find out everything you could about him. Because that was all you would ever have.

'Mia was beautiful, fun, a super-talented chef and liked to party hard and work hard like I did. I was smitten. I still didn't feel ready to settle down. But if I wanted Mia in my life I had to make a commitment or lose her. Those were her terms.'

'Quite rightly too,' Dell murmured in sudden solidarity with his late fiancée.

He paused. 'She would have liked you.'

'I think I might have liked her.' Would she have been jealous of Mia? It was a pointless question. Back then she'd been too busy with her marriage and her desire to start a family to even think about another man. No matter how attractive. No matter how unattainable.

'I can tell myself over and over that it was fate she was in the restaurant at the wrong time. But fate had nothing to do with me beginning to question if Mia was the right person to be my lifetime partner. And not being honest enough to tell her.'

'So that's where the guilt comes from,' Dell said slowly. 'But if you don't forgive yourself you'll go crazy. Mia loved you. She wouldn't have wanted you to live your life alone. It's been nearly three years, Alex. Wouldn't she have wanted you to move on?'

'Meeting you showed me I could be attracted to another woman, Dell. I thought that would never happen. You don't want to talk about that day in Athens. But I meant what I said. That doesn't mean I intend to commit to another woman ever again.'

'It's as well I'm out of bounds because of my pregnancy, then,' she said, trying to sound as uninterested as if she were discussing someone else.

For her own self-protection she had to do that. Did he realise how hurtful he sounded? Or was he still so caught up in his grief and guilt he didn't realise that the best thing that could happen to him was to let himself love again? If not with her then with someone else. And when that happened, she wanted to be far, far away.

CHAPTER FOURTEEN

THREE PEOPLE INVITED Dell to the party to celebrate Alex's Aunt Penelope's seventy-fifth birthday on the coming Saturday. Aunt Penelope herself. Alex's cousin Cristos. And then Alex.

Dell had told the first two she would have to check with Alex before she could accept. She hadn't missed their exchange of sly smiles at her words. She had protested that Alex was her boss and she was accountable to him. Aunt Penelope had replied, with a knowing nod, that in Greece the man was always the boss. Dell had decided not to argue with the older woman on that one.

When Alex invited her to the party she told him about the other two. His eyes narrowed at the mention of the invitation from Cristos. Surely he couldn't be jealous of his handsome cousin? She quite liked the little flicker of satisfaction she got from that. Cristos was, in fact, extraordinarily good-looking. But the only man Dell had eyes for was Alex. Much good that it did her.

'The party will be at the original Taverna Athina on Prasinos,' he said. 'Of course you will come. I promised to take you there one day, if you recall.'

'I'm honoured to be invited,' she said. 'But do you

think it's wise, considering the ongoing speculation about us as…well, as a couple?' She laid her hand on her gently rounded belly. 'It's getting harder to conceal my pregnancy.'

'Your pregnancy is your business,' he said. *And nothing to do with me.* Dell sensed his unspoken words. 'You don't owe an explanation to anyone in my family. When it becomes obvious you're expecting you can tell them whatever version of the story behind it you choose.'

'In that case, I happily accept the invitation. All three invitations.'

'But you'll be coming to the party with me,' said Alex.

An imp of mischief prompted Dell's retort. 'But Cristos said he'd take me in his boat.'

Alex glowered down at her. 'You will *not* go in my cousin's boat. You will go in my boat. It's much more comfortable and better for a woman in your—'

'Condition, I know,' she said. 'Of course your boat is far superior to Cristos's boat. Your boat is superior to any other man's boat I know. Not that I know another person who owns a super duper speedboat like yours.' What was lacking in his four-by-four Alex kept on Nidri, and the equally battered van he kept on Kosmimo, was more than made up for in his luxurious streamlined boat.

'You'd better believe it,' he said with a reluctant grin. 'Cristos can transport his grandparents Aunt Penelope and Uncle Stavros to the party.'

'Befitting as she is the guest of honour,' Dell said.

'The party starts in the afternoon and might go on quite late,' he said. 'The *taverna* also has rooms to rent.

I will book one for you so you can stay overnight. If you get tired you can slip away any time.'

'And you?' she said.

'I'll bunk down at my uncle's house. It's where I stayed when I first arrived from Australia. It's on the same street so I won't be far should you need me.'

'I'll be okay,' she said, hoping that was the case. Anyone she had met from his family had been friendly and hospitable, while being subtly—or not so subtly, depending on gender—interested in her relationship with Alex. 'I'm looking forward to it.'

Taverna Athina was set right on the beach at the southernmost corner of a delightfully curving bay. The water rippled from sapphire, to the palest aquamarine, to crystal clear lapping up on a beach comprising tiny pale pebbles.

The open-air dining area of the *taverna*—entirely reserved today for the family party—sat right over the water on a dock. A banner was strung from post to post with a message in the Greek alphabet that Dell assumed meant Happy Birthday but Alex explained read *hronia polla*, and was a wish for many more happy years of life.

The *taverna* was painted white with accents of bright blue and tubs of Greek basil at its corners. The effect was friendly and welcoming. Behind the *taverna* was a traditional Greek building with a terracotta-tiled roof. Its idyllic position with the tree-studded hill as background and the water in front made it look as if the restaurant could sail off at any moment.

'That's where you'll be staying,' said Alex, indicating the older building as he helped her off his boat, moored nearby. 'It's humble but comfortable.'

'The *taverna* is charming, Alex,' she said. 'No wonder you were so attached to Athina in Sydney if this was its parentage.'

Greek music, typical of the Ionian Islands, was echoing out onto the beach. 'It's what Tia Penelope likes,' Alex explained.

'I like it too,' said Dell.

She held back as she and Alex got near to the *taverna* entrance, suddenly aware of her ambivalent status as employee and yet friend enough to be invited to a family party. And then there was the persistent speculation about her and Alex as an item.

She need not have worried. As soon as she got inside she was swept up by Aunt Penelope and introduced to the family members she hadn't previously met at either the villa or on Kosmimo. She told herself she was imagining it that the first thing the women did was glance down at her stomach.

As she was being carried away Dell turned to see Alex in animated conversation with a tall older man with steel-grey hair and glasses and an elegantly dressed woman of about the same age who had her arm looped through Alex's as though she could never let him go. Dell had no idea who they were. But even from a distance, she could see Alex bore a distinct resemblance to the man. Perhaps they had come from Athens for the party.

'What are you doing here?' Alex asked his parents, still reeling from his shock at seeing them at the *taverna*. 'I had no idea you were coming.'

'A surprise for Penelope for her birthday,' his father said. 'She says she's getting too old to fly all the way to Australia so we decided to come to her.' His father's voice was husky as if he had a heavy cold. He was getting older now, surely he shouldn't have flown with a cold.

'We wanted to see you, too, catch up with how you're doing,' said his mother.

That made sense. But Alex detected an unfamiliar restraint to the tone of both his parents' voices and wondered. 'Why didn't you tell me?' he said.

'We thought it could be a surprise for you too,' said his mother, unconvincingly to Alex's ears.

'It's certainly that,' said Alex. 'Where are you staying?'

'Here at the *taverna*,' his father replied. 'Where we always stay when we visit the family.'

Alex's father was a highly regarded orthopaedic surgeon back in Sydney, his mother a sports physiotherapist of some renown. They could afford to stay in the best of hotels. Fact was, on Prasinos the two-star Athina was the best hotel. There were luxury villas and houses to be rented but the family would take great offence if his parents stayed anywhere but the family hotel.

'We saw you come in with that lovely red-haired girl Penelope has been telling us about.'

'You mean my assistant, Dell Hudson?' Alex asked, forcing his voice to stay steady.

'Is that all she is?' said his mother, sounding disappointed. 'Penelope led me to believe there was something more between you. You know how much we want you to be happy after Mia and—'

'Dell is a very capable employee, that's all,' Alex said through gritted teeth.

Was his aunt just speculating or did she at some level recognise how attracted he was to Dell? Whatever, he wished she would stop the gossiping. The sideways glances and speculation from the rest of the family were beginning to get uncomfortable. There were handwritten name-cards at each table place. Someone had thought it funny to strike out *Dell Hudson* to be replaced by *Dell Mikhalis*. He had grabbed it and crumpled it into his pocket before Dell could have a chance to see it.

His father frowned. 'Wasn't Adele Hudson the woman who gave Athina that bad review? When you sued the newspaper and lost all that money.'

'Yes,' he said.

'So why are you employing her?' said his mother. 'Is this a case of keeping your friends close and your enemies closer?'

Why was this conversation centring on Dell? 'She's not an enemy. In fact she was right about the falling standards at the restaurant. I employed her because she's really smart and switched on. She's proved to be immensely valuable to me on my new venture.'

'Oh,' said his mother again. Alex gritted his teeth even harder.

He looked over to see Dell helping out by carrying a tray of *meze*, an assortment of Greek appetisers, to the buffet table. Dell was laughing at something Aunt Penelope was saying. Among his mostly dark-haired family she stood out with her bright hair and her strapless dress in multiple shades of blue that reflected the colours of the Ionian Sea. She had never looked lovelier. Alex could see exactly why his mother was looking at her with such interest.

'Would you like to meet Dell?' he asked his parents.

'We would, very much so,' said his father. 'But first we need to tell you something important. News that we ask you not to share yet with the rest of the family. Come outside so we can talk with you in private.'

Dell was enjoying herself immensely. Alex's extended family were so warm and hospitable she hadn't felt once she was an outsider. In fact she had been embraced by them because she was his friend.

A lot of good food and wine was being consumed. No wine for her of course—she hadn't touched a drop since she'd discovered she was pregnant. She realised her abstinence was probably a dead giveaway but came up with an explanation that she was allergic to alcohol. Whether or not she was believed she wasn't sure.

She looked around for Alex. Despite what half the room seemed to think, she wasn't there as Alex's date. Still, it seemed odd that he would leave her so long by herself when he was aware she only knew a handful of people.

Several times she looked around the room but didn't see him. When the older couple he had been speaking with came in by themselves, she went outside to see if she could find him.

Night had fallen and light from the *taverna* spilled out onto the beach. Some distance away, Alex stood by himself on the foreshore staring out to sea. In the semi-darkness he looked solitary and, Dell thought, sad. He had every good reason to be sad in his life but she hoped from their conversation the previous week that he was beginning to come to terms with the tragedy that had brought him to Greece. He appeared so lost in his thoughts he didn't seem aware of her approach.

Softly, Dell called his name. Startled, he turned quickly, too quickly to hide the anguish on his face.

Shocked, Dell hurried to his side. 'Alex. What's wrong? Are you okay?'

Slowly he shook his head. 'Everything is wrong.'

The devastation in his voice shocked her. 'What do you mean?'

'My parents are here. You might have seen me talking to them earlier. A surprise visit, to share some news with me, they said. But the news was to tell me my father has cancer.' His voice broke on the last words.

'Oh, Alex.' After the tragedy he'd endured he didn't deserve this. 'Is it…serious?'

'Cancer of the oesophagus. He's started radiation therapy already. More treatment when he returns to Sydney.' He clenched his fists by his sides. 'Dad is a doctor. Yet when he started having difficulty swallowing he didn't realise it could be something bad. By the time he sought help the cancer was established. There…there's a good chance he won't make it.'

Dell put her hand on his arm. 'I'm so, so sorry. Is there anything I can do to help?'

'Actually there is,' he said.

'Just tell me, fire away,' she said.

'My father told me his greatest wish is to see his only son married before he…before he dies. My mother wants it too.'

Dell gasped. 'How can I help you with that? Find you a bride?' Her words were flippant but she couldn't let him see how devastated she was at the thought of him getting married.

'My mother has already suggested a bride.'

'But…but you don't want to get married.'

'I know,' he said. 'But it's my father's dying wish. I have no choice but to consider it.'

Dell dropped her hand from his arm and stepped back, staggering a little at the pain his words stabbed into her. She struggled for the right words to show her sympathy for the situation he found himself in without revealing her hurt that he would be so insensitive as to discuss a potential bride with her.

'An arranged marriage? Didn't they go out of fashion some time ago? And what has that got to do with me?'

'Not an arranged marriage. I would never agree to such a thing. But if I chose to get married to fulfil my father's wish, the obvious bride for me is you.'

CHAPTER FIFTEEN

DELL STARED AT Alex, scarcely able to believe she'd heard his words correctly. '*Me!* Why would you say that?'

'You know how much I like and respect you, Dell. That's the first reason.'

Why did *like* and *respect* sound like the booby prizes? She wanted so much more from Alex than that. Not *love*. Of course not love, it would be way too soon for that even if insurmountable barriers didn't stand in their way. She was certainly not *in love* with Alex. A crush on her boss didn't mean she was in love with him. Of course it didn't. But she would like some passion and desire to sit there alongside *like* and *respect*. Especially if it was in regard to marriage—though this didn't sound like any marriage proposal she'd ever heard about or even imagined.

'And the other reasons?' she said faintly.

'My mother, my aunt, my cousins—even my father—assume because you're pregnant that I will do the honourable thing and marry you.'

'*What?*' The word exploded from her. 'You can't possibly be serious.'

Alex looked down into her face. Even in the slanted

light from the *taverna* she could see the intensity in his black eyes. 'I'm very serious. I think we should get married.'

Dell had never known what it felt to have her head spin. She felt it now. Alex had to take hold of her elbow to steady her. 'I can't believe I'm hearing this,' she said. 'You said you'd never get married. I'm not pregnant to you. In fact you see my pregnancy as a barrier to kissing me, let alone marrying me. Have you been drinking too much ouzo?'

'Not a drop,' he said. 'It's my father's dying wish that I get married. He's been a good father. I haven't been a good son. Fulfilling that wish is important to me. If I have to get married, it makes sense that I marry you.'

'It doesn't make a scrap of sense to me,' she said. 'You don't get married to someone to please someone else, even if it is your father.'

Alex frowned. 'You've misunderstood me. I'm not talking about a real marriage.'

This was getting more and more surreal. 'Not a real marriage? You mean a marriage of convenience?'

'Yes. Like people do to be able to get residence in a country. In this case it would be marriage to make my father happy. He wants the peace of mind of seeing me settled.'

'You feel you owe your father?'

'I owe him so much it could never be calculated or repaid. This isn't about owing my father, it's about loving him. I love my father, Dell.'

But you'll never love me, she cried in her heart. How could he talk about marrying someone—anyone—without a word about love?

'I'm so sorry, Alex, about your father's illness. But perhaps the shock of his sad news has skewed your thinking. Perhaps it has even…unhinged you,' she said. 'Who would think such a sudden marriage is in any way reasonable or sensible?'

'My family would not question marriage to you. In fact I believe they think us getting married is virtually a *fait accompli.*'

Dell was too astounded by his reasoning to be able to reply. She fought to keep her voice under control when she did. 'What about me? Where do I fit in this decision-making process? Aren't I entitled to an opinion?'

He put up his hand to placate her. 'You're right. I'm sorry. It seemed like such a good idea and I've rushed things. You know often my best decisions are made on impulse.' She had become so knowledgeable about his business dealings she had to admit the truth of that.

'This is my life we're talking about here, Alex. I deserve more than a rushed decision.'

'When it comes to your life, I think you'll see it makes a lot of sense,' he said.

'Please enlighten me,' she said. 'I'm still not convinced I'm not dealing with an idea sprung from grief-stricken madness.'

He shook his head but it was more a gesture of annoyance that he should be so misunderstood than anything else. 'Let me explain my perfectly sane thoughts,' he said.

'I'm listening,' she said, intrigued.

'You help me with this and there are benefits to you. You'll be able to stay here to have your baby, surrounded by people who will no longer be strangers. I have dual nationality so you would be the wife of a Greek citizen. Your baby will have a name. And I will support him or her until he or she is twenty-one years of age. You wouldn't have to ask your parents any favours or perjure yourself to get government social security. In fact you would be able to enjoy the rest of your pregnancy and after the birth without worrying about money or finding a place to live. And I imagine it would be somewhat satisfying to stick it up the BX.'

His last point dragged a smile from her. Clever Alex with his charisma and business smarts made the crazy scheme seem reasonable. But there must be more to it than that, an ulterior motive.

'It would also get the media off your back regarding Mia,' she said. 'Quite the fairy-tale romance. The press would lap it up. The story would make great publicity for your new venture.' She couldn't keep the cynical note from her voice. 'I suppose you've considered that angle.'

Alex stilled. 'Actually, I haven't. You can't honestly think that's a consideration?'

'I'm hardly privy to your thoughts,' she said.

'My only motivation here is my father's happiness while he's battling cancer. Since Mia's death I've done my best to make reparation to the people I harmed with my aggressive business techniques and ruthless selfishness. People like you. I'll never get the chance to make amends for my behaviour towards Mia and I'll live with that for the rest of my life. But I can try to make up for it with my father by getting married so he can dance at my wedding before he dies.'

If Alex had said just one thing about how fond he was of her, and for that reason if he was going to have to marry someone he would want it to be her, Dell would probably have burst into tears and said she'd do it. But he didn't. So she toughened her attitude.

She remembered how she'd felt when he'd kissed her at the Parthenon. How exciting it had been, how happy being in his arms had made her. How she'd ached for more.

'You say it wouldn't be a real marriage. I guess that means no...well, no sex.'

'That's right,' he said, so quickly it was hurtful. 'That wouldn't be fair to you when our bargain would have an end.'

As if it wouldn't be fair to bind her to a sexless, loveless union with a man who even now in this cold-blooded conversation made her long to be close to him—both physically and every other way. It would be a cruel kind of torture.

'What do you mean "our bargain"?' she asked. Thoughts about his proposition spun round and round in her mind.

'This would all be done legally. I would get my lawyers to draw up a contract setting out the terms and conditions. How you and your baby would be recompensed. The marriage would be of one year's duration.' His face contorted with anguish. 'Less if...if my father were to die before then.'

A great wave of compassion for him swept through her. He had been through so much. 'Oh, Alex, is it that bad?'

Her instinct was to comfort him, to put her arms around him, to try and take some of his pain for herself. But she kept her hands by her sides. This was not the moment for that.

He nodded, seemingly unable to speak. 'It seems so.'

They were already standing very close to each other without being conscious of it. The nature of the exchange of conversation needed to be for their ears only. A cool breeze ruffled her hair and made her shiver.

He put his hand on her shoulder. In the semi-light he looked more handsome than ever, more unattainable. The stronger his connection to his family grew, the more Greek he seemed to become. 'Please, Dell. I think we've become friends of a kind. If you don't want to agree to this for the very real benefits to you, can you do it as an act of friendship? I'll make sure you won't regret it. Please say yes. Please marry me. There isn't anyone else I'd rather be getting on board with this than you.'

Was that a subtle reminder that he was so determined to do this that if she said no, he'd find another woman who would jump at the chance to be the make-believe bride of multimillionaire Alex Mikhalis?

Could she bear it if he married someone else?

She took a deep breath. 'Yes, Alex, I say yes.'

His sigh of relief was audible, even on the beach with the muted music and chatter coming from the *taverna*, the swish of the small waves as they rolled up onto the tiny pebbles on the beach. 'Thank you, Dell. You won't regret this, I promise you.'

Already she knew she would regret it. Everything about the arrangement seemed so wrong. On top of that, she was tired of putting on her fluffy-chick face, of pretending she was happy when she wasn't. Now she had signed up for a year of pretending that she didn't care about the man who was going to be her fake husband in a marriage of convenience.

'I guess I'd be working for you, still. A different job. A new contract.' She tried to sound pragmatic, to justify the unjustifiable.

Alex frowned. 'I hadn't thought of it like that.'

'It might make it easier if we did.'

'Perhaps,' he said, sounding unconvinced. He took a step closer.

'But right now I need you to kiss me.'

'*What?*'

His gaze flickered over her shoulder and back to face her. 'You can't see from where you're standing but there are interested eyes on us. In theory I just proposed to you and you said "yes". A kiss is appropriate.'

Appropriate? When was a kiss *appropriate*? Obviously in this alternate universe she had agreed to enter the rules were very different. That didn't mean she had to abide by them.

She looked up at his dark eyes, his sensual mouth she ached to kiss in an entirely inappropriate way. 'I've got a better idea. *You* can kiss *me*. And you'd better make it look believable.'

Dell was challenging him. Alex had been exultant that she had acquiesced to his admittedly unconventional plan. But it seemed Dell and acquiescence didn't go hand in hand. Somehow, in a contrary kind of way, that pleased him. Dell wouldn't be Dell if she rolled over and did just as he commanded.

It made him want to kiss her for real.

Her eyes glittered in the soft half-light, tiny flecks of gold among the green. Her lips were slightly parted, a hint of a smile lifting the corners—halfway between teasing and seductive. 'What are you waiting for?' she murmured.

He was very aware of their audience. The family members who must have watched her seek him out on the beach. They stood inside the doorway some twenty metres away, obviously thinking they couldn't be seen, but the lights from the *taverna* highlighted their shapes. It appeared the group had gathered hoping, perhaps, for proof that he and Dell were a couple. He would give them that proof.

He pulled her to him and pressed his mouth to hers with a firm, gentle pressure. In reply, Dell wound her arms around his neck to pull his head closer, her curves moulded against him. Her scent sent an intoxicating rush to his head—the sharpness of lemon and thyme soap mingled with her own sweet womanliness. It was a scent so familiar to his senses he was instantly aware of when she entered or left a room. She kissed him back, then flicked the tip of her tongue between his lips with a little murmur deep in her throat. Surprise quickly turned to enthusiastic response as he met her tongue with his, deepening the kiss, falling into a vortex of sensation.

Alex forgot he was on the beach, forgot they had an audience, forgot everything but that Dell was in his arms and he was kissing her. This was no meandering journey between gentle kiss of affirmation and one of full-blown passion. It raced there like a lit fuse on a stick of dynamite. Lips, tongues, teeth met and danced together in an escalating rhythm. Desire burned through him, and her too, judging by her response as that little murmur of appreciation intensified into a moan. He groaned his own want in reply, pulled her close, as close as they could be with their clothes between them. He could feel the hammering of her heart against his chest. His hands slid down her waist to cup the cheeks of her bottom; she pushed closer as she fiercely kissed him.

'Get a room, you two.' Cristos's voice, in Greek, pierced his consciousness.

Dell pulled away. 'What was that?' Her cheeks were flushed, her breath coming in gasps, her mouth pink and swollen from his kisses.

Alex had trouble finding his own voice, had to drag in air to control his breathing.

'My cousin trying to be funny,' he said.

She looked up at him, her breasts rising and falling as she struggled to get her breath. 'Alex...that was—'

'I know,' he said, not certain of how it happened, knowing what it meant for their bargain, realising he had lost control and that he had to take back the lead.

Her eyes met his as a shadow behind them dimmed their brightness. 'We can't do that. A kiss like that wasn't what you'd call *appropriate*. It wasn't fair. Not when I—'

When she *what*? Alex wanted, needed, to know what she meant. Because at that moment when she had moaned her desire something had shifted for him. Something deep and fundamental and perplexing. He had to know if she had felt it too.

But there was no chance to ask her. Because then his family, headed by his parents, were spilling out of the *taverna* onto the beach and surrounding them with exclamations of surprise and glee and, from his mother, joy.

'I knew from the moment I saw them together, they

were more than friends,' he heard Aunt Penelope explain. Not explain—*gloat*.

He looked down at Dell, who looked as though she had been well and truly kissed. In a silent question, he raised his brow; she affirmed with a silent nod.

He put his arm around her. It wasn't difficult to fake possessiveness. 'Dell has just agreed to marry me,' he announced.

There was an explosion of congratulations and laughter. He looked up to see mingled pride, relief and love on his father's face.

'Thank you, Dell,' Alex whispered to her. 'I won't forget what you're doing for me and my family.'

Her face closed. 'It's just a business arrangement between us, remember,' she whispered back, being very careful she wouldn't be overheard.

So she hadn't felt it. He knew he had no right to feel disappointed. Nevertheless, his mood darkened but he had to keep up with the momentum of excitement as he and Dell were swept back into the *taverna*.

The third time someone wished them *'I ora I kali'* Dell turned to ask him what it meant. 'It means, "May the wedding day come soon",' he replied. 'And we need to have it as soon as possible. My father needs to get back to Sydney to continue his treatment. Is that okay with you?'

She shrugged. 'You're the boss. But of course it's okay with me. The sooner the better really.'

'You have made me very happy, son,' his father said when he reached them. 'Dell, welcome to our family.'

That made it worth it.

His mother burst into tears. 'Of joy, these are tears of joy,' she said, fanning her face with both hands.

'Dell, I've heard so many good things about you I feel I know you already.' She gave another sob. 'And my son looks so happy. Happier than since…well, you know what happened.'

Dell looked to him for help, started to stutter a response but he was saved by his cousin Melina who had helped him with her contacts in Athens. She picked up Dell's left hand. 'Show us your engagement ring, Dell,' she said.

A ring.

He hadn't thought of that.

It was immediately obvious that Dell's hand was bare. She shot a look of panic to him.

'This all happened very quickly,' he said. 'I will be—'

His mother saved him by sliding off a ring, sparkling with a large diamond, from her own left hand and handing it to him. 'Take this. Your father bought it for me for our anniversary a few years back. Our own engagement ring is something much more humble, bought when we were both students.'

She shared a glance of such love with his father, Alex felt stricken. Was faking his own marriage really the way to do this? But there was no going back now.

He took the ring and slid it onto the third finger of Dell's left hand. Her hand was trembling as she held it up for his family's inspection. There was a roar of approval. 'I will get you your own engagement ring, of course,' he said to her.

'That would be the height of hypocrisy and totally unnecessary,' she murmured, smiling for their audience as though she were whispering something romantic.

'You can give this ring back to your mother when our agreement is over.'

To anyone but him, who had got to know her so well over the last weeks, Dell seemed to accept the exuberant hugs and congratulations with happiness and an appropriate touch of bewilderment at how fast things had moved. However he noticed signs of strain around her mouth, a slightly glazed look in her eyes that told him how she was struggling to keep up the façade.

He did the only thing he could do to mask her face from his family. He swept her into his arms and kissed her again. And again for good measure because he didn't want to stop.

Dell was tired, bone weary. Her face hurt from so much forced smiling and acceptance of congratulations. Aunt Penelope's birthday party had turned into a shared celebration to include an informal engagement party for her and Alex. She felt ill-prepared for the wave of jubilation that had picked her up and carried her into the heart of his Greek family.

She had long realised the truth that Greek people were among the most hospitable in the world. Their generosity of welcome to her now stepped up a level because she was going to be part of the family. There was a certain amount of unsaid *I told you so* that, even in her fear of saying the wrong thing and inadvertently revealing the truth about her engagement, made her smile.

One thing came through loud and clear—Alex was well loved by everyone. She heard of his many acts of quiet generosity, the hard work he'd put into family projects. Even the children, who were very much part of the celebration, seemed to adore him, flocking around him. He leaned down to listen very gravely to what one little cherub with a mop of black curls and baby black eyes was saying to him. The toddler could have been his own son. Her heart turned over and she felt very strongly the presence of the baby in her womb. Should Alex have thought more about this plan before sweeping her up into it? Should she have done the sensible thing and said *no*?

It also became obvious how deeply worried his family had been about him. His father, George, explained how, after the siege in Alex's restaurant, he had feared his son had been heading for a breakdown. How desperately concerned he and Eleni, his wife, had been about him. How happy they were that their son had found some measure of peace back in the homeland of his grandfather's family. 'And now this, the best news we could have.'

Eleni patted her hand. 'To marry into a big Greek family can be overwhelming, I know. I will do anything I can to help you. Will your own mother be here?'

Her own parents. What would she say to them? More secrets and lies. 'I'm not sure they'll be able to make the wedding at such short notice.' Her astute mother would realise immediately all was not as it should be. It wasn't a real marriage; she was tempted not to tell her parents about it at all.

'That would be a shame,' Eleni said, trying to hide her obvious shock that the bride's mother would not be in attendance.

Dell tried to play it down. 'Did Alex tell you I've been married before? I'm divorced. It's why we want to have a very simple civil ceremony.'

'He did mention it,' Eleni said. 'But it is his first wedding. I can't understand why he wants so little fuss made.' Dell wasn't surprised by the familiar female gaze as it dropped to her middle. 'Although we do understand the need to get married quickly.'

Dell refused to bite. 'George's treatment. Of course, I understand you need to get back to Sydney.'

Just then Aunt Penelope bustled up to take Dell's arm. Dell was immediately aware of an unspoken rivalry between Penelope and Eleni of the *I found her first* variety. Penelope pointed out that the matter of her wedding dress needed immediate attention. A lovely gown was not something that could be made overnight. Dell needed to think about it straight away. And her friend, a dressmaker, happened to be a guest at the party; she should meet her now.

'I'd thought I'd buy a dress off the rack in Athens,' Dell said, casting a helpless call for intervention to the more sophisticated Eleni.

Aunt Penelope didn't miss a thing. 'Ah, you think a village dressmaker could not make you the kind of wedding dress you want? My friend used to work in a bridal couture house in Athens. You show her a picture in any wedding magazine or on the Internet and she can make it for you.' As she led Dell away she added in a low murmur, 'My friend will help you choose the best style to accommodate your bump and allow for the dress to be let out if we need to do so in the days before the wedding.'

Dell stared at Alex's great-aunt, not sure what to say. Penelope laughed. 'You won't be the first Mikhalis bride to have a baby come earlier than expected after the wedding.'

Later, when she and Alex grabbed a quiet moment together Dell told him what had happened. 'Why didn't anyone tell me Aunt Penelope used to be a midwife? She told me she has delivered hundreds, maybe thousands, of babies and that she knew immediately I was pregnant that first day I went to the doctor. How are we going to tell them that the baby isn't yours?'

'We won't,' he said as he got swept away from her by the men to take part in the traditional male dances, some of them unique to these islands, that were an important part of any celebration.

As she watched Alex, as adept as any of the men in the dance, she knew she was there in this happy celebration under completely false pretences. Alex's motivations were worthy but how would these warm, wonderful people feel when they found out they'd been fooled?

Secrets and lies.

The most difficult secret for her to hide was her growing feelings for Alex and the most difficult lie was one she had to tell herself—that she didn't wish, somewhere deep in her heart, that this engagement party and the wedding that would follow as soon as they could arrange it were for real and she really was his much-loved bride.

CHAPTER SIXTEEN

To GET MARRIED in a hurry in Greece involved more paperwork than Dell had imagined, especially when Alex was being wed to a divorced foreigner. Then there had been issues with the venue. In Australia, you could get married anywhere you wanted by a civil celebrant. Not so in Greece. For a civil ceremony there was no choice but to get married in a town hall. The paperwork had been pushed through, expedited by the right people, so they were able to get married. But no one in Alex's family had been happy at the prospect of what they saw as a bland, meaningless civil union.

Before Dell knew it the ancient, tiny white chapel on Kosmimo had been re-consecrated and, two weeks after their impromptu 'engagement', she and Alex were getting the church wedding his family had clamoured for.

This was her not-for-real wedding day and she was feeling nervous. She had not spent much time alone with Alex in the past two weeks. The day after the party for Aunt Penelope, she had moved off Kosmimo and back to the villa. Her morning sickness was practically gone—though the weariness persisted—and the daily boat trips to the island and back to Nidri were bearable. Alex's family didn't think it appropriate they should be living on the island together so close to the wedding.

Dell might have put up an argument about that but in truth it was a relief. She hadn't been able to endure the close proximity to Alex sharing the pavilion with him. It was torture wanting him, knowing she couldn't have him.

She'd repeatedly reminded herself that the marriage was just a business deal. Another employment contract signed with the hospitality tycoon. It was the only way she could retain some measure of sanity among the excitement generated by his family, as they planned the wedding of their beloved son, nephew, cousin, to the Australian girlfriend they had given their seal of approval.

No one seemed to think it was unusual that the engaged couple had so little time together. George and Eleni had moved on to Kosmimo into one of the finished guestrooms. Understandably, Alex wanted to spend as much time as he could with his parents. Dell was always included and she did her best to be affectionate with Alex without anyone suspecting that her edginess was anything but pre-wedding nerves. She tried to hold herself a little aloof from George and Eleni because she really liked them. They were every bit as intelligent as her parents but in a warm, inclusive way. Losing them at the end of the year as well as Alex would be an added level of pain; the thought of losing George earlier was unbearable. Thank heaven she'd agreed to help Alex in his audacious plan.

She didn't have to feign interest in Alex's parents' stories and reminiscences of him as a little boy and rebellious teenager. She lapped up every detail and realised her obvious fascination with everything to do with her husband-to-be was noted and approved. George and Eleni, Aunt Penelope and Uncle Stavros made their delight in his choice of bride only too apparent. If Alex's kisses, staged in sight of some observant family member, got a tad too enthusiastic she was only too happy to go along with them. All in the interests of authenticity.

Two days ago, while working alone with Alex in their office on Kosmimo, she had felt a bubbling sensation in her womb and cried out. Alex had jumped up from his desk and rushed to her. 'What's wrong?' he'd said.

Then with sudden joy she'd realised. 'It's the baby moving inside me.' She'd put her hand on her small bump, waited, and felt the tiniest ripple of movement. 'My baby is kicking, I think.' She'd forgotten all about the complex layers of her relationship with Alex and just wanted to share this momentous discovery with him.

Alex had stood in front of her and she'd realised he was lost for words, a gamut of emotions rippling across his face. She'd been amazed to see shyness and a kind of wonder predominate. 'May I...may I feel it?' he'd finally asked.

Silently she'd taken his hand and placed it on her bump, her hand resting on top of his. The little tremor had come again. Then again. Alex had kept his hand there. When he'd spoken, his voice had been tinged with awe. 'There's a little person in there. Maybe a future football player with a kick like that.'

She'd smiled through sudden tears that had threatened to spill. 'Yes. There really, truly is. My little boy or girl. The baby I've wanted for so long.' Happiness had welled through her. The moment with Alex had been a moment so precious, so unexpected that she'd found herself not daring to say anything further, not wanting to break the magic of it.

Alex had been the first to end the silence between them. His hand had slipped from her bump and he had taken both her hands in his. 'Dell, I know this is something that I—' he'd started. But she never heard what he'd intended to say as the man tiling the kitchens had knocked on the door with a query for Alex.

The by now familiar shutters had come down over Alex's eyes, he'd dropped her hands and stepped back to turn and deal with the tiler, leaving her confused and shaken.

Now she stood at the entrance to the little chapel, in the most picturesque setting she could imagine near the edge of a cliff with perfect blue skies above and the rippling turquoise sea below.

The ceremony was to be a contemporary one, in recognition of the Australian background of both the bride and groom. But there would also be the traditional Greek Orthodox wedding service. She had been walked up from the resort to the chapel by her attendants, Alex's two sisters and his cousin Melina from Athens. His sisters had flown in yesterday from Sydney, husbands and children in tow. Aunt Penelope had organised dresses for all three as well as Melina's sweet little daughter, who had walked ahead strewing rose petals.

It was purely a Mikhalis family occasion and Dell was okay about that. This wasn't about her. It was about Alex and his love and loyalty for his father and her chance to help him right one of the wrongs he imagined he'd caused people close to him.

So here she was, surrounded by so much goodwill and happiness it was palpable, like a wave rushing through the wedding party and guests and whirling them around in its wake. But it was based on a false premise: that she was about to become Alex's loving wife and the mother of his child.

She was a fraud.

Could it be any wonder that, as she took her first steps over the threshold of the chapel, she was the most miserable she had ever been in her life? Her happy-chick face was threatening to crack from overuse. She took a deep breath to try and control her fear of the wrong she was about to do to this family and it came out as a gasp. Immediately friendly, comforting hands were upon her, patting down and soothing what they so obviously saw as a case of bride-to-be jitters.

She couldn't do this.

Then another step took her inside and she saw Alex waiting by the side of the small stone altar that had been festooned by his family with flowers. Her heart seemed to stop. He had never looked more handsome, his black hair and olive skin in striking contrast to his white linen suit. But it was the look of admiration and pride on his face as he caught sight of her that set her heart racing. It wasn't *love*, she knew that, but it was enough to let her decide to rip off that mask she was so weary of wearing and show him how she really felt. Later, she could put it down to what a good actress she had been on the day.

But right now she was going to let the truth shine from her eyes.

She loved him.

The person she had lied to the most was herself. Because she loved Alex Mikhalis with all her heart and soul and she could no longer deny it. She realised this was a make-believe wedding and nothing more would come of it but she was going to behave as though this were her real wedding.

To pretend just for this day there was love and a future.

She smiled back at him, a tremulous smile that she knew revealed her heart completely without artifice. Their gazes connected and held and there was no one else in that tiny church but her and the man she loved. But she could not tell him how deeply and passionately she felt all those things a make-believe bride should not feel for her pretend husband. There would be heartbreak enough when their contract came to an end—one way or another.

Dell in her wedding dress was so breathtakingly beautiful that Alex found himself clenching his hands by his sides in an agony of suppressed emotion. He wasn't aware of anyone or anything else. Not his father and his cousin Cristos by his side. Not the priest behind them. Not the tiny church filled with his Greek family and friends, the scent of roses and a lingering trace of incense, the sound of the sea breaking on the limestone rocks beneath. All his senses were filled by the beauty of the bride walking slowly towards him. *His* bride.

She was wearing an exquisite long dress of fine silk and lace, deceptively simple, cleverly draped to hide the secret everyone seemed to be only too aware of. Her hair was pulled back from her face and entwined with flowers at the nape of her neck and he knew the gown swooped low at the back and finished with a flat bow. She carried a bouquet of white roses and tiny white daisies, the traditional gift of the groom to his bride. Pearl earrings from her new mother-in-law hung from her ears.

He knew the whole wedding was a sham, although created with the best of intentions. But suddenly he ached for this marriage of convenience to be a marriage of the heart. For Dell to be his wife for real. As she took her place next to him and the traditional crowns connected by ribbons were placed on first her head and then on his, the realisation hit him.

She was his wings.

Dell was the one who would help him soar back into the full happiness and joy of life. Without her he would still be grounded, plodding along looking backwards and sideward, sometimes forward but never up to the sky where he longed to be. But he couldn't soar to great heights unless she was by his side. He needed her. *He loved her.*

How blind he'd been, how barricaded against ever finding love, ever thinking he *deserved* love that he hadn't seen it when love had found him. When had he fallen for her? At Bay Breeze when she'd been so kind at a time she'd had every reason to hate him? Or the day she'd zoomed up on her bike so full of life and vitality shining her own brand of brightness into his dark, shadowed life? Whenever it had been, he realised now that the job offer, the move to Greece had all been an excuse to have her nearby.

He had to tell her how he felt.

How ironic they were repeating vows—in Greek

and in English—to bind their lives together. Desperately he tried to infuse all his longing and love for her into their vows, hoping she would sense it, wanting this to be the one and only time he ever made these vows. Vows that made her his lifetime partner. When they were pronounced man and wife he kissed her with a fierce longing surely she must have felt. Then searched her face for a hint of returned feeling, exulting when he saw it, plunging into despair when he realised it could be all part of the game of pretence he had lured her into playing.

But telling her how he felt wasn't possible in a snatched aside between the rounds of congratulations and the endless photos. Then when they walked down the hill to the new resort he had created with her, where the party was to be held, they had to face the reception line that saw them individually greeting their guests.

He felt a pang of regret and sorrow when he realised she had none of her own family and friends there. She had point-blank refused to involve them in what she called the big lie. In all conscience he had not attempted to convince her otherwise. Now he wished he had done what he had wanted to do in the interests of authenticity—gone behind her back and invited her parents and Lizzie and Jesse. Because he didn't intend for her ever to have another wedding—this was it, for him and for her. He had every intention of claiming her for his bride for real.

After the feasting and the speeches, and before the dancing would begin, he managed to lead her out to the marble balcony that looked out over the sea. When a guest with a camera tried to follow them out he gestured for her to leave him alone with his new wife. He and Dell watched her depart and saw her tell others that the bride and groom needed some time together.

Alone with her, Alex found himself behaving like a stuttering adolescent. 'It went well,' he said. Of all things to come out when he had so much he wanted to say. Life-changing words, not inane chit-chat.

'Yes,' she said with a wistfulness he hadn't seen before in her and that nourished the glimmer of hope he'd felt at the church. 'I… I think we managed to…to fool everyone.' Fool them? Fool *him*? 'We both put on quite an act.' *An act?* Was that really all it was for her?

'Dell, did you…did you find yourself during the ceremony wanting…?' Where were his usual eloquent words when he wanted them?

Her brow pleated in a frown. 'Wanting what?'

Wanting our vows to be real. The words hovered on his tongue. But she seemed so cool and contained. What would he do if she denied any feeling for him? He had a year to convince her. He shouldn't rush into this—it was too important for him to get wrong. 'Wanting your family to be there?' he finished lamely.

There were shadows behind her eyes when she looked up at him. Her mouth twisted downwards. 'No, I didn't. There are going to be enough people disappointed and hurt when they find out the truth of what this wedding meant—or didn't mean. I don't want my side dragged into it.'

Her voice wasn't steady and he realised how difficult the deception was for her honest nature, how, although his father was beaming with happiness, perhaps his plan had not been in Dell's best interest. But how very different it might be if their marriage was for real. He had the crazy idea of proposing to her in earnest out here on the balcony. Going down on bended knee. But he thought about it for a moment too long.

She turned away from him, her shoulders slumped before she pulled them back up straight. 'We'd better get back to our guests. Act Three of this performance is about to start—the dancing.' Then she turned back, lifted her face to his in the offer of a kiss. 'We'd better do what our guests will expect us to do, Alex, a husband and wife alone together for the first time.'

When her cool lips met his, he knew she was pretending and he didn't like the feeling one bit. As she moved away he saw the moment she pasted a smile on her face and forced a brightness to her eyes he knew she didn't feel. Making her his bride for real might be more difficult than he had anticipated.

CHAPTER SEVENTEEN

LEAVING HER DISASTROUS encounter with Alex on the balcony, Dell retreated to the bathroom—the only place she could get a few moments to herself. She splashed her face with cool water, being careful not to damage her make-up. There would be more photos to come and she still had to play her role of the happy bride.

Back in the beautiful little church on the clifftop, there had been no need for her to pretend. After the fervent way Alex had repeated his marriage vows, not taking his eyes from hers for a second, her heart had done a dance of joy, convinced he might feel towards her something of what she felt towards him. And that kiss… He had really taken the invitation to kiss his bride to the extreme. Her toes in her kitten-heeled satin shoes curled at the memory of it. No wonder the congregation had applauded them.

But on the balcony his stilted conversation had proved anything but satisfactory. How foolish she had been to let the romance of an extravagant wedding catch her off her guard. And yet… For a moment she'd been convinced he had something important to say. Maybe he had thought it was important to talk about the fact her family wasn't there. But was it because he'd thought it mattered to her or because it might make people question the authenticity of their marriage?

She closed her eyes and let a wave of weariness wash over her. Actually, she'd let her personal feelings overcome her business sense. When her carefully worded press release went out announcing Alex's marriage and the news got out, people might question the lack of participation by her family in the wedding. She'd have to think of a way to explain it. So maybe that was what Alex had been trying to say. But she felt too tired to worry about that just yet. Not just tired. Unwell. She smoothed back her hair from her face and prepared to return to the fray.

Then the cramp hit her. And another. She clutched her stomach protectively. Saw her face go white in the mirror.

Please, not that, not now.

But when she went into the stall to check, there was blood.

Dell rested her face in her hands. Her baby was kicking. She'd allowed herself to believe everything was all right. This couldn't be happening. She couldn't get up, couldn't move, frozen with terror and disbelief and grief.

She didn't know for how long she sat there. But there was a knock on the door. 'Are you all right in there, Dell?'

Aunt Penelope. The woman who had been so good to her since she had arrived in Greece. She was a midwife. Aunt Penelope would know what to do. Dell opened the door.

'The baby?' the older woman asked.

Dell nodded. And let herself be looked after by her new family who weren't really her family at all.

Alex was talking to his cousin Melina about her four-year-old daughter who was their delightful flower girl. He hadn't even known Melina had a child until quite recently. Melina was explaining when his father interrupted them. Alex knew something was wrong when his father tapped him on the arm and took him aside. Dell needed to be taken to hospital urgently. She wasn't well and there was a chance she could be miscarrying. He heard the cry of anguish before realising it was his.

But his father told him he needed to be strong. How much had he had to drink because his speedboat was the fastest way to get his wife off the island? Fortunately all he'd had was a flute of champagne.

His wife.

Alex found Dell surrounded by the women in his family. His aunt, his mother, his sisters. She looked ashen, her eyes fearful, her hair falling in disarray around her face, stripped of her wedding gown and wearing the white dress with the blue tie she'd worn when he'd first kissed her in front of the Parthenon.

But when they saw him, the women stepped back so he could gather her in his arms. She collapsed against him and he could feel her trembling. 'Alex, I'm scared.'

'I know you are, *agapi mou*,' he said, scarcely realising he had used the Greek endearment for *darling*. 'Try not to worry. We're getting you to the hospital as fast as we can.' He knew how important this baby was to her. He would do anything he could to help her.

Alex murmured a constant litany of reassurance as he picked Dell up and carried her out of the building and down the steps leading to the water. But still he hadn't told her how much he loved her.

She protested she could walk but he wasn't taking any chances. He carried her to the dock where his boat, and the boats that had brought over the guests, were moored.

Then the women took over again as he took the wheel, released the throttle and pointed the boat towards Lefkada. People were worried about the baby. He was too. Since the day he had felt it move the baby had become real to him. But he was racked with the terrible fear that something might happen to Dell. He had a sickening sense of history repeating itself. Would he lose Dell as he'd lost Mia with her believing he didn't care about her?

The next morning, Dell lay drowsing in the hospital bed, hooked up to a number of monitors. She felt a change, sensed a familiar scent. When she opened her eyes it was to see Alex sprawled in a chair that had been pulled over by her bedside. He was still wearing his wedding suit, crumpled now, and his jaw was dark with stubble. Even dishevelled he was gorgeous. He wore a wide gold band on his right hand in the Greek manner. The ring that was meant to bind him to her.

Her ring—his mother's ring—was sitting tightly wrapped in her handbag inside the hospital cabinet. She would never wear it again.

'You're awake,' he said, his voice gruff.

'Yes,' she said.

'I didn't think you were ever going to wake up.' She hadn't been asleep the entire time. But she'd requested no visitors. Not even her husband. Until now.

He went to kiss her but she pushed back against her pillow to evade him. 'No need for that. There's no one here we need to fool.' Was that hurt she saw tighten his face? Surely not. She wanted his kiss, *ached* for his kiss. But she needed to keep her distance more.

'I'm sorry about our honeymoon,' she said. 'Have you managed to cancel the booking?' For appearances' sake, they had planned a short break in the old port town of Chania on the southern island of Crete.

His dark brows drew together. 'Why would I care about that when I'm worried sick about you? I haven't slept for fearing something would happen to you. And the baby.'

His reference to the baby surprised her. 'I'm okay,' she said. 'I don't want a fuss. I'm not miscarrying.'

He let out his breath on a great sigh of relief. 'Thank God. Are you sure about that?'

'Yes,' she said. 'But I need to stay in bed for a few days.'

She didn't want to discuss the intimate details with him. They hadn't been intimate. Hadn't made this baby together. It was nothing to do with him. As he'd made so very clear on several occasions.

He leaned closer to her. She could smell coffee on his breath. Noticed his eyes were bloodshot. 'Do you have to stay in hospital?' he asked. 'Or can you come home to Kosmima? I can organise nursing care for you.'

Home. The island wasn't home for her. Much as she had come to love it.

She took a deep breath to steady herself, braced herself against the pillows. 'I'm not coming back to Kosmima, Alex. Not today. Not ever.'

She expected him to be angry but he looked puzzled. Which made this so much harder. 'You want to go back to the villa? Why? That's not part of our agreement.'

'Not the villa. I'm going back to Sydney.'

'What?' The word exploded from him.

Slowly she shook her head. 'I can't do this, Alex. I'm reneging on our agreement. I'm sorry but I just can't live a lie. Your family are so wonderful. Aunt Penelope has been like a mother to me. Your mother too. I... I've come to love them. But I'm an imposter. A fraud. They're all so worried about me losing this baby because they think it's yours. Can you imagine how they will feel when they find out the truth?'

'But we're married now.'

'In name only. It's not a legal marriage.' She couldn't meet his eye. 'It...it hasn't been consummated, for one thing.'

'That could be arranged,' he said slowly.

She caught her breath. 'I know you don't mean that,' she said.

'What if I did?'

'I wouldn't believe you,' she said. 'You've never given any indication whatsoever that...that you wanted this marriage to be real.'

'Neither have you,' he countered.

'Why would I?' she said. 'This...this marriage is a business arrangement. I've signed a contract drawn up by your lawyers.'

'A contract you would be breaking if you went back to Sydney.'

'I'm aware of that,' she said. 'But the consequences of staying with you are so much greater than anything you could do to me by pursuing the broken contract. So

sue me. I have nothing.' She displayed empty hands.
'The marriage isn't registered yet. If a marriage in
Greece is not registered within forty days, it becomes
invalid.'

He didn't say anything in reply to that. His expression was immeasurably sad. 'So it comes full circle,
does it, Dell?' he said finally. 'Are we enemies again?'

How could he be an enemy when she loved him
so much her heart was breaking at the thought of not
being with him? But she couldn't endure a year of living with a man she loved so desperately in a celibate,
for-convenience marriage. And then be expected to
walk away from it with a cheque in her pocket, never
to bother him again.

'Never an enemy, Alex,' she said with a hitch to
her voice.

'So why this desire to run away to Australia? Surely
it's not just about my family. So we keep to our deal
and we break up after a year. Divorce happens all the
time.' He shrugged. 'They'll get over it.'

She glared at him. 'You don't get it. You just don't
get it, do you? You can't just play around with love,
anyone's love.' *My* love.

Her voice was rising but she couldn't do anything to
control it. A nurse came into the room. 'Are you okay,
Mrs Mikhalis? Is something upsetting you?'

The nurse looked pointedly at Alex, who stood
glowering by the chair. But Dell was too stunned at
the way she'd so matter-of-factly referred to her as *Mrs
Mikhalis* to really notice.

Alex towered over the hospital bed, over the hapless
nurse. 'I am her husband and the father of her baby.
I am not *upsetting* her. I'm here to take her home. To

the people who love her.' Now he completely ignored the nurse, rather turned to face Dell. 'To the man who loves her.'

The nurse knew exactly when to exit the room quietly.

Dell pushed herself up higher in the bed. 'Was that "the man who loves her" bit for the benefit of the nurse, Alex?'

He came closer to the bed, took both her hands in his. 'It's purely for your benefit. I love you, Dell. I have for a long time. It just took me a while to wake up to it.'

'Oh, Alex, I love you too.' She gripped his hands tight. 'I… I thought I had a silly crush on you but… but it was so much more than that.'

'Aunt Penelope, the family, they saw it before we did,' he said.

He leaned down to kiss her, tenderly and with love. The same love she recognised now from his kiss in the church. Her heart started a furious pounding.

'Alex, the wedding. The vows. You meant every word, didn't you?'

'Every word. I was hoping you would recognise that.'

'I meant every word too,' she breathed. He kissed her again.

'That means we really are married,' he said. 'Registered or not. I want to take you home with me where you belong.'

'But what about the baby? You said you could never take on another man's child.'

He frowned. 'Somehow, I have never thought of the child as anyone's but yours,' he said. 'Then when I felt your baby move beneath my hand, I realised it didn't matter who was the sperm donor. The father will be the man who welcomes it into the world, who loves its mother, who truly *fathers* it, like my father fathered me.'

'That's quite a turnaround,' she said, a little breathlessly. 'Do you really believe that?'

'Our little flower girl today, you know she is adopted?'

'No, I didn't know that.'

'Neither did I, until Melina happened to mention it today. I was in Sydney at the time. She said she loved her little girl the minute she first held her in her arms. Her husband felt the same.'

'She's a very loved child, that's obvious,' Dell said thoughtfully.

'That she is. So why would I not love your child, Dell? I love you so that's halfway there. I guess I won't know how I feel exactly until I see him or her but I guess no parent does. I'll be there at the birth if you want me to and be involved from the very beginning.'

Dell put her hand protectively on her bump. She smiled. 'He or she—I hate saying *it*—just gave me a hefty kick. I think he or she is listening and giving his or her approval.'

Alex smiled too, his eyes lit with a warmth that thrilled her. 'I think the baby is telling me to take you home and love you and make a happy life together.'

'That baby has the right idea,' she said.

She swung herself out of bed so she could slide more comfortably into his arms. 'We're already married so I can't really ask you to marry me, but I think I will anyway. Alex, will you be my husband for real?'

'So long as you'll be my wife,' he said.

She laughed. 'I think we both agree on that. I love you, Mr Mikhalis.'

'I love you too, Mrs Mikhalis,' he said as he kissed her again, long and lovingly.

CHAPTER EIGHTEEN

One year later

DELL RELAXED BACK in the shade of the pavilion near the swimming pool and watched as her husband played with their daughter in the water. Litsa squealed in delight as Alex lifted her up in his arms and then dipped her into the water with a splash. 'We'll have her swimming before she's walking,' he called.

The baby gurgled her delight. At just six months old, she was nowhere near talking but she was very communicative, as she'd been in the womb. She and Alex had had endless fun making up meanings for her bump's kicks and wiggles.

Dell waved to her precious little lookalike. Litsa had been born with her mother's auburn hair and creamy skin but with brown eyes. People often remarked that she had the best of both her and Alex. Husband and wife would look at each other and smile. Alex had legally adopted Litsa. They would choose the right time to one day tell her about her biological father.

Alex need not have worried about bonding with the baby. As he'd promised, he'd been there at the birth and had adored his daughter at first sight. So had Dell.

Motherhood was everything she had dreamed of. Even more as she was enjoying it buoyed with the love and support of the husband she grew to love more each day.

She and Alex had debated whether or not to move back to Sydney but had decided to stay in Greece, at least in the short term. Pevezzo Athina had been such a success that it was already completely booked out for the season and beyond. They still lived in the pavilion but Alex had started building them a magnificent new house out of sight of the resort but within sight of the little church where they'd married and Litsa had been christened. Her blog had taken a slight change in direction but had not lost her any readers—rather she had gained them.

The best news was that Alex's father, George, had gone into remission and was a devoted grandfather when he visited Greece, which he did more often. He and Eleni even talked of buying a house nearby when they retired and living between both countries.

Much to Dell's surprise her mother had become the most doting of grandmas—after she'd got over the hurt of being excluded from the wedding. When Dell had taken her into her confidence and explained why, her mother had forgiven her. She'd surprised Dell by telling her that she and her father had always disliked Neil but hadn't wanted to criticise their daughter's choice of husband. When they'd flown to Greece to meet their new son-in-law, her parents had given their full approval. Alex had taken to them too.

There was a friendly rivalry between her mother and Eleni over who would spend the most time in Greece with their granddaughter. When the grandmothers had met after Litsa's birth, they'd realised they'd met each other before at a pharmaceutical conference and a genuine friendship had formed.

Who knew? Dell now mused. She would have to figure out a time to tell both the grandmas her news at the same time.

Alex gave Litsa a final plunge in the pool and swung her up into his arms to a peal of baby giggles. As her husband walked out of the pool, his lean, powerful body glistening with water, Dell felt the intense surge of love and desire she always felt for him.

'Are you feeling okay?' he asked. 'Need more dry crackers, more lemonade?'

'Ugh,' she said. 'No, thanks.'

No one had been more surprised than Dell when she'd fallen pregnant. For so long she'd thought herself the problem in her battles with fertility. Turned out she'd been married to the wrong man. Or that was what Alex said anyway. She could only agree.

* * * * *

COMING SOON!

We really hope you enjoyed reading this book. If you're looking for more romance, be sure to head to the shops when new books are available on

Thursday 27th June

LET'S TALK
Romance

For exclusive extracts, competitions
and special offers, find us online:

 facebook.com/millsandboon

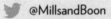 @MillsandBoon

@MillsandBoonUK

Get in touch on 01413 063232

For all the latest titles coming soon, visit
millsandboon.co.uk/nextmonth